Foreword

There is a song by Finglas band The Brilliant Trees called Home, a gentle tune that ambles along carrying its thoughtful yet depressingly accurate message.

Released in the early 1990s, the chorus contains the couplet, *'They're gonna rip it up and tear it down, for a shiny new face for Dublin town...'* It continues *'These are our homes, these are our streets, so please listen to me...'*

As I listened to it for the first time at my job in The Forum newspaper in the summer of 1993 the pleading message struck me hard as in the pages of the paper I wrote for was stories of plans to carve Finglas in two with a new road, to build this, that and the other in place of what already stood. The copious and lush green fields around my own home were to be covered with concrete and topped with hundreds of new houses. The community centre around the corner that played host to various childhood clubs and Christmas parties would soon be no more. The park behind it where we played football late into the summer evenings would soon be annexed and with it the old red barn where bands practised at will over the years. The quiet countryside was to retreat into submission.

Finglas had already been culverted and ripped apart. The news that more was to come made me think would we lose the spirit of this ancient town forever.

Out of Time is a memory book, images of the Finglas of long ago, the Finglas of my childhood and of my early adulthood. Not necessarily my memories, but the memories of the area, of what has now long disappeared. The fictional characters mingle among the factual and are involved in events that, in places, actually happened.

This may never be the best book you read, it may never be the most memorable and it may be the only book I ever write. But it is my book, my story, my characters. I hope you can take something from this book and that the characters and events, factual and fictional, come alive in your mind.

'We have to know where we've come from, to know where we're going...'

the author...

Alan Bird was born in 1974 in Dublin and is a native of Finglas, spending the majority of his life in the area. Having worked primarily in the newspaper industry, he cut his teeth as a journalist with *The Forum* newspaper, a fortnightly publication covering Finglas and its surrounding areas. From there he tried his hand with a variety of local and national publications before moving into desktop publishing and newspaper design, where he spent 17 years as production manager of the *Northside People*.

A member and voluntary editor and designer of the Bohemian Football Club match day programme, Alan has also contributed to *Finglas: A Celebration* in 1998, a book celebrating the many aspects of Finglas' history, and *One team, One Dream, One Friday Night*, a collection of articles by fans of various League of Ireland clubs.

Out of Time is his first novel.

He lives with his wife Sandra in Ashbourne, Co. Meath.

with the most sincere thanks...

'Thank you, don't mention it, I'm pleased to meet you...'

An obscure 1980 b-side by a Dublin band who went onto bigger and better things sums up the following people who have been gracious enough to assist me on this endeavour.

Aidan Kelly, Declan Cassidy, Darren Kinsella and Ger Guthrie of the actual and unfortunately short-lived Forum newspaper; many good times were had back in the day. Thank you for your editorial, moral and publication support and mostly for lending your names to this piece so I could bring The Forum alive once more.

Huge appreciation to Cheryl Connor, someone completely out of the geographical loop who could cast a blind and honest eye over the text; your recommendations and advice at the final stages helped so much.

To Avril Glavin, many thanks for allowing me the use of your wonderful image on the cover.

To Moira Cassidy and her endless vault of historical Finglas information; thank you. So much to learn, so little space to use it.

All at the Finglas Historical Society, I'm very grateful for your endless photographs, maps and for digging deep with information on the surprisingly secretive Jamestown House.

To Christy, Billy, Joe, Alan, Rod (not forgetting Tony), namely Aslan, a big thumbs up for allowing the use of your lyrics in this book.

To my patient and ever supportive Sandra, long hours in the office researching and typing away have finally produced this tome.

To my family; my father Bernard, mother Ann, brother Conor, sister Elaine, Godchildren, nieces, nephews and of course in-laws.

This may not be your cup of tea but still, it's my legacy.

...dedicated to

my Godson Daniel Bird, whose hopes and dreams will pave his future
and to the memory of the inspirational Shane MacThomais,
who made the past come alive in the present

"All I have is everything to me,
but everything could change real soon..."

Goodbye Charlie Moonhead, 1993 - Aslan

Out *of* Time

by Alan Bird

560 AD

Within the boundaries of the Upper and Nether Crosses lay a monastic settlement, a vital seat of Christianity in the land. On this night of Samhain the holy men were on edge, praying, watching and listening amongst the sounds of the late winter evening.

They knew the importance of the dark evening as it approached and enveloped the wild landscape around them. It would test their work. They sought to purge the long-held rituals still evident in the land and instead open a new world of Christian teaching to the people. The yew trees on the banks of the crystal stream which trickled through the settlement played a major role in the area's pre-Christian past. Now in this time of Christianity, they were holy trees, freed from their pagan usage of times past but still sought by those who practised unholy rituals; a ritual perhaps like the one in progress deep in the forest on top of the hill that stretched up from the settlement.

Two men had been dispatched by the shrouded woman and had stealthily negotiated their way into the grove, extinguishing their lanterns made of hollowed turnip and illuminated by crude lumps of coal. The silver moon lit up the scene below. The stream guided them, bolts of random silver glistening in the now abundant moonlight. Silently they collected their bounty, the gentle wind rustling the leaves and branches around them, masking their presence.

A plentiful supply of branches in hand, they crept past the random huts of wattle and daub, the glow from the moon a welcome help in their return uphill to the weary party of travellers who had journeyed for days from the Hill of Ward. In the huts they passed, some monks sat silent in prayer and reflection. Flickering, scant light was their only comfort as they sought solace and guidance on this testing of nights. Others slept until early morning devotions.

Young scholars from the scriptorum were sent to patrol the area. They weaved silently, naively waving their lanterns. The foragers remained calm, watching the bobbing and burning coals as they meandered around them.

Two watching lanterns proceeded to separate, leaving the chosen path free for the crouching men to return uphill. They slowly began their silent trek away from the settlement, every step filling them with confidence as they left the pillaged yew trees and oblivious holy men behind. One of the patrolling scholars heard something untoward and stopped still. He blew out his lantern. There it was again. Slow, muffled footsteps over the damp ground beneath.

He scoured the blackness around him. The yew trees rustled in the wind and the boggy footsteps quickened. He stood still, his cloak flapping at his ankles as he blindly scoured the landscape. He knew what he had heard. He listened attentively.

A sudden, muffled cry carried on the air. One of the intruders had tripped, spilling his bundle. His companion cursed him, all stealth and calmness forgotten as he hissed at the fallen man to pick them up and run.

The scholar's head darted towards the sound. He hailed the abbot loudly. Inside his tiny hut, the superior's eyes shot open, his deep silent prayer disturbed. He knew what this meant. He grabbed his cross. He scampered outside, pausing outside a neighbouring hut. Easing inside, he saw Canice, deep in prayer. He looked up, his greying eyes emitting wisdom and devotion.

He looked silently at the abbot for a few seconds, his mind churning, his stomach flipping as he knew what was about to unfold.

'Not in my settlement. Not here…'

He nodded back at the abbot and returned momentarily to prayer. The abbot stepped back into the cold night. Canice opened his eyes again, unclasping his hands that were locked together in devotion and drawing them slowly over his unshaven face.

'How can a great town arise here if our beliefs are compromised? This must not be allowed to happen here…'

He looked over his shoulder and thought about going out to look at the trees but shook his head and cupped his face again in his hands, returning once more to his reflections.

The intruders ran, clutching their prize taut to their chest. They left the noise of confusion and flickering coals behind as they continued up the hill, hidden by the unending forest. They sought out the fire in the fairy ring that the others had gathered around, the priestess chanting over the blaze that burned high within, embers floating upward gently and dancing at will, finally coming to rest on soil that would change and nurture over time. In the grove of the yew trees, Canice's eyes shot open as the pain swam through his prayers. A terrible event had just happened. He had sensed it. He unclasped his palms, bowed his head and held it within his hands as he sought answers from his God.

I

1902

Beginnings

Fire raged within his skull. A harsh sound, screeching and grating beyond anything he had ever experienced before was about to burst his eardrums. His whole body contorted in the most unbelievable pain, his head felt like it would split in two. He held his hands to his temples, vainly trying to stifle the destructive pain searing throughout his skull.

He felt as if he was being thrown around, jerked from side to side, up and down, non-stop. He had no control over his body, no control over his emotions, no control over the pain, no control over anything. He wanted it to stop, he wanted to give in. At this moment he wanted to die.

A sudden and sinister shooting, piercing sensation caused him to throw his head back and scream an unmerciful, haunting scream that seemed to scorch his larynx.

'Death. Death, please, death'.

He yearned to be free of the unimaginable sensation he was experiencing.

'Can they not see me? Can they not see what is going on? Can they not help me?!'

He collapsed to his knees, two hands clutching either side of his head. His body arched forward in a new, unbearable spasm of pain, with his elbows touching the floor. This wasn't pain. This was beyond agony. He wanted death. That would be his only mercy now.

'Let me die. Or kill me…'

He didn't know whether he was shouting those words or thinking them.

He felt his eyes bulge, his insides churn and twist, his muscles burn like hellfire. An unknown weight slammed down on his head again and again and again, pushing his brain to bursting point within his skull.

Visions shot past him, blurred faces unknown, landscapes changing and evolving but moving too fast to make any sense. Laughing faces with no eyes, no features. The laughter and incessant cacophony of voices grew louder and louder, making no sense.

'Death. Death, please, death.'

Silence. Calm. Peace.

He lay on his side, unable to move. The pain that ached mercilessly through his body went no further but didn't initially subside. For how long he had been lying there, he didn't know. Where he was, he didn't care. He just lay silent, still, and motionless. He was alive though.

Kaleidoscopic colours flashed behind his tightly closed eye lids. Disappearing voices called out for him, grating waterfalls of white noise hissed continuously. Time now meant nothing to him as his mind vainly sought control over his emotions and senses. Minutes, hours, days; he had no idea of how long had already passed.

The turmoil within his mind delayed him noticing that pain had begun to cease, the mental gaggle and white noise dissipated, the grating sound in his eardrums abated. He began to notice new sensations and softer sounds. Something wisped into his eardrums, something cooling, offering minute but welcome relief to at least one tiny fraction of his battered body.

He could hear his own breath again, the agonising, heaving gulps forcing their way out and in to his lungs. He became aware of a thunderous noise, bouncing out of his temples and chest. It was his heart, beating mercilessly within him, beating uncontrollably and rapidly.

He knew he wasn't dead. But what condition was his body in?

He remained in the same position. More relief came to him. His heart slowed, his lungs relaxed, the pain throughout his body subsided. He could feel the breeze whispering gently over his face. He tried to open his eyes. They were so heavy. His eyelids flickered for some moments before he closed them again. His head swam, he felt nauseous.

Sensation and mobility slowly returned. He realised he could lift his arm, move his legs. His heart rate was returning to normal, the erratic fibrillation now a steady regular rhythm. He tried opening his eyes again. Powerful light filled his eyeballs, burning them as reflexes shut them tight again. He waited, felt his body temperature cool, the gentle soft air fanning his smoking skin. He knew he was now alone. Vulnerable. He was powerless to prevent anything happening to him while he lay like this.

He opened his eyes again slowly. The blur in front of him was a bright one, a soft distortion that, coupled with the serenity of sound, gave him hope. Something soft flickered in front of his eyes and he focused on the soft fluttering until he could gaze upon it for a time. Grass. Lush, green grass.

His steadying heart leapt. He was outdoors.

He slowly turned his head, blinking as the brighter light swam into his tiny pupils. His eyes fell on a virgin scene. A deep blue endless ceiling, wisps of soft white dotted here and there. The sky. The clouds. A beautiful, warming light in the distance, bright enough to cause him to throw his forearm in front of his eyes again.

He felt a gasp of laughter well up from deep within his dry throat but he could not yet let it escape. His ears picked up every sound around him, the low and gentle rustle of the wind sifting through nearby trees and grass, the sweet cacophony of bird song echoing around him, the droning buzz of a hovering bee. Beautiful scents filled his clearing nostrils, sweet, clean smells of a new world. But also the pungent smell of burning.

Dark, random wisps of smoke rose from the ground around him but segued into the fresh, welcome breeze. He hunched up on his elbow and immediately felt dizzy. He squinted in the bright light of the sun.

He sat up fully, winced at the effort as his body stiffened. He took a breath, gazed around him some more at the new landscape before him. Excitement grew within him as he tried to get to his feet. He fell back in a crumpled heap, gurgling in pain as he hit the ground hard. His head still hurt, his body ached. He hunched himself up again, head spinning at the attempt. He tried to cough but almost choked with the effort.

The silence amazed him. Just the gentle call of nature resounded in his ears. The air was so different, so clean, so sweet. Straining his neck, he tried to look around, all the time shielding his eyes. A smile crossed his face, but disappeared as an icy chill shot down his spine.

It was then he saw the girl.

She was standing stock still, staring right at him, only metres away. He stared back, eyes fixated on hers. She stood, eerily and silently, a ghost from a vision he gave time to in the past, an unmoving yet living, breathing relic. Flesh and blood, right in front of him. They exchanged frozen glances, two faces from two completely different walks of life yet the only two faces in existence in this world right now. The simplicity of her appearance appealed to him. The fine skin, her flowing, wispy brunette hair answering the gentle call of the breeze, her worn dress. He tried to raise his arm to her, to call out to her, to offer an exchange but a fit of coughing overtook him and he landed back on the scorched grass with a dull thud.

He rolled over, helpless, but in need of help.

He hadn't died. But he had been seen. His head spun. He closed his eyes. Powerless. He stared up at the sky, the scent of an untouched landscape in his nostrils, the sounds of a beautiful, peaceful place in his ears, and the expression of a young girl dominating his mind. A shadow slowly fell in front of him, his eyes darted towards it. She was standing only feet away, her footsteps made no sound to alert him. Her face had lost the shocked look. She was expressionless, motionless.

His head began to hurt as panic welled up deep within and flooded every pore. He shook his head from side to side, uselessly held up his forearm in some form of vain self-protection. After all that. After all he had been through. She came nearer, leaning in closer. He felt dizzy. He was sure he could see the beginnings of a smile on her unblemished porcelain face but his eyes closed and he slipped into an unwilling unconsciousness.

One

The noise was incessant, a babble of voices, screaming manically. Visions of lost, tortured souls in agonising pain, their withered arms outstretched to him, their ghostly, haunted faces, with mouths wide open, begging him to help them, their stained tears of a sobbing long since past. All shouting, calling, crying, 'help us, help us'. Bony fingers stretched out, their flimsy efforts to grab him forcing him to back away into nothingness. Still they came. He screamed back at them. 'Stop, stop, I cannot help you' yet still they came, in greater numbers. Behind them stood a woman, always silent... he threw his hands in front of his face, shielding his vision from the spectres almost upon him. They had caught up to him, their arms wrapping themselves around him, their fingers scratching at him, all the time wailing, screaming, begging for help, for deliverance. He struggled to be free, to escape, to run, to hide. All the time the woman stood in the background, watching, commanding...

The silence was a gift. He lay still, curious yet terrified. Memories surged back, of the brief beauty he had experienced, of the girl edging closer to him, her visage one of shock then nonchalance.

His mind, as pained as his body, tried to make sense of time. How long ago had that been? Hours? Days? Something was different. The air. The light. He eased his eyelids open. He was in a room. He had been moved.

Heavy eyes took some seconds to adjust, but this time to darkness. At the far end of the rather large room was a dim square of light. He focused on it, staring at it for some time, its stained, yellowish, appearance morphing into a window, curtained from the outside world.

To his right, a chair silently guarded a small table on which an enamel jug and bowl, side by side, were carefully placed. A single cup stood beside them. The surrounding walls and ceiling were nondescript and plain. The room looked vacant, uncared for as if it hadn't comforted an occupant for years. Behind him to his right was a door, heavy and still, a single dull doorknob keeping him from the outside world. The air in the room wasn't as soft or the smell as sweet as he recalled from his brief memories.

It was musty and stale. His throat and nostrils stank as he took deep breaths, the stagnated air irritating him. Dried sweat added to the pungent mix.

He was on a bed, under heavy, taut blankets. He pulled them back and swung his legs over the side. He glanced down at his body, which was wrapped in a sheet. Underneath he was naked. He stopped, stared at his legs, his feet, his stomach. They bore no mark of pain or suffering. Hope entered his heart. He lowered his legs until his feet touched the hard surface underneath him. It was so cold to the touch and a blessed relief. A dark floorboard creaked as he applied pressure with his foot. He tried to stand up but his legs were weak; before he could collapse he grabbed onto the iron frame of the bed and eased himself back into a sitting position.

He listened. Silence. Nothing. He gazed around him at the few surroundings. The basic room was like nothing he had seen before. He was enthralled yet uncertain.

His tormented mind was awash with feelings, emotions, all fighting for supremacy in the tortured soul of a man who did not know how to think. Or dare to think.

He stared at the window, itching to draw the curtain back and survey what world awaited him. The brief glimpse he took in was fresh in his mind; the clean air, the serenity of the sounds of nature surrounding him, the bright, warming hold of the sun on his face, the, mischievous, gentle wave of the wind cooling him, the crisp colour of the grass. Wonderful new sensations, ones he only dared believe he would experience.

His meandering caught him off guard as he failed to notice the soft footsteps outside the door approaching slowly, the tarnished, brass doorknob turning gently and the heavy door gliding open before his mind had time to react tho this new event. He sat frozen as the door slowly creaked open. He felt his heart beating in his chest again. Sudden pricks of sweat escaped on his temples. He stared at the light, eyes darting back up again as a woman entered the room.

"Oh hello, you're awake I see!"

He remained silent, repeating her words over and over in his mind, their meaning, their warmth, their manner. Her beaming smile soothed the tension. She wasn't the woman he had glimpsed previously, this one was older. She looked bashfully away, towards the floor.

"I must fetch you some clothes…"

She disappeared as quickly as she arrived. He didn't move, reliving this initial contact.

Her simplistic words, the kindness and thought in her tones. He pulled the cover over himself again, the look of relief on the woman's face when she arrived with a small bundle was evident.

"These are my son's, he's about your size, put them on if you will. Your own clothes were in an awful state."

She departed the room again with a weak smile, cautiously closing the door behind her. He took the bundle in his hands, gazing at the unexciting clothing he was presented with. He patted his hands over the folded items, scrutinising the coarse material. He placed the neat pile on the bed and laid them out, staring at them. Shirt, pants, waistcoat, socks. Simple garments. Dressing was an effort, low grunts and winces escaped his sore throat and it took him some minutes to do that simple task.

A soft, shaky voice followed a brief rap on the door, asking was he presentable. He tried to reply but his arid throat wouldn't allow. The same woman poked her head around the door and on asserting the guest was decent, glided back into his company.

"It's good to see you awake at last. You gave us an awful fright. Can you walk?" She held out her hand, clasping it gently around his and put her other arm behind his back. Her hands were clammy. The touch of another person excited him; he could feel the life in the woman, the warmth of her body.

"Up we go."

He tried to stand again but slipped back, missing the side of the bed and ending up on the floor. He let out a raspy moan. A look of panic crossed her face as she bent down beside him.

"I'm sorry sir, I didn't realise you were so weak."

She cupped him in her arms, her strength surprising him as she hauled him back into a sitting position on the side of the bed. He tried to say something, to thank her.

"Hold on, I'll pour you some water."

She softly poured some water from the plain porcelain jug on the table, staring cautiously into the cup as she did, head tilted sideways. Satisfied, she placed the jug silently back onto the table and held the cup and held it up to his lips.

"Sip this, take your time."

Her gentle hand cradled his back as she helped him clasp the cup and drink. She oozed gentleness, care. The first few sips made him splutter and cough the water onto the floor.

"Take your time I said. Sip it, slowly."

Her voice bore authority, but one of a kindly matriarch. He tried again, the cooling water welcoming and so refreshing on his parched lips. He cleared his throat, tried to talk again.

"Thank you," he rasped.

"Oh that's better, sir!" she beamed as she placed the cup on the table, refilling it. "You're welcome. I'll leave some more here for you."

He pointed to the curtain.

"You want me to open it? Yes, of course. It's a lovely day out."

She drew back both curtains quickly, the incoming light taking him by surprise. He threw his arm up in front of his eyes and grunted disapprovingly.

"A bit bright for you, yes?" she chuckled. "Well you have been in this room for two days."

Two days. He stared back at her in disbelief. His eyes allowed him to take his first proper glance at his visitor. She was old, quite old. Her tight silver hair sat under a small and simple white cloth bonnet. Her face looked weathered, but her grey eyes sparkled in the protruding sunlight, betraying a long life but one of experience. Her clothing was simple, nondescript, faded perhaps from overuse. She clutched her hands together. Her chest heaved gently as she inhaled and exhaled the musty air. He gazed into her grey eyes, tried to see into the soul of a woman whose life was so far along and would continue for a number of years more, but whose life in the great scheme of things would wither, die and be reduced to crumbling bones and a dusty afterthought. A name that one day would never be spoken of again. But here she was alive, vibrant, interactive. This was her time, her moment as she stood in front of a man whose life had unequivocally altered forever and whose being she knew no different of.

"Well, it's good to see you awake, sir. Rest up 'til the power returns to your legs." Her voice trailed off.

"A fright," he repeated quietly. She looked him up and down.

"Yes, a fright, sir, you got a nasty going over, didn't you? You were in an awful state. Have you a name?"

He gazed at her in confusion. His name. At that moment he realised he had no idea what horrors his face betrayed to her. His eyes darted around the room. He needed to see himself, to see what she saw.

"A mirror?"

"Of course." She made to leave but stopped and turned back.

"Where are you from? You're not from 'round here, that I know. I've never seen you before and you talk, well, peculiar. Can you not remember your name a'tall, sir?"

She blushed at her closing sentence and hurried out of the room, the door closing gently in her wake. He sat transfixed on the bed.

'A good going over'. What did that mean?

The adrenalin that coursed through his veins gave him a welcome injection of strength. He was now in the thick of it, not ideal but seemingly safe. The door opened once more and the lady held a small round mirror, attached to a wooden stand, in her hand. She handed it to him silently and left the room again. Her footsteps were gentle, ghostly almost. He took the mirror and looked.

He saw pain. He saw fear, exhaustion, unkemptness. Stubble broke through his always shorn jaw line. His always neat dark hair was wild, dirty and his face was tarnished with days of dried sweat. A dark, purple inflammation encircled his right eye. He moved his fingers to touch it and winced.

His lips were chapped and flaky. He looked at his eyes, the eyes of a terrified man stared back at him. Their deep green had waned, in the reflection of his eyeball he saw the image of the ghouls of his dreams reaching out to him again, pleading, begging. He jumped back, dropping the mirror. He stared at the shattered pieces on the dark floor, their shards glistening. The woman hurriedly returned, followed by a young man, who looked at him with disdain and tutted before walking back out.

"Are you alright, sir?" She spotted the remnants of the mirror.

"Oh dear... never mind, I'll clean that for you." He swung his feet back onto the bed as she returned with a small brush and pan.

"It's ok, it was old, no matter, you must rest." She hunkered down on the floor and began swiftly removing the tiny shattered fragments. "Pay no attention to my son. He's young, impertinent, they all are at that age, you were too I'm sure!" the woman chuckled, not once raising her head.

She stopped for a moment, looked him up and down properly.

"Oh the clothes are perfect. They'll do you for now." Her body weaved across the floor, partially under the bed until she finally stood up.

"If you're up to it you may have some dinner soon."

"Dinner?"

She stared blankly at him.

"Dinner? Yes dinner… you must be starving, sir?"

She paused for a moment, glancing at the jug of water.

"Though maybe some soup first, your throat doesn't appear to be great, does it? Anyway…" she concluded, "I'll get you a bath organised and a blade if you want to have a shave. You'll feel better once you've cleaned up."

He stared back at her and smiled weakly, nodding. She surveyed him cautiously.

"Maybe you need some more rest, I'll fetch the doctor again."

Her eyes had narrowed, her worried gaze also betrayed a hint of suspicion. He understood her nervousness, he felt she understood his. This stranger from nowhere, and in presumably her home, looking wretched, haggard. She turned to go. He had to ask. He must know!

"When is this?" he rasped, his voice improving.

"Pardon?"

"When is this?"

She stared at him.

"The late morning…"

"No, no, when is this, where, when?"

Her eyes widened, betraying fear. His words were very pronounced. She could hear no accent. She stood quietly, staring him up and down again, before losing herself in the window for a moment.

"You did get some knock out there. Two days lying in that bed, you must be very confused."

He wasn't satisfied. "I must know, when is it?"

The confused pools of her eyes dropped their veil of suspicion. She tutted, lifted her left hand gently to his bruised eye, without touching it.

"Lord Almighty, what have they done to you out there?" she muttered.

"Today is Friday afternoon, the thirteenth of June."

He stared blankly at her before his gaze peeled away to a vacant spot on the wall behind her.

"What year?"

Her mask fell into place once more. "I may get Dr. Ryan to have a look at you again, just to be sure."

At this stage he had to find out before anyone else became involved.

She stared at him for some seconds, her eyes searching his for a clue to the question, but she could only find a blank expression, an innocent reflection in them. "You got an awful clatter…" she said, more to herself.

"Please, lady, the year?"

She stared back. Her face changed to one of a defensive nature, her eyes narrowing to little beads, her lips pursed in an admonishing manner.

"My name is Devine, sir, Mrs. Devine, I would hope you would show me some good manners when in this house. We have cared for you and I do not yet know your name. I'm fetching Dr. Ryan again, your mind must be affected. I think you should lie back down on that bed." She wiped her hands on her dress and hurriedly turned to go. "Lord have mercy. What the hell happened to you..."

She closed the door behind her, footsteps, while shallow, sounding thunderous as they slowly degraded out of earshot. He sat still, hands clasped tight at the side of the bed, head staring at the ceiling, eyes wide shut. He was afraid to open them, as if to see the room would acknowledge what had already been confirmed.

The voices came back, at a distance, the blunt images of ghouls but a pale shadow of themselves. He opened his eyes and stood up. His legs were steadier. He tried to walk and slowly shuffled to the window. He inhaled, pulling back the thick net curtain and gazed out at the world.

The sun shone bright and high overhead, wisps of gentle cloud lazily patterned the sky. His fingers pressed down at the base of the wooden window frame. Two small brass hooks allowed him leverage to pull the window up which he did with effort. Flakes of chipped paint fell from the frame as it rose higher with a grating sound that made him wince. Placing his hand on the base of the window, shoulders hunched, he stooped and pushed his head outside into the new world.

Clean air filled his nostrils and cooled his face. Below, acres of varied greenery lay in abundance, the lush grass, the vast selection of trees in their oddity of shapes and sizes. The peace of that moment was heavenly.

Save for a gentle crescendo of beautiful bird song and the rustle of the wind in the trees, there wasn't a sound. He closed his eyes, the rays of the sun warmed his face, the gentle wind breathing new life not only into the room of dead air behind him, but also into him. He inhaled deeply, repeatedly, filling his lungs.

His nostrils widened, his chest rising as the clean, welcoming air was sucked deep into him.

Opening his eyes, his gaze fixed on a bird in the sky; wings outstretched, it appeared to be simply floating on the gentle breeze, uncaring. Eventually it's wings flapped, but only to steady itself, it continued to drift as birds around it kept diligently to their path.

'To be as free as that bird' he pondered. At this precise moment he felt safe. He was in a strange room in a strange house but right at that time felt secure; the open world in front of him, the silence of the peaceful setting protecting him, looking out for him. He closed his eyes again and wanted to give in to that moment in time, that precise moment which he knew he surely couldn't experience for much longer. But for now, he was safe. Happy. Giddy at what he was seeing with his own eyes.

A tap on the shoulder startled him. He jerked upwards, banging his neck off the underside of the opened window, causing him to mumble in pain. The beautiful moment broken, he ducked his head and quickly turned it back inside, scooping the net curtain away.

A young girl stood to his left. His eyes narrowed and he gathered himself and eased back into the room.

She stood there smiling.

"Did I frighten you?"

He couldn't be sure, not for certain. He searched his memory to place her, he had previously only caught a brief, painful glimpse. His wide eyes that darted up and down her young form, betraying what he was thinking.

"Do you remember me?"

A hint of a grin formed on her face as her eyes bore deep into his.

He searched for words yet found none. He gazed over at the jug of water, abruptly brushed past her and, with a shaking hand, poured the jug back into his mouth. She chuckled and, holding the sides of her soft her dress, swayed her hips from side to side slowly. He put down the jug, the sudden rush of water down his throat causing a fit of coughing.

"You'd want to be careful drinking that fast, you'll harm yourself."

Her eyes studied him, her head tilted thoughtfully to her left. She brushed some of her brownish hair to one side, holding it firm in her hand before pulling her clasped palm downward past the length of the strand.

She moved nearer.

"You don't look bad for a man of your ilk."

She stepped back and stretched herself out on the bed, feet on the pillow, propping herself up with her left elbow.

"My ilk?" he ventured.

"Well, I can't pick a better word to describe someone like you. Do you know what I told them? That I found you in a field, not far from this house. Which I did. But that's all I said…"

His fear was realised.

"I told them you must have been in a fight, that's why I had to give you that black eye. Your clothes were in tatters anyway. Don't want them getting suspicious, do we?"

His hand touched his swollen eye again.

"It's a good one, isn't it?" she chuckled. "I learnt well."

To his left was the open door of the room. The dark corridor stretched away out of sight. He could hear activity and distant voices, audible yet indecipherable. He pleaded silently for the older woman to walk in.

"You thinking of running away?" the girl smiled back at him, her head tilting up toward him. She set her gaze on his, never broke it, as she stealthily stood up and walked over towards him.

"It is good to see you back on your feet."

"What did you see?"

She leaned towards him, cocking her head to his right ear and whispered "Oh everything, everything… I saw it all, stranger."

She drew back and turned away to the window. His heart leapt. Sweat flowed on his forehead, his palms clenching and unclenching without thinking. He stared at her silently. The silence hung in the air for some time. In the distance of his mind he could hear garbled voices again, never rising in tone but there, babbling away. What were they saying to him? Why?

"If you would be so kind to go back about the work you are here for."

Both turned to see Mrs. Devine stand in the doorway.

"You shouldn't be up here," she said nervously, staring at the newcomer.

"Now now missus, that's just not fair, is it?" the girl's voice condescended.

"Mrs. Devine to you, and you know that well!" the matriarch hissed, placing emphasis on her title.

"You may leave and return to your work. How did you get up here?"

"Your son was kind enough to let me up, he's such a good boy!" she mocked. "He will do anything for me if I ask nicely..."

"Get out, get out!"

The girl brushed passed him, stopping to eyeball him.

"I'm sure I'll be seeing you again, won't I stranger? You must tell me all about your adventures someday, I'm sure we'd all love to hear them."

The threatening sarcasm dripped from her tongue, her presence biting the air surrounding them. Her tone was musical, confident and she winked at him as she sauntered out of the room with an air of superiority.

He was shaken by the encounter. Mrs. Devine, flushed with anger, maybe embarrassment, went to close the window. He followed her path, expecting an explanation but had to settle for a curt few words.

"She works here, sometimes, and found you nearby. We helped you up to bed."

She turned back around, her eyes meeting his.

"She's a funny one, she'll drag you down, be careful of her."

"What do you mean?"

She didn't answer, instead fixed the curtain and smoothed out the bed covers. "I'm sure you'll be wanting to contact someone who knows you, sir? Or continue on your way? You'd nothing with you though, no possessions. Robbed I presume?"

His mind built up a picture of their version of events. For some reason the girl hadn't mentioned anything else but had concocted a plausible story. That in itself begged a greater mystery. A few days ago he was in complete control, of everything. Now that control had been wrenched from him and by a girl he knew nothing about nor what she could do.

"We'll have to do something for you, sir. Can you remember where you're from?" His host interrupted his thoughts and he turned to face her. A seemingly decent voice of reason in this new world to him. She began listing off some local town lands, names he recognised but he shook his head at her suggestions.

"Well no-one recalls seeing someone new come through the village, and they notice everything!" she remarked.

She walked towards the door. "I'll make sure you get a hot bath and you can shave. Clean yourself up a bit, you'll be called for some food soon. We'll be eating in the parlour and as long as you're here, you're very welcome in Jamestown House."

She closed the door behind her. He was left alone with his thoughts, his fears. Her words excited him.

'Jamestown House,' he repeated to himself, his mind beginning to chart a basic map in his head. He turned back towards the window, craning his neck, searching for the bird that was earlier drifting along. But there was no sign, it had either drifted out of sight or taken a definitive path. He turned away from the window. The stranger knew where he was at least and began to form the nucleus of a plan.

'This turn of events is unfortunate,' he thought, *'but, that is the peril of what I have undertaken. I have survived. Survived! I am a pioneer!'*

He smiled to himself then turned back towards the window, pondering what path lay ahead for his life from now.

Two

A tortured soul called out to him, eyes pleading, hands clenching open and shut as the wiry, pained figure edged ever closer. No matter how far he ran, the spectre was always at his shoulder, his rasping voice causing a thunderous concoction of noise in his head, his bony hands grasping at his shoulder making him beg the ghoul to leave him alone. The phantom laughed, head thrown back in gleeful mirth, his arms elongated and entangling, drawing him closer and closer to his gaping, open mouth inside of which uncountable eyes looked upon him and voices, forever damned to Hades called out for him to join them; yet still the woman stood silently, expressionless, motionless...

"Are you alright sir?"

He awoke with a start, his head jerking back from the slumped position he was in, gasping for breath as his arms fought invisible enemies.

He had slept, again for how long he didn't know, this time in the hot bath prepared for him. He looked back towards the voice he had just heard and saw Mrs. Devine peeking around the door.

"You dozed off. Be careful the water doesn't get too cold on you, sir. Dr. Ryan will be along shortly, he'll take another look at you. I hope you haven't hit your head or something and that's why you keep on nodding off. Food will be ready downstairs very shortly, if you want some of course sir, in the parlour. When you've finished make your way down, first door to the left as you come off the stairs."

She closed the door behind her and he sat back into the metal tub, alone once again with his thoughts and demons.

This room was brighter and airier than the one he had awoken in and the sun shining through the window illuminated everything within. A large cast iron bed sat snugly against the wall, by the window a small table stood with a new mirror, razor and simple white towel resting beside a bowl. A bare but ornate fireplace dominated the opposite wall, coloured mosaics of tiles stretched around a cold grey hearth.

Above it a large mirror hung, reflecting the sunlight and brightening the room. Faded patterns adorned the walls and light, emerald green curtains, that once match the faded emblems on the walls, moved gently in the breeze that cooled him through the open window. He stood up in the tub, dirty water falling off him and stepped out slowly. His legs were stronger. He took the large towel from the back of the wooden chair on which it hung and slowly began to dab himself. It was good to feel clean again. All the time he stared at his face in the mirror except this time he saw a more presentable face, one shorn of days of growth and wiped clean of grime. Pulling clothing onto a clean body made all the difference. He smoothed his hair with a comb and laced up the dull boots. He had his wits about him now, it was time to learn more about this place.

His boots resonated deeply on the polished wooden floorboards as he slowly strode towards the open window. He hauled it up further and against stuck his head out. The sun was higher in the sky now, the sight that greeted him again one of peace and serenity. In the near distance was a gathering of buildings; the village and beyond that the sloping azure haziness of the mountains. Far behind was the harsh pyramid of what was an extinct volcano, silent yet still watching over the city. Far to his left, the unmistakable cut of the sea as it eroded a soft yet recognisable bay at the cusp of the city. His mind pondered on the activities of the city beyond but he was drawn back to the nearby village further down the hill.

It sat silent, as if waiting to be discovered. He withdrew his head from nature, pulled the window down again with his fingertips and walked over to the door. The outer corridor was cool and dark. He glanced at the other doors shut tight, longing to find what was hidden behind them. Below he could hear voices, unfamiliar and loud voices carried in the echoes of the walls. One hand on the rail, he descended the stairs, noting every item in sight; the semi-circular table with a variety of flowers in all colours, the light wallpaper with the golden patterns that played a trick with his eyes.

Mrs. Devine appeared from a door at the far end.

"Ah you look much better, in this way sir," she gestured as he followed her outstretched hand into a large room. His boots clumped on the shiny floor as the smell of polish and freshly cooked food hung in the air. A large, heavy table with ornately carved legs dominated the room. A painting of a faded landscape hung on the far wall, still figures pointing to a distant cabin as women in fantastic dresses fanned themselves as they lounged under a tree. Above the fireplace a huge, tarnished mirror sat, carvings of minute cherubs scattered around the frame. An empty basket sat by the hearth.

Nestling on the mantle under the mirror was a clock, it's sweeping wooden sides encasing a dull, golden face that ticked ambiently. A sideboard guarded the far wall, trinkets and a dusty glass bowl its only decoration. Above him, a large Gothic light fitting hung, pointed tentacles of tarnished gold and brass branching in all directions like a wild tree. It sat unlit, dormant. Generous decorative coving capped the high walls and supported a dull plastered ceiling. Tiny atoms of dust floated in the sunbeams that filtered in through the window, dancing gently without a care as to who he, or anyone, was.

He sat down in the chair that was drawn out and a hot bowl of soup was placed before him. He surveyed the steaming, limp liquid. He ran his tongue between his lips as the scent awakened the hunger in him.

Three others followed him into the room; the young man he had briefly encountered in the small room after he came to, a younger boy and a young woman. Following behind and expertly carrying five plates of food between them was his host and another younger woman. Both women carefully placed the hot plates at set places already laid out, a small towel shielding their hands.

"I hope you like your soup," she smiled as Mrs. Devine sat down at the head of the table. The woman who accompanied her sat at the far end.

"I know it's a hot day in summer but, well, I don't think you're able for solid food, yet anyway, it's chicken soup, made fresh. When you're ready for some proper food, you can have it, it just needs to be heated on the stove."

A plate of bread was placed beside him by the woman who had followed Mrs. Devine in. He felt nervous, faced with five people all of a sudden. He was hoping to minimise contact.

"This gentleman is our guest," Mrs. Devine announced. "These are my children," she offered, her hand lazily waving in their direction, "Thomas, Kathy and Michael." The three murmured a low, polite greeting.

She then gestured to the lady sitting quietly at the far end of the table. "This lady is Eleanor, sir, a help around the house for us! I couldn't run it without her, it's big for a woman my age to run it these days!"

Eleanor smiled softly and uttered a simple greeting. She spoke differently than the others, her accent had a northern English lilt.

He stared at her for some seconds making her blush as Mrs. Devine said a small prayer over dinner. She noticed her guest didn't join in.

"Don't you pray, sir?" she enquired innocently.

"No."

She nodded slightly, to herself, and instructed the others to begin.

He watched the eyes of the others study him as they began to eat. He lowered his head and began his meal. All five ate silently. He picked up the tarnished spoon and began to sip slowly, dribbles of the soup dripping back into the white bowl that was adorned with faded flowers of many colours. He dallied the ornate spoon in the bowl and slowly brought some more to his lips.

'*Slowly, slowly…*' he thought. He dreaded the sense of nausea that may overcome him at any second. He noticed the younger diners throwing him curious looks from time to time as he sipped, trying not to notice yet trying to take in everything about the situation.

They were tucking into full meals of meat, potatoes and a small selection of vegetables. The soup set off the hunger in his belly again and a low rumble escaped. He continued to look into his bowl, avoiding eye contact.

'*I must converse… should I?*'

He turned his gaze on Eleanor, she noticed and began to blush again, staring into her plate.

"You are not from here?" he asked, looking at her as the three children giggled.

"Enough, please!" Mrs. Devine ordered her offspring.

"Eleanor's not from around here sir, she's from England you see. She moved here some years ago. Anyway, please let's eat."

The gentle clanking of cutlery on the plates was the only sound in the room outside of the hypnotic movement of the clock. He began counting the seconds as the hands ticked by; one, two three, four. A beautiful creation of springs and coils was counting by the seconds as they passed into minutes, minutes would morph into hours, hours into months, to years, centuries.

"Unfortunately this man cannot remember his name, such was the going over he got," she continued, her summary to those around, he gathered, the only official account of what happened to him, "but Dr. Ryan is coming back to have another look."

'*That name again, Dr. Ryan…*'

He decided he had enough of the soup. He sat back, wiping his mouth with his napkin as Mrs. Devine had done after her meal, which she had eaten quickly and heartily. He was relieved. No reaction to the food.

The silence was awkward. He had never felt this uncomfortable before. He searched his mind for things to say. The young boy stared back at him, the older lad out the window. The girl caught his eye shyly, then looked away.

"This place is small."

A variety of giggles answered him.

"Children, please! Manners! Small, sir?" Mrs. Devine grinned back at him. "Well, I've never heard of this house being called small I will say, but each to their own! What did you expect? I thought you weren't from here?"

He was caught off guard, cursing himself for not thinking before he said anything.

"Did I say something wrong?" he asked.

"No of course not, just a strange thing to say! This house has never been called small before, not that I know anyway!"

"Is this your house?"

Mrs. Devine was silent for a moment. "I look after this house sir, I have done for many a year. Another man and his family owned it until recently, yes it is mine now I suppose if you must ask. However…" her voice trailed as she gazed around the room. "This house has seen better days, grander days, but sure…"

She didn't finish her sentence, instead getting up from the table.

"It is quite bare," he ventured daringly. The eldest boy continued to gaze out the window as he smirked and shook his head silently.

"Like I said," she replied, gathering up the plates, "this house has seen better days. Not much use for all the rooms now so no point in furnishing them."

"It used to be a mad house!" the youngest child piped up, delight shining in his young eyes.

"Enough of that!" his mother snapped, glancing at the guest with uncertainty.

"A mad house?"

She sighed and he felt a reluctant explanation was needed.

"Ah, a long time ago… an asylum. Poor unfortunates, what's gone has gone. Can never happen again. Now it's a home again."

"Can I see the house?" he asked.

The matriarch gazed at him silently, studying his face before deciding on her answer.

"My daughter Kathy will show you round the outside," was her decision.

"It's a lovely day, a walk will do you good, you being stuck up there for a few days, yes?"

Her daughter looked at her with a slight uncertainty, but readily agreed and asked him to follow her out when he was ready. He got up from the table and followed her back into the hallway, his boots tapping sharply on the wooden floors. The eyes of a man followed him from a small photograph as she opened the door. He stared back, the stern face, adorned with a neat, curled moustache that hid the hint of a smile beneath. He sat, legs crossed, one arm resting on a decorative table, his elegant suit dull in the sepia toned photograph he looked out from.

He stopped, staring at the picture hidden behind a dull frame with dirty glass. Behind him, a pictured backdrop stood.

"That man," he queried, forcing the girl to stop as she held the door open, "who is he?"

The quizzical look on her face dissipated as she re-entered, catching sight of the photograph.

"That will be Ben," she said quietly. "Mammy likes to keep his picture there."

"Who is Ben?"

"Ben was an old friend of my mother," she whispered.

"Is he dead?"

"He could be, he moved away years ago I believe."

She turned away and beckoned as she stood in the doorway.

"Won't you come?"

Her slim frame was still, one arm holding the door open, her head turned. Complimenting her long navy shirt and boots was a neat blouse, buttoned tightly to her neck. He wondered momentarily on the choice of clothing given the weather. He descended the steps and followed her out into the world, his first proper foray into this land he had woken up in.

Beyond the initial open courtyard a wavy sea of green was back-dropped by deep blue. The door closed behind him. Kathy dropped her gaze when he passed her.

It was a heavy door, snugly bordered by large decorative bricks that separated the door frame from the regular brickwork of the house. Above the door, a fanlight window glistened in the sunlight. He stood gazing at the façade, captivated by the craftsmanship and brickwork. A driveway swept away to the left before turning sharply to the road, the entrance guarded by a small, badly kept gate house. He turned back to Kathy. She was small petite, pale skin and dark hair neatly tied up on her head, yet the wind caught thin wisps which danced slowly, dreamily. Her skirt fluttered in the wind as she turned back to him. She spoke softly, a musical lilt to her tongue.

"Come on, I'll show you around," she chirpily requested.

He followed her, the wind ruffling his almost dry hair and lifting the shirt gently from his torso, cooling him under the hot sun.

Trees of all shapes and sizes were dotted around, oak, sycamore, cedar to name but a few. Now and again she pointed out things; the village down the hill below them, the mountains still coloured in a blue haze, the faraway elegant curl of the bay at the edge of the city, far away from where they stood but within view thanks to the high ground. He surveyed the wildflowers, ran his fingers back and forth through the grass, making Kathy chuckle.

Apples hung from various trees as horses and cows ambled and rested in the fields beyond, the incessant clucking of poultry offering a musical alternative to the sound of the wind lazily rustling the leaves. Kathy paced herself just ahead of him, turning frequently to keep watch on the strange visitor, more than often catching him immersed in the surroundings. He stopped, head cocked to one side, listening.

'This is truly remarkable, this is just beyond what I dreamed.'

"Kathy," he ventured, catching her by surprise. "May I call you Kathy?"

She blushed again and smiled. "Yes, yes of course."

She knew the story of how this mysterious and unusually pale man had arrived at her home. She sensed no danger in his presence.

"Is everything alright?"

He didn't look at her. "This is really the countryside, yes? I mean, we are nowhere near the city or anything?"

She turned her head, then giggled softly. He looked at her, surprised as she cupped her hand in front of her mouth.

"I'm sorry," she said, "but that's funny."

He stared at her, confused. She gathered herself and stared back up, nodding her head as the ethereal sound reoccurred. "Well yes, we are, the city is a bit away alright. Here it's quiet, peaceful. You hear that sound, just in that tree behind you? A pigeon, some sort of one anyway. I've been listening to that since I were a young girl, beautiful, isn't it? I used to go to sleep in the warm evenings, I still do quite often, with the bedroom window open and listen to that. You couldn't do that in the big city."

She led him along the curve of the sweeping pathway that led to the road, then suddenly stopped, her hand shielding her eyes from the sun.

"Come here, look!" She grabbed him by the hand, leading him to the left of a tall copper beech tree.

"Do you see, up there, in the branches, the bird with the huge eye and beak? In between the leaves there, you've got to look real close."

He followed her direction, squinting his own eyes, seeking for what she was trying to show him.

"I do not understand," he replied.

"It's not a real bird, I always thought it was... look closer. You'll see a giant bird! Stand here, where I am, and up there, you can see the shape behind the leaves."

He gazed up at were she was pointing, surveying the network of branches until this mysterious creature revealed itself to him. Hidden away, only to be viewed at a precise angle, the branches collated to form the ghoulish image of a bird's head. It had a menacing look, its wide open beak and huge eye staring down at him. Another branch resembled a long, thin arm, picking him alone out from where he stood, like a ghoul from a dream.

"I was terrified of that when I was a young girl," Kathy continued, " that it would come down and grab me." Her description was apt, the illusion harboured threat, fear as he stared transfixed.

"That girl who found you, she climbed up the tree to get it one day but fell, she didn't hurt herself badly but blamed me..."

"Do you know her?" he asked, cutting her off.

"Not much anymore, we used to be friends as young girls, she was always strange though.

"She would be in the fields playing from early. No-one really liked her, they still don't, mammy doesn't like me near her, which is silly because she pays her to do some work around the back. She was going home when she found you, she lives in the village down there."

"Where was I found?"

Her brow furrowed. "Around there I think," she guessed, again vaguely pointing to a spot away from the house and perhaps towards the road outside.

"I didn't see, I only heard when they brought you inside."

"They?"

"Mammy, Eleanor who joined us for dinner, Tom my brother, a farmer."

"Did they say anything, did they…" He sought for the right words. "Did they say there was anything unusual about where they found me?"

"It was in the fairy fort and…"

"The girl who found me, I met her today, she was in the house?"

Kathy looked surprised. "In the house? Where?"

"Yes, she came into the room where I was put to bed."

"She's a whore's boot," she murmured, eyes wide blushing at her language. "Don't tell mammy I said that, will you sir? She got Tom into trouble …"

"Trouble?"

"Behind one of the horse stalls a while ago, mammy was going to send her away home for good but, well mammy was good friend's with Rowena's mother when they were young, God rest her."

"Rowena? Is that the girl?" he interrupted again.

"Yes, Rowena Whyte, that's her name. Her mother died soon after Rowena was born. Mammy was very fond of her."

"And she lives in the village?"

"Yes, in the cottages on the main street. Not far from the crossroads."

He smiled faintly and looked in the direction of the village. He relished the opportunity he had stumbled on.

"Thank you Kathy, really, I cannot remember much, you see..." he lied. "I would like to thank her," he offered, "for getting help for me."

Kathy didn't batter an eyelid.

"Come on, I'll take you to see if she's still here."

The rhythmic call of the unseen bird in the tree grabbed his attention once again as he followed the young woman back in the direction of the house. He had to confront Rowena Whyte.

Three

The bird sat in the tree, watching him, teasing him until it leapt to life, pointing down at him. No matter what way he moved it's wooden, elongated arm picked him out as peels of cackling laughter fell from it's long beak. Behind the ghostly avian a small army of skeletal minions waited patiently, uncurling their arms as they sough to encase him in their dread and fear forever…

A tap on the shoulder made him jump. He swung around, fists drawn, startling Kathy.

"Oh my God!" She gasped, backing away,

"Sorry, my mind… my mind drifted," he explained, panic in his voice.

In truth he didn't know what had happened to him. He waited at the side of the house while Kathy went to search for Rowena and found himself gazing up at the tree with the hidden bird, the optical illusion. He stared into the naturally carved eye of the tormentor, transfixed as images of the tortured soul entered his hypnotised subconscious.

"Rowena, she's gone for the day. But mammy says do you want a real dinner, some proper food? I said you sound so much better now."

His stomach rumbled. He accepted and followed her though the back of the house. He touched the wall before he entered, it was warm in the high June sun. He held his hand on the brickwork for some moments, pondering on the many who had lived here before and those yet to call this place home before it would fall forever.

Mrs. Devine sat in a small room at the back of the house, just off the kitchen that faced out towards the fields. A simple wooden table, some chairs and a bare wooden dresser were the only items.

"What do you think sir?" she asked as Kathy slipped away, exchanging a smile with him.

"It is, beautiful, peaceful."

She smiled and got up from her seat. "It is, yes, very quiet. The house had a good few owners in the recent past, for why I'm not really sure."

"Your young son said it was a 'madhouse'?"

She sighed and looked back at him. Her eyes gazed out the small window behind as her mind recalled a past she had lived through and one she been told about. He knew she wouldn't reveal much. She seemed a proud woman, proud of this beautiful red-brick house she resided in and kept well.

"Once, for a while, many years ago sir, I think every godforsaken big house round here ended up being one at some stage. Some still are, most of the unfortunates were from overseas or outside Dublin and were from the upper classes who wanted to hide them away for their own, well, selfish reasons, if you ask me."

"Were the houses built purposely as asylums?"

"It was to do with a road sir, well as much as I know."

"A road?"

"A business man, and I use that term lightly sir, built a new town some miles up, along the north road. Ashbourne he called it. He said the road was the quickest way into the city. It's an old road, see, built so a king could see his mistress, sir. The businessman charged money for those who wanted to travel into Dublin through his town, but the road was left to rack and ruin. I know nothing about road building but I heard he didn't do such a good job and the gentry who lived in them originally complained. The state of the road and the cost of the tolls was the reason why most of them left their houses and moved to the city or beyond. Travellers to and from the city started to use another road, you see sir, the houses that they left behind fell into ruin or were turned into asylums or fever hospitals, including here I'm afraid but, for this house, all in the past thank God. Some other fine houses around here though still operate as so. I don't agree with it, never have, but anyway. My sister moved up to the town when she married one of the locals, she works in the Hunt House now."

She eyed him for some moments, searching for any cue to his identity.

"Anyway I'm rambling sir, but that's the bones of the story. I'll get your food." She left the room and returned promptly, plate in hand.

"I had this made for you earlier, it'll fill you up, for your journey," she said, as she placed it on the table in front of him, "presuming you're moving on sir, of course, or going home. You're looking a lot better. That eye will go down in no time, I'll fetch some ointment to help. Dr. Ryan said he would be up to check on you again."

He gazed down at the steaming food. He was starving by now.

He slowly began to eat, his first real meal in a long time. It tasted bland but his stomach didn't react. It was obviously prepared well. His throat was better, it was still an effort to swallow but he did so carefully.

"So…" Mrs. Devine began, "you still have no idea of who you are I suppose?"

He looked back up, in time to see her move in closer. "Or are you just pretending not to know who you are, sir?" Her voice carried suspicion.

"Jonathan," he lied.

"Jonathan what?" she asked, her eyes widening, hoping for more.

"Whyte," he continued to lie, plucking the girl's surname from his memory.

"Jonathan Whyte? Any relation to the girl here, Rowena?"

"Girl?" he asked innocently.

"The one who found you?"

"No, no, I have never seen her before."

"Not a common name around here. And you say you're not from here?"

He ate some more before answering. "I did live near here once…"

"Ah, must have been a long time ago as you didn't know any names I asked you?" she smiled, happy to be finally getting some answers.

"Yes, a long time. It has been years since I left."

"But the village hasn't changed much in a long, long time. You must have been a child when you left."

He knew more questions would come. He tried to calculate answers of questions he expected to hear. In the distance, he could hear a clock chime. Further still, other voices could be heard, different voices than those he had been earlier introduced to droning on, other voices that went about their business, but other voices that perhaps would never make themselves known to him. His host sat back in her chair.

"You must understand why I asked you these questions. I keep a good house sir, a quiet house. I just want to go about my business here and the same for my children. I want no trouble."

"I bring no trouble," he stated, his words drawing a swift nod from her as she placed her hands in her lap once more. "Kathy is very kind."

Mrs. Devine smiled as she withdrew the empty bowl he had just finished.

"She's a good child, a sweet girl really."

"She told me about Rowena Whyte, they used to play together as children."

"Yes, well, that was a long time ago. She's a peculiar girl, let's say, between me and you, sir.

"Her father God love him is no use, he just works and drinks, but he did ask me to give her some work not long back, otherwise she'd spend all day rambling the fields and village. She had some housekeeping work in the village right enough, place called Rose Hill House, she didn't last long, the senior maid never took to her. She complained to the owner and they got another young girl in instead. So I took her in, gave her a warning, you see, I did feel sorry for her at one point, she was a bit of a touched child…"

"Touched?"

"By the hand of God," she continued. "Touched, you see…" tapping the side of her head with an index finger. "Just a term, a harsh one maybe."

"Her father never got over her mother dying. Rowena was very young when she died, people said she broke her mother's heart with her temper and ways and that her mother couldn't cope with her. They said she died 'cos of her, but that's just village talk, I don't approve of that, sir. How can a young child be responsible for her mother's death, outside of childbirth? Anyway I did, yes I did feel sorry for her but she grew up, the cow in her heart and when I caught her and Tom…" She stopped for a moment, anger in her face.

"She's streetwise, if you know what I mean, charms the men. I wanted to get rid of her I was persuaded not to, some feel sorry for her too, you see. She's still here, but I forbid her wander around in the house."

"That is why you were angry when she came into the room."

"Yes," she cut short, "she had no right. She found you, we did the rest."

"What happened?" he asked, trying to piece together a more truthful version of events. "That day, I mean."

"She ran in saying she found a man in the fairy fort, dead. So we ran out, my you were a sight. We got a few people together to take you into the house. We didn't know what to make of you. We got Reverend Hackett and the doctor, to have a look. You were alive so they agreed to let you sleep and you'll come around in your own time. The priest blessed you. You're the talk of the village I hear!"

"I want to thank her."

"Leave her be, best thing for you to do is go about your business, don't humour her or she'll follow you around. Have you plans to go?"

The question was abrupt he felt, but she waved her hand and shook her head. "I mean, were you on your way somewhere when you were attacked, sir? The constable figured you were waylaid, robbed and left to die, but the mystery is how you ended here.

"You'd nothing on you, no money, coins, nothing. Robbed by whom God knows."

"A constable was involved?"

"Yes, Reverend Hackett told the police, he had too, we haven't seen such excitement round here in a long time!"

He clasped his hands on the table and lowered his head, adding up the new names to his story. It wasn't meant to be like this. Too many were involved.

"The constable, will he want to see me again?"

"I imagine so, yes sir. He did ask us to let him know when you came round. Dr. Ryan would have told him when I sent for him. Sure than can only be good, can't it? Unless you're on the run from the law..."

The atmosphere changed as a question Mrs. Devine was wanting to ask finally found a rightful time. She had laid the groundwork with her earlier sortie on the matter, she felt justified in asking it outright now.

"I just want to be about my business, no, I am not on the run from the law or anyone, I just want to be left be."

"That's fair enough," she replied as she opened the door to the kitchen.

"I'll get you some tea now."

"One thing, I still have not been able to remember properly? You have told me the date, but I cannot remember the year."

She nodded gently and turned to leave the room.

"It may be better to see you go into a proper hospital, for care I mean." She gazed at him for some moments, feeling sorry for the stranger who seemed odd but harmless. "It's nineteen hundred and two."

He clenched his fist and allowed himself a smile. He was left alone with his thoughts.

'1902! Remarkable!!'

He knew he had to slip away but knew that his appearance in a tiny village wouldn't just go away. He had to make them go away.

Rowena stood on the main street of the village, leaning against the wall of Heery's pub that sat by the crossroads. She gazed down the hill in front of her, past the thick greenery of the woods and onto the looming smoothness of the mountains south of the city. She watched as the local sergeant and doctor cycled up the hill from the barracks, talking quietly to themselves as they eased forward and up the hill towards Jamestown. Her eyes followed them, her mind knowing where they were headed and why.

Three men strolled past and entered the inn across the street, Upper Floods, one didn't give her a second glance, the second snorted, the third, younger, betrayed a smile behind lustful, searching eyes.

"Get us a drink?" She walked towards him, fingers playing with her hair. The young man stopped for a brief second.

"I can't. I'll be killed."

"Killed? A strapping man like you? Go on, get us a drink, sneak it out, I won't tell. I'll make it worth your while."

He hesitated, smiled again. Her hand brushed off his face.

"I mean it. I'll be in the field over there." She winked at him as she nodded back across the street and sauntered slowly away to laze on the wall beside Heery's. The young man glanced across to where she indicated, looked back at her, looking her up and down and abruptly, imagining her well-worn scarlet dress over her head. He turned and pushed the dirty, squeaking door in as she sat on the low wall bordering the field that belonged to the publican.

The village was unusually quiet for the time of day she thought; a horse and cart trundled by from the bottom of the hill, shuffled past her and continued on up the North Road. Three young children stood playing some unknown children's game at the junction, now and again one would sprint off only for another to follow, before they all rejoined back at the same spot, laughing and calling wildly as they spun around in circles.

She watched them intently. She remembered such random acts, games she would play all day, on the street, in the woods, by the stream until her mother would come looking for her, claiming that if she didn't get home before her father she would be taken by the devil under the small stone bridge.

How all the children fell for that tale, endorsed by adults; *'the devil lives under there, if you get too close he'll take ye…'*

She gazed back down the street by the old church, trying to remember the rhyme they used to sing at an always safe distance.

It was on days like this, beautiful, warm sunny ones, that the village was alive with squeals of her laughter as she played and ran for hours.

Her innocent thoughts were interrupted as the young man came bounding out, a small jug in his hand.

"Here, quickly, hide it!" Behind him an older man stood at the door, hand covering his eyes from the sun.

"Are you giving that one drink? Are you bringing drink out to that thing?!"

His voice was hard, authoritative. The young man stopped, horrified eyes transfixed on Rowena's smiling face, and turned back.

"No, no, I'm having it out here."

"Not with her you're not. Get back in with that you fool, she'll have you doing anything for her." The landlord turned to walk back in through the doorway when she shouted across.

"Aww, I love you too, you old fucker!"

He stopped for a moment, turned slightly and shouted what she thought was 'whore' back at her. She laughed. The young man walked sheepishly back towards the inn door. He took one last look and went in. She stood up, running her hands through her hair and began walking down the street, skipping past the three children now playing by the site of the old May pole.

At the back of the old graveyard wall, a courting couple guiltily edged in as close as they could, afraid of being seen in the daylight hours in the shadow of the abandoned church that sat at a lazy angle, the remaining few wooden roof beams slowly vanishing over the years through rot or theft, the shiny slates that once canopied them long disappeared. Rowena made a shush gesture with her lips and forefinger, winking back at them as she reached a small bridge that crossed the crystal stream and sat down, legs dangling over, listening to the gentle torrent of water flow under her. She leaned forward, enough so she could see straight down and almost under the arch of the small bridge on which she rested. The devil lived further up, at the waterfall, she was told, but he moved silently, watching out for misbehaving children.

"Are ye there devil," she called out to no-one, "Are ye there devil, because I'm coming to find out who you are you bastard!"

She laughed, jumped down, cursing angrily as she landed hard on the rocks under the water below and began following the trail of the stream. Two elderly men lazily sat in the adjoining field, glances exchanging as they puffed on their tobacco.

"Won't be long 'til she's gone to the madhouse. Her poor mother would turn in her cursed grave if she knew what that she was like today."

"She's trouble, stupid girl… her mother was none the better." His voiced raised as he spoke the last sentence, catching Rowena's attention.

She stopped and stared at them for a minute, they remained impassive, glaring back. "Did you mention my Mama?" she challenged, dress hitched up as the water cascaded over her bare feet. They ignored her, continuing to puff away.

"You never knew my Mama."

"Everyone knew your Mama!" they laughed, triumphantly as she seethed.

She gazed down, a loose rock caught her eye. In one quick motion she had the rock freed from it's watery base and flying through the air towards them. Her aim was good as they scattered, cursing back at her and calling her every name under the sun.

"You bitch! You're as bad as your mother! That mad old bitch was bad but by Christ you're ten times worse!"

"Say what you want about me, but never talk about my Mama or I'll cut ye, ye dirty bastard!"

They waved her off and strolled away, ignoring her obscenities that carried on the gentle wind and broke the natural silence. She stood still in the water, silent, breathless, cheeks burning red with rage.

"I'll never let them talk about you Mama," she whispered quietly to herself and splashed on slowly, head bowed. She turned back towards the graveyard where her mother lay. "It's ok Mama, I'll always stand up for you."

Mrs. Devine handed Sergeant Linden and Dr. Ryan cups of tea in ornate cups with matching saucers, the best service wear for important visitors.

"Kathy's gone up to fetch him, he said he wanted to rest again. He has eaten a meal today and took a walk. He said his name was Jonathan Whyte."

"Whyte?" the sergeant repeated. "As in Matthew Whyte below?"

"He said no, anyway they never had a visitor since the mother died."

Their conversation was interrupted as they heard loud footsteps descend the stairs. They glanced up as the door opened and Kathy stood before them.

"He's not there!"

"Not there?" her mother asked, eyes widening. "Did you check…"

"Yes, everywhere. I'll check the grounds but I think he's gone!"

Four

A tight circle of haunted faces surrounded him as he crouched down, their bony arms outstretched, pleading with him, begging him to follow them as the world swayed around him. Song birds sang a dreamy air, leaves rustled in the wind and the droning bee became a cacophony of noise as he slammed his hands against his ears and squeezed his eyes shut. But still they came, under his eyelids, ghoulish faces pleading, fingers reaching him and overpowering them, pulling him away to their hell, faces from eons ago who still wander and plead to him, all the time a woman watching silently…

He shook his head to clear the haunting images as he eyed the two men cycle past from his crouched position behind a hedgerow, one in uniform, the other well dressed. He knew they were for him.

'That must be Dr. Ryan himself'

He regretted leaving the kindness of Mrs. Devine and Jamestown House without any notice but he needed to. He had to find this Rowena.

The abundant summer foliage of trees and bushes in the rough, untouched and coarse fields offered him safe cover. Where men laboured in the toiled fields, he was sure to avoid their line of sight. Safe in his solitude, he stayed off the dusty road that led from Jamestown to the small village, squinting in the hot sun as he felt it burn his face. He couldn't afford the time to rest and sit in the cooling shade, time was against him, but he made sure to savour this new scene he found himself in. Birds of varying stature sang sweet tunes, the warm wind teased his burning face as he cautiously made his way through the landscape of lush green and soft yellow, random cottages dotted here and there. It was so peaceful, so quiet. The lowing of the cattle added a baritone sound to the sweet, shrill songs from above. Alone in this solitude, away from prying eyes, inquisitive questions and unheard words about him, he felt safe, secure. He was at peace in this place of a beauty new to him.

The small village loomed at the bottom of this hill, he longed for the city that lay beyond and with it the chance of anonymity. He would experience the streets, the noise, the clanking of metal trams snaking their way through the cobblestone streets, the screeching call of accents piling on top of each other as each person strived to make themselves heard over the other. A world away from where he stood now. The world he wanted to stay in and experience, but one which now he had to flee. Because of her.

He would first have to negotiate the sleepy, almost forgotten village. No-one would care who he was in the city. It was in the hamlet of Finglas he needed to worry about.

A small row of cottages sat snugly together as the road levelled out. Behind them farm animals lolled about, swishing their tails in the heat as labourers sporadically populated the scene, hands busy toiling at the caked earth as they lustily swigged refreshing, cold tea from flasks and wiped their soaked brows with their forearm. Their work was hard, but it was work.

He joined the road as hedgerows lined at either side, bigger buildings in the distance indicating the village was near. Women sat outside the cottages nodding a greeting, others eyeing him without moving a muscle. Young children danced and squealed under their watchful mothers' eyes, dogs lapped the attention or lay idly by whitewashed walls. He quickened his pace, his shirt sticking to his back with the sweat. He was almost there.

The cluster of houses increased, small cottages and farmsteads on the left and grander houses to the right. A big grey house stood with it's back to the peaceful cottages, itself facing towards sinister walls of a bigger house where clumps of ivy slowly crawled over the walls as if to escape from whatever lay within. Hidden behind those safe walls and dense trees and sitting at an unusual angle, the red bricks of this tall building stood out from the grey walls it hid behind. He passed the prohibiting walls until he reached heavy wrought iron gates, shut tight. He surveyed the name, Gofton Hall, painted in black on a white band and spread across two pillars.

Gofton Hall stood still, stark and strong in the hot afternoon sun. It reminded him of Jamestown House but on a bigger scale. He stood back, marvelling at the splendour in front of him and imagining unseen eyes looking out from the numerous windows or a grounds keeper emerging from the well-kept and lush gardens. He touched the gates, ran his hands along the cool and decorative cool iron bars that were painted a crude black. He closed his eyes and from deep within his soul heard distant screams and cries, all scattered, ridiculous voices echoing those that swam into his mind. His fists gripped the gates as he bowed his head. He stood back, the waft of greenery and mixed aroma of flowers reaching his nostrils on the breeze.

He placed his right palm on his forehead, his mind questioning whether all this was real. But it was real. Completely real and he was amongst it, breathing it. He cupped his hands around the gates once more, surveying the dominant arrogance of the building for a final moment. It stood alone and reclusive amongst all the others. The wind whipped up but the trees remained eerily still, loyal sentinels keeping watch for a strange face. His face. The windows were sealed shut, there was no sign of life within.

'Help us...' distant voices cried. 'Help us...' Those voices. Coming from within his head and from behind the windows. He couldn't help them, he didn't want to help them. He wanted to leave them behind.

Giggling broke the spell on his mind as he slowly turned around, his hands still clasped firmly on the gates. Two girls, of teenage years perhaps, stood watching from across the street.

"Are you locked out mister?" the tallest and thinnest piped up, causing both to squeal with laughter again. He studied them. Neither was Rowena. He began to walk away towards the crossroads. The girls followed him, whispering and giggling to each other as they pointed at him.

"He's one of them!" the smaller one sniggered, no effort to hush her voice.

"He's gonna get you!" the other sang as they approached him with gleeful eyes and cackling faces.

"Here madman, give my friend a kiss!" the smaller one howled as her companion laughed wildly and ran up to him.

"Come on, kiss me madman, I won't tell!" She held on to his arm and he tried to pull it away but she clung tighter, dragging along beside him. "Come on handsome, plant one on me!"

He stared at the thin girl who clasped his arm, her clothes ragged and old, feet bare on the dusty street, unkempt hair straggling across her face. He pushed her away, sending her toppling back onto the ground. Both girls burst out laughing. He gathered his stride and walked away as they laughed behind him, his actions catching the attention of an old man smoking outside the nearest tavern who stood and watched as he puffed on his pipe. The two girls called after him, singing childish tunes and laughing.

He stood in the middle of the crossroads, nearby three young girls played on a small patch of grass beside a water pump as they sang a song. As he stared, he felt his mind slip away, bringing him to a different place, yet his feet remained on that spot.

Eyes narrowing, head swimming, he saw the same patch of grass but the girls had gone, replaced by abrasive shouts and roars. Cackling laughter and the foul stench of body odour reeking from underneath filthy clothing assaulted his stunned senses. The place was full of people of all ages, none minding him, none paying him any attention.

Where the girls played only moments earlier, a huge, thin Maypole stood as women danced and fell around it, shouts from the men coming from everywhere, dogs barking, children squealing and a sudden rush as one heavily drunken man pulled a knife on another. The stench overpowered his senses as a fight broke out under the Maypole. People rushed by him, into him, bumped off him yet he felt nothing. An acrid atmosphere fell upon the scene as the noise intensified, yet he felt nothing.

His head jerked back and eyes snapped open as the sweaty drunken hoard was gone. He staggered a little, holding his palm against his temple, trying to understand what he had just seen. He shook his head quickly and blinked in quick succession as the scene faded from his mind.

'Another bad dream...' But this was too realistic for a bad dream. No ghouls or spectres haunted this image, this was of people like any other. Flesh and blood who surrounded him moments ago.

He looked down a hill directly in front of him, the ruins of a church sat awkwardly, rotting roof beams balancing precariously. He turned to his left, looking down another hill where sturdy and well built two-storey structures gave way to small, irregular whitewashed cottages on either side as the short road stretched on. Coming up the hill a cart with two men ambled by, both men staring at this newcomer before eventually nodding a greeting.

Such a difference in such a small area, great houses a stones' throw and in their shadow limp, random buildings. The crossroads was exposed to the heat of the sun, dust lifted from the ground in the wake of footsteps and the stale stench of dried horse manure flooded his nostrils. The mumble of voices unseen was a low one. A woman stood outside the tavern in front of him cradling a small child in her arms, watching him. He stared back at her, their eyes locking. She looked of similar age to Rowena Whyte. Would she know her? He walked over to her. Her eyes widened and she looked away. She glanced at her baby, swaddled in heavy blankets and he noticed she stepped back as he approached.

'I'm the talk of the village...' he remembered Mrs. Devine telling him.

But nobody betrayed an unease towards his appearance. Except this one girl. Did she know? Her eyes darted up and down, her black hair long and sitting wildly on her shoulders. She gently rocked the bundle in her arms, muttering soothing words. She wasn't much older than twenty he surmised. Word could get around that a strange man was asking questions. But he needed to know. The smell of stale ale and tobacco wafted from the pub as the door opened, another old man wobbling out and spitting onto the ground.

He found the scent peculiarly pleasant, warming. The aroma from the man's freshly lit pipe enthused him, his eyes following as he slowly ambled away up the north road. He turned back to the girl.

"Do you live here?" he asked. She was silent but her eyes betrayed her uncertainty.

"Do you?" he repeated.

"Are you alright Phoebe?" One of the girls who moments ago mocked him called over from across the street. "He's from the madhouse him, watch him!"

She glanced back at the girl and back at the stranger standing in front of her. "I have to go, my brother..."

"No, no, answer me, do you know Rowena Whyte?"

She nodded in recognition of the name before backing towards the door some more and calling out "Are you ready Conor? Mammy wants you to come home now."

A curt expletive was shouted out in response.

"Where can I find her?"

She darted past him, shuffling down the hill in her long skirt, occasionally glancing back as she hurried away.

"What did you say to her mister?" the thin girl called out. He turned and approached them again.

"I am searching for someone."

"Who mister?"

"A woman, a girl."

"You've found a good one here so you have, hasn't he Joanie?!" They exploded in laughter again. "You're lookin' for a woman, or a girl... you a soldier? Are you here for a good time? Cos I can tell you what house to go to for that, but we can do just as good, for free, but if you want to give us a few pennies then we won't say no! Even to an English bastard soldier."

Both cackled harshly. "C'mon, just over there, behind those trees."

"You are not the girl I am looking for."

"We not good enough for you?!" Joanie piped up.

"Y'hear that Mary, we're not good enough for him! Finglas country girls not good enough for ye, no? If it's more you want, off to the Monto with you on the next cart out!"

Their voices were quite loud. Attention would be stirred.

He turned back to face the sloping hill with the woodland lying just beyond and began to walk away.

"Ah yeah, walk off, go on!" Joanie shouted as he continued down the hill, ignoring her. He'd be safe in the woods for the moment, he would have to think of another plan. He could run, yes he could follow the road and get a lift into the city. But Rowena would still know. She would always know. How long before she would tell someone? The local police were involved, the doctor, the priest. Too many people.

Phoebe Hedderman rounded the cottages that sat in the shadow of the graveyard at the bottom of the hill at the main street. As she carried her baby into the crumbling, decaying building she and many others called home she glanced up at the Nether Cross peering over he graveyard wall. She uttered a quick prayer and entered the house. Yards away lay the gate house and walls of Farnham asylum. Facing her home, the Bayly family watched scornfully from the windows of their grand Rose Hill home which sat atop a small height. The occupants of Phoebe's tenement home often shouted curses and sang unsavoury songs as they stumbled out of Lower Flood's which sat in Rose Hill's shadow, their meagre labourers wages disappearing in a haze of alcoholic warmth as their children went hungry. Charles Bayly would often silently watch the comings and going from an upstairs window, tutting and shaking his head as the wind carried the foul language.

Once a police barracks, the locally-known White House was now a stopgap haven for the unfortunate and the vagrant. Decadent, damp and rotting, inner walls charred with the black soot of cheap coal. Curtains used as bed sheets. Doors used for firewood in the winter. Leaks in the roof, in the ceilings below. Decent people, hard-working men and women did reside inside but were out-shouted by those who felt they were owed a living.

As Phoebe entered the building shouts, cries and arguments abounded from all corners, the stink of full chamber pots filling the narrow corridors as she climbed the rotting stairs to the room she and her husband shared with her family. Settling the baby in the stolen crib she told her mother that her brother was on his way

"The strangest thing happened to me…" she began.

Five

Nature offered a brief respite, a protective coating around him to keep the demons at bay. He could still see them though, feel their presence as they called on more of their kind to entwine him, but this time he felt safer. He laughed in their demonic, skeletal faces. For the first time in a long time, he was in control of his dreams, his destiny, his future and his past…

He knelt by the bank of the stream, looking down, staring at the dim reflection of his own face that he could barely make out as the dominating trees cast a watchful shadow overhead. Bubbles from unseen water life below would interrupt the shadowy image. He dipped his fingers into the gently babbling stream, allowing the clear water flow run through his fingers. It was gentle; soft, alive, not contained like within the bathtub of the house he had since turned his back on. It sang to him, reminded him of the freedom he believed he would soon achieve.

On his knees, his hands grasping the ground firmly either side, he dipped his head into the gaggle of cooling water, submerging it, shaking it from side to side before jerking it back out, drops of water falling on his face and into his open mouth as he let out a howl of joy. He ran his hands through his hair, over his face, smearing the cooling water over him, a welcome and cooling relief from the baking June sun. He bent forward again, gulping down mouthfuls without a care as to whether it was safe to drink or not. He cupped his hands and threw water over his face, his neck again and again until he sat back, refreshed, relieved, and for the first time, experienced real happiness.

He closed his eyes, let his mind drift away and welcomed comforting thoughts. Giddiness took over him once more, he took off the borrowed boots that were now practically stolen, steeped his feet in the water and watched as a wild rabbit surveyed him from a safe distance on the other side.

Tall, thin trees, wide, knotted trees with knarled roots, unseen ditches, a carpeting of fern and moss, wildflowers, all surrounded him. Scant sunlight filtered through the high foliage illuminating certain areas in a beautiful bath of soft, welcoming, green light. He felt secure, hidden away from the lives of those he had unwillingly interrupted.

For the first time since he awoke in this place, he had the upper hand. He knew of these woods, the great woods of the area, yet had never set foot in them, or rather what remained of them when he was near. But today they were his woods.

He begged his memory to recall key events that led him to where he was found near Jamestown House. Garbled images surfaced, some clear, some muddied in the surrounding meditative solitude. Vital moments were missing in the lead up before he came to in the field some days ago. He remembered that so clearly, the girl, Rowena.

He mulled over her. He wanted to never see her again, to be but a memory in the rudimentary lives of those he had contact with. A sudden sense of euphoria washed over him as he immersed himself in the solitude. What if Rowena were to talk? He had learnt a little about her, about how she was scorned by some. If she were to talk, chances are she would not be believed. She would end up in one of the asylums, her brief, unwelcome interruption to his grand plans dying in a dark room with her, never to be acted upon. He smiled and let out a chuckle. Would that not be better? To leave her and her fantastic tale to the jury of her peers?

He looked to the heavens above him and shook his head in disbelief. Why hadn't he thought this through earlier? His was hell-bent on pursuing her, eliminating her from the equation before he could move one. He could just leave her to her rambling tales, the fool girl. He would still have to move on though, into the city but he was comforted by these new thoughts. He would never have to see her again. Leave her to her fate. He would be gone as quickly as he appeared.

He stood up and gazed down at his clothes. They would have to go. He needed a fresh start after the false one. He concocted a plan he knew the approaching evening light would assist him with. He filled his pockets with wild, colourful berries he recognised in the green tint of the slight sunlight. He followed the stream for direction. He would eat, bide his time, and make his next move. He regretted not being able to spend more time in the sleepy village he wanted to see, but he had seen and endured enough.

Rowena swayed in the gentle wind that fought its way through the foliage around her. Her arms outstretched, she hummed a tune to herself as she picked out her steps towards the asylum by the woods. She followed the wall until she found a hidden opening around the back. Sitting with her back against the wall she picked the white petals from a daisy she plucked. She concentrated on the wild flower in her hand, tearing the petals and flinging them away until the creak of an opening gate caught her attention. She looked up as the young man eased out, closing the gate gently behind him. He smiled down at her, looking around before kneeling and kissing her on the cheek.

"Hello Rowena," he whispered as she sniggered.

"Dawson's out the front, I don't have long, if I'm found missing he'll sack me, I can't afford to lose…"

"Oh shut up!" Rowena ordered as she took his hand and helped herself up.
"Not here. Let's walk."

"I don't…"

"Then fuck off Robert, I'll be off."

He grabbed her hand. "No, no, please, don't."

She chuckled at the fool who admitted he had fallen for her the other day. So easy to play. "I need some more money," she teased, as she curled a lock of hair around her finger.

"I can't keep on stealing you money!"

"Give me some of yours then."

"No, father would crucify me if he noticed a penny missing!"

"Well then, you'll have to find some, won't you? Daddy drinks his, I need to eat you know, and I need a new pretty dress. I can't wear this every day."

"I'll lose my position!"

"You'll lose me too you poor fool, plenty of men around here would gladly give me what I want." She leaned in closer to him, gleeful smirk on her face "I have the knack, you see, of getting what I want! Now, do you want to make use of these few minutes with me or not?"

"Yes, yes, course I do!"

"Some shiny coins then?"

"Yes, yes, a new patient came in today, I don't think his stuff has been stored yet, I'll see what I can do."

"Good boy," Rowena scoffed, patting the taller lad on the head as she led him deeper into the darkening woods.

He hunkered down under cover of the branches of one of the trees he had scaled, watching the patients amble about in the well-kept gardens below.

Vacant, empty and soulless eyes mirrored the images clawing within his own soul. The embodiment of the phantoms that tormented him. This place was as sinister as Gofton Hall. The air temperature had dropped, he felt a slight shiver as he watched the patients in the light wander aimlessly.

He followed their pointless steps, as if they lacked a soul, a meaning, a reason. Whatever meaning their life once held was now washed from their mind. He felt no sympathy for the motley crew staggering below him. What were they but unwanted relations and embarrassing social connections that lumbered too heavily on someone's regular life. Mrs. Devine's brief explanation was of benefit; institutions like this were tailor made for them, a release valve from familial intrusion and care, a recognised domain of high walls, manicured gardens and still glass windows so their vacant eyes could stare from day after day. Inside tiles would be counted over and over, friends would be made of birds gliding by in the world they were no longer welcome in. Men and women of all ages having seizures would be held down under force as physicians scribbled in notebooks that were held under spectacles balanced half way down the bridge of their noses. Treatments and cures yet to be examined would be the curse of these patients in the here and now.

To the outside world they were homes of rest to some, homes of respite. To others, more gullible citizens who swallowed the story. Tales of screams and disembodied howling would be spoken about in hushed tones then dismissed. Young, outcast girls would be parted with their newborn children, screams of pain morphing into howls of anguish as they sought to catch a glimpse of the swaddled bundle they would never see again. Pathetic lives all.

Externally, they were daunting places of high walls and imposing edifices, secure behind wrought iron gates. They separated the real from the surreal. What people could not see, they could not ponder on. Behind the shackled gates, under the protective covering of oak, cedar and sycamore trees was the canopy under which a different world lay.

Below him, aimless paths were followed. He watched carefully until he noticed two men slipping away from the marshalled pack. As the others, they were indifferent to anything else around them. Now and again a well-dressed gentleman would glance in their direction, but he was too caught up talking to another and watching the main group.

His disinterested glances would seal the patient's fate.

'Poor fool' he thought as he selected the perhaps forgotten man below who would assist him in his plan which he carefully worked out. He would escape by a wooden gate. He observed set deep into the walls further up. He watched earlier as a young man eased quickly through it, leaving it ajar. Ideal for his escape. The whole thing should take moments. He'd done it before.

He waited; poised, ready. Gradually the duo of patients separated sufficiently, one weak looking man of similar size straying close by.

He edged out over the branch some more. He would have to be quick. He jumped down, his feet landing on the shoulders of the unfortunate, collapsing him to a pathetic heap on the ground, his neck twisted expertly and mercifully in the same swift action. He dragged the body behind a bush and began removing him of his basic attire. Seconds had elapsed as silently he stooped and ran a tight path by the surrounding wall as it arced around the back of the building. The tight and plentiful growth of trees and hedges would disguise his escape. The gateway loomed ahead, just as the cries of *'he's dead'* could be heard behind him. Cries turned into howls of male voices as he reached the gateway. It was still ajar. He pushed it cautiously and went through.

Robert Hart panicked when he heard the commotion. He jumped up, fear in his eyes. He didn't know what the cries were about but something was up, something big.

"Where are you going?" Rowena enquired.

"You crazy bitch, where do you think? Can you not hear?! Somethings's happened. Christ, I'm gonna get killed!"

She jumped up with him and followed his scurried path back to the gate. Shouts of *'dead'* and *'murdered'* reached her ears as they neared. Robert stopped, turning back to her, hissing.

"Go away, get out of here!" Rowena stepped back behind a tree. Robert turned back to the gate and almost collided with the stranger emerging. Both men stopped, stared at each other, shock in their eyes, beads of sweat palpable on their foreheads. Their lives had unwittingly intertwined.

"Who are you?" Robert blurted as his eyes darted into the stranger's, who stood, frozen, a look of uncertainty in his eyes before he pushed past.

Robert stood in shock, his mind worked overtime in a panicked state of delusion. Had he looked into the eyes of the one unseen voices were calling a murderer?

If he was seen coming through the gate, he would be caught. He would be one caught in the centre of it all, his name bandied about the small village and gossiped upon to the shame and sorrow of his hard-working family. Sweat poured down his forehead. Robert didn't look back, instead concentrating on his own predicament. He turned to enter the gate. The crumbling, splinter-filled planks against his palms was the last thing he experienced as a rock crashed down on his head, sending him slumping against the gate and falling within the walls of the asylum.

The stranger ran, away from the gate, bundle under his arm, as fast as he could, his mind thinking ahead to his next move. His original clothes would have to be destroyed but not here. He knew another small village lay out to the west beyond the woods, Cardiff's Bridge. He would make for there for the moment. He could avail of his more innocent appearance for a short time, at least until the early hours of dawn. As he ran, darting between tall trees and low-hanging branches his mind wandered back to his actions. He regretted what he had done to that poor soul but it was an action taken out of necessity. His wandering mind dulled his senses and he was cursing his slip of concentration and over-confidence as his foot caught in a protruding root, sending him tumbling down a steep slope, the sharp pain in his head the last thing he remembered before slapping hard against the sleeping trunk of an ancient tree, his bones making contact with the ages past, a random shoot of nature long ago playing a pivotal role in the here and now.

Nearby, the limp body of young Robert Hart lay in a tangle, a look of horrified shock and surprise forever etched on his face until someone had the good grace to close his eyes.

Six

The eyes of the slain patient pleaded with him, boring deep into his own soul. As his own hands, bigger in the near distance, made way around his neck he was pulled back by an unknown force; a force that was laughing, gaggling, crying, pleading. His head spun around and he saw a void of lost, vacant faces, bony arms holding him tight, pinning him to the ground, their incessant chanting and pleading bursting his eardrums as the asylum patient stood over him, a wicked, evil grin expanding across his face. Yet as he clasped his own hands around his neck, his eyes remained sad, lonely, unloved. The woman mourned for him, the anger and vengeance in the her eyes bored deep into his soul...

The soft orange glow crackled and randomly spat tiny fireflies into the cool night air. It was the first thing he saw as his eyes slowly fluttered open. It was comforting. It was warm. He lay on his side, head throbbing, throat rasping for water.

"He was someone, you know..."

The words resounded around his head, the voice gentle, musical, yet familiar. He turned his head to see Rowena sitting cross-legged at the other side of a small fire.

"He was someone. You bastard."

He held his head as he nudged himself up awkwardly with one elbow. He looked around, the place was dark. His eyes focused he could make out the heavy trunks of surrounding trees. Rowena stared at him, her hair swept to one side, her hands playing with a small stick that she was rolling around inside a flame. She took it out and inspected the smouldering tip, before returning it to the flames. He cursed to himself.

"What happened?" he asked, head thumping, tasting dried blood.

"You fell, I guess," she replied, all the time staring at the stick. She was wearing the same dirty dress. Added to the glow of the small, comforting fire it gave her a sinister look, her hair a stark raven-black in the altered light.

"You're lucky I got to you first."

"What do you mean?"

"It's all over the village you know, the murder. Doesn't happen here," she explained, grinning cheaply. "They're after you, the police, the villagers, doesn't take long to add things up. Probably the newspapers in a few days too. The doctor said the fool died by a broken neck, but a break by another person. So's the talk anyway. Strange really. The men working there claim they took their eyes off him for a few seconds, when they looked back he was gone. They ran to where he was last seen and spotted him lying there, feeble, head twisted and eyes as empty as they ever where. That's what I heard anyway." She stood up, dusting her dress down.

"Where am I, how did I get here?" he demanded.

"I should be asking you that, you devil."

She smirked and hunkered down beside him, her hand brushed his forehead. "That's a bad fall you took, you're very unlucky."

He stared into her eyes for some seconds. They were shadowed by the glowing embers of the small fire, her smirk betrayed an upper hand.

"Did you push me?" he ventured.

"Oh no, you did this one all by yourself."

"Where am I? Still in the woods?" he repeated.

"The woods, yes, I found you crumpled against a tree over there."

He had never experienced a fear like it, the dim glow of the warm fire made the penetrating blackness that surrounded them even more imposing. He propped himself up on his elbows, looking around to gain a sense of perspective in the surrounding blackness. He remembered the clothing, a quick glance downward revealed he was in the patient's clothes.

"They're burnt," she continued, "all young Tom's finery! Hah, he'll be looking for those back one day. Anyway, the lunatic's clothes are a better fit."

"Who dressed me?"

She laughed and threw her head back up in the air, shaking it from side to side as she slowly lowered it and met his eyes.

"Who do you think?! Slattery? Stafford? No, not the holy men, let me see…. Hmmmmm oh yes…" She leaned almost into the fire, reflections of flames blazing in her pupils and adding to the intensity of her presence.

"Me, that's who."

He was silent, inspecting the carefully buttoned shirt, laced shoes.

"Oh it's not as if I haven't done it before you know. I've seen it all."

"How long have I been here, unconscious?"

"The early hours. I cared for Granny when she was ill, you know that? I can certainly look after a man who hit his head again a tree. Some knock, that'll be a bump for days. You were saying some strange stuff in your sleep, night hags maybe?"

"Night hags?"

"Bad dreams."

"I cannot remember."

"You're not from round here, I know that," Rowena offered, her eyes making sly contact before turning back to the fire. "You never even heard of the night hags for a start, and you talk, funny?"

He took the opportunity to study her features in greater detail in the glow of the comforting fire. She was young, delicate looking, perhaps the subject of a lovingly-painted portrait of times past, echoing whatever turmoil she kept locked away in her mind. Her face was sculpted, elegant cheekbones covered in soft pale skin. Her eyes sparkled, with what though he was unsure.

"The man," he eventually asked, "the man who was killed, was he known in the area?"

She eased round beside him and gently poked him in the ribs with her bare foot, causing him to wince. She smiled, leaning in real close, eyes centimetres apart, her stale breath wafting up his nostrils.

"Which one?"

Her words chilled him.

"What?!"

"Which one? Two men were killed, you know. Probably lynch mobs leaving the taverns looking for you, with a feed of ale on them."

He searched her motionless face for a clue. "I do not understand...?"

"Two men were killed, a patient and a worker. Oh such a fuss you've caused mo stór! I wonder who could have done that now," she mocked.

He sat bolt upright, grabbing her arms, causing her to gasp in surprise but her smile to widen. "I only killed one man!"

She laughed, wriggled her arms free and cupped his face in her hands.

"Your first mistake, stranger. Admitting it."

He shook his head free and threw her arms away from him, the sudden movement of air caused by her tumbling to the ground causing the small fire to wave and shudder briefly.

"Oh angry again? You gonna kill me too?!"

"Who was the other man?! I did not kill another man!"

She got up, swept her tumbling hair from her face and walked up to him.

"The young boy you met at the gate."

Her words caught him off guard. He narrowed his eyes, searching his memory until he could picture the brief encounter.

"I was there too, you devil, I was nearby, when all hell broke loose. I was hiding away and saw you rush out, almost knock him over. I don't know who looked more afraid, Robert was afraid of losing his position, you see…"

"He worked there?"

"Intelligent man I see, he did, yes, he shouldn't have been away."

He searched his mind, his memories, his tortured brain for reasoning. His head was still hurting but he had crystal clarity on the events at the asylum.

"I did not kill another man."

"That's cos you didn't."

"Then who did?"

"I did."

He stared back at Rowena, her sculpted face smiling as she twirled the edges of her dusty dress. "You?"

"Well, couldn't have him telling on you now, and you been taken away from me?"

He felt his heart rate increase, he felt threatened, isolated. Rowena was cunning and she held a secret he needed to destroy. She displayed a stealth and a craft he needed to meet head on. She was dangerous; whereas he felt comfortable with his hosts and even a patronising superiority over the villagers, she was a different story. She was the most sinister.

"You said take me away from you, that you did not want them to take me away from you?!"

"Oh no, that wouldn't do, would it?"

"Why?"

She walked to his side, standing on her toes, and whispered in his ear.

"I don't want anyone to take you away before you tell me everything, besides, I know who you are…" she retreated, with a smirk.

"You say you know me…" he offered the words more in hope than expectation. She was wily.

"I do, everything, and the village are out to kill you, if the sergeant doesn't get you first. You can't stay in this place forever. But I can help you."

"Help me? How?"

"I can hide you." Her voice was suddenly gentle, lustful, yet one he couldn't trust.

"I do not need it."

She bounded back towards him, the force of her outstretched palms pushing him back to the ground. She sat astride him and leaned in close to his face.

"Oh but you do, you do."

She smiled and brushed his hair back.

"You need because you see, I know everything about you."

"You know nothing of me... Rowena."

"Ha! You know my name, good boy! But I know some things and I need you to tell me everything! I'm the best person for you to know now. What you gonna do, tell them I killed Robert?! Half the fuckers don't care about me, think I'm bad, mad, no-one would believe little Rowena could kill someone when a stranger has just been found and disappeared again. But, to tell them would mean facing them and the cells for you before the hangman. With me, you and your secret will be safe."

"What secret?" he bluffed.

She leaned back, sizing him up. "The one you're gonna have to take to your grave, Devil, when you tell me."

"Devil. What is this devil? Why are you calling me that?"

She leaned in so close to him, smiling, her breath sticking in his throat.

"Because you are a devil, my devil. Some would have me believe you're the devil, the real devil, living under the bridge. Stupid fools who believe that tale grow up in fear, but the devil wouldn't live under a bridge would he?"

"The devil, as you know him, does not exist."

"What devil are you talking about now?"

"Your devil."

"But you are my devil and my devil alone. I know things about you..."

She stood up and walked around to the other side of the fire. He staggered to his feet, shaking dirt from his clothes which stank of an institutional washing product. "Who am I then, girl?" he demanded.

She turned back, stifling a giggle. "Oh girl is it now? Well you've got that right Devil, I'm all girl under here and the only one who can help you. My Mama christened me Rowena. I'd rather be called by my name."

"I know your name. I do not need you Rowena, I do not want your help."

"You do! Stories spread fast in this village, everyone knows, and the kind old fool of a lady who's bed you woke up in has been telling tales of the stranger who was found in a field near her home, then vanished as quick. People make up their own minds. But this time they'd be right!"

He grabbed her wrists and held them level to her face. "Then why have you not reported me then? Told the authorities? Told the villagers?"

She laughed and wrestled her wrists free with a strength that took him by surprise. "I can you see. I can, sure was me who found you. But I need to know who you are first. I can hide you. I can protect you but you must tell me everything. I cannot tell the villagers how I first saw you though, they will cart me of to Farnham. But I can tell them everything else."

He thought back to what Mrs. Devine told him about her. "Those who would send you to the asylum, are they the ones who blame you for your mother's death?"

Her face twisted with rage, fingers contorting as she lashed out at him, grabbing his hair, scrabbing his face, kicking, punching, cursing with such ferocity he fell back. She loomed over him, eyes blazing, hair tossed asunder as he counteracted her arm movements with his own until his strength won over and he sent her crashing in a heap against a nearby tree trunk. All the time she resisting his fight back.

"Don't you ever talk about my Mama! Don't you ever talk about my Mama, you bastard!"

He had to be rid of her. She was too much trouble. She knew too much. Now was time. He jumped towards her, but she was crafty. A sudden kicking foot caught him between the legs, downing him as she rained kick after kick into him, screaming about her Mama until she relented and slumped to the ground, arms resting on her knees as she began to sob.

He lay where he fell, breathless, pain searing throughout him. He watched her, head bobbing as the sobs flowed before she wiped her wrist across her eyes and got up. She stood looking at him.

"Pathetic. You let a girl beat you. You wanted to kill me, didn't you? Didn't you fucker? I'm trouble, amn't I now? Yeah, yeah, well you need me now Devil, as much as I need you."

She turned and walked away but stopped almost instantly. The fire cracked weakly. He sat up, allowing the pain to recede.

"Don't you see?" she asked gently. "I need to know, I must know about you. I saw it all, I saw everything. Robbed and left for dead in a field. That was clever of me, wasn't it? My old schoolmaster once said I was a clever girl."

She stood stock still, staring into the nothingness of the darkness. She swiftly turned, grabbed his hand and began to lead him away.

"Let the fire go, it'll be getting bright soon. Daddy will be away to work."

"Where are we going?"

"I've got to hide you. The house is empty during the day, no-one comes near it."

"You are bringing me back to the village?!" he exclaimed, her boldness catching him by surprise.

"Well we can try the tunnel under the graveyard to the castle up the north road, but you'd have to find it first," she chuckled.

His mind perked up. "A tunnel?"

She smiled, nodding her head slightly.

"A legend, another from round here. According to some people there's an old tunnel that runs under the graveyard and right up to the big castle, a while away…"

Her tone descended into a mocking one, "…but like most stories, no-one knows anyone who has walked it. Like I said, another story."

"I can take care of myself. Disappear."

"Hah! Oh you can wander Devil, if you like, but we're not so backward out here in the country, you know. The city isn't far and word spreads quick, everyone'll be looking for you. A stranger who killed two innocent people in the country? You'll be wanted high and wide, you'll have no rest 'til you are caught and hanged. And you will be."

Her words bore deep into his heart. She was no fool.

"They wouldn't think to look for you in the village, though."

"They could…"

"After two murders? Oh no. The police in the city have been informed by now. They think you're dangerous, that you'll flee. There's so much they want to know about you. They'll want to know why you left Jamestown House so quickly, if you've nothing to hide. And now two people murdered, in this sleepy little place, Oh you're wanted alright. But you'd be mad to stay here, wouldn't you? To hide in the village. That's why they wouldn't think it. That's why you're safe with me."

They remained silent as she led him towards the edge of the wood. He felt low, defeated, not in control of the situation. Her argument made sense. He had tried to be rid of her, what if he did kill her? Then she would be missing, the girl who found the stranger in the first place. The search would intensify. He was on his own here, no protection and as he was discovering, all his schooled knowledge counted for nothing in the reality. She knew his secret. She was intriguing, perplexing... beautiful.

The woods gave way to open space. Overhead, the dark of night was segueing gently into the lull of pre-dawn, one of calmness, serenity, one whose beauty captivated him. The sharp blue of the emerging sky, still holding the twinkling stars caught his gaze, the fresh morning air revived and soothed him. The azure thrill of the oncoming dawn was one he wanted to spend every moment in. Bird song gently filtered through the air as the sun sought to creep over the horizon. Shades of yellow, red, merging to purple, blue, navy were the canvas he stood under now.

Rowena turned eventually and looked at him.

"You look like you've never seen dawn before."

She stared back at him for a few seconds, before releasing him from her gaze as she concentrated on the oncoming day once more. In the dawn of a new day a peace arose between them. Rowena moved to stand beside him.

"What's your name?"

He stared ahead. "It does not matter, to anyone."

"To me it does." He continued to search the sky, eyes darting back and forth among the constellations, seeking any potential slight shift. To see the stars in such positions was a wonder to him. Of all the things he had seen in this new place, the emerging dawn was the most beautiful. He turned to her.

"The sky is so beautiful."

"I know, every morning I leave the house, talk to Mama. Mornings like this are the best; no-one sees you, no-one cares, it's just me, the stars and Mama."

Her voice had softened, representative now of a girl her age.

"What happened her?"

He knew the answer, Mrs. Devine had told him back at the house, but he wanted to hear it from her.

She looked away, before looking back at him quickly, her eyes betraying an uncertainty for the first time.

"She died. When I was little. Daddy never recovered from it. Some blamed me for Mama's death, said she was never right after I came along. Others, kinder people, say she never recovered after a boy she sought married another woman. My aunt told me he broke her heart. Ben was his name, I think, he liked Mama, Mrs. Devine liked him too. She still has his picture on the wall."

He thought back to the photograph he had studied, of what Kathy had told him about the young man seated at the table confidently. How intriguing they were all linked.

Rowena continued. "He liked Mama more, when Mama was a girl, but he went off and married someone from the country. Then she met my father one day. That's all. Come on, we must go, Daddy will be away soon and we can stay in the house."

She took his hand in a kind grasp, echoing the gentile nature of her story. He remained rooted to the spot, surprised.

"Don't make me fucking drag you..."

He seceded and they both began walking in the direction of the village.

"Do you know where you are going? It is still quite dark out."

She laughed. "I've spent more time walking these fields than perhaps anyone in the village. I know my way. But we got to go now, while it's still a bit dark. You can stay in the house. Daddy will never know. No-one will ever know. It's the safest thing for you."

Her hand remained taut around his as she skillfully negotiated unseen bumps and hedgerows. "Ben. I think I'll call you Ben."

They continued silently across the fields, the ever expanding dawn forcing them to quicken their step across the countryside as a new day awakened until they were running silently up the main street, heads bowed as she led him to behind the small cottages and asked him to stay low until she gave a signal. He hunkered, shivering in the cool air of the dawn, pondering on whether he should run or stay. What had he to gain? What had he to lose? His thoughts were interrupted by her whispering voice as she beckoned him inside.

The house was simple, unloved. It served as a shelter and that was it. She led him into a small bedroom, a single window allowing the emerging dawn to illuminate a faint light on the bedroom floor. There was a small table and a washbasin.

"Stay there. I'll get you some of Daddy's's clothes to change."

He was letting himself be lead back into the heart of danger. He panicked and stood up.

"I have to go."

"Go?"

"Yes, I have to leave."

She laughed and patted him on the chest. "You are some fool aren't you? Have you not listened to a word I said? Word spreads quickly through here. I told you. It's morning now. People will be about. You're in serious trouble. Only I can help you."

"I have ways of hiding."

"Oh yes, you do, when you're not killing fools or somehow knocking yourself out against a tree."

She leaned in closer to him. "Walk out if you want, but it will be in the lunatic's clothes, not father's. You won't get far, not here."

"The village is small, I know my way."

"Then have fun looking at your picture on posters in windows then. Oh you'll get caught, maybe not tomorrow, but you will." She pushed him back onto the bed and leaned in close, face to face.

"Do you not understand?! Must I say it again? Staying with me is the safest thing you can do! For both of us. I need you to stay!"

He cursed to himself, cursed the village, cursed the girl.

She left the room, returning shortly afterwards with a change of clothes.

"Get into them, give me the ones you're wearing." She smirked and leaned against the wall, playing with her hair, occasionally gazing out the window. It made him uncomfortable. She enjoyed it.

He undressed silently, in the darkest part of the room he could find and hurriedly dressed again in the new clothes. She giggled.

"You're pathetic, you know that."

She stepped forward slowly, looking him up and down as she took the discarded clothes, saying nothing as she gathered them in her arms.

"Stay there. Don't look out the window."

She left and he could hear a key turn in the door.

He slumped back onto the bed, head bowed, defeated.

'How? How? How did it come to this?! What have I done wrong?'

He had no answers. He had no-one to help him or answer for him. He recently relished the solitude in this world; now he feared it.

Seven

Tears welled up in his dry eyes, tears that were never meant to fall now fell openly and freely. The emotion got the better of him; in his mind's eye he could see the ghouls that haunted his sleeping dreams cry with him, their wails rising incessantly to drown out his own sobs as the turmoil and trauma of a new life so quaint and unsuited to took hold of him. The deceased fool stood silently at the back, eyes crying but silence defeating his sobs, the woman smiling…

Outside the tiny cottage, the world lived through another day. Muffled voices passed, the sunlight of another beautiful day filtered through the small window, the floating dust the only other action in the room. It was cool, the stone walls offering a welcome respite even though the window was hot to the touch, when he dared to cast an eye out.

His mind, alone with nothing but permutations that day, concluded he still had a lot to learn. Maybe he grossly underestimated his situation. These were decent, smart people, not the rabble he perhaps thought they were. He hadn't planned for what happened, it had evolved so differently, but here he was, falling deeper into a trench of uncertainty and entanglement. He sighed heavily as he rose from the bed, his height forcing him to stoop under the eaves. He spied the plate on the floor by the door, where she had left it earlier. Food apparently, nothing edible. His thoughts were interrupted as he heard the key turn in the door. Rowena stepped inside.

"So how's do you find your lodgings, Devil?" she chirped on returning.

"You cannot keep me prisoner here."

"I can do whatever I want with you…" she began and, eyeing him up. "Daddy will be home later. Not a word, you here? You're safe here."

"As your prisoner."

Her demeanour changed instantly and she bounded over, cupping his startled face in the palms of her hands.

"Oh you can walk out of here if you wish, but you'll have to get by me first! And anyway, do you know what the talk of the village is about today?

" The dead fool. And the dead worker in the asylum. His mother is howling, wailing down at the church. His brother wants blood, his friends want blood, young girls playing told that peeler Scollard of the strange man they saw outside the Flood's. Those two trollops Joan and Mary too, they say they saw someone acting very strangely, and he was very physical with them, throwing Joanie to the ground. They say he spoke to scared Phoebe Hedderman too, but she's too frightened to say anything. Good enough for her, bitch... her family are no help either, filthy fuckers living in their own shit down there.

"Devine gave a good description alright, as did her squeaky clean daughter, her two sons and that English one. You see, it's all out now! They want to talk to me now but I've been avoiding them. The telephone office has been busy, the peelers knocking on doors talking to the villagers, interrupting the workers in the fields. They've talked to their lot in the city too, they've got people searching the woods and helping out here. They spoke to Daddy and his fellow workers in the next town too. Some innocent boy was cartered off to the barracks but got let go now. Oh wait til the papers get a hold of this. You, devil, will be infamous! All the time I could just tell them to come here and that'd be you finished. Do you not see that I'm trying to help you?!"

He flung her away from him. "Why? Why are you helping me?!"

She brushed her hair from her face and faced him.

"Because I saw everything. You didn't exactly walk into my life, did you?"

She stood up, wiping her mouth with the back of her hand.

He had to face it. "Are you talking about the field, up in Jamestown?"

"Yes I am. Quite a strange day that was, you see, if word gets out, what'll that mean for you? They'd probably get the Brits in, at least they'll enjoy their stay with some of the girls around here! I can easily find out, but, I'm drawn to you and your strange way of talking. Like it or not, I'm the only friend you'll ever have around here. You're a stranger, a murderer..." She placed slow emphasis on the final word, "...and God knows what else. Only I know the truth, about Jamestown, about that day, about you; isn't it best for you to keep it that way?" She stood right in front of him, staring straight up into his eyes, unblinking.

"So you see, it's better for you to do what I say. I have many questions, I think I know the answers, but I want to hear them from you soon."

She smiled as she pushed him back onto the bed.

"Shhhhh, quiet now. People are around. You don't want to be hea..."

70

A rap at the front door startled them both.

Rowena stared out the doorway, the sudden interruption confusing her. She swiftly turned to the visitor. "Stay here. Under the bed. Don't move," she hissed.

She gently slipped out, pocketing the key of the door she locked behind her and answered the main door. Flecks of dry blue paint loosened and fluttered away as she lifted the heavy door inward.

"Constable?"

"Sergeant," Robert Linden corrected, tucking his helmet under his arm. Beside him Constable William Scollard stood.

"Can I help you?" she asked noticing their identical moustaches.

Under the tatty metal bed, he dared not to breathe. He heard the boots of the men pass outside the door, only feet away. Muffled voices. Quiet voices that continued to talk. In his confinement he felt sweat drip from his forehead onto the dusty, cold floor under him. How had it come to this? He had no-one to help him, those who could, he would never set eyes on them again. His dream was a nightmare. His strong heart beat in his chest, echoing in his eardrums. He had knowledge, vast, superior knowledge, far beyond what those surrounding him now would ever know. But it was useless to him as he lay, alone, afraid, hidden under a bed like a common criminal, a prisoner in a primitive cottage of stone and slate. He felt tears fall.

Matthew Whyte sat in Upper Flood's bar, nursing another drink as he stared into nothing behind the counter. The proprietor, always eager to get a rise out of him, finished cleaning a glass and smiled.

"Haven't seen you in here in a few days. They run out of drink down the hill?" The scattered few drinking around them gave various and mixed grunts of laughter.

"I seen your one the other day, across the way, trying to get drink bought for her again."

Matthew didn't move. Didn't blink.

"All she does is wander the area during the day."

Matthew sat motionless, continuing to stare ahead.

"She's been sending people in to get her drink, a few times now…"

He leaned forward over the bar.

"I don't want that kind of trouble here, you know, with her sort."

Matthew's eyes darted towards the middle-aged face staring back at him.

"Her sort?"

"You know…"

"I don't, tell me."

There was a silence, broken only by a voice at the end of the bar.

"She's a whore."

More stifled guffaws of laughter followed. Matthew's eyes sank back into the glass he now gripped with anger. The stale smell of beer, tobacco and old wood filled his nostrils as he began to breathe heavily.

"She found that murderer, you know, up by Jamestown House, came to see him and all again I heard. She's probably with him in the woods now, doing what she does best!"

Matthew stood up straight, sizing up the speaker before draining his glass and firing it down towards him. The sudden movement caught the young man by surprise as the glass crashed into the side of his head, followed by Matthew's bulk laying fists into him.

"I'll kill you, you little bastard!" Matthew roared as repeated attempts to pull him off the young victim proved futile. Rowena's father was a big man, he had been in a few scraps before and knew how to win them. His unkempt beard added a menacing look to his face as his eyes bulged with anger.

Cowering on the floor, the younger man shouted at him to stop until a mass of arms finally managed to halt the assault. The customers dragged Matthew away, the owner ordering that he be thrown out.

"She's only a little whore, everyone knows, half the village have had her!"

The young man's words reached Matthew as he was brought through the door but try as he might he couldn't break free and found himself settling onto the ground outside in a pile of dust.

"That's my daughter!" he roared at the now closed door. "That's my daughter you bastard!"

Two constables, drafted into the village in light of the recent events were standing outside the barracks.

"What will we do, or should we do anything?" the youngest asked.

"A warning will be enough. Drink that's all." They wandered towards him, urging him to quieten down or spend a night in the cells.

"Come on now, go home, now."

"He should be in the cells!" Matthew roared, pointing vaguely back at the bar. The watching public stood quietly, not surprised at the latest outburst.

Women whispered to each other, their eyes staring at the crumpled heap of one of the village drunks, their heads nodding slightly as they spoke.

Matthew looked around at them. His head was heavy, his throat raspy, his eyes fighting to stay open.

"Havin' a good look, the lot of ye, are ye?!" he roared. "Havin' a good talk about me?"

"Go home, Matthew, now, or I'll make sure you lose your position!" the voice of Constable Scollard added as he walked towards him. He had heard the shouting, recognised the voice at he sat at his desk near the window in the barracks by the crossroads.

"Now!" he ordered firmly. "Go now Mr. Whyte! Rowena's there, we were talking to her earlier in the day. Go home to bed."

Matthew waved them off and stumbled up, staggering towards the cottage while uttering a litany of mumbled curses. Rowena could hear everything as it echoed down the street. The front door opened with a lunge.

"Rowena!" Matthew barked.

"I'm resting…"

"Rowena come here." His voice was softer, quieter.

She gestured at her guest to stay stock still under the bed.

"In a moment."

She waited quietly for a few minutes before leaving the room, making sure to lock it behind her once more.

He could hear murmured voices, raised slightly at sparce intervals. What sounded like a slap, followed by a sharp howl, echoed through the key-hole. There was more shouting followed by muffled sobs. The door burst open and Rowena stood in the doorway, hair askew, slamming the door just as hard behind her.

"You aul bastard!" she roared back.

"What happened?" he whispered.

She sat on the floor, staring into the corner. "He came home with a feed of drink on him again, this time got into a fight because someone said I was a whore. He's after asking me was it true."

He pulled himself out from under the bed. "What did you say?"

Rowena let a stifled, surprised laugh and turned back to face him. She got up and eyeballed him again, both hands resting either side of him on the bed. "I'm no whore!" she snarled trough gritted teeth. Her voice was soft, quiet, but venomous.

"I've had my way with a few lads round here, but I'm no whore. Years ago my Mama was called a whore, Daddy nearly drowned the man who said it in the stream... my Mama wasn't like that, I'm not either."

She pushed herself back up. "He'll be asleep soon. We'll go for a walk."

She lay back on the bed, he sat on the floor by its cold frame, staring out the window as slowly the evening melded into the first dark of night and the whiteness of the moonlight gradually crept across the cooling floor.

She hummed gently to herself, twirling her hair around her finger.

Earlier he had waited under the bed for what must have been half an hour while Rowena expertly spoke to the policemen, telling them she had found him in a bad way in a field off Jamestown House and had visited him again when he had come round. No, she had only spent a short time with him so couldn't pick up anything of interest. She had no idea where he had come from, he said nothing. She couldn't tell them any more but agreed that the presented sketch was uncannily accurate. Of course, if she saw him again she would report it. The policemen left, impressed and amused at her co-operation and recollection of events. Maybe she wasn't as bad as people make out after all. Seeing the two RIC officers out, she gently unlocked the door and closed it softy behind her. He thought back to her standing there, smiling, her two hands behind her back, as if to ensure the door was shut.

'Johnathan Whyte, is it now?' she had chided. 'Are we related then, devil? A simple, country girl I may be...' she had begun, her voice betraying a mocking tone towards him, '...but I know how to add things up. You asked Kathy Devine who I was and later used my surname alongside such a common name! Johnathan! It isn't a name common to a devil like yourself, but now I know that you were looking for me. I suppose, knowing what I know, you had to.'

He recalled that last sentence over and over in his head.

Back in the moment, she moved down beside him and began brushing his cheek with her fingers. He turned his head slightly at this. She eased onto his lap, sitting astride and facing him before pushing him back onto the floor.

"I'm honoured. You chose my own name to fool people, yet you can't fool the girl who's very name you stole."

She leaned forward, her face right in his.

"That's exciting, that is, to know that, you know…" She sat back and began to undo his shirt. He grabbed her wrists violently, startling her.

"Ooooh Mr. Whyte, aren't you the surprising sort!"

She shook her wrists free and continued unbuttoning his shirt. He resisted.

"Help! Help me!" she screamed, her face looking towards the window. His heart leapt. "What are you doing?!"

"Help, the murderer, the murderer…"

He clasped his palm over her mouth and flipped her over, slamming her back onto the stone floor. She bit down on his palm, causing him to wince in pain and retreat.

"You do what I want or I'll scream and shout and have the neighbours kicking in the door. You'll be caught then. Dragged out, beaten, thrown in a cell then hung!"

His eyes darted around the room.

"Go on, go on! Hit me with something, a poker or a chair or something, go on! I'll scream and scream and even if you kill me, you'll be heard. That'll be it for you, Devil… or…" She stood up and grabbed the lapels of his shirt. "Do what I desire and I'll keep quiet and save your life. Again. Your secret will be safe with me. I won't tell…"

His eyes bored into hers. Her smile remained.

He shook his head, glancing back out the window. She lifted him up off the floor and towards the bed. "You're too good looking for me to ignore. Wherever you came from, welcome to my world."

Mrs. Devine knelt by her bed, elbows on the covers, hands clasping rosary beads tightly and her head bowed as she prayed and prayed.

A tear escaped as she begged the forgiveness of her God for harbouring a murderer. She wasn't a bad woman, she explained. She was good, a good Christian, a kind, hard-working soul who was taken in by the devil incarnate as she saw him. Twice now the law had visited her about him, the second time to reveal the brutal double murder he was being sought for. She had never any dealings with authorities before.

Now the whole village knew she harboured the stranger before he slipped from her grasp to wreck havoc on the sleepy village below.

She had been taken in by him, fooled by his manners, his conversation, his questions. She was as responsible for the two murders as he was.

She raised her head, facing the crucifix on the wall over her bed, failing to notice her daughter knock gently before slipping the door aside. She poked her head and a small candle holder round the door, the light enough to catch the glow of a great candle burning on her mother's beside table.

"Are you alright mammy?" Kathy asked, worried about her mother.

"I'm praying, love," she whispered as mumbled pleas for forgiveness continued to slip off her tongue.

"It's going to be alright, isn't it? No-one will blame you."

Mrs. Devine shut her eyes tight. "They already do, Kathy love. He was in my house, my care and I allowed him to walk away. I even shared a meal with him, had him as my guest. A murderer, can you believe it? A murderer. I let you walk alone with him in the grounds, I gave him Tom's clothes…"

"People wont think that way, you know they won't."

"A murderer and I gave him shelter… God forgive me."

Kathy knew to let her mother pray until sleep called. There was no point in convincing her otherwise. She would face her own demons and all she could do was pray her mother would realise she was not to blame. It would be hard, a village as small as this one, for her involvement to slip from the mind.

Eight

The demons stood either side of the temptress as she sat on a chair of bones, her head bowed, eyes glaring, mouth curled in a sweet but evil smile. Her cohorts danced and goaded at either side of her as she beckoned him forward into her lair, her world… behind him the dead fool and worker grabbed an arm each, pushing him towards the temptress as he begged to be released. She stood from the chair and extended an elongated arm, wrapping it around him as she smiled and drew her to him. In her other arm she held a small bundle, a child, skeletal in appearance…

He opened his eyes and felt her hair on his face, her lips against his. He gasped and moved away as she giggled. His eyes focused on the tiny room once more. Rowena slipped away, pulling her dress on before she left the room, her feet not making a sound on the floor. He noticed his shirt open and remembered, what had happened, what they had done.

'*Curse her…*'

He sighed a reserved yet pathetic sigh and closed his eyes. It was a disaster. The planning, scheduling, thought that went into his journey and for what? To be holed up in a primitive stone cottage by a young woman? The same woman who witnessed everything and who held such sway over him, a woman who threatened to throw him to the wolves if he didn't obey her. The old, fictional-bred dictations of not interfering with anything or anyone were prominent in his mind and something he and the woman had agreed, but how, honestly how, could anyone but he know that those rules governing his unique journey were useless? Not that it mattered, not that anyone knew what had become of him. A small passable village this may be, but lives had been altered forever, ended prematurely. Too much had gone one.

'*This journey was meant to be enlightening, pioneering, a new beginning, now what has it become but an unbridled mess of warped sequences, events happening that should never have, people intertwining in an unplanned and dangerous way, lives that should have been straightforward changed utterly for the worse…*'

Rowena returned to the room, stifling his thoughts. She nodded deftly in his direction and opened the front door. He slowly rose and followed.

'I can kill her now, I must, I should, but am I defeated?'

Closing it behind her, she took his hand as they ghosted onto the dusty hill, he not seeing or caring but allowing himself to be led blindly by Rowena.

 "The churchyard tonight, we'll sit awhile and talk to Mama!" Her smile was hidden from him in the shroud of night.

Just as in returning from the woods in the pre-dawn light, she knew her way around expertly in the dark, leading him up the hill of the main street before turning down the hill of Church Street and to the wall of the churchyard, which she skillfully climbed. She sat atop, looking back down on him.

"Come on!" Rowena gestured.

He hesitated, paused, looking around at the silent cottages, sensing a forlorn chance.

"Come on!" she snarled. "Do you know what it's like to be chased down by a mob with flaming torches in the dead of a night? You'll be struck dead before you hit the ground. I will shout out. Join me."

He clumsily climbed the rough stone wall, scraping his arms painfully as she took his hand and they jumped down onto the other side. She grabbed his hand again and led him briefly through the dark until they sat against the cooling wall of the nave beside the old porch at the entrance.

The now disused abbey sat silent at it's peculiar angle, left for the stone to crumble and the timbers to rot since the new church that stood across the sloping street was built almost sixty years earlier. For centuries the abbey and the surrounding area was a place of adoration, worship, wealth, pillage; originally a monastic settlement and one of the two Eyes of Ireland. On this mild June evening at the turn of the 20th century, it was alone, pitifully standing guard over the dusty bones of the long forgotten buried arbitrarily in its shadow, their grave markers harder to read as time moved on.

"We can be at peace here," Rowena whispered, "no-one can go near us here 'til the morn. Better than the woods, they've searched them today, probably one or two still there be they peelers or people looking for a reward. We can sit inside the church if we hear voices. You're safe here 'til we go home.

"Over there, at the other side of the church, poor Robert, will be buried soon, in his family's grave. Mama's grave is the other side, near the big cross. I'll bring you in a bit. We'll walk through the church."

"Poor Robert you said?"

"The boy who you ran into at the gate. And killed."

"But you killed him…"

"Not according to the village, Devil. Remember that."

He didn't reply to that statement.

"You say your mother is buried here, are all your family here?"

"Some. A few were dumped in a mound, up the hill in the big cemetery as you head out to Phibsboro. Cholera killed them. Cholera killed many round here."

"Dumped?"

"Dumped, disease-ridden poor souls, you know. They were all dumped into a pit. No holy rest for them…"

He recalled tales of such burial; infested corpses, some with the grace to be wrapped tight in cloths, unceremoniously slipping from an upturned handcart as they tumbled into a hastily dug pit. Gruesome, frozen and pained faces staring back, lifeless, as the living hurriedly got to work with their spades. Occasionally a frail arm would lift from the rotting pile, a person not yet quite dead, silently pleading for mercy as the clodding earth slowly filled their mouth, throats and lungs, suffocating the little life left from them. Etchings existed, only scraping at the true horror of the operation.

"All that suffering from drinking dirty water in the stream. People drank from it always back then. Strange really, was only around fifty years ago, some remember it well…"

She stared up at the bright orb of the moon. "Some say it will fall." She touched his arm with a tenderness he was wary of.

"What?"

"The moon, will it fall?" He followed her gaze, forcing a brief smile at her astuteness replaced, in one sentence, by naivety.

"No, it will not fall. It will remain in orbit."

She turned to him. "What? What are you saying?"

"The term for the moon, the orbit, what keeps it, well, floating…"

"You've been well taught," she giggled as she turned to face him.

"Tell me more of the moon!"

He searched his mind for the right answer. "I don't know much more."

Naivety again. A chink in her armour.

"Oh but you do, you must!" she squeaked with excitement.

"Why must I?"

"Cos you're not from here, are you?"

He couldn't see her face clearly but knew she was smiling.

"I am."

"We both know that's not true, don't we, Devil?"

"I am from here, but it was at another time. I know this area."

She moved around so she was sitting astride him again, pinning him firmly against the soothing cold stonework.

"Time you told me I think."

Her words were plain, straight to the point. He closed his eyes. He gazed back at the stars. "I am from here, but I have been on a journey…"

"A journey?"

"Yes, a journey, a long journey, the greatest journey ever, to get me here, to bring me back here."

He was surprised when she slipped off him and back to her original position. She began humming.

"That sounds very romantic. The greatest journey ever, you say. I'd believe that, knowing what I know."

Silence fell on both of time for a while, his mind calculating responses to questions that ultimately never came.

"What are you singing?" he enquired.

"An old song I used to sing as a girl, Mama taught me, I don't really remember the words anymore."

She moved forward to face him again. "Do you know of the fair? The fairs that used to be here, by the maypole, just up the hill over there?" She was giddy, excited as a child.

"I have heard," he replied.

"Oh I would loved to have been at one, there was killings at them, you know? Great fun! You've brought the excitement back to this forgotten place! We haven't seen as much excitement since then!"

His mind shot back to the vision he had as he entered the village, the long, tall pole, the carnage, the man with the knife in his hand, the pungent smell of sweat, alcohol and manure… had he been there?

She stood up, taking his hand.

"Come on, Mama's grave, and Granny's, I'll show you."

She took him by the hand and led him through the porch where once heavy oak doors kept all inside safe, doors claimed perhaps for firewood long ago. They continued into the deserted, tiny nave where only half a century before, another generation filed in slowly for adoration, kneeling on old timbers and praying for their needs. Locals, much like the villagers today, facing forward into the chancel where the priest held court. His voice would drone on and reverberate against the close stone walls and timbers of the arched roof, timbers that were all but gone now as the stars from the clear night shone on the deserted and ghostly scene.

"Watch the grave now!" she chided as she skipped over a tombstone within the confines of the church, unseen in the dark night and snug against the wall before leading him through a low doorway.

"This way is shorter," she giggled, "down this way." She pointed toward the ground. "That's a vault. Down the steps there."

She led him around to the right.

"I cannot see it."

"It's there, right in front of you, the Bayly vault, another step and you'd tumble all the way down. What great sport that would be!"

She moved to stand in front of him. "But what a great place that would be to hide you, wouldn't it? If things got worse for you, I mean. You could help me break in that door and hide there. You'd never be found!"

He could see her outline in the moonlight. *'One push…'* That's all it would take. One quick shove and she would tumble back down those steps, certainly hurting herself at least, leaving him with an easy job to finish her off.

"I know what you're thinking," Rowena ventured.

He hesitated. "What are you talking about?"

She skipped daintily to the side, to safety as the quiet call of an owl eerily sound-tracked the moment. "You want to push me down there, kill me and you could have, you could do, but I'd scream and scream and wake up the dead lying around as well as this village! I'd make sure they heard your name before you snapped my neck. Those in the White House would wake up, the drunken bastards stumble out of bed with a lust for your blood. The cottage people, you'd be quite surrounded. Nice idea but you are best with me, besides…" He saw something catch the light in her hand.

"I'd plunge this into your gut as sooner!" she hissed the sentence, spittle shooting up into his face.

She took him by the hand and led him through the darkness, between headstones and graves in the pitch black.

"Over here," she whispered as they snaked to a spot by the wall.

"Hello Mama! I've brought a friend this time. Say hello to Mama!"

He felt a sharp object in his side, pressing deeper until he cried out in pain and jumped to the side. But her other hand held him taut.

"Say hello…" Her words had a musical tone, she stared at him but he couldn't see her face.

"Hello," he replied, cautiously, with one of her hands practically blocking the flow of blood in his wrist and the other positioning a knife in his side.

"I've called him Ben, Mama, he says his name's Johnathan though… oh he won't break your heart, he won't break mine, but Mama you should see where he comes from!"

Her words caused him to swallow with uncertainty. "What's that? Oh no Mama, he hasn't told me, but by God he will, won't you?" she demanded, turning to him. The knife jabbed deeper into his side as she closed the sentence.

"What did you really see Rowena?"

"Shhh, not now, were talking to Mama!"

She continued a frightening, one-sided conversation with the ghost of a woman only she could see or hear. He understood why he was warned away from her, why she was 'touched' as Mrs. Devine described her. He thought back to his plan to run and leave her to her tales.

'They may commit her, but they would still search for me…'

He felt the knife in his side all through the exchange.

Early morning birds had begun their sweet chorus when she decided to bid her dead mother goodbye and urged him to return to the cottage with her.

In a tree, an owl ominously hooted. The cool air offered a brief respite to what was to be another intense hot day ahead. They scaled the wall where the faded Nether Cross stood, clamped together years before by locals having freed it from it's earthly grave where it lay since Oliver Cromwell's troops lazily marched through the village. Smashed in two, it was buried for fear it would fall victim to their destructive force. It lay forgotten for years, it's discovery the result of the lucky ramblings of an old man.

They scuffed across the dirt on the street, the dry soil crunching softly underfoot, the odd loose stone being kicked inadvertently as they ghosted silently by the sleeping tenement house, its drunken howls quiet in these dawn hours, past the dormant houses and pubs, the babble from the stream a soothing reminder of the nature he was in awe of after his arrival. Rowena expertly weaving her way until the cool whitewash of the small cottage she called home was reflected in a fading moonlight.

He had enjoyed his respite outdoors. She glided through the unlatched door, leading him in again to the musty, dank room where she made her bed. She gently shut the door behind her and quietly turned the key in the lock.

She slipped it back into the pocket of her dress and her silhouette gestured towards the small bed tucked away in the corner.

"I'm tired," she yawned, her eyes sleepy.

"I was about to ask if you ever sleep…" he whispered.

"Not so much, I have no need to, I sleep on and off but I have the night hags sometimes."

He sat down on the bed alongside her, sleep overcoming him rapidly, his body was weary once more. She lay him back on the bed, alongside her, the knife still in her hand, though her grip had loosened. His mind drifted. Tonight would be ideal to rid himself of her once and for all. But she had proven her worth as a fine foe. If he attempted to tackle her, under the spell and desire of sleep himself, it could be his end.

She wasn't about to kill him, that he knew. She wanted to know his secret. The longer he strung her along, the more time he would avail of to gather his strength and think his way out of this whole sorry mess. Sleep overcame him, already her young body was heaving gently beside him yet her fingers gripped the knife still. He pondered, as he did sleep washed over him with a gentle soothing relief. He was slipping out of this existence, vaguely aware of the waking man elsewhere in the building, pulling his clothes on for another day of work, oblivious to his daughter's guest in the next room.

He let his mind drift. Memories returned to him, he was back in familiar surroundings, back among his own as he sat facing them in conversation. His body jerked in response to a deeper sleep as the images began to change, grotesque beings forming over the faces so familiar to him as he cried out to be left alone. A lone, ghoulish woman with fiery hair sat in the background, holding a tight bundle in her arms.

Her image grew bigger, grinning wickedly as she led her cohorts towards him. His flailing arms could not protect him as he was held down.

The lone spectre drew an unending sword from a scabbard of skin and, throwing it's head back in evil, churlish laughter, brought the weapon down heavily into his stomach as he howled in pain. He clutched his stomach as he was propelled from evil nightmare to the land of the living once more. He was sitting bolt upright, Rowena on the floor beside the bed, her knife drawn.

He looked around, saw familiar but unwelcome surroundings as Rowena leapt back onto the bed, snarling and posing the knife in a threatening manner. Adrenaline rushing through his veins as he grabbed her wrists and threw her back on the bed as the sound of a boot kicking at the locked door filtered through both their sub-consciousness. They stopped, startled, as the door flung open, sending splinters and shards of wood from the violently forced lock spinning at them. Rowena's father stood there, sleepy eyes peering out under bushy dark eyebrows, eyeing the intruder.

Matthew saw the glint of a weapon, his daughter pinned under a stranger and made a run, sending her guest crashing against the wall as Rowena screamed.

He dragged him off the bed and lay kick into kick into the prone intruder as Rowena pleaded with him to stop. His response was to unleash a forearm sending her flying back onto the bed. She tried again to stop the attack but he threw her back onto the bed.

"You're a fucking whore, bitch, your mother is spinning in that grave you put her in!"

"I didn't put her in any grave you bastard!!" Rowena roared back through tear filled eyes.

"Once a whore, always a whore!" he retorted as he grabbed the knife and turned back to the man lying splayed on the cold floor. As he turned him over, his daughter landed on his back, arms around his neck. He dropped the knife, grabbed her arms and slammed her against the wall.

"You bitch!" he roared again and again as he slammed her repeatedly off the wall before picking her up and throwing her on the bed. She lay there, legs exposed under her dress as he looked her up and down.

"You're not my child, you killed your mother with your touched ways. I lived with you in silence for years, never thought you would bring one of your men in the house. Oh I knew all about you, but refused to believe. No child of mine does that, not to me, not to their mother's memory. "

"Daddy, please," Rowena cried, eyes screwed up as the tears flowed.

"Who's your latest fancy boy?!"

"Leave him be!"

He stood over the crumpled form of the stranger, oblivious he had the most sought after man in Dublin at his mercy.

"Out. Do you hear me? Get out. Out of my house."

The battered man raised himself from the stone floor, exchanging glances with Rowena.

"Go," she repeated, "please, go…"

"Out I said, of my house before I throw you out!"

He got up and glanced back at the crying girl who was nodding quickly, a deft message for him to adhere to her father's wishes.

Matthew sneered as he watched the battered man leave the room and listened as the door shut behind him. Matthew stared at the floor for some seconds before returning to look at his daughter, his face betraying pain, anguish, betrayal.

"Do you know what they say about you Rowena?" he asked, calm restored in his voice. "Am I to believe it, after what I have seen now?"

"Don't listen to them Daddy."

"It's hard when I hear it so often. I don't see you much any more, I don't even know you." Rowena wiped away a tear as she realised this was the most she and her father had spoken in years.

"Daddy please…"

"I don't know you, maybe you're not my daughter at all anymore."

He turned to leave and noted the shattered lock. He looked back at Rowena and left, returning with some rope. Her eyes widened in horror and she cried and begged some more as her father shoved her to the floor and tied her two hands to the bed frame, causing her to wince as he bound the rope tighter.

"That'll make sure you don't go anywhere."

"Daddy please…"

"You'll learn your lesson Rowena, by God you will. You'll stay there 'til I return. You can piss yourself there for all I care."

He ignored his daughter's sobs as he closed the door as much as he could and calmly finished dressing before blindly leaving the house for his usual lift to the fields he toiled in. He ambled down the empty street, head lowered as the taunts of those in Flood's haunted him.

He hauled himself on the back of the cart, Patrick Cummins gruffly nodding as he watched in case Matthew knocked over the churns destined for Halligan's Dairy. He flicked the reins and the pieball horse slowly drew away, arcing by the woods where the stranger who he had caught with his daughter was now fleeing to, gripped with panic.

The cart trundled over the dusty ground as he kept his head down, Cummins giving up on their usual brief conversation and instead concentrating on the negotiating the road out of the village, onto the junction and small little village where the crystal stream met the flowing Tolka abundant with trout at Finglas Bridge, and ascending the hill by the silent great city of the dead where rich man, poor man, pauper, cleric and great leader all lay under the one soil. But this morning he didn't pay attention, he didn't care.

He ran down the hill blindly and in pain, passing the bemused man waiting patiently with his cart, towards the ancient celtic cross that stood at the edge of the graveyard that was bathed in an eerie early morning glow, nestled beside the still quiet tenement. He stumbled on, by the gate house to the Farnham asylum, lumbering back and forth until he entered the woods, pathetically negotiating the woodland by hand, arms flailing out against unseen trees as the minute morning glow vainly tried to penetrate the green canopy above his head. The soft carpet of moss and ferns often gave way to a sudden mound of gnarled dry mud with a stray root lounging across his path. He brushed aside gentle waterfalls of green and yellow that hung from arbitrarily pointing branches.

He stumbled into an unseen ditch, another succession of protruding roots catching his unaware foot and not for the first time. He wandered aimlessly, the brightest, friendliest part segueing into a darker, more threatening environment where giant trees blotted out any realm of sight. Unseen branches scratched his face and tore at his shirt.

The smell turned from pleasant fauna to one of dirty stagnation. He knew he could be found at any time. But he needed out of this hell. He found a small clearing in a dark part and crouched as an unseen embodiment snapped twigs underfoot and pushed aside branches as he pleaded with his eyes to adjust, giving him some sense of location.

All the time, he was fearful of people stumbling upon him, or he stupidly into them. He could not go back and get Rowena in the daylight.

He would have to remain here and cower. But he also knew he could be hunted, discovered and set upon by the law or a mob. He shook as he pondered his next move in this world, a simplistic world but one so difficult to adapt to. His cohesion of thought was gone. Nerves took over as he leaned his head back against a tree and began to weep. He must take his chances or he would die in this place. He grimaced as his rib cage throbbed and wiped away blood from his lip.

"Please, please, someone…" he begged softly, but no-one he knew could hear him as he crouched pathetically in the darkness, all alone yet with everyone seeking him out. He was barely here a week and everything was so wrong.

'What is worse, my dreams or my reality, there is no escape from this torture, this will haunt me in my nightmares and at every waking second…'

Matthew sat in Heery's nursing his ale. Whispers weaved their way towards him. His neighbour could never keep a secret and thrived on gossip with his friends over ample portions of porter he hadn't the means to buy. He spoke of the furore in Matthew Whyte's house that morning, the argument heard through stone walls, the sound of the girl screaming. A careful glimpse saw a wounded stranger limp away, in the light of the emerging dawn sky it was difficult to make him out but he must have been another fancy men they all thought she entertained.

Matthew ignored what was carelessly and audibly discussed, he continued to drink. He called for more, only getting up from his table to relieve himself.

Anger welled inside him as he finally left, shouldering the door frame as the peels of laughter echoed behind his inebriated hulk. He staggered past the silent grey cottages and down the hill toward his house.

Rowena would, should, still be there. He stood outside the cottage for a moment before punching the wall repeatedly, bloodying his knuckles as his curious daughter lifted her head to the noise outside.

"Bitch…" he mumbled as he clumsily opened the door, slamming it shut behind him, making the imprisoned Rowena's heart jump into her mouth. Matthew was greeted by a pathetic sight, his daughter crumpled on the floor.

"You locked me in here all day, how was I meant to go to the toilet, to drink, or eat, or anything?!" she pleaded, a weakness in her voice.

"Mama would be ashamed of you, you drunken bastard!"

He clattered her across the face, sending her sprawling back against the bed. "Ah yeah, go on, hit your little girl, go on, beat me around the place…"

"You're no daughter of mine," he slurred. "they're all right, you're only a fucking whore!"

"Rather be a whore than daughter to a man who beats her around…"

"How many times, in this house? How many times have you taken a man into this house, and while I slept in your mother's bed?!"

"What do you think I am?!" Rowena snarled.

"You're not my daughter!" he roared. "You're a cheap village harlot!"

He left the room, taking his place in the chair by the fireplace outside. He stared out the window for a moment, tears running down his face as he called his dead wife's name. "Elizabeth, Elizabeth…" he mourned. "Forgive me, she must learn, she must."

He wrestled himself from the chair and picked up his father's old walking stick he kept in the corner since he had passed. She needed to be taught a lesson. He approached his daughter's room, her eyes widening with fear and head shaking quickly from side to side as she mouthed the word 'no' over and over again, too scared to utter the words out loud.

Nine

Slow the dead marched, bony arms linking as they silently went down the hill, the casket of bones held aloft as unseen women wailed. At the head of the procession, a woman led the way, weeping, looking around... he lay hidden, the one they sought, hidden from this unknown life. Dead, soulless eyes looked around, searching, seeking for an answer...

The procession of doffed caps and heavy woollen shawls filed quietly down the hill to the bottom of the main street before turning at Chapel Lane where the small Catholic church stood atop a neat line of steps. It looked towards the tenement house and Lower Flood's; the grandeur of Rose Hill stood to its left beyond the alehouse. Across the stream, the graveyard was silent, save for the quiet sound of soil being unearthed. Muffled footsteps and the quiet, random murmuring of prayers were the only sounds from the attending congregation to break the silence of the early morning. People approached from all directions and merged into a neat line as Reverend Hackett waited by the doors, prayer book held in crossed palms, a nervous looks on his face.

This was a big deal in a small village, a funeral of a murder victim, a local boy, the perpetrator still at large, angering and frightening the sleepy community in equal measure. Reverend Hackett would make sure to include reference to the asylum patient slain at almost the same time, his corpse having been collected quietly by his family and spirited away to a burial at Mount Jerome.

Now and again a sob escaped the throng as they cautiously filed up the steps, heads bowed and into the dull grey barn-shaped church where the coffin containing the body of Master Robert Hart lay, candles standing guard either side. The tiny village was shaken, gossip blossomed and word was out of the stranger taken into Mrs. Devine's care. The early morning sun formed rays of peaceful light as they beamed gently through the long, dirty windows onto the incoming congregation below.

Silently the villagers filed into the wooden pews, the church half-filled while people outside still approached; men, women, eager children who stared at the simple wooden box despite their parents eyeing the floorboards.

Little Tony Salinger walked down with his family from their tiny cottage on the long road up to Jamestown House. He was wedged between his father and brother, not understanding what was happening but fascinated by the candles. Now and again he asked his father what they were for; each time he was hushed. He was oblivious to the day yet cautious at the sobs. When the mass was over he would run out to play as he always did, perhaps never to mention or think about this horrendous day again.

Mrs. Devine, flanked on either side by her daughter Kathy and Eleanor, walked slowly towards the crowded steps. Behind them her two sons walked dutifully

"I must leave you here now," Eleanor insisted in her broad northern English tones. Distracted, Mrs. Devine stopped and stared at her companion for a few seconds.

"Oh, of course, yes, yes of course…"

"I'll go to my church and light a candle for 'im," she ventured, bringing a smile to the pale face of the old woman.

"That would be lovely Eleanor. I'll see you later, dear."

Eleanor turned away and began walking back up the quiet hill in the early morning sunshine, before turning left at the top and continuing down onto Church Street, crossing over the small bridge over the stream, past the old church that was falling into disrepair and ruin and its graveyard that held souls of both Christian denominations that were buried centuries ago. She continued until she was filing through the gates of the St. Canice's Protestant church, its sharp spire pointing to the Heavens above where she would pray at the Eucharist for deliverance in her own faith.

Rowena waited until the church was full and silently climbed the steps, staring up at the sharp angular roof with a solitary circular window looking out at her. Her mother's faith was very strong, knowing that she quickly blessed herself before easing the great wooden door open gently and slipping in. No-one glanced at her, she maintained a low profile, finding a decent vantage point looking over the shoulders of two unkempt labourers. Despite beams of light from the morning sun, it was dark inside. The two lone candles illuminated the area around the coffin.

Standing between their flickering luminosity, Reverend Hackett had begun his homage, bible held high in his raised hands as the congregation followed his every uttering with a dutiful response.

The prayers blurred into one long drone as Rowena's exhausted eyes stared at the coffin. Poor Robert, poor Robert, she mused to herself. The stifled sobs of his mother and sisters carrying audibly down to the back where she observed.

She hadn't slept, her mind drifted with ease as she fought to stay awake, the highly charged atmosphere of the previous days catching up with her. The celebrant's voice seemed to get louder, the responses grew as she found herself wedged into the group of people standing at the back. The heat rose to an uncomfortable level in the small sealed church; she could feel sweat dripping down her back, dampness forming under her armpits as the sun rose higher and with it spat out a greater stream of light which gathered heat from the windows. Her fuzzy brain entered a state of confusion.

Now and again someone coughed, all the time the celebrant continued the mass. The heat was playing tricks with her mind. She licked her lips desperate for a sip of water but could not move, dehydration forced upon her having being bound in her bedroom causing her to wither and shake slightly. She must not move, to leave now would be noticed and scorned upon.

'That harlot who found the murderer, she left early, it's her fault, she should have let him be in that field, Robert would be alive today…'

She could hear the accusations, the opinions yet to be whispered and conclusions still to be drawn. If only they knew. God if they knew.

Robert was a nice lad, she thought, easy to get around, handsome, sought after, but it was her he sought. Their dalliance was brief, only a few weeks and unknown to anyone else. She would meet him occasionally by the walls of the asylum. Now and again he would sneak into her house. He was never improper, never forced his desire. He would have sat and talked had she wanted. Sometimes she did. Sometimes she didn't.

She felt an emotive cry from within her. Poor, poor Robert, a simple lad, a foolish lad and now he lay, skull smashed in, inside that wooden box. She stared at the coffin, felt a little dizzy because of the heat and closed her eyes. Her body began to fall limp and she wasn't adverse to her being propped up by those around her, their hefty workman shoulders holding her in a standing position.

Her head drooped, but lifted when she saw her mother crying at the top of the altar. She stood, head in hand beside Robert Hart; his eyes as wide and surprised as the time she left him on the dirt.

'Please Mama,' Rowena begged, *'please don't be annoyed with me, please…'* but still her mother Elizabeth wept silently.

'I had to Mama, I had to!' she pleaded, trying to go up to her but finding herself rooted to the spot. Instead Robert approached her, his eyes, his expression the same, his outstretched palms asking of her why she did it.

'Mama please, I had to, I must know the stranger's secret Mama, I must know it!' Robert floated towards her, through unseeing people, all the time his ghastly eyes fixated on her, until he was in front of her, his palms moving slowly to cup her face until she could smell his rank breath. His face turned, eyes narrowed as his expression changed into one of disgust, of anger. His hands dropped from her cheeks and formed a tight ring around her neck.

She screamed, those around her shuffling and allowing her to drop to the floor. Muffled voices turned around. Reverend Hackett, halted in full deliverance of his sermon, looked up from the pulpit. "What is going on?"

The voice of the new parish priest boomed throughout the tightly-packed church. "Who is interrupting me during this sad occasion?!"

Two men lifted her from the floor and managed to carry her outside, the air reviving her and the gentle wind soothing her brow that was caked in sweat.

Surveying the scene for some moments, the celebrant picked up exactly where he had left off, once more commandeering his captive audience as he spoke of deliverance and redemption. This was his first funeral having being drafted in to the area only two months ago to replace the popular Rev. Slattery who died suddenly one spring night, slumping against the door frame having given directions to a messenger boy. Hackett was keen to assert his authority, keen to spread his work to his flock, and his word was of an angry God who would punish all those who held even scant knowledge of the crime that took the young man's life. His voice thundered, his clenched fist thumping on the open bible in front of him as he warned anyone in attendance of the eternal perils of hiding the stranger away.

In her pew midway down the church, Mrs. Devine began to weep silently.

Kathy put an arm around her. "It's ok, mammy, you weren't to know, you weren't to know…"

Outside, Rowena opened her eyes, staring unknowingly around for some moments before regaining a hold on the events that had brought her to be seated in the dry dirt of the street. She sat still, the morning sun on her neck, arms stretched around her bent knees as she sought to know what had just happened. She wiped away a falling tear with the end of her palm. She had seen her Mama and more worryingly Robert, who demonstrated his disdain.

She lifted herself up and knelt under the shadow of the church, hands joined, head bowed but not knowing what to say, not knowing what to ask for but knowing she must say and do something.

She began uttering prayers she hadn't said since her school days. She needed direction, she needed citation. She needed to do something to save her knowing soul. She still had a soul. She began praying with greater ferocity as the tears began to fall. His fault, the bastard, it was all his fault. He came into her life in the most unusual way and now her simple, selfish ways were turned upside down. She had been turned into a killer, her mind clouded with a desperate yearning for an unknown path that she was tumbling down. And for what? For confirmation from him of what she had seen? For him to confirm she wasn't a mad woman? For him to admit he was a so-called devil or spirit of some sort? She knew what she had witnessed that day, she must know why and what. He wasn't going to give his secret away easily, she would have to use other ways, other means to obtain the secret she badly needed affirmation of. Since she had interfered with the happenings up in Jamestown she had blood on her hands. Real blood that wouldn't wash away but blood that needed to be washed away.

'I must know who he is, Mama, why he's here…"

Eleanor stood outside the graveyard as the solemn procession weaved among the headstones towards the reopened Hart family plot. She blessed herself and entered through the separate Protestant gate, across the churchyard from where everyone else filed in silently, the only sound sobs and footsteps on the soil.

She turned left and made her way along the dusty pathway that arced between the ancient tombstones and abandoned church building. The graveyard was a small one, a cluster of graves sat on the opposite side of the old church, a mix of those recently dead and those centuries gone.

The freshly opened plot was near the back wall by the entrance to the Bayly vault which sat adjacent to the church, steep, greasy steps led downward to a heavy door. Eleanor shivered as she cast a quick eye down.

She elected to stand under the shade of a yew tree that generously offered respite from the heat. The hot morning sun baked the mourners' skin as prayers were mumbled and the simple coffin gradually lowered into the grave. Everywhere she looked, pathetic limp flowers lay withered from the heat even on the most recently visited graves.

Elsewhere, long neglected ones remained still, the only interaction a rat waddling over the forgotten mound or the stretched legs of mourners, blessing themselves as they step over the forgotten corpses to seek a good vantage point to the latest incarceration.

Birds sat atop dirty and stained headstones, lacquered in transient green mould that had dried into the stone in the summer heat. Headstones leaned dangerously, carved names of the deceased almost unrecognisable anymore, slabs tilting, ready to slide off the plinths they rested on. Family plots with no more family to attend to them. Year after year they remained still, unloved, untended with no living memory of the bones covered in tatty, degrading clothing. They would remain forgotten forever more, future generations casting an occasional interested eye on the faded, neglected name of someone who once walked through the village as they would do.

Prayers droned on as the sun rose higher, not a sound to be heard otherwise except for the wind in the trees and the occasional singing of a bird. Eleanor squinted in the sun and looked around her. Often she pondered how she ended up in this place, doing the job she currently held, each time feeling more foolish at having pursued a man. Where would she be if she had let it go; perhaps still teaching in England, happier than she was at the moment. She sighed and smoothed her dress as the sobs drifted on the wind. She waited on her friend before taking her arm gently, patting her hand and accompanying her to the waiting cart for the return journey to Jamestown House.

Rowena sat with her legs dangling over the stream below, glancing occasionally as the crowd dispersed. The publican Heery would do a roaring trade today. He stood at the door and nodded in satisfaction as the men made their varied way towards the two taverns at the crossroads. Mr. Flood stood likewise outside his premises, each doing their best to coax as many people in to their pub as possible.

Both landlords nodded over at each other, a denied yet silent agreement to throw out a selection of punters who would then waddle over to the neighboring pub. Everyone would be happy.

The fresh water still dripped down Rowena's face as she plunged her head into the river again, drinking the cool water like a dog. She was so thirsty. She washed herself quickly before sitting on the small bridge to watch the cortege filter away. She bade Robert a swift 'bye bye' before following the course of the stream down through the woods. She knew he'd be there. Now and again she submerged her head under the cooling, babbling flow, forcing her eyes to remain open a little longer. She knew these woods well but even today she found it difficult to concentrate. But concentrate she must. It must be today. Her path was sullied; she sought deliverance but would accept punishment.

What price another? What price another if it delivered her the truth about the whole sorry affair.

He was so easy to find; curled up, cowering and carelessly hidden beneath a pile of ferns covering a shallow and uneven ditch. He wasn't far from the stream. *'The fool, he knows nothing of us or this place…'*

It was a dark, threatening part of the ancient woodland. He was sleeping. Should she wake him? She needed sleep, but sleep would wait. She knew what she had to do. She lay beside him, gently caressing his face until his eyes bumbled open. He jerked back until he recognised the dark figure lying beside him in the smudgy ditch.

"I came back for you."

He sat up, eyes adjusting to and memory recalling where he was. "How long was I here?!"

"Since yesterday I think, that's if you ran and cowered straight here. Robert was buried this morning. You're really not hidden well at all. You could have been caught."

"What happened?"

"I'm ok."

"What happened. Your father…"

"He kept me tied up in the room after you left, afraid I'd run off, he came back, we talked. It's ok now though. He was angry. But it's ok now…"

She broke her gaze and knelt beside him. "Ben. Johnathan, Devil, whoever you are, why me?"

He was confused. "I do not understand."

"Why me? Why involve me?"

"Involve you?"

"Yes, me. Why arrive when I was there?"

"I do not understand you?"

"Yes you do, your silly way of talking doesn't hide your lies. I saw what happened, I saw you, I was there. Why did you come when I was there too though?"

He sat up, eyes barely refreshed from broken sleep and unable to focus properly in the dank woodland around him. The scent of damp pine was overpowering. A warm summer it may have been, but the darkest parts of the woods remained musty. "Maybe you dreamt it…"

She signed a smile, shaking her head from side to side as she glared at him and moved in closer. She shot forward, right in front of his face.

"Don't call me fucking stupid, I'm not one of those fools in Farnham or Belle Vue or the Lodge! I'm not foolish. I saw what I saw! Others may think I'm a fool, but I won't hear it from you. You have too much to lose from me!" The last sentence was spat out, venom and intent evident.

Then she moved back, her demeanour changing, and began caressing his cheek with her hand, her soft skin arousing him once more with it's sensuality. She eased her face into his again and kissed him gently.

"Please, tell me, it'll be our secret, or I'll be signed into the madhouse with questions and tales. It's dangerous up there you know, in the village. Very dangerous. People will hear of the man who ran out of Matthew Whyte's home, the knife in the room. I told you before the woods can't offer you safety for long; there's people always around, people are still looking and a reward needs to be collected. Think about it, a reward that could set me up with a pretty penny for life. I could tell them everything. Everything. Time is running out for you, I have hid you as long as I could in the village, I have protected you, but that is running out."

"I cannot, you were never meant to be there."

"You can…"

"No…"

She sat astride him and pushed him back onto the damp ground.

"Please... tell me your secret. I thought you were a devil, but a devil doesn't have eyes like you, or a devil won't hide in the woods like you. A devil certainly wouldn't let a drunk man beat him in a fight, a devil wouldn't let a simple girl like me tell him where to go and when. You are no devil, are you? But what are you?"

"A devil can take many forms..." he stammered, fear entering his mind again. The beating had left him sore, bruised and badly shaken.

"But not yours," she replied instantly. She leaned forward onto him and began kissing him with greater force before she sat back up. His eyes widened, his face flushed.

"You like that don't you Ben? You don't have a forked tongue, I noticed that the other day."

"Why did you do that?"

She laughed gently and tutted. "You kiss strangely."

He stared at her as she laughed. "Definitely not a devil."

She sat back up straight, looking around cautiously, identifying the faint noises before glancing back down at him and unbuttoning his shirt.
He grabbed her hands but she forced them away. She closed her eyes. In her mind the events of the last few days replayed as she sought to make sense, but no sense would come. She opened her eyes once again and smiled. He was so attractive, so unlike the other men in the village. He was unique; tall, piercing eyes, perfect features, so unusually pale... different and alluring to her.

"Do you like me? You must like me, I think you do. The other night in my room, you looked at me with eyes that never looked on me before..."

'Stop it, stop it, please stop it, I cannot, cannot again, why is she so alluring...'

She followed his darting eyes, his surprised face. She leaned forward and kissed him again. He tried to break free but he couldn't. She had him pinned taut, he tried to resist but alluded to her charms, to sensations he wanted to experience again. Her form pleased him. Not in his life had he ached so much with pleasure or lust. He was giving in yet again to a knowledge he had seceded to in another existence. *'I cannot, I cannot, I have to resist...'*

She was all over him, her dress flung in the dirt beside them as he gazed at her form with desire, allowing her to have her way, her whispers and questions finally beginning to draw some answers from the mouth of a strange man who was overcome with temptation and sensuality.

II

1982

Ten

"Up. Get up!"

He felt a sharp kick to his hip.

"Get up. Now!"

His hands instinctively covered his head but when there was no more contact, he lowered his arms and squinted upwards. A tall, dark figure stood over him, the glow of a streetlight behind offering a powerful orange aura around his body. It was cold, very cold.

"Come on now, up. Both of you!"

Ben held up his arm weakly. The figure standing above him hauled up the drunken young man from where he sat slumped against the graveyard wall.

"And you, Miss."

Ro had awakened and was staring at the mysterious arrival, a puzzled and stupid looking expression on her face.

"Who's that?"

"If you hadn't downed all that drink you'd be able to see who it is."

Ben was limply leaning against the wall for support and uselessly offered Ro his hand. She took it but the Guard brushed his hand aside.

"Look at the two of you, for God's sake. What's your name?" He barked at Ben. Turning to Ro, his voice lowered. "Jesus Rowena, what are you like?!"

Rowena focused her eyes, the familiar voice recognisable to her.

"Eamon?"

The Guard cleared his throat before replying. "Yes."

"Jesus have you nothing better to be doing?? Catching royjiders… or something."

Ben giggled. "Joyriders you twat!"

"Enough you!" Eamon barked. "You're just as bad you, look at you. Shameless drunk. Well you do what you want but by Christ you won't drag her down with you!" he hissed with intent.

"Leave him for fuck sake!" Rowena slurred before slumping against the wall.

"I'm taking you home," Eamon offered.

"You," he glared at Ben, "can fuck off yourself."

Eamon eyeballed him, teeth showing. "I'm telling you now son, go home. One more word and you'll be sleeping this off in the station. GO!"

He gestured to his fellow Guard sitting in the squad car, who started the engine. He helped Rowena over towards it and eased her into the back seat.

"I can get home meself," she stated.

"No you can't, you're in no fit state, drinking again. Jesus Rowena, come on. Mary is gonna go mad. The top of Jamestown Road!" he barked at the driver. "I'll show you from there."

The car pulled off gently, turning away from Church Street and out onto the dual carriageway. Ben remained propped against the wall, completely out of it before slumping to the ground again. He turned over on his side, arms folded across his chest.

"Fuck them all…" he mumbled as he fell into a restless slumber once more.

The look on Mary's face turned from dread to anger as Eamon explained why he had called into her at 1am.

" Get that bitch in here!" she hissed as she pulled her dressing gown closer over her. "Jesus Christ I didn't know if she was fuckin' dead or what! Back the car down the driveway, will you, I don't want anyone seeing this!"

"I can't really Mary, I'm on duty…"

"I couldn't give a flying fuck if you're guarding the Pope, back the car down and we'll take her in through the back gate. You didn't have the siren or lights on, did you?!"

"No, no need for it."

"Thank Christ; please, for me, let's bring her in through the back door."

"Ok, just the once, ok?

"Oh this won't happen again I can tell you. Jesus if her mother could see her…"

"That's what I said," Eamon added before turning back down the path.

Mary stared at him through narrow eyes for a moment, not happy with his comment before she closed the hall door, darted back down the hallway and straight into the kitchen, fishing under the light of the stark white fluorescent bulb for the back door key. Through the vent in the wall she could hear the blue Cortina reverse down the driveway and smell the grisly, pungent fumes from its exhaust as she gently opened the door before stepping out into the cold back garden, sliding the bolt of the back gate across.

Eamon and his companion were helping Rowena out of the car.

"I think she's fast sleep now," he exclaimed. "Best leave her to sleep it off."

"Oh I will, thanks for the advice," Mary cattily replied. "I've been dealing with this fool long enough to know how to handle her, thank you."

She led the Guards inside to the back room where they gently lay her on the sofa. "We'll turn her on her side so she doesn't choke, best get a basin in case she gets sick…"

"Yes I know!" Mary thundered as she stormed out of the room, rattling around in the kitchen until she returned with a blue plastic basin which she placed by the sofa. She pulled a coat over her younger sister who had begun to snore loudly.

"Ok Mary, we'll be off. Sorry about this."

Mary nodded and smiled weakly, touching the Guard on his arm.

"It's ok Eamon, honestly. Sorry for being annoyed."

"Ah no it's grand."

"No it's not your fault. It's just difficult at the moment."

"I understand Mary. Well you get off to bed now."

"I will. Tell your ma I said hi."

"I will. Goodnight."

He placed his cap back on his head and nodded to his partner who trooped out the back door ahead of him.

"I won't say a word about this I promise."

"Thanks Eamon, night."

She followed them out to the back garden, shutting the back gate before stepping back inside and locking the kitchen door. Turning off the humming light, she returned to the room where her sleeping sister lay. She turned off the overhead light and sat on the armchair in the dark. On the wall hung a picture of their deceased mother. She gazed up at it for awhile, unable to see the picture in the darkness but knowing every contour and colour of it. She smiled weakly, before surrendering to her emotions, to the tears.

She wondered to herself could she manage anymore. Was it all getting too much for her?

The milkman woke Ben.

"Come on son, get up will you?"

Ben turned his pounding head and recognised the kindly face. Above him, the footsteps of an early morning worker making his way to his job thundered across the dirty iron footbridge.

"Jesus Ben what has you like this?" He shuffled up against the wall and took the elderly man's hand for support. "Ben go home son, please."

"I don't live there anymore."

"Well go back to the flat then, please, for me?"

Ben had known Billy for years, he was the local milkman round his way and had become a family friend. His worn, tan coloured coat covered the frailty of age. He visibly struggled in helping the young man from the ground. His glanced across at his young assistant clanking the fresh bottles on the doorsteps of the neat row of shops across the road on Church Street. He thought about calling him for help but declined. He could still do it. He didn't need anyone else in the dairy knowing he was slowing down. He wanted this job. He needed it.

"Look, here's a bottle of milk ok, get it down you, say nothing, ok? I'll drop you off at the flat."

Ben gratefully accepted the bottle and tore off the foil seal. He took a seat in the milk float as it hummed into life and, with a wave for the assistant to join them, the three took off up the road in the dim autumn morning.

"Who's this?" Billy's companion asked.

"It doesn't matter. Ah, I know him a while, to see, said something about getting a hiding…" he lied.

"Shouldn't we bring him…"

"He wants to go home, that's enough for me."

"But…"

"But nothing. We're milkmen. Up to him if he wants to see a doctor or a guard." The young companion nodded and leafed through the pages of his notebook as Billy maneuvered the almost silent milk float away from the graveyard wall and across the dual carriageway before swinging left in front of Rosehill House and up the incline of the main street.

"You'll catch your death out here, you know that?" he said to Ben.

Ben didn't answer, just swallowed the milk, rivulets escaping out of each corner of his mouth as he gratefully accepted the drink to satisfy his raging thirst.

Billy looked the young lad up and down, tutting as he shook his head. His jeans were filthy, there were tears on his leather jacket which, when added to the white t-shirt he wore underneath, was totally insufficient to keep out the morning cold.

"Johnny, like I said I know this lad. Not a word about this back at work, you hear me?" he nodded to his assistant.

Johnny nodded and smiled to himself.

'Wait 'til they hear about this at work…'

They pulled up outside a shop in the middle of the street, Billy thankful there wasn't a soul about. Ben stumbled out and glanced at the milkman.

"Thanks."

"Go into bed now will you?"

Ben coughed nervously. "If you see me ma…"

"I won't tell her," Billy affirmed as he watched Ben clumsily fish the key out of his jacket. Once he was safely inside, he returned to his route. "And you, not a word, yes?" he pointed to young Johnny.

Johnny nodded but Billy could see the smirk. The electric float hummed back into life and turned back down the hill, turning by the public toilets that stood by the shoemaker's cottage, once the old gate lodge of the long gone Farnham House and onto the dual carriageway that split the old village in two. They turned left after the graveyard and continued on their route along Church Street.

Mary held Rowena's hair as she vomited into the basin.

"Oh Jesus Christ I'm in tatters."

Mary said nothing as her sister lay back on the sofa, wiping her mouth and gazing at her as the soft light filtered in through the net curtains.

"Why Rowena?"

"Why what?" Rowena croaked, resting her palm on her forehead.

'The dying swan…' Mary snorted to herself.

"Why are you doing this?"

"Doing what?"

"THIS!" Mary screamed as she stood up and wrestled another cigarette from the packet resting on the bare wooden mantelpiece.

"Going out, getting hammered. And being found asleep by the wall of the old fucking graveyard?! What are you like?"

She lit her smoke and stood facing out the window, her back to her sister, furiously dragging away at the cigarette that was gone in minutes. She lit another.

"I'm sorry." Mary said nothing. "I said…"

"Oh like the last time? And the time before? Come on Ro, for Jesus sake, we need to work together, you know. You're better than this, girl, you know you are!"

She turned around and leaned back against the windowsill. In the greyness of the morning light she could see her sister's face, pale with sickness but with eyes that radiated so much hope.

"You're the image of her, you know…"

"Of ma?"

Mary nodded. Rowena swung her legs onto the floor and sat forward. "Can I have a smoke?"

"Absolutely not."

Both women were silent for a moment, nothing disturbing the calmness but the waft of a freshly lit cigarette.

"I was only out having a laugh, Mary, God I needed that."

"Rowena to be found by Eamon of all fucking people slumped under the bridge…"

"Under the bridge?"

Mary exhaled and lowered her cigarette, a sarcastic look crossing her face.

"Too pissed to remember I see."

"Was I on my own?"

"No with Ben."

The young woman closed her eyes slowly as she remembered, albeit partially. "We were just talking, must have fallen asleep."

"Fallen asleep my arse. Look, go to bed, I've to get ready for work now. I stayed up all night watching you, I'm exhausted. Please, just think of others next time." Mary stood up and stopped at the door. She turned back towards her sister. "I know it's hard, being around Mammy's anniversary and all that, but I'm missing her too. I can't go out and get rubbered to forget, can I? Just, for me, think next time, eh? We're in this together. What would Mammy say?"

She left the room and Rowena stumbled back onto the sofa, forearm rubbing gently back and forth across her forehead as the headache took command. She had met her pal Ben for a drink the night before, they had been the last to leave and had gotten a takeaway of cans and vodka from Ben's brother behind the bar before clambering over the wall of the old graveyard and continuing their splurge. How they ended up outside she couldn't guess. As she began drifting into a needed sleep, her eyes shot open; wide, scared and regretful.

She lifted her head, looking around the dark room as if to search for a memory she badly needed confirmed or denied. She glanced back out the window, staring at the dull greyness of the late autumn morning sky, her mind trying to act coherently before a sinking realisation hit her and she slowly closed her eyes. She turned back around and lay on the pillow, opening her heavy eyelids and staring up at the ceiling.

'Fuck… oh fuck'

"The state of you."

"Fuck off."

"Where'd you end up last night?"

"The pub and then the Outdoor Inn..."

Des laughed and went to leave the room. "Well, I'm off to work, don't sleep too long." Ben didn't reply, he just smoked away staring upward at the ceiling. Parts of the previous night were coming back to him.

Rowena stared at her reflection in the mirror. A tired, drawn face surrounded beautiful piercing eyes set into porcelain pale skin; her dark, thick hair uncombed and rough. The excesses of the night before showed on her face. A few hours sleep, after she dragged her weary body to her own bed didn't do her any favours. She turned on the tap and let the cold water flow before cupping her hands under it and splashing her face. She repeated the movement, again and again and again. With wet hair sticking randomly to her face, she gripped the sides of the sink and gritted her teeth in anger and frustration

"No, no, no NO!!!" she screamed as she swiped at the make-up mirror, sending it flying from the window ledge in front of her and crashing against the tiles of the bathroom wall, dropping into the bath below, small shards of cracked glass slipping into the bottom of the aqua-coloured plastic tub. She stared at the shards for some moments before she began sobbing.

Mary sat at her desk during lunch, supping her sixth coffee of the day. The tiredness had dulled her senses and her desire to work. She starred out the window of the cold office block, across the shopping centre car park below, out across the junction at the main street and onto the ruined church that poked out from behind the overgrown foliage surrounding the dull Celtic high cross that was the War of Independence memorial.

Rowena had taken her mother's death badly, as she had, but Rowena had youth as her side as an excuse. There was fourteen years between them. Mary, now in her early thirties, had assumed the matriarchal role. With no father in their life, she felt alone, desolate. She had to hold everything together, taking over the crippling mortgage that her menial job just about covered as well as feed the two of them. Her younger sister, while holding down badly paying part time jobs since she left school the previous summer, relied on Mary for income and support. Pissing it away was not what Mary wanted when she handed her a few bob from her pay packet at the end of the week.

She was angry at her sister, hurt; but extremely protective.

The other problem on her mind loomed like a spectre in the background. It would have to be addressed sooner rather than later. First she had to tell Eamon.

'What fun that will be…'

She couldn't continue like this. She didn't want to turn around in thirty years time and look back upon a life of regret and failure. Rowena would have to step up to the plate this time. She needed to do this. It wasn't running, she comforted herself time and time again. It was a fresh start. She needed it and Rowena would comply.

Eleven

"Just what the hell are you like?!"

Ben wished he hadn't opened the door.

"Just look at you, the state of you! I thought you were going out today to get a job in one of the factories?"

"I will do Ma, I am, later."

"You need to pay your way, properly. Well you can't be relying on Des to bail ye out forever. And I know about last night. Don't be coddin' me now"

Ben glared at his mother, busy tidying up the small flat over a shop he shared with his school-friend as he sat nervously in the borrowed and tattered armchair. "That old bastard."

"Enough!" his mother retorted sharply, turning on a sixpence and pointing at him. "You should be lucky he found you, God knows what could have happened you! What were you doing? Well, the reek of drink off your breath kind of answers that."

"I just went out for a few…"

"Few too many you mean. Jesus if your father finds out, all your labour money gone, yeah?"

Ben's mother was a small, slightly stooped woman who had given up working some years after his birth due to constant ill health. Her husband's comfortable wages more than saw them happily through life. She enjoyed being at home, having worked since she was sixteen. This was meant to be her time to relax. Instead she found herself worrying about her youngest.

"Part of the agreement with you moving out was that you'd pay your own way."

"I'm trying Ma."

"How much did you spend last night?"

"Not much."

"And did you give the rest of your dole money to Des for rent?"

"Yes."

"So are you going to look for a job?!"

"Jesus Ma it's a recession you know?"

"Plenty of jobs out there."

"Where?"

"Thought you were looking?! Have you tried H Williams, Superquinn?"

"Yes. Not hiring at the moment."

"It's autumn, won't they be hiring for Christmas?"

"I asked them that, they said try again in November."

There was a silence for some minutes.

"The pubs then? The Drake? Jolly Toper? Can Declan do anything for you in the Drake?"

"He said he'll try."

Ben decided against telling her that his older brother had facilitated their take-outs the night before.

"Well keep at him, I've asked him to keep an ear out. What about up the west, anywhere there? Or up the other way, the Ballymun House? The Fingal…"

"What, where Malcom McArthur skulked into during the summer? Oh yeah, that'll look good won't it?"

"What do you mean?"

"Me working where a murderer hung out…"

His mother dismissed his argument with a swipe of her hand. "Ah now Ben, God's sake, that's a stupid thing to say, no-one will be thinking that. What about the shops round there, even for something part-time? I'm just trying to help, to put ideas into your head. You tried Unidare?"

"Yes!" he drawled, eyes to Heaven.

She stayed silent and glanced out the window onto the busy street below. "How do you stay here with all that noise?"

"It's quiet in the evenings."

"And the dirt of those windows."

"They're ok."

"Give them a wipe, some newspaper and vinegar."

"Yes."

"Are you eating a'tall? You look very pale."

"I'm eating Ma."

"Do you want to come up for dinner one of the days then?"

The though of a nice home cooked dinner appealed to him as his stomach began rumbling. "I think I will, yeah…"

"Good. Look, please, look after yourself, son?"

His mother drew her lips inward, a sudden wave of sorrow washing over her. She hated Ben living like this. He was her baby.

"I have to go Ben, but please, for me, just try will you? Look I just had to drop in after Billy talking to me. He was worried Ben, he's known us since before you were born. Wouldn't be worse if he left you there. I left a pot of stew in the kitchen. That should do youse for two days."

She stood in front of him, worry in her eyes, as she tied her head scarf back over her permed hair. Ben was her weak spot.

"Clean yourself up and look after yourself love, ok?"

"Thanks Ma."

Mary sat uneasily at the table as she and Rowena ate.

Eamon was dropping up later. They were due to go to the cinema in town but she cancelled. She had to tell him what she had been planning, keep him in the loop. Rowena she could deal with later. One step at a time. Rowena ate silently and finished her meal, washing the plate and cutlery in the kitchen sink when she'd finished.

"What happened the bathroom mirror?" Mary asked.

"I opened the window and it fell."

"The window opens outwards?"

"My arm caught it."

"So how did it end up in the bath?"

"How'd you know that?"

"I stood on a few shards when I had a shower. You didn't tidy as well as you thought." Mary decided not to pursue it. She commented that a broken mirror was seven years bad luck and went out to the back garden to have a cigarette. The evening air had a chill. Broken clouds mapped the azure evening sky, the last fading remnants of what was a scorching summer. The clocks would go back shortly and then Mary would be going to and returning from work in the dark. A short ten minute walk to the village but she hated the dark evenings.

She lost herself in her thoughts as she sat on the cold step dragging away at her cigarette, gazing at the sights that she knew too well; the wooden fence separating the neighboring gardens, the faded motley collection of flowers, not a patch on those here mother once planted.

The garage loomed on the opposite side, just beside the back gate, a garage that was only used for storage now since both her parents has passed and she had sold the car. The garden path stretched beside the rough wall of the garage and beyond into the rest of the long garden.

A wall of giant, thin pine trees stood to attention just behind the back garden wall, blocking the view of the houses behind them. She turned her head the other way, at the first of the two giant trees that stood in adjacent gardens, all that remained of the old country estate that used to be located in the immediate area. The incessant call of a pigeon vibrated from deep within the fading burgundy leaves. The dull noise of a plane disappeared as soon as it begun. High above, the faint trail of a jet scorched the dim sky. She followed the trail and wished it could be her soon.

She stubbed the remnants of the cigarette underfoot and on top of a small diamond-shaped patch of dark paint that had been there for years longer than she could remember. She climbed the two small steps and closed the back door behind her. Rowena had sat back at the white breakfast bar-style kitchen table, finished her glass of Coke and stared ahead down the hall, catching fleeting glimpses of shadows on the pathway outside through the two arched frosted windows of the hall door. She had thought about last night a lot. She knew there was something up with her childhood friend but it took a lot of drink to get it out of him. Deciding to clear their head and talk some more they decided to climb into the old graveyard again, as they frequently did over the years, but Ben insisted on getting more drink.

As children both often stole into the graveyard on long summer nights, telling each other secrets, laughing and joking, not caring that the bones of long dead neighbours and ancestors lay metres away. Rowena had always laid flowers at Granny's grave but she found it harder to go back now that Mammy lay there. She had always liked the graveyard, she was well up on her local history. She loved telling Ben stories. She must have told him tales and legends many times over the years.

Last night, though, was different. She ran the events over and over in her mind to ascertain a reason, a part in this for her. She knew she had to talk to him and soon.

She went back into the living room and curled up on the sofa watching a programme she didn't really care for.

"How's the head fucker?" Rowena hugged Ben as he answered the door.

"Better now Ro, you?"

"Ah, was sick as a dog."

She followed him silently upstairs into the small living room that looked out onto the main street.

"My Ma went apeshit."

"How'd she find out?"

"Billy told her. The milkman. He found me asleep."

"Could be worse. I was apparently brought home in the back of Eamon's fucking squad car. Mary was seething. Luckily she had the cop on to ask him to back down the driveway."

"You say that on purpose Ro?"

"What?"

"Cop on?"

"Oh piss off."

They sat silently as the noise of daily business and traffic resounded outside the window.

"So, what do you think?" she finally asked.

"Of what?"

He knew what she was talking about but despite all he had prepared in his mind left it as he went for a safer option.

"Ah come on Ben, of what you said?"

"Was the drink…"

"Really? Well I don't believe you."

"Well you're gonna have to."

Rowena stared at him for a moment. "I don't know how to take that. A lot has happened in the last few days, you know that?"

"Yep."

"Well?"

"Well what?"

"We have to talk about this."

"Well what do you want to say?"

"Oh I don't know, for fuck sake Ben! You tell me! You started this!"

Ben lit another cigarette and offered Rowena one.

She took it and sat back in the chair, eyes locked on her friend who looked very rough and pale, his brown hair growing out and uncombed over an unshaven face.

They sat silently. "Want to go out for some air?" he finally replied.

"Better than staying here; don't know how you live in this kip."

The village was cold as they sat on the shopping centre carpark wall at the crossroads at the top of the main street sharing chips from a bag. Behind them the hulk of an ugly office block where Mary worked stood, a perfect, red brick rectangle structure with unending windows that caught the glint of the sun and rendered the heating system inside unnecessary. It stood guard over the L-shaped shopping centre promenade it was built over and faced the glass tower which held the slippery stairway leading into the library. Below the layered concrete and individual parking spaces marked in careful white paint lay the foundations of buildings long gone, a small row of cottages and the post-office: the former hub and centre-point of the village, now re-located to a dark, dusty building on the main street with the greying wooden floor with frayed and greasy mail sacks, the relentless dull thump of the rubber stamp on the wooden counter a constant sound. Memories long since buried under the curse of progress spearheaded by faceless planners who couldn't care less about the beauty of the disappearing village that had stood for millennia.

"Really beginning to hate this place."

"Why?" Rowena asked him.

"Ah, just get in on top of you. Wouldn't mind leaving."

"I'd like to stay, well, won't be going anywhere for a while anyway."

"Just cos you've got family roots here."

"What's my family got to do with it?"

"Well they've been here for yonks, you've more attachment I suppose."

"Suppose. I've always like it, loved it. Ah Ben I don't know anymore."

She took two chips from a bag and ate them slowly, swigging from a can of Coke, which she suddenly held up in front of her.

"This one still has a World Cup promotion! Fuck sake. Either they don't sell much Coke or bought way too much earlier. Don't know how, I drink gallons of the stuff. That mascot freaks me out, big head on him…"

"It's meant to be a Seville orange, it's his head."

"Still…" She swigged some more and stared over at the ruined church.

"Ben, the other night."

"What about it?"

"Us."

Ben stared right ahead, eyeing two young women at the celtic cross memorial.

"Ben please…"

"Ro, look, I'm not sure, I can't really remember."

"You know what happened, you just don't want to admit it."

"We were drunk…"

"That we were… Jesus."

"Maybe we didn't, completely..."

"Yes Ben we did. Trust me, I know."

"How?"

"Are you seriously asking me that fucking question?!"

"I'm sorry, can we forget it?"

"It's not as easy for a girl you know, not that simple. You said things…"

Ben searched his mind, snatches of the night coming to him. "The always staying together part?"

"No, the 'I've always loved you part'…"

"Oh yeah."

"Heat of the moment? Cos if you say it was I'll fuckin' kill you, I swear."

"Well, I have, you're me best pal."

Rowena shifted on the wall to face him. "It was more than that the other night, or was it a cheap shot? Cos I can't deal with a cheap shot right now Ben, you know that, there's too much going on in me head."

"You said the same right back."

Rowena froze. She genuinely could not remember saying that. Her voice lowered and she emitted a small squeak. "Did I?"

"Yep."

"Fuck." Both stared ahead at the passing evening. The crowd filed by, youths wasting time, men and women wandering to and from the pubs, people buying cigarettes in the ugly, boxy shaped newsagent that replaced the demolished Duck Inn pub across the road from where they sat. Rowena's parents drank in it in their younger days, her grandparents before then when it was known as the Widow's, in her great grandparents time it was Heery's.

Now bored and surly assistants sold newspapers, books, bread and what not where a decade previous, people had sat and drank, laughing, talking, remembering.

The trees swayed gently in the breeze around the old war memorial, a memorial that, fenced off by rusty iron railings painted in harsh green, no one bothered about anymore.

It served as a rubbish pit mostly now, discarded chip wrappers, empty beer cans littering the base where Eamon DeValera once stood to commemorate a martyr of the War of Independence. The two girls giggling to themselves paid the granite structure no heed. It was there yesterday. It will be there tomorrow, no big deal. Not many cared anymore. Beyond the trees, neon orange lights stood sentry by the dual carriageway that cut a swathe through the village, forcing the crystal stream underground. The heavy trucks that passed constantly in close proximity to the silent graveyard were loud enough to wake the long dead. Rowena didn't like the change. The small village she once loved was disappearing.

"Ben can we, I don't know, forget it?"

"Ok"

"Just like that, Ben?!" Rowena exclaimed.

"Jesus you just asked could we forget it?!"

"Yeah but, I mean…"

"Look Ro we made a mistake, we were pissed, beyond pissed, things were said, things were done, please, we've known each other too long."

"So you do remember it all then?"

Ben shook his head and looked out ahead.

"I'll walk you home," he eventually ventured.

"Nah, You go on, I'll wander up meself. I'll be grand."

"Still friends though?"

Rowena smiled weakly. "Yep. But Ben, c'mon, we have to… I'm a bit annoyed. I can't easily let stuff wash over me like this."

"Look Ro, what more can either of us say? Let's just, I don't know, move on?"

"As if it never happened?!"

"Ro this can't come between us. We were pissed."

She nodded, disappointed but at least something had been exchanged.

They hugged, as they always did when meting or departing. Ben began walking down the hill of the main street towards his freezing bedsit.

Rowena turned and walked by the carpark, passing the huge rock that sat in the fountain. A tear ran down her cheek. The conversation hadn't gone as well as she hoped. But she had got something out of Ben. *'Oh Mammy, please, what will I do? He's me best friend'*

Eamon sat back in the armchair as Mary finished telling him of her plan. He rubbed his forefingers over his chin and stared at the window.

"Wow. That's a lot to take in."

"I know."

"Why you only telling me now?"

"I've only really decided," she lied. "I have to try."

"Ok, I'll give you that, but you can move in with me."

"Into you pokey flat in Phibsboro? Maybe not Eamon. Besides, like it or not, I have Rowena to think of, I always will."

"It's in a big house."

"Yes but you have a room Eamon, a room."

"It has its own sink."

"Eamon, seriously."

"Just a quick walk to the bus out here…"

"Eamon!"

"Ok, anyway, how will Rowena respond?"

"Badly I imagine but the offer will only stand for a little while longer."

"Do you not think you're going over her head?"

"What other choice do I have?! I'm more or less her guardian anyway, I feed her, clothe her, pay the mortgage. She doesn't bring in any money for God's sake. It's my decision to make. The way I see it, it'll be a fresh start."

"Maybe she won't see it that way?"

"That's what I'm working on, the way to tell her."

"And what about us? A year is a long time."

Mary knew her lie would only be a lie for so long. She wasn't interested in thinking about telling him the full truth yet. Letting him think they were heading away for only a year would do for now.

"Eamon just leave it, I've enough going through me head."

"I have to ask."

"Yes I know, but not tonight Eamon, please? Just come over here and sit beside me will you? My head is all over the place."

Twelve

Rowena and Ben only spoke over the phone for the following two weeks. He was marshalled into the city centre by his brother to help him look for work, she flitted between applying for part time work here and there, work that she had no interest in but something to keep Mary happy. It looked like she bagged a few days in the small newsagent up on Jamestown Road, just around the corner from where she lived.

"It'll give you a few quid, a wage..." Mary smiled.

She spent most of her hours rambling through the area, past the industrial estate that sat across from the newsagent where she'd pick up a few pounds, down the hill towards the ever expanding village, the twinkling lights of the city and mountains looking as if they all lay snugly right behind the village from her vantage point. She loved it after dark. She felt the ghosts of the past would come out and reminisce with her. The silo of the bakery hummed as the yellow Butterkrust vans filed in and out of the gates. The giant bakery never slept, it was constantly busy, lights ablaze in the early hours as the scent of freshly baked bread and cakes wafted into the houses around. It stood guardian over a row of tiny and long-standing cottages on the sweep of the road to the village.

She continued on, crossing the busy junction by Ashgrove House that now held a compendium of businesses before stopping once more outside the imposing walls and gates of Gofton Hall, letting her mind wander to times past; times she heard about but wanted to experience. She felt a deep connection to the past, a past that was being buried under tons of concrete and steel, a feeling not many gave time to, always citing *more important things to worry about* whenever she struck up a conversation on the matter.

She wrapped her hands around two of the iron spikes on the rusting gates that were a remnant of a time when they stood to keep people in. The faded Gofton Hall signage that adorned the two pillars was disappearing slowly, echoing the disappearing town. A crowd of teenagers interrupted her thoughts, giggling and shouting as they passed. She huddled into the collar of her denim jacket and crossed the main street, continuing down to the shops that lay in the dip to the right of the iron bridge, down the hill of Church Street which was now dissected by that bloody dual carriageway.

She went into the chipper, ordered a can of Coke, hoping to take that strange taste in her mouth away.

She began swigging as she crossed the iron bridge, stopping to gaze down at the busy roadway out to Dublin. The bridge shook in the wind and with the resonance of the trucks heading towards and coming from the North Road. She walked a bit further until the bridge began to slope as it declined towards the old graveyard. The ruined church looked desolate, bare, but the graveyard was very much alive. Her mother was buried there, in an old grave that held up to four generations, close to the wall near the carriageway. She would end up in there too, she would request it. She wanted to continue the tradition. There wasn't much of that left anymore.

"Love you Mammy," she whispered as she blessed herself and started her journey back home, repeating the private prayers she uttered in her head during her short ad hoc visit. Her Mammy would look after her, that she knew. She was safe. All would be well.

Ben took his jacket from the hall.

"I'll be off now Ma, thanks for the dinner."

"You going already?" his father asked, peering over his Evening Press.

"Yeah, gonna get me head down, tired you know…"

Mrs. Hedderman got up from her seat in the corner of the room.

"Ok love, but wait, take some of the apple tart home." She disappeared back into the kitchen while Ben stood awkwardly in the room with his father.

"How's Rowena these days?"

"Fine, she's fine, the usual…"

"Good. Tell her I said hi. Haven't seen her around in a bit."

"Ah she's looking for work and helping her sister."

He nodded and returned to the sports pages. "Will you watch the Ireland match? It's on telly I presume?"

"What? Which one?"

"Iceland. A few of us in work might go. Been a poxy year for results."

Ben nodded. "Yeah, yeah, will have a look."

"Better than watching that shower of shites in Dalymount, " his father murmured, head buried behind the broadsheet pages.

'*Whatever you say…*' Ben thought, knowing it best not to get dragged into an argument with his father when he was in moods like this. *'Poxy bad day at work again, eh? Union rep on at your again about conditions and break times yeah?'*

Ben's mother hadn't uttered a word to his father about what Billy had told her, something he was grateful for, he was in no mood for an everlasting lecture. She returned from the small kitchen, holding the remnants of the home-cooked apple tart, generously wrapped in layers of tin foil.

"Have this with a cup of tea later. Is Des on nights?"

"Yeah Ma."

"OK well you look after yourself."

"I will."

"Seeya Da."

"Bye."

He afforded his mother a thin smile and opened the door before descending the three steps at the hall door and the three more that led to the garden gate. He closed it behind him and waved as his mother stood leaning against the door frame, arms folded, looking around at the street before waving back and retreating into the warmth of their home. He walked up to the top of Ballygall Crescent as it curved by the green. He crossed over onto the grass, following the path and steps that would bring him to the back of the Bottom of the Hill pub, passing the old church that served as a drinking den these days as opposed to a place of worship for generations past, unashamedly sitting within view of the grand parochial house. He turned right onto the main street, past the harsh inner light of the newsagent where a bored woman was doing her nails behind the counter. He ignored the temptation to sneak into the pub for a drink and turned the key in the door.

The stairwell was cold. He fumbled around for the switch which sparked the flickering bulb in the hallway to life. He climbed the stairs and into the room facing out onto the street, the depressing yet comforting neon glow from the streetlight directly outside enough to bathe the room in an eerie, cautious and mellow orange.

He placed the apple tart in the fridge before throwing his jacket down and plonking in the tattered armchair beside the window, smoking and staring He thought back to the last time he had met face to face with Rowena. The things she attempted to sort out but which he wasn't eager for her to say. He remembered well enough that particular night.

Playing dumb in parts made the reality easier to grasp. It bought him time. Time he hoped to allow things to slip by. They would move on, forget the brief, drunk dalliance that he feared would wreck their friendship.

He though back to the early, innocent and sepia-toned memories of childhood. Their respective mothers were friends, always in each others houses and gradually the two children began to play together, share toys and eventually call into each other's houses. Their friendship blossomed, with that Rowena also blossomed into a beautiful young woman. Primary schools sat metres apart, secondary schools further but they met regularly. They were never an item. It was never an issue, neither felt uncomfortable as teenage hormones kicked puberty into life and washed their mind with new sensations and emotions. Friends they always were, friends, he hoped, they would always remain. Sneaky nights were spent nervously in the Drake and Ballymun House on borrowed money. Money they could never pay back but they stretched the leniency as far as they could.

So he thought. So he hoped. Whatever was going through his mind, he knew Rowena would amplify the same thoughts. She was that kind of woman; a deep thinker, one who would spend hours in books and though nothing of wandering around the town on a bright Sunday when all he wanted to do was go to Dalymount to see Bohemians.

She ventured there with him once, he regretted not forking out the extra few bob for the seated main stand, instead they huddled together on a crash barrier whose paint was jaded and flaked. They stood under the multiple eyes of one of the four towering floodlights, in the fine, misty drizzle on the Tramway End. She asked questions about the ground, questions he never really knew the answer too but questions quickly forgotten as he joined the chorus of boos and shouts. He was more interested in what Bohs weren't doing on the pitch. She leafed through the match programme before burying her hands in her pocket, counting down the minutes until the referee's shrill whistle signalled the end. Yes, this would all blow over he thought. A lesson learnt. He could see the imposing bell tower of the Catholic church just metres away, its green, angular peak, topped off with a cross, reminding him of a rocket ship. Below him in the street, muddled voices and dull thuds on the path strode alongside the rapid, sharp clicks of high heels as couples passed on their way to wherever.

He sat forward and pulled the net curtain aside. Two drunks were slouched against the clothes shop once again, swigging from a bottle of God knows what. Another welcome mat of vomit for the well-to-do manager to order an assistant to clean up in the morning no doubt.

He walked over to the radio and lazily turned it on, slumping back in the chair and caught the tail end of a song he recognised, a recent enough effort from an up and coming Dublin band. The singer grew up near Rowena, weird bloke with a weird accent. Proddy too. Ben bumped into him a few times over the years, him and his weirdo mates acting the arse in some stupid gang, dressed up in such a way to invite a hiding.

He preferred the other crowd, clattering and banging away in a garage at the end of her road. Leather jackets, slicked hair, they looked the part.

He went to the fridge, snapping open the ring pull of a beer and began drinking slowly. The apple pie sat where he had left it on the shelf. It would wait. Later, maybe. Fuck it. Fuck it anyway. Things couldn't get any worse. All would be well. He eased back into the chair and watched as the droplets of cold autumn rain began forming on the dirty window.

Rowena sat staring through her bedroom window. Through the gap between the two semi-d's across the road she could make out the AnCo training centre bathed in neon orange. She'd have to drop around and sort something. Move on. Make something. She was still young, so very young but times were harsh and wouldn't get any easier for her unless she did something. She lay back on the bed, tapping her foot to the end of the song on the radio. She narrowed her eyes as she suddenly asked herself if the band were that crowd at the end of the road, always practising in the drummer's garage. The singer sounded familiar. *'State of them in their leather jackets...'* She racked her brains to remember their name. They were called after a concentration camp, that much she knew. What was it they changed their name to? Didn't matter. They wouldn't last. Looking the hard men.

She looked across at the patch of ground that was left to its own devices when the realigned road to the long demolished great house was bricked up. It split the neat road and divided it from the acres of fields behind it.

She remembered the house before it was levelled, well the red brick shell that stood withering for years. Gone now of course, like most beautiful things.

She wondered who lived there down through the years, who worked there, what their names were. She saw a drawing of the house in a local history book and imagined all sorts of well to do people going to and fro. What a time to live in. Now whatever remnants were left of the foundations were long gone under the crop of estates that sat on the once free land. She remembered the story of the fairy fort her mother told her when she was very young. You never disturbed the fairies, that was very important. You always said hello and left them food.

However one day the devil appeared there and brought shame and blood to the village, according to an old story anyway. She smiled at the thought. She missed her mother. Too many years, too many years ago since her cancer-ravaged corpse was put in the damp ground.

'That wasn't Mammy' she would run through her mind. *'That wasn't really Mammy…'*

She preferred to remember her mother as the beautiful radiant woman of her childhood before her sickness took a cruel and unrelenting hold.

'Where is the fairy fort now?' she asked her Mammy once.

'In the fields somewhere,' her mother replied, leaving her young self to seek undiscoverable clues in the acres of remaining fields around the corner. Innocent days.

Rowena switched off the radio and descended the stairs quietly as Mary was asleep in her own bedroom. She turned back down the hall, straight into the kitchen. Her sister's purse complete with wages lay on top of the fridge. She rifled though it and took out a five pound note, holding the fresh brown paper in her hand for some moments as she stood at the kitchen window. She could see the outline of the tree with the giant bird in the moonlight. All those years it sat looking at her, pointing at her.

'Is that the devil Mammy?' she asked once, thinking he could have taken the shape of an evil bird. *'No love, that's just branches in the tree, that's all, they look like a bird, there's no devil around anymore.'*

No devil. Yeah. Tell that to a sobbing Rowena, held tight by her older sister as they stood by a freshly opened grave in the old graveyard.

She peaked inside and saw the top of her grandmother's coffin, resting crookedly on the rotting wood of coffins underneath. Mary tugged her back sharply and rubbed her hair as her beloved Mammy was put in the ground by strange men. She howled out for her, bringing tears to the stoniest of eyes gathered on that wet day. She looked around, pleaded for people to take her out of the ground, that she didn't belong there, but she was met with glassy, averting eyes and wobbling mouths nestled into scarves. If God was good, then the devil must have taken her Mammy. She remembered seeing her mother for the final time, waving cheerfully at her from a window in the Mater hospital as she and Mary set off for home after visiting hours. She looked wretched. Rowena didn't know it would be her last time seeing her. Their mother was very weak, very gaunt, yet here she was, knowing they'd glance back up at the window, waving cheerily at them, her broad smile beaming. They were heartened by that.

'She's getting stronger Rowena, I get that feeling. She's not going without a fight. She'll hang on!'

Both sisters were to sob into each others shaking bodies in the hallway in the early hours of the following morning, before the taxi arrived to take Mary and a kindly neighbour to the hospital. Old Mrs. Collins from up the road was good enough to stay with Rowena, but she wanted to go with Mary, she couldn't understand why she had to stay.

'It's alright Rowena, they won't let young children in. Mary will be home very soon. Remember your Mammy wants you to remember her smiling and happy…' Mrs. Collins comforted. She told her stories of her own mother, an English woman who lived and worked in the big house that used to stand nearby, telling the crying child how she was sad too when her mother passed away. 'Your Mammy isn't sick anymore, she's with God now. She's happy and she's safe.'

The young girl was always told to listen to and be polite to old people, but on that of all mornings she couldn't understand why her Mammy would be happy to be dead. The young Rowena couldn't fathom why her mother had smiled so vigorously as she cheerily waved out the window only hours before. How could she die?

Now, years later, she knew though, that her mother recognised it was time to go, to be rid of the pain, she could take no more.

She would give her girls one last big effort then slip away while they slept soundly at home. The devil had taken her lovely Mammy, her kind Mammy. Rowena's thoughts collapsed around her as she realised that the anniversary was in a week. She began to cry again. It wasn't fair, none of this was fair.

She rubbed her hand over her stomach and took a drink of water from the kitchen tap. That bloody taste was back. She turned off the light and went back upstairs to bury herself beneath the covers where she sobbed gently, remembering her mother. This would pass, she promised herself. This whole sorry episode in her and Ben's life would pass and they could move on.

'Isn't that right, Mammy?'

Thirteen

Mary ate her sandwich at her desk as she leafed through the holiday brochure, carefully concealed in a magazine. She needed to see the pictures of what awaited her. She traced her finger excitedly along the spire of the Empire State Building that took up most of the page.

Her best pal Debbie lived nearby, a neat apartment on 34th Street. 34th Street! A smile stretched across her face as she guiltily glanced at the woman in the desk next to her. Soon she'd be free of this place. A job it was, yes, hardly taxing, but nothing to excite either. It paid the mortgage, put food on the table. But there was more to life then a carriage clock and handshake in thirty-odd years time.

New York! She wiped the crumbs from her keyboard and sipped her coffee, checking her watch before tidying the magazine away. Time to get back to work, but she wasn't thinking of the job. Debbie had done well over there, she now managed a boutique on Fifth Avenue. The shop was expanding within the year, Debbie had a lot of pull and hinted at securing jobs for her childhood pal and her younger sister should they want. Mary needed to do it. Breaking the news to Rowena would be one thing, breaking it to Eamon that she may not be coming back would be another.

He wasn't really impressed when she told him they'd be taking a year-long trip but it cushioned the blow. She could maintain the lie, once she was over there what could he do? The house though, how to explain the estate agent's sign in the garden. They had been going out two years, he was head over heels but she never felt the same. Being a Garda he enjoyed his boozy nights out in the city centre with his colleagues, something which she was never into. She stared out the window towards the monument.

No, Eamon would be collateral damage. Fuck him anyway. She was tiring of him. Rowena was more important, this chance in life was more important. She gave up on the idea of having a child years ago, it never really troubled her. She had nursed her mother and helped raise her sister. That wasn't an issue with her. Tentative enquiries in the estate agents had gauged a general price on the house, an impressive one for a recession ravaged country. She planned sell it outright, the cash would finance the trip and keep them afloat.

Time to move on. She toyed with her conscience many evenings, on whether she was doing the right thing for her or Rowena, but deep down she knew this was the next step. It would give Rowena a chance. That's all the young girl needed.

She quivered with excitement at the thought. Back to the green screen in front of her. Not for much longer though. She would be able to tell that bitch of a boss where to go.

"Ah c'mon."

"Sorry, an extra 10p."

"But I'm always in here, the owner knows me da!"

"Sorry, I need the full amount."

Ben stared the young assistant out of it, intimidating her.

"It's just a fuckin' package of cigarettes and a Press, c'mon, I'll get it back to you."

The young girl's voice quivered as she repeated the tally to him. She wasn't going to mess up this job, it was a gift after the other girl never turned up. She wanted to impress the owner. This chancer wasn't getting away with it.

"10p."

Ben slammed the paper on the counter, making the young girl jump in shock and attracting the attention of the middle-aged owner lining up the orange gas bottles outside. His lean, wiry frame filled the doorway.

"What's up Sharon, is everything ok?"

"This man owes us 10p!" she stated confidently. Here was the owner. He'd sort this out and be proud of how she dealt with it.

"What are you getting?"

"Twenty Major and a Press, that's all."

"And you're 10p short?"

"Yeah," Ben smiled, "just 'til dole day, y'know…"

The owner towered over him, his impassive mouth sitting within a short, grey beard. "I can't do that, I'm sorry," he said softly.

"I'll get me da to drop up the money."

"I can't son."

"I haven't got it! C'mon."

"Sorry son but I'm owed money all over the place."

"Aul bastard..." Ben muttered as he looked away at the door.

"What?! What did you say to me?!"

"Nothing."

"No, you said something, what did you call me?" the shopkeeper demanded, eyes wide, poking Ben in the chest.

"I heard it, go on, tell me!"

"If you heard it why are you asking me!?"

"'Cos I want you to be man enough. Tell me."

"No."

"You called me a bastard didn't you?"

"What?"

"You called me a bastard. Wait 'til I tell your dad!"

Ben burst out laughing.

"Funny is it?!"

"I didn't say that!"

"You did…"

Ben looked the middle-aged man right in the eye. Chances are his father would find out anyway. He turned and left the shop without his paper or cigarettes. "I said aul bastard, ya daft aul bollix!" he shouted as he stormed across the courtyard in front of the shop, merging with the crowd of AnCo trainees who had clocked off from the training centre further up the road. He kept his head down and inadvertently shouldered a young woman, purely by accident.

"Watchit will ya?!" she shouted as Ben blindly began to make his way down Jamestown Road.

"You, you, ya prick!"

A hand swung him around violently, almost toppling him over as three men in denim jackets stood in front of him. The middle one eyeballed him.

"That's me girlfriend, ok. Watch it!"

Ben turned away but was spun around just as quick. "Fuck off, leave me alone!" he roared back but the three men had him against the wall. Workers coming out of the industrial estate across the road gazed interestingly at the scene but continued to walk on.

"You whacked into me girlfriend!" the middle one continued, flanked by two taller men either side, cigarettes in hand, egging him on.

"I didn't mean it," Ben replied, the odds rapidly calculated in his mind.

"Don't mess with me, ok, I'll fuckin' do you!"

"I won't, I won't!" Ben rasped as his opponent's fist clutched his throat tighter. The snarling apprentice eyeballed Ben before shoving him away, almost sending him toppling. Ben fixed his collar and walked a few steps.

He was good at running. He wasn't going to let this fucker get away with it in front of his mates. "Your bird's in bits anyway, fuckin' sniper wouldn't take her out!" he offered as he began to run across the road, back turned.

"Didya hear that? Didya? Didya hear what he called me?!" Ben glanced over his shoulder and saw that the small gang were almost upon him. He tried to outrun them but they caught up, clutching at his coat and leading him into the courtyard of the small factory that lay behind the deep red-brick walls with high railings. They dragged him around the side, unseen as fists and boots reigned in on his curled up body. As he tried to shield himself he could hear the woman shouting "Go on! Fuckin' kill him, cheeky bastard!"

Mary was in jovial form as she sat chatting with Rowena after dinner. She brought Debbie into the conversation, told her of how well she was doing, how they were invited over for a visit. An oblivious Rowena sat, curled up in the armchair, blanket over her as the fire blazed in the hearth, glued to the Late Late Show.

"You looking forwards to starting in the shop?"

"Haven't heard back from him yet," she lied.

"You will do, yep, a few bob. Sure you can pay for your trip to America, when we go to see Debs."

"Maybe…"

Mary turned towards the television but the banal guest lost her interest after a minute. She carefully shovelled some lumps of coal from the brass scuttle and replaced the fire guard. She stared into the fire for a moment and chuckled.

"Do you remember Mr. Hand?"

"Who?"

"Mr. Hand, he put in that fireplace."

Rowena's eyes darted back and forth for a few seconds until a slight smile crossed her face.

"Ah I do, old guy glasses, that right?"

"Yeah that's him," Mary smiled

"Yeah he used to say to you, *'if anyone ever hits you, give them a bet of this!'* as he held up the poker!" she chuckled.

"God help anyone that crosses me then!" Rowena winced as she laughed, her hand rubbing her stomach.

"You ok?"

"Yeah." Any day now. Would have to be.

"I wonderer whatever happened to him?" Mary pondered as she gazed over the polished, staggered rustic brickwork of the fireplace her mother paid for shortly before she fell ill.

"Ah here, you remember, what was he called, Feeney? The old guy, used to stand at the gate of his house on Jamestown Road and get Mammy to buy him his whiskey in the shop? You were in your buggy, you'd remember him."

"Vaguely," Rowena replied.

"He used to gave Mammy a few quid to get some in H Williams or Superquinn or wherever. She was mortified until one day she told the old moaner behind the counter who it was for!" Mary laughed at the memory.

"Whatever happened to him?"

"Not sure, haven't seen him in years, dead maybe."

"Ah right."

Mary chuckled away to herself in good humour. Rowena smiled weakly, not really sharing Mary's sudden trip down nostalgia lane.

'C'mon mammy, please. Please.'

"It'll be good to get away, won't it Ro?" Mary asked chirpily.

"Suppose."

"Course it will. We've never been on a trip like it… beats Kerry! You never know, you may want to stay there?"

She eyed her younger sister for any reaction but got none. Rowena stared straight ahead. "Maybe…"

Mary lit another cigarette and sat back in the chair, staring at the television but not taking in what was going on. She felt guilty. God she did. Her and Rowena had always gotten on, they never seriously fell out and her younger sister looked up to her. She was sure if she explained her reasons, Rowena would understand. She would have to pick her moment carefully.

"Fancy some tea? Or coffee?" she asked. Rowena looked across at her.

"Ok, yeah thanks, if you're making it?"

Mary patted her sister on her arm as she got up.

'What the fuck will tea solve for me? Mammy, c'mon…'

Ben was lucky to get away when he did, some overall-clad employees rushing out to prevent him from being severely beaten. Bastards.

Did he need an ambulance? he was asked. No thanks. Would he like some tea? A lift? No, no, thanks.

As Ben sat alone in the cold flat, he knew he had got away lightly. He could have been pummelled. Over what? A stupid argument with a shop-owner that clouded his judgement when he walked out, a shop he couldn't go back to in a hurry and one he was terrified his father would drop into soon to collect a gas cylinder. What if he bumped into that crowd again? Rowena lived up that way. He put his hand up to his cheek, the throbbing had subsided and the bruising on his side would remain hidden anyway. He daren't let his mother see him like that. It was bad enough skulking by the people in the village. He had to lay low for a few days. He could say he fell but his mother was no fool. Anyway his father was bound to drop into the shop in time. He hoped that by then, either the shopkeeper would be otherwise occupied or have forgotten.

Des commented on his face when he arrived home.

"Do you want me to get a gang and wait for them?"

"No, no, Jesus Des, who like?!"

"I know a few of the skinheads, well to see like, I can organise…"

"What, a fight at half four in the evening, in front of everyone, when they're walking down the Jamestown Road?!"

"Just asking, I can, don't let them get away with it."

"Ah it's done now, leave it…"

"Well you're very lucky."

"I know. Thank the guys that work there. Handy that one was a huge bloke, hair growing out of his teeth kinda man."

"You remember Keogh?"

"The aul lad who lived at the back of me ma's?"

"Yeah, you hear what happened to him?"

"He got a hiding one night, that's all I heard, a few years ago."

"Yeah, he knocked into someone's bird one night coming out of the Toper, accident, but Keogh being a cantankerous bollix, gave back cheek when yer man challenged him. Turns out the fellah knew loads of the heads from the West. They waited for him one night, coming out of the Toper, beat the living shit out of him, left him under the bridge."

"That what happened?!" Ben asked surprised.

"Yeah, in hospital for ages. Very lucky. Totally changed him. He's still living shit scared. So easy to happen, could have been you. Fucking stupid talking back."

"Ah look I know…"

Des stirred the two cups of tea he was making and handed one to his friend.

"What's on your mind buddy?"

"Nothing."

"Ben, c'mon, I know ya years. Is something up?"

Ben glanced across at his friend. Good old Des. Dependable Des, would never let anyone down.

"Ah a few things, nothing major, nothing to worry yourself over."

"You sure?"

"Yeah, just a bit down, the jobs and all that stuff."

"Well it's not like you to get into a fight like that. Did you tell Ro?"

"No, nor will I be. The bruises will be gone in a few days. She'll never know, no need for her to either, ok?"

Des held his two hands up.

"Sure buddy, no bother. Just worried about you."

He got up and went to his duffle bag and pulled out a small brown paper bag. "I met one of the Doobie Brothers last night. Wanna roll a few?"

Ben smiled. "Fuckin' sure."

"Okaaaaay, now we're talkin'…" Des chimed.

"First though, a bit of doobie music."

He went over to the record player than sat on a cheap plastic table by the covered fireplace. "So, Neil Young? Dylan? Sergeant Pepper? Bob himself?" he asked as he flicked through the records.

Ben sat back in the chair, sipping the tea.

"Leave it to you ," he decided as he relished the welcome escape from the throbbing pain as well as reality that the next few joints would bring him.å

Fourteen

Rowena opened the heavy door of the doctor's surgery in a daze. The evening traffic at the junction outside Ashgrove House hummed and beeped as her mind swam. Her world had just collapsed, her mind was a vortex of fear, anger and indecision.

The sickness welled up once more and she had no option but to vomit in front of the hardware store that occupied the bay window section of the building.

"Ah you fuckin' scaldy bitch!" a harsh voice carried to her as a young woman came to the door of the store, magazine rolled up in her hand.

"Ah Jaysus, why here? You're only ourra the doctors! Clean that up!"

Drivers and passengers alike watched as Rowena wiped her mouth and turned sharply by the side of the building and began walking home.

"Hey! Hey! Are you gonna clean that up?!"

She ignored the calls as the tears began to flow.

'No, no, no, mammy, NO!'

Hands buried deep in the pockets of her coat, her feet couldn't take her quick enough up the hill, past the closely set two-storey houses and old cottages that harked back to another era. All passed in a blur as the news she had just received made her heart bounce in her chest. The constant lights from within the bakery gazed past her as the hum of the giant silo segued into background noise of traffic. The fresh scent that would cause a young Rowena and some pals to hang around looking for fresh cakes lingered in the air but she cared not today. Stan the old baker who always sneaked a few cakes to the kids as he left for the day in his battered old Morris Minor could be long gone for all she knew. She hadn't thought about him in years but today, this day, his smiling face was before her again; albeit a memory but something to take her mind away from her predicament, if only for a second.

'Innocent days, good days, good people… all gone'

The halcyon days of the early 70s disappeared in a mire of a cold, wet and wintry October evening in 1982. She felt her stomach heave once more. She bolted towards the bricked up old gateway of the bakery and vomited again.

No question now, it would explain everything.

Her mind was a haze of confusion. Visions of the past and of circumstances yet to breathe through her young veins tormented her, swarming through her subconscious as a pitiful, sickly laughter threatened to erupt in her conscious. Tears fell as she scrunched up her face against the cold air and the insecurity of everything that lay ahead.

How could her mammy let her down? How?! Rowena wished she was going home to the warm comfort of her arms, her maternal scent a blanket of warmth and security that Rowena missed yet needed so badly. Instead she would walk into a cold empty house, dark shadows in the hallway her mother once stood in, opening the door for her as a young girl when she danced home from school. Only memories danced through the hallway now. She craved a memory, a sign that her mother was at her side.

The dull evening offered no such memory, no such solace. Heavy clouds loomed overhead like a shroud of doubt and uncertainty. The hill was steeper than usual today, her legs turned to jelly. Her head sunk into her coat as the rain fell bitingly sharp yet she was in no mood to go home yet. Her mind needed time to work through what she had just been told. She continued on up the hill automatically, not raising her head to see who passed by for fear they knew her and would see her tears.

She continued on by the turn for her home, past the dilapidated red-roofed barn, the dirty curved iron topping resting now on quickly laid blocks of concrete, a solitary, heavy rusty door, heavily bolted, the only way to gain access now. Beside it was the local community centre and the freshly built training centre. She paid no heed today, memories of the youth club she attended weekly in the boxy building not enough to bring a smile to her face now. Ahead of her lay fields, across the road the barely visible ruins of a gatepost and wall of one of the long gone farmsteads. She often was allowed go up to see the cows that grazed in the field during the hot summer months of her childhood, today she didn't care to remember.

The badly surfaced road twisted, an occasional cottage dotted here and there as the road continued to rise at a slight incline. The rain fell with greater ferocity now, stabbing icy shards mingling now with the tears that flowed with such horrific ease. She clasped her hands around her sides, shaking her head and crying forlornly as the few curious motorists gazed at the hapless figure in the dim light, her hair slowly matting in the freezing rain.

Had her mother let her down? Had she forsaken her?

'Why Mammy, why?? Why?? Please God, why?? Not now, not now…'

She reached the junction at the top of the hill, having walked a mile from the doctor's. To the left a small farm sat, a curved green-roofed barn, in full use, the smell wafting down each morning during the summer months.

Sitting in the back garden on her summer holidays the faint lowing of the cattle carried through the air on the breeze, and with it the pungent smell of manure. Another memory, another simpler time. Today though she felt no emotion at the thought. Raw bitterness, hatred and fear was forcing her heart to beat at a furious rate, she could almost taste it in her mouth.

She stood at the junction, arms folded tight for what seemed to her an eternity. Trucks and cars passed her, curious onlookers caught sight of her tearful face yet none stopped. She wanted to escape, to continue walking, past Dubber Cross, continue onto the fields out to Ashbourne until she dropped. If she fell into a sleep with which she did not awaken from, she would have welcomed that. Rather that than face the reality.

The country scene on this cold day mirrored her mood, her train of thought; long removed from the walks she, Mary and her parents used to venture on. There was a photo somewhere of her standing beside this very barn as a young girl, her smiling face in a blue summer dress as Mary beamed beside her. That memory warmed her heart, briefly, but not enough to snap her out of her delirium. She realised she was soaked, freezing cold and under-dressed for this evening. As car and truck headlights approached she wondered what would happen if she just stepped out onto the road. She lowered her head and rubbed her belly, the immediate feeling of guilt washing over her like a welcome tide, the warming sensation of having a child growing within her.

'I have to protect you. This is not your fault'

She spun on her heels and began the journey home, jogging part of the way as a sliver of renewed hope entered her heart. She knew this wave of euphoria wouldn't last, she knew the fear would return soon. She had to get home before it did. She was still terrified and angry, she had to figure out how to tell her sister, but the empty, abandoned feeling of earlier was being replaced with something more beautiful.

She craved the warmth and coal fires spewing from neighboring houses as she closed the creaking gate by the path to her door. The key slipped from her hand twice as she fought with it and the lock. She cursed loudly, not caring who heard.

Behind the house she could hear the leaves of the ancient trees that stood behind neighboring walls hiss as the wind took up. The still bird was awakening and coming out to mock her, its mouth in a perpetual expression of laughter. Mary was still at work. She flung her keys onto the telephone table and ran up the stairs into her room. She threw herself on the bed and the tears began again.

Cheap eye make-up began to stain the white pillow. Anger. Disbelief. Fear. *'Oh Ro why so fucking, fucking stupid?!'*

She turned the radio on and closed her eyes, calling upon those happier memories she conjured up at the green barn. Her mother would have helped her. She would have guided her though this. She would be disappointed, yes, but would have been the shoulder for her to cry on.

Mary was going to kill her.

More beautiful, soft images returned to her mind. Memories of helping her mother plant her cherished flowers during the bright spring mornings as music resonated on the old Bush radio in the kitchen. She would carefully show her youngest what to do, how to dig the soil, plant the seeds or immature stalks and nurture them.

Rowena could see her mother's soft smile, hear her cheery laugh and smell her unique, perfumed scent. Everyone said she looked like her. Old photos proved it; the same long, soft brunette hair, porcelain skin, high cheekbones and piercing eyes. Mirror image, she would recall being told.

Her mother's hugs, yes, she remembered them. How she would hug her and Mary together but, when alone, would whisper with a cheeky smile and wink that Rowena was her favourite hug of all. A wan smile creased her face only slightly, at the thought that she could become that very mother to her child.

The image in her mind retreated to the present cold autumn evening, her mother's plants lay long withered, the only care taken in the garden anymore was the cutting of the grass. Her mind drifted, the emotional exertions giving way to sleep, a sleep Mary would encourage when she returned home from work and carefully placed blankets over her sister's peaceful body. She failed to notice the tear stains in the darkness.

Mary was sound asleep when Rowena left the house through the back door. She relieved her sister of that five pound note, still carefully positioned in her brown leather purse. She stole up the driveway carefully and turned left, walking to the end of the road and beginning the journey down to the village. The night was still, the rain had abated and a ghostly calm ensued.

'That dream…'

The dream she had perplexed her. A woman in a pure white dress and a child, the child crying as eerie skeletons danced around them, the mother protecting her child yet piercing through Rowena's dreaming soul with intent.

'Your child, your child…' the woman repeated over and over again.

The child's face became clearer, dried tears refreshed by a new fall, piercing blue eyes betraying a melancholia echoed within Rowena's soul.

'Your child, your child…'

The woman, a young, beautiful one, moved to the side. Behind her stood a man, hollow eyes, tattered clothes, bloodied hands moving gently over a bloodied face. His legs faded below his knees. He glided towards her, menacingly.

'Your father, your father…'

It was then she awoke with a start and a gasp, beads of sweat prickled on her forehead as her top stuck to her back. She shot out of the bed, opening the curtains to reveal a world that to her was as normal as ever.

The dream spooked her. She changed her top and decided to get out of the house. It was still relatively early in the night but her sister was fast asleep in bed, the toll of sitting in front of a green computer screen taking it's toll on her eyes.

Ben needed to know. He needed to weigh in with this. She walked down Jamestown Road, ignoring all around her, not stopping until she reached the Drake at the village crossroads.

She stopped outside. She shouldn't drink. She shouldn't. The baby. But she needed a drink. She needed the courage to tell Ben. She thought of the consequences. One drink. One drink. It was before last orders.

She poked her head round the door. Ben's brother was on duty. Shit. She had a quick look around and saw Lucy there.

'That freak. Who was she out with?'

She'd do. Lucy saw her and Rowena jerked her head to the left as she stepped back outside. Lucy followed her out.

"Rowena?"

"Lucy, hi. I need you to do something."

"What?"

"Get us some drink. Bottle of vodka if you can."

"Ah here…"

"Do it, please, and say nothing to no-one."

"Ah I don't know…"

Lucy Jones had been Rowena's pal through primary and secondary school though she viewed her with suspicion now. As children, Lucy was a loner but gave Rowena her chocolate bar when she returned after her mother's funeral.

'My mammy says I'm to give you this,' she always recalled her saying.

Their friendship grew, they drifted as they got older and these days only chatted briefly if they met. Lucy had reverted into herself even more, it was said she was a bit of a manic depressive. She had bouts of it; happy one day, in the doldrums the next. She had an eye for the men though, she was mad into Ben but he was having none of it. Now Rowena found herself asking her former close friend for a favour.

'The fuckin' state of her dolled up like a whore's boot…'

"Go on…"

"What's it for Rowena?"

"For fucking drinking?!"

"No, I mean… is there a party?"

Her tone indicated she sought company.

"Who you in their with?"

"Just my sister."

"Get the vodka Lucy, please, here's the money." She dug into her pocket and handed over the money she had. Lucy slipped back inside as Rowena stamped her feet against the cold, her breath forming wisps of condensation as she looked around nervously. The door opened again, causing her to jump. Lucy stood there with the tightly wrapped brown paper bag.

"I had to tell the barman I'd meet him 'round the back afterwards to get that! He took it from the storeroom, fuck sake, here. I've no intention of going anywhere with that ugly prick. If there's a party can me and Susan come?"

"I'm going to check now, stay there, have another drink, I'll poke me head back in for you," Rowena lied.

"Thanks Rowena."

Rowena turned away. For fuck sake, Ro. Ro. Not Rowena.

"Rowena?"

She stopped, looked skyward and turned around.

"What?!" she said sharply.

"I don't want to go 'round the back with him!"

"Yeah I know, you told me, well fucking don't then, Jesus, Lucy!"

"So you'll come back for me for the party?"

"Yes!"

Lucy fucking Jones. Loopy Lucy. Jesus wept. Rowena allowed herself a sarcastic laugh as she walked away.

'I wondered which Lucy that was then, the good or the bad one…'

Drink to forget or Dutch courage? She could choose either. But only one could help her. She glanced at the bottle in her hand. A few shots. Then that would be it. The baby wasn't far gone, it would still be in its bubble, the doctor said. Or something like that. She wasn't sure, she'd have to read up.

'Women have drunk loads further into their pregnancy, until they find out. I'll be ok, just a few…'

But fuck it she needed this. She took a deep breath as she began the walk down the hill towards Ben's.

The empty bottle dropped onto the footpath behind them with a terrific smash as both the giggling adults stooped under cover of darkness.

Rowena let out a howl of laughter as she leaned back against a tree.

"Yayyyyy!!" she cheered.

"Let's walk, c'mon, see if we can avoid any tombstones!"

The two staggered through the small, ancient city of the dead that lay silently in the shadow of the ruined abbey.

"They have to give us a plot for free, we're always in here," Ben mumbled, the effects of the vodka playing havoc with his sense of direction as he sat on a cracked flagstone that covered a grave of a soul long forgotten.

Rowena took his hand and led him through the darkness, deeper into the maze of mounds and headstones until they were near the wall that separated the eerily quiet necropolis from the rolling dual carriage feet away.

"Let's say hello to Mammy!"

They sat awkwardly beside the family plot. Rowena patted the grave silently, rearranging the flowers she couldn't see but guessed were there.

Her beloved mother lay silently under the earth.

The drink and the surroundings took control of Ben's mind.

"Is there much more room in the grave?"

"A lot," Rowena replied, over-pronouncing her words as she continued to pat the grave as she gently sang a song her mother used to sing to her.

"Graves were dug much deeper years ago, not like now. Grannny's in there, my great-granny too. Not much known about her. They never talked about her really, well my granny didn't. Mammy told me though, said she was a beautiful woman who died very young... same name as my name. She was a Rowena too. Hate the fuckin' name anyway... Rowena. Jaysus. Why couldn't I have been called after me mam, or Granny? Elizabeth she was. Lovely name. Lovely, like me mammy. A mammy's name..."

Rowena buried her head in her hands as she began to cry. Tears cascaded down her face as the awful, sickening sinking feeling swept through her once more.

"Fuck it, fuck it anyway!!" she screamed

Ben moved to her side and put his arm around her.

"It's ok, she's not in pain anymore."

"What?!"

"You mam..."

"It's not me mammy, Ben."

"What is it Ro?"

"Ah fuck off!"

She brushed him aside roughly and stood up, stumbling in the darkness and coming to a collapsing halt against the wall. She slithered down it until she was in a pathetic heap, sobbing.

"Oh Mammy, ... have to tell you something, I really do, I'm so sorry."

"What? What do you have to tell your ma?"

"Not her! She knows! YOU!! You!! You inconsiderate, fucking arsehole!"

She began swinging arms wildly at him as he stooped to be with her, eventually falling into his awkward embrace.

"What Ro?!"

"That night, a few weeks ago..."

Ben remained silent. He had it worked out. Rowena's next words didn't register. He didn't need to be told. He held his sobbing friend as a spear of terror welled up deep inside him.

"Is this really going on?" she repeatedly sobbed.

"Is this really going on?! Is it just make believe?! Is it Ben?!"

Ben remained stoic in his silence. He wiped his hand in his eyes and, practically sobering up, stared at the moon that was creeping through the billowing cloud overhead.

"You sure?"

"Yes."

"How sure?"

"I was at the poxy doctors. All the signs were there, apparently. Been late a while…"

"For what?"

"What?!"

"Late for what?"

Ro shoved her childhood friend hard, sending him collapsing to the dirt.

"Oh Jesus Ben, Jesus Christ, are you that clueless?!" she howled.

His mind clouded with disbelief and irrational thoughts he couldn't control. Alcohol spurned them on, egging the words he would never normally say to his tongue. "How'd you know it's mine?"

He slurred the words, trying to pronounce them with authority. Rowena stood before him, silent, unable to see the expression on his face but his expression was irrelevant now. The word, those words. They repeated again and again in her mind as she swayed over her best friend. The tears continued to stream down her soft cheekbones, flowing with a torrent, echoing the now almost totally buried rivulet that once weaved its way through the village, now as scarred as her soul.

"Did you just say that, Ben? Did you? Did you?!"

Ben couldn't reply. The bravado of vodka and cheap cans of lager provided him with a wisdom he would normally scorn upon but it was too late. He had said those words. Rowena's flailing, aimless and pathetic punches and kicks were a testament to his lack of judgement, her angered limbs failing to connect more often they did.

"You bastard! How could you?! How could you?!" she roared.

Ben moved away from her, skulking over graves and bumping into headstones toward a wall which he eventually climbed over, leaving his close friend and expectant mother of his child in a sobbing heap on the ground, her back against the far wall as she shrieked loudly while staring into the inky black sky. "Leave me! Go on, you fucking coward! Leave me here!"

Ben stumbled across the dual carriageway, shaking his head as he refused to accept what Rowena had spelled out for him. No way. No way. He wasn't the father. Bitch. Lying bitch. Just because he was her lifelong friend, she wasn't going to tie him down with this one. He stumbled onto the road in front of Rosehill House, past the Bottom of the Hill pub and across the road where the neglected old church that occasionally served as a parish hall sat on it's plinth. It served as a parish hall now these days. Beside it and hidden behind a row of neat mature trees, the parochial house silent in the night, facing out onto a forgotten Rosehill House. Years of neglect showed on the weather-beaten façade; rumours were rife in the village that it and Gofton Hall were next to be knocked in the name of glorious progress.

Save for elderly voices of discontent and concern, the younger generation didn't care. There were too many problems to face first before caring about a building that was a relic of prosperity long gone. Memories of business dealings and commerce that once occurred within the high walls when the Bayly's were one of the wealthiest families in the county now faded to dust and crumbled with their bones that lay behind a heavy door down the steps to their vault in the old graveyard.

A voice called him. "Ben?"

He turned towards the old church building.

"Where you at the party?"

"Who is it?" he asked.

Lucy Jones stepped out of the shadows, her sister Susan nervously at her side. "Me. Lucy. Just having a fag before we go home. Want one?"

"Why you smoking in here, in this dump?"

"Me ma will kill us if she sees us."

"Your ma always up this late?"

"You know what I mean, some neighbour could see us."

"No, don't want one. I need to go home."

"So do we Lucy," Susan snapped. "Work?"

"Ah I'll be there soon."

"I'm going then? Knew I shouldn't have stayed this late," Susan replied, clacking her way down the steps onto the sharp bend once known as Chapel Lane.

"Go. Ben will walk me home."

"And me?"

"Susan you can see our house from here!" she admonished as she pointed across the green and behind the back of Rosehill to the houses beyond.

"Fine!" she snapped. "If I'm attacked on your head be it!"

Susan clacked off, her high heels becoming less audible as she negotiated the wide steps up the hill where the green space lay, before giving way to a winding path that led to her house on the corner of the large estate near to Ben's.

"She's mad," Lucy smiled. "Have you any smokes Ben?"

"No, need to go home Lucy."

"Ah Ben, you serious?!"

"Lucy I have to…"

He was distant, looking anywhere but at the slim girl in front of him.

"Well I'll walk up that way with ya, I fancy chips."

"Whatever."

Both silently descended the steps, the glass of smashed beer bottles crunching under their feet, the smell of stale urine assaulting their nostrils. The stepped by the carefully stored wooden pallets and tyres gathered for a Hallowe'en bonfire. As they turned back up the main street Ben noticed the haze formed by the crass neon streetlights. It added an air of uncertainty to the night, to the season, a spooky omen. He began to cross the street.

"Where you goin'!?"

"Home."

"You not walking me home after I get chips?"

"No."

Lucy ran across the silent street after him, tugging his arm as he fought to wrestle the key from his pocket. The happenings of the night and the cold night air were playing havoc with him; in his head, a dull ache resonated as his tongue begged for water.

""What Lucy?!" he exclaimed, turning to face her for the first time.

"Are you ok?"

"No."

"Why?"

"'Cos I'm not Lucy, I don't need this shit, ok?"

"Shit?! What shit? Fuck sake Ben I only asked you to walk me home, or to the chipper. What's up? Did something happen at the party?!"

"What party?"

"Where you not at the party Rowena was at?"

"What?!"

"She got me to get her a bottle of vodka, said she'd be back for me, never was though. She looked weird."

"I was with her a while, went for a walk."

"Where was the party?"

Ben chuckled to himself. "The graveyard, and what a fuckin' party it was…" he replied, more to no-one than Lucy.

"The graveyard?! Which one?"

"Ah Lucy, look, I'm headin' in, you can get yourself home, it's only across the way."

"Ah yeah, and what if I'm attacked?!"

"By who? There's no-one around!"

"Some pervert lurking?"

"Then scream."

"Scream? Are you for real?!" Lucy stood with her hand on her hips, eyes wide. She relaxed her stance and approached him softly.

"You're locked, Ben."

"Ten outta ten. You were always the bright spark Lucy."

She grabbed hold of the lapels of his coat, looked him up and down and smiled. "Let me stay with you."

Ben laughed. "You fuckin' serious? After the night I just had?!"

"Well whatever it was I'll make it better for you," she whispered as she moved her hands down his torso.

"How?" he admonished.

"Let me show you."

His head swam as he allowed Lucy Jones kiss him. He knew she had perhaps been plotting this moment for many a year. He felt nothing, no passion, no excitement.

Lucy was pretty but without being beautiful. She had a petite figure but he never was attracted to her. Now he found himself standing outside the door of his flat with Lucy kissing him and her hands wandering aimlessly.

His head swam as spectres of the evening circled him; realisations, daunting, horrific realities of a world that faced him, a world that would turn his, and his family's life upside down. Panic welled up inside him. Beads of sweat formed on his forehead as he strove to push Lucy away.

"Ben, c'mon, let me inside, please."

He took one look at her. From tomorrow morning he would have decisions to make, hard, rash choices about his future.

"I want this," Lucy whispered as she kissed his neck.

"I don't."

"You're turning me down Ben?"

"Lucy my head's not right at the moment, please go, will you?"

She stood back, arms folded, looking up and down the street.

"Can I use your toilet first?"

He signed and turned to open the door. "Then go, ok…"

She nodded and followed him up the dark stairway, patiently waiting as he fumbled with the lock to the small flat. The smell of cannabis still hung in the air.

"Through there," he grunted, pointing to his left yet not turning to face her.

She said nothing and locked herself in the dingy bathroom. Her mind swam as urges, amplified by the night's drinking, took hold of her. She stood up and stared at her reflection in the mirror. She knew she was selfish, that Ben was obviously in a bad place, but she enjoyed being a bad girl. She would get what she wanted. She began to undo her skirt. Ben sat staring out the window in the freezing flat, dragging slowly on a cigarette as he sought to make sense of the turmoil in his mind. He didn't turn around initially when Lucy called him, but she attracted his attention soon enough.

Mary put the phone down and smiled. It was good to hear from Debbie. She had just spent the last hour chatting to her, seeking and receiving reassurance. She decided to tell Rowena soon. Debbie could guarantee them jobs if they gave a promise to be over. She giddily skipped up the stairs to her bed. Strange to find Rowena asleep like that so early. She was out cold so she went to bed herself, soon slipping into a deep, happy sleep. She wasn't to later hear her sister cautiously descend the stairs and out the back door.

Fifteen

Rowena's heavy eyelids flickered as the dim unwelcome grey light filtered through. Everything was on its side; not right. She was freezing cold, her arms huddled around her, clothes damp, hair stuck to her face.

For a few minutes she remained in that tight, pathetic foetal position on the damp ground. Bits and pieces of the night before began to return to her mind, spectres that she could not drown in the alcohol she gulped down hours before. The pain returned. The guilt. The terror. Her eyes darted towards her mother's grave. It lay eerie, silent, calm in the early morning grey. She had slept by her mother's side for the first time in many years, but no comfort could be offered now. Nothing but the cold wind whistling around her, animating the looming shadows of trees that stood nearby; the chill bouncing off the dull grey stone of the ruined church. She was alone in this world. The dead surrounded her, those she once loved and could share a smile with now lay in rotting coffins feet below her.

She tried to ease herself to a sitting position as her bones shook uncontrollably. She looked around, the early morning dawn and bristling chill of a cold east wind of another wintry October day brought everything back to her. She crossed her legs under her with some effort, her teeth chattering as a sharp breeze invaded every part of her body, swimming through her stiff frame with ease and delight. She huddled up in a pathetic effort to warm up but knew she couldn't. She slowly stood up, with great difficulty, her dull head not wanting the physical effort and leaned against the graveyard wall. Early morning traffic droned by only feet behind her.

The streetlights were still on. She thought back to a few hours before. She had told Ben, his reaction? She was sure it would come back to her. The knowing pain in her gut intensified as the realisation of her actions sank in. The fear, it was known as; the immediate insecurity of someone waking from a drunken stupor. She looked down at her stomach, her hand patting it maternally. Oh God, what had she done? What had she done!? Had she killed the baby?!

Footsteps on the iron bridge by the graveyard alerted her. She sunk into the shadows, carefully finding her way along the wall until she reached the familiar crevice she knew she could easily scale. Listening for more footsteps, she hauled herself over, grunting and with effort and discomfort. Her frame jolted as she landed on the footpath.

She huddled into her jacket, buried her hands in her pockets and turned to cross the iron bridge that would take her across the dual carriage way and back to her side of the village. She never looked up once, terrified again that someone would recognise her.

Early morning starters were few on the dull streets, anyone who passed didn't offer a second glance to the freezing, hungover young woman. She crossed the village, raising her head once as she passed the old red-brick asylum. In another time she would be dispatched there, sent in shame as her family turned their backs. In a twisted way she longed for that option. She stared at the iron gates; powerful captors to keep people in and out. She buried her head deeper into her damp coat turning away from Jamestown Road into the estate leading off the busy road in an effort to remain undetected. She hadn't time to think. She must get home before Mary woke. She walked at a ferocious pace, nervously glancing at her watch again and again, skulking up the laneway at the back of the houses that she often used as a shortcut in the past. Skipping through back gardens at this hour would be easy. She hid under the cover of the tall pine trees backing onto her garden; no sign of life in the house. She glanced at the neighbours. No lights, no sign of movement. She scaled the wall with ease, creeping stealthily down the long path, fumbling carefully for the key to the door before gently letting herself in. As she closed the door behind her, she glanced up at the demonic bird in the tree, pointing at her, mocking her, its face twisted into a grin as it singled her out for admonishment.

'*You bastard, you're enjoying this…*'

The second hand on the blue-faced clock on the kitchen wall thundered in her head as she slipped her coat off, carefully placing it back on the same hook she took it from and removed her Doc Martins to began the ascent up the stairs, terror forcing her heart out of her chest as she slowly conquered every step. She daren't make a sound. She stood for what must have been minutes on the landing. A plan crossed her mind. She opened her door and walked to the bathroom.

Finishing on the toilet, she used the noise of the cistern refilling to remove her clothes and bundle them into the laundry basket. She quickly brushed her teeth and stepped out and confidently strode back to her room.

"Rowena?"

Her heart stopped.

"Yeah?"

"You ok?"

"Yeah? Just going to the toilet."

She squeezed her eyes as tight as they cold shut, praying she wouldn't be found out now.

"Ok. Better be getting up meself soon."

She slipped back into her room, threw on her pyjamas and sighed with relief as she slipped under the covers. They were cold but would soon soothe her mind and warm her bones. Had she gotten away with it?

Mary got up and ready for work, the sound of the early morning radio filtering through the house. She could hear her elder sister come up the stairs. She knocked on the door and slowly opened it.

"Cup of tea?"

Rowena, warmth returning to her body, sat up as Mary turned on the table lamp and placed the tea on the wooden stool beside her bed.

"Oh Ro, you look knackered!"

"I didn't really sleep Mary."

"Stay in bed a bit longer. I went out like a light last night, woke up in the same position."

Rowena smiled wanly, guilt etched with relief visible on her face.

"Anyway, I was thinking Rowena, if you want, we could go out for dinner tonight? The two of us?"

"Why?"

Mary had her plan prepared for a long time. She would gently break it to Rowena about the move to New York.

"Oh, just to have a talk, we never really chat anymore. You fancy a pig out in Phibsboro? Emma's?" she smiled.

"Really? Oh Mary yes, thank you!" Rowena smiled.

Mary leaned in and gave her sister a hug. Rowena sealed her mouth shut, just in case.

"Ok, back to sleep, I'll see you later."

Mary closed the door behind her. She clenched both her fists and skipped back down the stairs. Rowena was no fool, she knew that, but they had been the closest in months in those few moments. She knew that she had taken one more step towards New York.

Rowena sat back, her head tilted towards the ceiling. She raised her hand to her eyes and began to softy cry. The world was about to come crashing down.

Ben had been awake for hours. He stood by the window smoking as the early morning light painted the inky sky a dull, tedious grey. The smell of cannabis he and Lucy smoked still hung in the air, as pungent as the moment they sparked up the joints. The neon lights still shone their comforting orange glow. He felt his jaw, rough, unshaven. He felt unclean as the demons from the previous night danced around his fragile mind and thwarted him. His face was still tender form the beating some weeks ago but the bruises had healed. The room was freezing. He hadn't bothered with the gas heater.

A noise behind him interrupted his thoughts. Lucy walked into the room, the bed-sheet wrapped around her. She rubbed the back of her head and walked over to him.

"Why you up so early?"

Ben said nothing. He looked Lucy up and down. Her eyeliner had ran, the remnants of a once forensically made-up face giving her an edgier, dangerous appearance. He stubbed the cigarette out and walked passed her.

"Come back, Ben."

He walked out of the room and back into his bedroom, throwing himself back onto the rumpled sheets. The room smelt of stale perfume, long-smoked cigarettes and alcohol. Lucy followed him back, sitting on the edge of the bed. She looked at him for a few seconds, smiling then looking away. She twisted her fingers around each other, patting her bare feet on the floor.

"Ben…"

"Don't."

"Ben you have to…."

"No I don't."

She glanced back at him, nervousness in her eyes.

"Ben we shouldn't…."

"Too late," he scowled as he sat up.

"Jesus Ben, what have we done?"

He refused to look at her.

"Lucy, best go."

"What?!" she cried, springing over to him, her hands on his shoulders as she sat at his turned back.

"Ben, we can't, we…"

She began to weep softy. All her dreams of being with Ben became nothing but a stark, ugly reality in the cold room. She cursed the extra drink and joint she had in his apartment. She cursed kissing him at the door. She cursed following him. She cursed calling out to him by the parish hall. She cursed meeting Rowena. She cursed going out at all last night. She was due to go into work shortly. She would have to go home, face her parents, her sister who had the Guards probably called by now. Oh what had she done. Sensible Lucy led astray by her own wont and now facing the harsh realities of her actions. It wasn't meant to be like this.

She couldn't look back on last night with a secret smile. She was so stupid, so, so stupid. Careful Lucy, sensible Lucy had perhaps thrown everything away in a few stolen minutes. Ben remained with his back to her.

"I want you to go Lucy."

"Please…"

"Go."

His voice bore no emotion, no tone, no inkling of care. His eyes stared fixed at the wall. She got up from the bed, gathering her belongings as she slipped silently down the stairs and out on to the street below.

Ben continued to stare at the physical wall. The mental wall was tougher, a wall that couldn't be climbed over, traversed around or dug under. He was a prisoner. Demons danced around him, pointing, laughing. He was trapped, a damn fool trapped in a hell he himself had foolishly participated in.

Lucy crossed the narrow main street as the tears flowed like a gully. Arms folded, head bowed, she turned at the parish hall, crossed over and began scaling the steps by the green. Her hand shook as she took the key out of her bag and closed the gate gently behind her. She climbed the three small steps and was walking up the path when the door opened.

Her sister stood in her dressing gown, a look of relief on her face as she ushered Lucy indoors and up the stairs.

"Mam and dad had to go out in the early hours, Auntie Jean was taken to hospital. She's not well at all. They came into me, asked me to let you know in the morning, they wouldn't disturb you.

"You're fucking blessed you stupid bitch! Where were you?! Where were you?!"

Lucy allowed the tears to fall freely as she buried her head in her surprised sisters shoulder. She guided Lucy to the sofa and hugged her tightly, demanding to know what was wrong.

Lucy eventually spoke. Staring at the fireplace, she squeezed her sister's hand tightly before uttering. "I've been so bloody foolish, oh God what have I done?! What have I done?! What a stupid bitch I am, what will I do?!"

Sixteen

Mary paid the bill and sat back down facing her sister.

"Thanks," Rowena said, smiling softly.

"You're very welcome. Still don't know what I did with that fiver. Hate breaking a big note. Ah well…"

"What was all this about anyway? Not my birthday 'til next year?"

"Ah I just felt like it. Why not. I'm in good form, can't bring the money with you anyway, can you?"

Rowena drank some of her Coke and stared out the widow at the busy junction. Mary must be told. She had to be.

"Anyway Ro, did you ever feel the house is too big for both of us?"

"What?" Rowena turned back at this surprise remark.

"The house, you know, it's hard to maintain, hard to keep."

"It's Mammy's house."

"I know but, well, we're two young women, struggling for money, what I get covers the mortgage and so on, well, there could be more, couldn't there?"

"Suppose…"

Mary gazed into her younger sister's eyes. They were the window of opportunity. Both sisters looked quite alike, Mary always conceded though that Rowena was the better looking. In her mother's image.

Rowena looked back out the window, Mary's words suddenly sinking in.

She turned back to her sister and leaned across the table, her eyes widening.

"Mary, are you thinking of moving?!"

Her tone was a surprised one, not one of anger.

"I've been thinking about it Ro…"

Rowena sat back in the chair, her perplexed gaze fixed on her sister.

"Oh, well that's a shock, Mary!"

"Why, would you not like to?"

"Mammy's house Mary…"

"Yes but too big, too much to run."

"It's only a three bed."

"Doesn't matter, it eats the money. Look, doesn't matter, just speaking aloud, that's all, don't be worrying about it."

"You want to move then?"

"One day…"

"Soon I take it?"

Mary looked at the table then slowly out the window before turning back to her sister. She searched her eyes for a hint of what was going through her sister's mind. She reached over and took her hand, softly yet enough to translate how both of them needed to be in this together. "I know Ro, would you consider coming with me?"

"Mammy's house, Mary, Mammy's house… plus she's buried down the road, if we moved far we couldn't go. "

Mary looked back out the window, pointing at the abandoned cinema across the busy Phibsboro Road. "You see the old building?"

"The old cinema?"

"Yeah, the Bohemian; mam used to go on dates there, and the Casino in the village too. Being brought out here was a treat for her, Daddy brought her out here the night he proposed. Probably knock it down soon I guess, like everything else."

Rowena gave her sister a quizzical look. "Mary if this exchange ends with, 'sure everything changes', I'll whack you with this poxy menu."

Mary nodded, released here sister's hand and grabbed her purse, stuffing it back into her bag.

"Come on, let's go. See if there's a 19 bus on the way."

Rowena finished her drink and put her coat on. It still smelt damp even though she had put it on the radiator. Her heart was racing, Mary's sudden bombshell only added to her own stress.

"You didn't eat much, are you ok?" Mary asked.

"Yeah, just one of those days."

"Oh ok. Once you're ok though?"

"Yeah I am. So your mind's made up about moving I guess..." Rowena's statement trailed off.

"Just a though love, I can't go on like this, money-wise. I'm taxed to fuck as it is, tonight was out of my savings. Go on outside and wait, I just need the loo."

Rowena stepped outside, looking at the dilapidated, unused Bohemian cinema sat across the road, waiting for the wrecking ball. She pondered Mary's words. This had come very suddenly. She always thought they'd live in that house forever. Mary was the breadwinner, the sole earner. She had aspirations to improve both their lives; the only thing Rowena would bring to the equation now would shatter everything Mary had been building up to.

"Let's go!" Mary stood smiling, tying a head scarf round her. Both women crossed the car park and stood by the bus stop on the Phibsboro Road.

"Grandad used to work out of the tram sheds that were once there," Mary added, pointing back to the ugly shopping centre that now stood in it's place. Behind it, the towering floodlights of Dalymount Park stood.

"Forgot about that I think."

"And you the family historian!"

Both stayed silent in the freezing evening as they sat on the wall, glancing past Doyle's Corner for a bus, each thinking their own thoughts; Mary on how the new opportunity would be a blessing for both of them, Rowena on the stark, frightening future that lay ahead for her.

"Mary, where are you thinking of moving to?"

Mary closed her eyes momentarily and exhaled gently.

"Oh look, here's one, a 19!" she chirped, the subject kicked to touch for another moment. They hailed the orange bus and took their seats on the uncomfortable blue leather. Rowena stared out the damp, condensation coated windows. Her mind was as confused as ever. Mary would be devastated.

'Jesus Mary why think of moving now?! Your timing is up your hole...'

Mary stared ahead, oblivious to the torment in her sister's mind, happy with the evening. She felt guilty but had made the first steps, put the feelers out. She could work on Rowena. She would talk to Debbie more, ask her advice. New York was not to be sniffed at. She was sure Rowena would love it. Yeah, it would be fine. She smiled and linked her sister's arm.

Rowena turned and smiled back.

"Thanks for tonight Mary. You're very good to me."

Those words, as true as they were echoed in her soul. Mary was good to her. She had to tell her. She had to.

Lucy filed into the church with the old women as the rain pelted her face. She took her soaked woollen hat off as she eased into a pew in the centre of the church, placing her bag and hat down beside her. The huge orbs that served as lights hung steadily from the sturdy brass arms that clung to the thick pillars supporting the ornate, arched ceiling above them. Dark wooden confessionals were spaced evenly either side of the church separated by elaborate, Renaissance-style paintings of the Stations. The priest came out and began the mass; old women were scattered in small clusters throughout the cavernous church. His voice droned on as she looked around at the delicate paintings. The large altar ahead of her was impressive, the thick red cross with the Saviour hanging still as it has done for years.

On either side of the altar, a smaller collection of pews lay empty, the inhabitants at this hour of the morning deciding to face the elderly priest who muttered indecipherably, hands raised in perpetual adoration as he continued with the prayers.

She didn't follow the course of the mass, she hadn't the time. She mumbled a few prayers, all the time nervously looking around at the elder generation sank into deep devotion, rosary beads alive in their hands, heads moving back and forth as silent words came from their mouths, praying for a life lived and the life their descendants had yet to live. She recognised a few faces from around the village through the years. The old woman directly to he right was always old, even when she was a young girl skipping off to school herself. She wondered would the hardship-beaten face, one obvious of her generation living in a poorer Dublin, live forever.

Lucy buried her head, pleading for help, for calm, for serenity. She had told her sister everything, she had agreed what a stupid bitch she was but she also agreed to stand by her and not say a word until the tests came through. What would happen would happen, she said, and they'd deal with it after that.

Lucy poured her heart into her pleadings. She had a nice life, good job in an office on Usher's Island that she wanted to keep. She had a few pounds in her purse, more in the bank. She was terrified that all that should be ripped apart for a few stupid minutes with Ben. She couldn't blame the drink, she never drank that much; it was her fault. She wanted him, gave herself to him on a plate. She took advantage of him, he was in a disturbed frame of mind. She felt guilt. Terrible, terrible Catholic guilt for a churchgoer like Lucy. Seconds could alter the path of her life.

She blessed herself in a hurry and grabbed her belongings, choosing to slip out the church by the side aisle. As she passed the small alcove with the statue of Our Lady at the back of the church, she paused to squeeze her hand through the slot in the railings and put a few coins into the brass box as she lit a candle. All the while the elderly Canon Deasy droned on, ignoring the loud clank of metal on metal as the coins dropped in. She felt guilty that there were a few half pennies in the bundle. She didn't have much on her and needed her bus fare.

She hurried back out the entrance, allowing the door to close loudly behind her as a sudden gust of wind that found its way into the hallway. The priest stopped for a moment, pausing from his homily as the noise echoed through the church, before he droned on in the same manner.

She stood outside the doors, fixing her hat on her head under the statue of St. Canice before running down the steps towards the bus stop.

She just made it. She found a seat at the back and closed her eyes in hope before the conductor rolled out a small ticket with damp, purple inky squares.

Ben lay on his bed, the soft night light creating a projection of his bedroom window on the opposite wall. He swung his feet down to the floor and twitched the net curtain aside, gazing out at the neighboring back gardens that he could see from the window in the family home. Above them the fireworks of this Hallowe'en night exploded in an array of colour, the varied sounds created by bangers of numerous strengths echoed in the background. The heavy rain that had been falling since early evening wasn't offering a deterrent to the entertainment of children or youths.

It was something he always did as a child; creating stories and activities for the houses backing onto his street that had lights on or homeowners who could be seen carrying a bucket of coal in from the back yard. Bathroom lights flashed on sporadically; gradually lights dimmed and went out as the night wore on. There was always one that remained though well into the early hours. Ben imagined a party in the house; fire blazing, happy people, sharing a beer, crisps, a smoke as they laughed and danced. He let the curtain rest and lay back on the bed.

His parents were surprised when he announced he wanted to come home. He told Des he couldn't stay in the flat, he wanted to go.

He moved his meagre belongings back to his old bedroom. His mother was made up. He was happy for her but he wanted to experience his old room, the home comforts again.

His mind was awash with the thoughts of two women, neither of whom he had been in touch with since that accursed night a few weeks ago.

They had dominated his mind; the actions of a foolish, drunk man had altered his path in life. No longer could he breeze by day by day, what had happened in the graveyard and his flat would haunt him for the rest of his days. He walked the streets late at night, mulling over what had happened. He stayed away from the pubs, ignoring the challenges of drunken youths gathered by the memorial. A lifelong friendship had been shattered, he had also contributed to possibly damaging the life of another.

He grabbed his jacket and slowly descended the stairs, popping his head around the living room door.

"Just goin' out for a walk."

"You're not going to cause trouble are you?" his dad asked, face buried in the paper as usual.

"No Da just a walk."

"It's lashing out!" his mother stated, looking vainly through the front window from the far side of the room.

"I won't be long, just a bit of a headache. I won't be long."

He looked at them for a few seconds more, before nodding and letting himself out. The walking helped him think, helped him navigate the muddy corridors of his mind as he strove for an explanation, a reason, a solution. He often spent time standing in the middle of the iron bridge looking down the dual carriageway towards the city. He wished the woods that were ripped up to create the busy road and surrounding estates were still there as he needed somewhere to hide. In their place now lay bricks, mortar and concrete. The long road that stretched past Premier Dairies and out into the city only offered him regular trips to sign on in Gardiner Street.

He looked beyond at the faint lights at the base of the mountains, a different world, a new world, perhaps opportunities lay out there for him. During the days his mind was drawn towards young mothers and their infants as they were wheeled around the village. He gazed at happy young couples as he wasted hours sitting on the small wall of the car park. He stood silently outside the padlocked gates of Gofton Hall as he remembered what Rowena had said to him about the place, you would be sent there by your family for minor matters. A few generations ago Rowena and now possibly Lucy would have been dispatched there to see out their pregnancy. Lucy. Was she pregnant too? Panic rose inside him again, a cold sweat pricking his forehead on this wet night as his stomach heaved and he vomited over the side of the bridge.

He didn't even know if she had told anyone. He didn't know anything. That gnawed at him; but, strangely, comforted him. Would it go away? Would they realise he was a waster and cut him out of their lives and get on with it? He would be freed of the responsibility, but never of the guilt, of the stupidity.

He turned off the bridge and down the hill. He stood in front of St. Canice's Catholic church, staring up at the dominating spire. On the ground to the left was a large stone grotto, its landscape carefully nurtured by a select but avid few eager to please the parish priest. To the right and beside him at the entrance to the esplanade was a full-size crucifixion scene, the white figures depicting accurately the sorrowful emotions of a scene drilled into him since he was a young boy in the local primary school a stone's throw away. He stared up at the crucified saviour, the stark whiteness of the figure seemingly floating, the dark wood of the cross having melted into the darkness of the night. The wind rustled the trees that stood at the side.

He tilted his head at the apparent floating figure and a sense of calm washed over him. For the first time in weeks he had a clear thought.

Mary was sitting laughing at the television as Rowena entered the room. Walking over to it, she turned the sound down. The room was cosy, the fire crackled warmly in the fireplace, the side lamp added a comforting glow.

"Ro, I'm watching that?"

Mary sat up in her chair as Rowena pulled over another, almost touching off her sister's fireside armchair.

She began to cry. "Mary, I have…"

"What is it?"

Rowena wiped her eyes and clenched her fists.

Her voice wobbled as she stared into the fire. "Ok Mary, just let me finish, don't interrupt me, just let me talk."

"Ok, are you…"

"Just let me talk!" she gulped. Her body shook, tears ran down her face as she sniffed repeatedly, glancing at the large picture of her mother that hung over the fireplace. "I'm so stupid Mary, so fucking stupid, and I'm sorry Mary, by Christ I'm so sorry, I've let you down, I've let me down, I've let mammy down…"

Mary was startled. "What? What's up?!"

"Shut the fuck up Mary, please!! Just listen. I've been so stupid, so stupid, I'm sorry, I'm really sorry, I'm sorry, I was wrong and I was a fool…"

Mary sank back in her chair, mystified.

"I was drunk Mary, really drunk and didn't plan it, I swear, didn't want it, don't fucking want it now! Stupid, so stupid, me and Ben, Mary, so fucking stupid and I've fucked my life up, I've fucked your life up, I've fucked everything up, I've fucked my fucking life up!"

Her words spilled out of her mouth at a waterfall's pace; no let up, no gulp of air, no rational thought of reasoning to the obscenities she was spewing forth, she just emptied the fear she had been carrying around with her.

"And the doctor confirmed it for me, I'm so sorry, I've made a shame on the family."

Mary's face was impassive as she sought to decode the incessant ramblings of her young sister. Then she saw the tearful woman rub just below her stomach almost subconsciously. Her heart let out one frightening thump before it began to sink in her chest. Sweat formed on her forehead and hands as her sister continued spilling words and incoherent phrases. But she knew. Now she understood what Rowena was saying to her.

A fire of confusion and anger burned deep in her mind. She sat, mouth opened, as Rowena continued to talk, rocking back and forth in her chair. She pushed her chair back and got up, Rowena's eyes questioning this move as Mary walked out of the room and into the kitchen. Her sister jumped up after her, following her out into the back garden as the rain fell, battering her face courtesy of blustery winds.

"Mary, wait, Mary…."

Mary said nothing, she walked out to the garden and stood silently by the flower pot that had sat for years, embedded in the soil beneath. She looked up at the large tree, its branches noisily swaying as the wind caught her hair and blew it askew around her face.

It was cold, it was raining, but she stood still, trying to comprehend what her younger sister had told her.

Rowena had followed her out to the garden, crying, begging her to understand and not argue with her. Mary didn't hear the words, she just stared at the outline of the giant tree, its sparse burgundy leaves that sprouted for generations falling onto the gardens below once more, falling asunder like her plans.

Behind her, Rowena pleaded and sobbed, placing her hands on her shoulders. Mary felt nothing. Then anger welled up from within. Anger. Hate. Spite. Jealousy. She swung around and cracked Rowena across the cheek with her outstretched hand, the force of the blow sending her sobbing sister back onto the wet grass.

She turned and stood over her.

"You stupid, selfish bitch! Do you know what you've done?!"

"Please Mary…" Rowena wailed.

"Do you realise what you have done?! What you have done to us?! To me?! Jesus Christ Rowena!"

Mary grabbed her hair and pulled tight, a sinking realisation of her future hitting home. "Oh Rowena, you stupid, fucking bitch!!"

Mr. Devine in the attached house peered through his curtains, trying to see what was happening next door, the inky darkness of the night and the dividing grey fence blocking his view. He put down his cup of tea and stepped out into the garden towards the fence. He could hear cries and shouting.

"Is everything ok?" he called, more concerned than nosy.

"Everything is fine, Charlie, just an argument. Go in out of the rain, just an argument." Mary retorted through gritted teeth.

Charlie Devine shrugged his shoulders and went back inside. Upstairs, his wife peered through the curtains of the back bedroom, the light from next door's kitchen offering some illumination on what was happening. She saw the two women from next door, usually quiet, gentle girls, shouting at each other, their blouses beginning to stick to their skin with the falling rain. She watched the scene for a few moments then left.

Mary held her head in her hand as she spun around, seeking comfort, solace, a way out. But she knew there was none. Rowena sat sprawled on the grass below her, sobbing uncontrollably, repeating that she was sorry over and over again. Mary began to sob herself as he dreams came crashing down.

New York. The escape. The dream.

'All gone…'

Did it matter that she never got round to telling Rowena the full plan? Of the destination? Did anything matter anymore? Years of barely getting by were due to come to an end. A new path awaited, one in which she and her sister would benefit… gone.

She stared down at Rowena once more.

'You cheap, calculating, stupid bitch! What have you done?! Oh dear God what have you done?! I'll never get out of this shithole…'

Mary clenched her hands tighter on her head as her own tears began to fall. Dreams ruined, fallen asunder. She wanted to leave her pathetic sister where she sat, to leave her sobbing, get into a taxi and go to the airport.

'Leave her. Leave her behind. Leave it all behind…'

"Oh Rowena…" she sobbed. "What have you done…"

She leaned forward, grabbed her hand and squeezed it tight before she returned inside, climbed the stairs and shut her bedroom door.

She sat at the side of her bed and stared vacantly out of the window. New York could not happen now. She could never leave her sister, the silly, stupid woman. She gazed as the flickering lights of a plane ascending from the nearby airport and began to weep softly.

Outside Rowena remained on the grass sobbing, clenching the cuffs of her blouse as she pressed them tightly against her eyes. She rocked back and forth as the rain fell hard. *'Come in, you'll get pneumonia'* her mother used to warn her as she played in the rain. Tonight there was no warning voice, nothing but cold rain and strong wind and the background soundtrack of Hallowe'en bangers and rockets.

Mary now stood by the back bedroom window and watched her sister as her own tears continued to fall. Dreams. What was the point of dreams? She was foolish to think she could have any. She should have known they'd be taken from her. But by Rowena? Of all people, her own flesh and blood. She sat back on the bed, slowly letting her body drop back. Once her mother's bed, yet one now void of comfort and support.

Rowena would be soaked to the skin. She didn't care. She just didn't care. The squawk of a bird, the type that can only be heard at night, pierced the wind as Rowena looked at the giant tree. It was the bird, gloating at her. Gloating high up.

'Go on, gloat… I've nothing to offer anymore…'

Her world collapsed in those moments. There was nothing. She stood up, looking back at the house and began walking to the end of the garden. The static evil bird laughed down at her as she scaled the back garden wall and began walking delicately along it towards the trunk of the tree. If she survived the climb she wouldn't be discovered maybe until the next morning.

'Plenty of time, it'll be all over then. I'll see you again soon Mammy...'

The random explosions of fireworks and leaping flames of scattered bonfires in what fields remained around the village were visible to him. Knocking at the doors of houses, children dressed up in plastic masks, witches hats and black bin-liners and hollered "Help the Hallowe'en party!" with each opening door. Squad cars hovered around bonfire sites, keeping a keen eye on them and the crowd gathered around. The rain would make sure they couldn't get too out of control, the Guards hoped. Bags of sweets, apples and nuts were mixed when siblings arrived home, apples bobbed for in basins of water carefully placed on tables before fathers everywhere took their children out to see the local bonfire.

Ben chose the night well. Too many distractions.

"Get down you gobshite!"

Johnny Heery couldn't believe what he was seeing. The crowd gathered below alerted him as he passed by Church Street. Shouting from the bridge drew his attention. He walked on a bit, down to the lights by the cottages that still sat snugly outside the graveyard. A man was sitting on the rail of the bridge, his two feet dangling on the outside.

A small group of people stood either side of him, a bigger crowd below. In the corner of his eyes he could see the flashing blue lights of the Garda car. He scrunched his eyes; an oncoming truck, full beams on and lights blazing from over the windscreen lit the face of the person responsible for the crowd. It was his neighbour's son Ben. His heart leapt.

"Ben? Ben? What are you doing?"

Ben looked down, then back out at the motorway.

"What's going on?" Johnny asked a woman gathered beside him.

"Someone walking their dog spotted him sitting like that, legs dangling. Shouted at him to get back on the bridge. Said he was going to jump..."

"What?"

"Yep. More people gathered, then of course the poor fuckers who happened to be walking over the bridge after him. Said if anyone goes near he'll jump."

"We could wait for a gap in the traffic, make a try."

"Tried that, he just stood on the rails, swaying back and forth, said he'd jump if anyone came near. No-one's gonna be responsible if that fella falls, I can understand that."

"Well if we try when there's no traffic coming, at most he'll break his leg…"

"Or his fuckin' neck!" the woman answered. "More Guards on their way. Up to them."

Two Garda cars stopped, one either side of the dual carriageway. They assessed the situation before one crossed over to the second half of Church Street, beside the graveyard wall and turned onto the bridge. Another vaulted the wall and ran up the hill towards the village to turn onto the bridge from the opposite end. A few bystanders had approached the Guards waiting below, speaking into their car radios.

"They're gonna stop the traffic!" a young girl shouted.

Ben saw the commotion and once more stood up on the rails.

"Don't go near me!"

"Does anyone know him?!" one of the Guards on the ground called.

"Me, I do, his neighbour," Heery replied.

"Will ye try and talk sense into him?"

Johnny nodded and called up to Ben.

"Ben, look, I'll get your mam, come down, ok?"

"You leave her out of this!" he roared back down.

"Ben, just sit back down!"

"Leave it!"

He looked around and was alerted to the two Guards making their way slowly along the bridge.

"I'll jump!"

"No you won't son, don't be silly."

"I will…"

Eamon reached him first.

"Ben, it's me, Eamon, Mary's boyfriend? C'mon man, sit down, please? We can talk. What's up?"

Ben smiled weakly.

"That's typical. A few weeks ago you were kicking me in the ribs at the wall down there."

"Ben that doesn't matter, c'mon, listen to me, the wind might take you over, look at all the people, you don't want them to see that do you?"

"Couldn't care less!"

"Come on now Ben, don't be like that."

Eamon held his spot, about five feet away from Ben. If he could lunge and grab him he would. He exchanged glances with his colleague, the street lights showing a glimpse of fear on their faces.

"Leave me be Eamon!" Ben replied, a calmness in his voice. "There's no way out for me."

A chill ran up Eamon's spine.

"Nonsense Ben, none of that talk. What about your family? You dad, your mam? Your brother? What do you hope to achieve? Why are you doing this?!"

"It's the only choice I have," Ben continued as he stiffened his legs.

"No you don't. Come on, come down, come back with me, I'll get you a cup of tea. We won't tell your folks, it'll just be me and you."

"You're talking bollox!" Ben laughed. "Won't tell me folks? Fuck off!" He stood up firm on the rail, arms outstretched. He knew the Guards below would stop the traffic. He could see a flow of headlights approach him and he could hear engines behind him.

"Everything's falling apart!" he roared, head tilted upwards. "Nothing for me here anymore!"

"Ben don't talk like that, c'mon, climb down. Think of the people, think of your family, please…"

"I have done. They're not me," he cried. "They don't have what's going through my head right now."

"We all have problems Ben, we all do."

"Not like me."

"What do you mean? Whatever it is…"

"Whatever it is, it's finished me."

Both men were silent. Ben gazed below. The traffic was still moving under him, but not for long. The bright lights of the thundering truck got closer, closer, closer. He arched his head back as much as he could to see what was behind him. He couldn't see, he would gamble.

'Look where gambling got me. I got no fear now, no fear anymore. I'm nothing. I'm haunted by this at every waking second. No more…'

He stood straight, eyes focused on the truck. To the left, unseen in the distance was the floating figure of the crucified Christ, floating perhaps, at peace, but not of this world anymore to be judged. Eamon realised what Ben was about to do and going against the advice of his colleague, who was shaking his head from side to side in a frenzy, he lunged at Ben. The back of his hand brushed the young man's ankle as it sprung outward, towards the yawning chasm, the air cleansing Ben's mind and soul as his eyes remained shut tight. The cries of horrified onlookers below bellowed in his ears. Eamon's desperate cry became more distant as the wind cushioned him now.

Through eyelids sealed shut, the light grew brighter and brighter. A sense of calm enveloped him; crackling radios in the blue Garda cars below, cries and shouts from those gathered below and behind him, the thundering of car and truck horns blending into the screeching of breaks as the waft of burning rubber entered his nostrils.

He felt like he was floating gently, sailing away from his worries, his tribulations and those he caused pain and discomfort to never again to question him. He would cease to have responsibility, he was free of the shackles of his dull, boring life, he was alone with himself in this moment of serene calmness. He felt warm, safe, comforted. He heard no other sound but the relaxing beat of his own heart, echoing like that of an unborn child on a monitor. A smile crept across his face, the wind was fresh and the rain a soft, soothing waterfall washing his troubles away. He was happy, calm, at peace.

His mother's sobbing face segued in under his eyelids and his relief and joy twinge to sadness, a sudden, sharp guilt and a stabbing fear crossed his heart. He would never again see her, feel her arms around him, hear her laugh. Memories of his life with her ran through his mind like a film reel on a fast loop; the sounds, smells, sensations he experienced through his young life with his mother now out of reach forever. She would wait in her Heaven for him but neither would ever meet again as her God would not allow it. She and her husband would meet their God one day, heartbroken, pathetic people having lived the remainder of their days broken by the loss of their beloved youngest.

He would seek solace in drink, he would never recover but blame himself. Ben's mother would sit at the fireside on Christmas Eves to come in a room she would refuse to decorate again, willing her own passing knowing she would never again see her son's face on Christmas morning. Ben's mind was in turmoil as the horror made a home in his previously calm mind.

'Stop. Stop. Reach out. Grab something!!'

Flailing arms vainly attempted to grab onto something he knew wasn't there. He hoped it would be his mother's waiting arms. It wasn't. There was nothing there. He was alone, too far from home, mindless, a cursed fool. He called out to his mother, she would help him, wouldn't she?

So wrong. The Christ figure hovered always in the background, behind it, figure, a ghostly pallor of a woman who opened the door to the world of the dead on the same night centuries ago beckoned him, arms outstretched, to join her.

'Rowena, what have I done?! I'm sorry Lucy, I'm sorry...'

The real world flooded back into his mind in those final moments as he let out a cry of despair, of horror, of regret and revulsion. A bright light filled his eyes, burned his retinas as a thundering cacophony burst his eardrums.

"Mammy!" he sobbed. "Mammy, help me..."

III

1993

Seventeen

The stale smell still hung in the air, the acrid reek of last night's alcohol and tobacco that minutes earlier was wafting from the breath of the man who had just left the room.

Declan leaned forward, elbows on his desk as he watched the rain patter against the window. The greyness of the December day outside merged with the forgotten stone of the ruined abbey barely in his eye line up the street.

He glanced at the latest copy of the paper on his desk. His paper. It had taken him time to build it up but it was his baby and he wasn't going to let a pickled old hack tarnish its name.

A slight rap on the door broke his concentration.

"Yep."

Aidan strolled in, carefully shutting the door behind him and sat in the facing chair as Declan stared back out of the window, his hands clasped behind his head.

"So what to do now?" the young assistant editor asked.

"Did you hear all that?"

"Through those walls you'd hear anything."

"So what you think?"

"Declan he's a liability, a loose cannon… I'm all for investigative journalism but c'mon, he's taking the biscuit, waving his 'great name' around the office as if we owe him something?"

"Yeah. Told him again but he's adamant we'll be throwing away a scoop."

"And what did you say?"

"The same I've always said; we're a local paper, we cover local issues, we stick to that. If he wants to work on that particular thing he may do so in his own time, not ours."

"Good."

"Funny thing is, it does sound like a very interesting piece, but not for here. We've built up a great base for God's sake, took us a while, a great following and we give the readers what they want, current local stuff. I don't think an exposé like that will do us any good; how much copy and time will that eat into?"

"Am I to neglect St. Canice's in the football finals so he can publish his piece? No. Told him that. People want to see their kids' photos in the paper, not a photo of a grave or some half-baked story from a century ago. Told him where our priorities lie. God knows there's enough bad press and crime around the area, never mind dragging up something like that. Plus the relation he's on about who lives around and is connected with it mightn't want the family name in print again over something long forgotten. Am I right, Aido? That it's just too dodgy for us at this time? That's my stance, anyway."

He lowered his hands and placed them on the desk in front of him, looking our the window again. "And he went apeshit."

Declan leaned forward once more, cupping his hands nervously on the desk. His eyes mirrored irritation and tiredness.

"You know, I regret taking him on. I should have listened to you."

Aidan nodded and glanced out the window. "What's done is done, we gave him a position, I could see your point about having his name associated with it when we started in fairness. His name is well known, I'll grant him that, but, well he's becoming a dead weight. He told Darren off last week for taking a picture of the kids bring and buy sale. Like, who is he to comment on anything like that?!"

"What did Darren say?"

"Fuck off."

"And rightly so."

"So where's he gone now?"

"The Drake I'd imagine. Carruthers, not Darren."

"Seriously though Declan, if he starts, or perhaps continues for all we know, bad mouthing us, we have to be rid of him."

Declan stared back out the window. He was 24, The Forum was his second attempt at starting a local newspaper. His family were well-known in the area and a gift of the gab managed to blag some support and bank funds to get the business off the ground. The tiny staff were all younger then he, save for James Carruthers, the architect of Declan's current angst, a reasonably known name who penned for the various nationals over the years.

The bank loan afforded them a small premises over a bookies' on Church Street and some second-hand hardware, with enough to secure a modest printing contract with a small scale printer. The paper had taken off and received generous support in the area.

It was building slowly since its first issue a year previous. He couldn't afford to let someone bring it crashing down.

The income was supplemented by the sub-letting of a back room to a young electrician who was setting up his own small business, bartering advertising space in The Forum for maintenance checks on all the equipment and some rewiring the old building needed. It was working well. A small team of contributors added to the editorial variety, one being Michael, a fresh from school rookie who joined in the summer to beef up his portfolio for the journalism course he was taking. He had completed his Leaving Cert. the previous June, knocked on the door of the paper the following day and was a regular fixture in the offices. He took advantage of the extended and early Christmas holiday due to storm damage at his college.

He sat in the opposite newsroom as Declan and Aidan spoke, a small room with three desks at varying angles and an assortment of boxy Apple Macs, fax machines and filing cabinets. Yellowing wallpaper over the bricked up fireplace was covered by a huge map of Dublin.

He was aware of the argument between his editor and James Carruthers. The middle-aged man had tried to coax him into assisting with his research for this famous piece but he was warned off. James refused to give up on it. There was a bad atmosphere hanging in what was until recently a very laid back and fun place to work.

Darren stirred his tea and entered the room, with electrician Gerry in tow, and placed his camera on one of the desks.

"Just saw James steaming across the bridge, look of thunder on his face! Another argument?"

"Yep," Michael nodded.

"He's a poxbottle," Gerry added, twirling a screwdriver into the back of a small cassette recorder.

"You any jobs he can do for you?" Darren laughed.

"I'll fuckin' electrocute him first, always hated him, smells of drink and sick almost every day," Gerry replied. "Thinks he's a big wig 'cos he worked in the Herald and Press... you know why he worked in a whole load of places, don't you? Cos of his drinking, he made a lot of enemies. My ma's cousin's neighbour lived next door to him for a while. He hated him."

"Declan shouldn't have brought him on board," Darren added.

"Well he did because he was a well-known name didn't he?" Michael asked.

"Yeah, initially, but he's been nothing but trouble."

Declan and Aidan filed into the room.

"You heard?" Declan asked generally

"Met him on the bridge," Darren added, sipping his tea.

"Did he say anything?"

"No, just thundered by."

"Prick," Aidan muttered as he sat down.

"He called us amateurs and even criticised the way we dress!" Declan laughed.

"I says so, what, jeans and t-shirt aren't acceptable? Even in a town where no-one gives a shit what you look like? He was on about his days with the Press, how they all wore ties and all that shite. Said you looked like a hippie Aido!"

The others laughed as Aidan's eyes widened.

"Hippie?"

"He's old enough to remember anyway!" Darren laughed.

"Just be careful what's he's saying to others..." Aidan added with serious tones, not looking up at anyone.

"I'm on it, don't worry," Declan nodded.

"You're definitely not gonna run with that story?"

"No, sure I can't, can I? Never mind what it'll replace or keep out of the paper; fucked if I'm going through it with a fine tooth comb. You never know who he'd be offending. It's too heavy, we've only been going a little over a year... I don't want to rock the boat. Maybe in time, but not now."

"Interesting story though, in fairness," Michael offered cautiously.

"Yes but not for us," Aidan remarked echoing his editor's stance. "We're too small an operation to have a loose cannon like him dedicate his whole time to something that happened a century ago. When I studied journalism we did a module on law and stuff, it can sink a publication. This story could be a tinderbox. It'll gain us nothing, earn us no advertising and probably piss off any remaining family members."

"Agreed," Declan added. "I asked him to interview Fr. Tyrell about the food collection for the poor before Christmas. He snorted, actually, really snorted and said he hadn't covered a story like that since the fifties. Like what a cheeky bastard."

"Ease him out?" Darren offered.

"The way he's going he'll be eased out the fuckin' window."

"Just keep saying no, no, no," Aidan pointed, stabbing his finger in he air with each declaration of the word 'no'. "He'll get pissed off eventually."

"That's the problem," Declan sighed, staring out the large window, "he won't. I just know he won't. Besides that gobshite will get up off the ground, after being fucked out the window I mean, get up and dust himself down."

"He'll climb the wall back in!" Darren laughed.

"The undead!" Gerry piped up as the whole room erupted in laughter, breaking the tension and offering some light relief.

"Anyway," Declan laughed, "anyone for lunch in Wilde's? I'd murder a plate of curry chips."

The pot-bellied old man drained his drink and called for another. The bar was quiet and he only needed to nod to Bill. The barman, paying more attention to the match on the tv that sat on a questionable shelf over the bar, gruffly nodded back and began pouring.

The customer returned to the tattered old folder laid out on the table and searched for a particular page. James Carruthers was the eldest of the tiny newspaper staff. In his early sixties, he wasn't from the area and formerly worked as a freelance reporter in the nationals. Rumours of drinking and harassing people for stories circulated to explain the unusual job turnover throughout his career. He carried an unnerving face; his nose red, balding, grey hair unkempt and clothes permanently rumpled and stained. He approached the paper shortly after it's inception, offering experience and privately hopeful of obtaining the editors position within a year but a move which would continue to elude him. He did it for 'pocket money' he always said. He was near retirement age and wanted to wind down. Declan's suggestion that winding down a career as an investigative reporter on a local newspaper covering a large area with its fair share of social problems wouldn't be the holiday he had hoped for was met with derision and planted the seeds of resentment between the two.

Declan could see his uses though, with the Forum staff all under the age of 24, his experience was beneficial in parts, when he felt like offering it. His CV added a string to the bow of the fledging paper as it sought for recognition and sales.

Having a journalist who worked for almost all the dailies at one point was a powerful marketing tool. James loved the idea of having the power on his side, of being a reasonably recognisable name. At the best of times he was often a rather helpful aide to have, particularly when a crime story broke. At the worst, he was a mess who grunted his way around the office, mumbling about being surrounded by amateurs and kids.

James lit another cigarette, flicking the still burning match into the yellow ashtray on the table in front. His brow was creased in lines of thought and perplexity as he studied the photocopied document in front of him.

A police report, dated Wednesday November 12th, 1902, signalling the end of the investigation surrounding the mysterious murders in Finglas village the previous summer.

He had read through the report countless times but remained baffled at the 'case closed' conclusion. His fresh pint was delivered to the table, he nodded to the lounge boy who lingered momentarily for the customary tip. James didn't as much glance up at him, instead burying his head in the page.

'…suspect has disappeared from local area and no other division have had any reported sightings throughout the county or beyond, we have no further cause to continue the investigation with these resources at this moment…'

It was signed Sergeant Robert Linden, a name James has cause to curse again and again. "Typical" He muttered, placing the well-read photocopy on the table as he gulped from his pint. Bloody RIC. Did nothing right.

He sat back and recalled his conversation with Old Tony. Senile old bastard, he was dubbed, but James did like to sniff out a story that afforded him time to study. But that very time was also an enemy. As it stretched on people would die. Interest, difficult enough to encourage almost a century after the event, would pale and, as he was discovering, no-one would care about an unsolved murder or two all those years ago.

But he did. Ever since he spoke to Old Tony Salinger, what was he, ninety-five? Living in the same cottage on Jamestown Road since he was born there. He weaved a wonderful tale of the changing old village. Urbanisation grew around the old row of cottages that still stood from a time long gone. The dusty track that led into the village was gradually widened and laden with tarmac as more and more families made the area their home, be it from a relocation project to escape the accursed city centre tenements or private sales as young couples sough to begin their lives and rear families in the quiet country village.

The village became a town, the giant silo of the bakery hummed and stood guard over the hive of activity within its white, pebble-dashed walls and loomed ominously over Tony's whitewashed domicile.

The cottages remained, modernised over the years, except for Old Tony's. He still had an outhouse in the back yard despite the protestations and offers of conversion from his neighbours. He kept poultry and subsidised his pension by selling his fresh eggs to Donal, the old greengrocer who worked his stall from a van across from the supermarket. Everyone knew Old Tony, but as the years passed he became more isolated. Old friends died, his siblings passed on or were sent to homes. He had no family of his own, just memories and his beloved disappearing village.

He was at the funeral of the former village mayor when he began talking to James, who had been resentfully sent to cover it for The Forum. Old Tony discovered he worked at the local paper and began talking about that, about how he read it every week in Wilde's Café beside the iron footbridge. They began talking, drinking some more, James fascinated with tales of the old village; how the old dairy house in Church Street was bulldozed to build the dual carriageway which split the town in two, how the once abundant stream that Tony played in as a child was slowly disappearing underground, the neat row of cottages that sat snugly beside the Drake razed to the ground to make way for the shopping mall and car park. He told the story of Gofton Hall, one of the last remaining great houses of the area, it's beautiful red brick structure dismantled in the name of modernisation and development to be replaced by the soul-less red brick of yet another banking institution.

The personal stories fascinated James the most, the people that had long since gone; the Wren Boys at Christmas, the Luby sisters of the Post Office and the land-owning Cragies who gave much employment to the area, all names barely floating in a haze of memories yet names once predominant throughout the village. The rumours made James chuckle; the underground tunnel from the old graveyard to Dunsoughly Castle some miles north, the Viking that Old Tony was convinced lay buried under the same graveyard, because he heard it as a child and of course the person buried alive there. All rumours and tales but ones which he and his childhood friends accepted as fact. Different times, he echoed again and again, his glassy, watery blue eyes staring our from behind his thick rimmed glasses, cataracts clouding his current vision but not his visions of the past.

Then he went on to talk about the murders. Mysterious murders by a mysterious stranger who arrived in the village one summer day, spent time in an old, long-gone house and disappeared as quickly as he had arrived. James quizzed him further on this. Old Tony recalled the story his father had reluctantly told him in his old age. How he was one of the young men of the village who went in search of the murderer. Two people had died on the same day and at the old asylum where the Spanish nuns would later build their convent. A patient and a young man from the area. A third would die shortly after, from natural causes allegedly but whispers spread in the tiny hamlet. A local girl was spared by good fortune.

Old Tony had been at young Robert Hart's funeral he was later told, the young man from the village killed outside the asylum at the same time the patient was murdered. Tony was a small four year old boy at the time, but couldn't remember. The small and sleepy village that always minded its own business was a mixture of anger and dread.

The locals were dissatisfied with the progress of the police at the time. A mysterious stranger was the chief suspect but he was never heard from again and no-one would later speak of it. It was a story long forgotten, but one that Old Tony remembered and he pressed his father on in years to come.

Occasionally someone would refer to it, Old Tony learnt in later years that a helping of porter would often loosen someone's tongue. That's when he learnt of the girl. A young woman who had discovered the stranger in a field by the long-gone Jamestown House and was accused of hiding him from the others. She died not long after apparently, buried without noticeable ceremony in her family plot, save for a few token people. She held the key to the story though, people reckoned. The investigation was closed, nothing ever came of it.

That's when James's fascination took a hold. He fed the old man drink and pumped him for every other bit of information he had; what he thought had happened, what he believed in. The ramblings of the old man were rarely taken seriously by anyone but an interest sparked within James; he saw a golden opportunity to show that Forum crowd just how good he was.

James went home, writing down everything he could remember down as soon as he got in. He called into Old Tony again, collecting the paper for him, bringing him drink, offering him company which in reality was false company. Anything to get him to talk further. But even the old man's memories had a limit. Until a new light emerged.

Talking one day about the girl, and who she could have been, Old Tony randomly announced that one of her relations, a great-grandaughter maybe, still lived in the village.

'*Where?*' James demanded as the man rambled once more. He wasn't exactly sure, somewhere near the top of Jamestown, but she had the same name as the girl whose name was forever linked with the case; Rowena.

Thumbing through a heavy copy of Thom's Directory with the added advantage of an unusual name on his side, it didn't take James long to find her. Her name and address was in front of his eyes in black and white.

That was when he approached Declan. Declan had never heard of the tale. He listened with interest, took a few notes but decided against pursuing the story.

'*Leave it,*' he argued, '*the women in question probably doesn't know anything about it. No point raking up what could be a non-story.*'

'*But it's a great story!*' James counter-argued.

'*Yeah has potential,*' Declan retorted, '*but maybe if she does know about it, she doesn't want to talk. It's been too long. Plus we're a small newspaper; local news, events, sport, that's our priority. We're only after starting out too. Best leave it.*'

But James wouldn't. He conducted his own research, at home, in the pub and in the office. He wasn't going to let it lie. An unsolved murder case? He would earn his corn once more, show the upstarts he shared an office with what stuff he was made of. He wasn't past it yet. He would retire on a high.

He ordered and swallowed a quick whiskey, paid for his drinks and, notes under his arm, left the Drake and turned onto Jamestown Road, crossing at the busy junction and began his trip up the hill.

It was time to accelerate things.

Eighteen

Rowena sat in the back room, dragging occasionally from a cigarette she didn't really want but lit up out of boredom. She sat awkwardly in the chair by the fire, facing the television and flicked through the remote to see if she could find anything interesting. Anything Christmassy to lighten her mood. She was enjoying some time to herself; she had worked a hard day in the drapery shop near the village and picked up her daughter afterwards from her friend's house before arriving to a cold home with the dinner to prepare. The same drill day after day. But it had to be done.

She enjoyed her young daughter's company. Sandra had turned ten that summer and Rowena always made a fuss out of her. It was just the two of them and she wouldn't have it any other way. Brief romances came and went but nothing would ever get in the way of her little girl. She was too precious to her. The mortgage was almost paid off, they were comfortable. Approaching Christmas she tried to gauge whether her sleeping daughter's belief in Santa Claus was but a pretence now. She wished it wasn't, that her baby would believe for just one more year before part of her innocence would disappear forever. *'Just one more Christmas…'*

As he stubbed her cigarette out and leaned forward to throw some logs on the fire, the doorbell rang. She checked her watch and made her way to the front door, throwing on the hall lights as she eased the door her father had installed many years before open. Through the panes of the porch doors, she could just make out a man's shape in the gloom. She pulled her cardigan tighter over her and, remaining on the hall step, leaned forward to open the porch door.

"Yes?"

"Rowena Brennan?"

Her heart entered her mouth as she played a variety of scenarios in her mind. The man was middle-aged, in an untidy suit, a folder under his arm. A Guard? Who could have befallen of an accident?

"Yes? Who are you?" her voice quivered as she stared down the stranger. She had learnt the hard way to be tough. She knew the baseball bat lay just out of sight to her right. No-one was going to harm her or her baby.

"May I come in?"

She clocked the smell of drink. "Who are you I asked?"

"My name is James Carruthers, senior reporter with The Forum newspaper. Have you heard of us?"

"Yes, yes I have. What can I do for you?" She tried her best to maintain an icy tone and disguise the quiver in her voice.

"I really need to speak to you, can I come in?"

"ID?"

"What? I mean, pardon?"

"ID? Identification please."

He swapped his tatty folder back and forth between his hands as he searched for his wallet. He plucked an orange journalists union card from it and held it near to her face. His hair in the photograph was as unkempt as in real life, his cheeks as flushed.

"What's this about?"

"It's in relation to a story I believe you have some involvement in Ms., Mrs. Brennan?"

"What story?"

"If I can come in, I can explain."

Her eyes darted around his face, searching for a reason to let this relative stranger into her cosy home on this cold night.

"I can call into your office tomorrow and talk to you then."

"No, no, Ms. or Mrs. Brennan, I'm out tomorrow. If I could just have a few moments of your time now, it would be of great help? I've come a long way? Is it Ms. or Mrs.?"

"You've come from the pub by the smell of you. It's Ms. if you must know." Her cautious mind scolded her boldness but she was secretly delighted she managed to say those words. *'Show him who's in charge...'*

James smiled weakly. "Press launch. You have to go and show your face. And accept a drink."

She hesitated. Mulled over the idea. He girl was safe upstairs. What did he want? "I have no idea what story you're referring to Mr. Carruthers."

"Well not you personally, Ms. Brennan. It involves your family though. If I may?" he gestured past her with his hand. Rowena's eyes scanned him once more. She stood back, blocking the sight of the carefully positioned baseball bat as he thanked her and stepped into the hallway.

She directed him into the front room that twinkled in the multi-coloured lights of a generous Christmas tree.

She turned on the main light, revealing a neatly kept parlour, a neat suite of leather furniture, the walls adorned with old family photos and a bare red-brick fireplace as centre piece. The glass, orange coloured lamp shade completely covered the main bulb in the centre of the ceiling, offering a gentle glow and patterned shadows across the ceiling.

James glanced at the wall before settling down on the far armchair.

He admired the tree in the corner. He noticed how tastefully collected decorations were complimented by those made by a child; a small lantern, a pipe-cleaner Santa. A healthy collection of cards adorned the mantelpiece and glass cabinet by the far wall. A succession of Christmas accessories dotted the room.

"Very cosy," James beamed as he scanned the photos hanging in an assortment of frames around the room.

"They your family?" he asked.

"Yes. What can I do for you?"

Rowena's face could sink a ship. *'Be firm...'*

He opened the folder in front of him before taking out a thick pair of glasses from within his coat.

"I'm working on a story regarding a murder in the village some years ago."

"Oh," Rowena exclaimed, searching her mind for some information or memory of an event.

"What murder? When?"

"Well, quite a number of years ago in fact. You won't remember it, that's for sure!" he chuckled.

"You family have lived in the area for many years, yes?"

She was wary that some of his words were slurred. Keep it short and sweet, ring the paper tomorrow either way. "Yeah, why?"

"Do you know how long they've lived in the area?"

"A while. What's this about Mr. Carruthers?"

She folded her arms and sat poker straight, adopting an offensive position. She was regretting letting him in. She saw him noticing the ornamental sword hanging over the fireplace. She'd use it too.

"Well, I have reason to believe, on reviewing police files and interviewing a witness, that one of your family members was involved."

Her eyes narrowed.

"My family?"

"Yes, that's right."

"When was this?"

"A good many years ago."

"When?"

"Ninety-one years to be precise, 1902."

Rowena snorted as she stifled a laugh, cupping her nose in her hand.

"Are you having a joke with me? 1902?! It's 1993! And a witness, the fuck?!" she giggled, shaking her head.

"Ok. Well an elderly gentleman still living in the village has some memories of that time."

"And he's your witness?"

"He has memories, like I said."

"Who?"

"I can't divulge."

"Oh yes you fucking can, if he's bringing my family into it?"

"There's no need for language Rowena."

"It's my house and you're on the way to being thrown out. Christmas time or not. And it's Ms. Brennan to you. Remember that. You're going the wrong way about this, you know that?"

Any uncertainty in her mind when she opened the door was replaced by a steely defensive determination. James remained silent, licking his lips more in response to them drying after the feed of pints he downed earlier.

"May I have a glass of water?"

"No."

James nodded and consulted his notes once more.

"Erm, Rowena, Whyte I think?" James asked, eyes peering over his glasses.

"Don't know." She would be damned if she was going to feed this old man information.

"Yes, that's her. My investigation has cause to believe she, well, how shall I say, may have had a hand in the murders…"

She swallowed hard and tried to maintain her steely expression.

"No murderers in my family Mr. Carruthers."

"I didn't say she was a murderer, that she was involved, maybe having helped him, certainly she, as we now say, hung around with him, according to these files anyway."

Rowena glanced at the photo of her mother; her favourite, taken in the 1950s when she was in her thirties. She was outside her aunt's house in Ballygall, her chin resting on her palm, elbow resting on the pillar by the gate, her smiling face covered in a head scarf, the tall steeple of St. Canice's Catholic church in the background. The evening sun casting a wonderful burst of light on the scene. She looked so pretty then, so pretty. She wasn't too dissimilar in age to Rowena now, but she was a beauty. People said they looked very alike. Rowena often looked at herself in the mirror wishing for her mother's beauty. He mother had shared her love of history; local history and family history, passing on valuable knowledge. She knew what her visitor was getting at. But it would be none of his business. All so long ago, long forgotten. Why was he pursuing this?

"Can't help you," she smiled, placing her hands on her knees as she prepared to stand up.

James glanced at the photos.

"Who's the girl in the middle?"

"My sister."

"Nice girl."

"She was."

"Was?"

"She died some years ago. What's it to you anyway?"

"And that's you little girl I presume? The school uniform."

Rowena stood up.

"Please leave. Now, Mr. Carruthers. I have no knowledge of this story, it happened a long time ago. Me and my girl just want the quiet life. Whatever happened ninety fucking years ago has no concern to me now. Tell that to your witness. Let me guess, that Tony bloke?"

"I cannot divulge."

"Divulge me arse. Betcha it was him. He's ancient, decrepid, not without his illustrious past if stories are to be told. Told you with a feed of pints did he? Yeah, your best pal by the smell of you."

James stood up, eyeballing her.

"How dare you, how…"

"How dare I?!" Rowena responded, darting forward so each word she spoke spat into his face. "In my own fucking home, and you say how dare I?! Let me tell you this!" She jabbed a finger into his chest.

"I don't know anything about the story, God knows why you're bringing it up now, I'm gonna ask the editor tomorrow…"

"You see, you cannot tell him I was here," James interrupted,

Rowena stood back, throwing her arms in the air.

"I'm sorry?! I cannot tell him?! Why, you not allowed to go annoying people close to Christmas about this? Are you not? You been warned? Listen pal, I've a good friend in the Guards down the village, want me to tell him too? Actually, how the fuck did you know where I lived?! I'm not in the phonebook!"

"Thom's Directory."

"You sneaky fucker. C'mon, out, out now, don't attempt to call at this house again, you here me?!"

She pushed him towards the front door, brushing the hall curtain back so he could see the baseball bat.

"Out of my house now, please don't come back. Out. Out."

As furious as she was her voice remained calm. To shout and scream would alert her daughter. She pushed him out the door and closed the doors behind him. She turned around, her back to the door, shaking.

"Mammy who was that?"

She craned her neck upstairs.

"Nothing love, just a man looking for another house. Go back asleep now."

Sandra said a brief good night as Rowena turned off the front room light and settled back down in front of the telly in the back room.

She lit another cigarette. *'Not now,'* she mused to herself, *'why's all this being brought up now?'*

She got up and went to the phone in the hall. She picked it up, took another drag and dialled a number. She glanced at herself in the mirror, brunette hair tied back in a pony tail, wishing she looked like her mother did in the photograph.

"Is Detective Eamon Ryan there please? It's a family friend."

She paused until a familiar voice crackled on the other end of the line.

"Eamon? Hi, it's Ro."

"Hello Ro, long time no hear! How are you?"

"Fine thanks, and you and the family?"

"Good thanks, getting ready for Santy, you know yourself! Is everything ok Ro?"

"Yeah, well, just took a chance you'd be on duty! You're still one for the night shifts anyway!"

"Something serene about working them," he chuckled.

"Anyway, sorry to bother you..."

"It's no bother?"

"Just want to run something by you. Had a journalist from The Forum up, the local paper, Carruthers, smell of drink off him, asking about some murder that happened a century ago, reckons my great grandmother was involved."

Eamon was silent for a moment as he repeated the word murder lowly to himself. "Ahh, I remember, I think anyway, Mary mentioning something briefly to me, well it was more she let slip after a drink, God rest her."

"Two, three people died, is that right, and it was reckoned the relation knew the murderer or something? Yeah I remember that, she never spoke of it again and shushed me everytime I brought it up. I'd forgotten about that. Blast from the past, eh?"

""Something like that," Rowena replied, playing along with the vagueness.

"Why, what's he want?"

"Well not a hundred percent sure, says he's investigating it so I imagine some sort of story. Anyway I think he was trying to scrounge info out of me, intimidated me sort of, asking questions about the photos of Mary and Sandra."

"You want me to rough him up?" Eamon laughed.

"Seriously, Eamon. I'm just asking can he do that?"

"Well he's entitled to go to your home, he is a hack, I'm not too up on that form of protocol to be honest, never personally come across something like that before. I can ask around though."

"No, no, don't, Eamon just keep this between me and you."

"Ok... I don't know what you mean about the photos though, was he saying them in a, I dunno, threatening manner?"

"No, just creeped me out. Like he was in my house. Just a bit worried. He had a few on him alright."

"Few what now?"

"Drinks, like I said."

"Ahh yeah, sorry. Ok, first thing tomorrow ring the editor."

"I'll be in work so might call over at lunch maybe, or just ring, I'll see, suss out what's this all about. He said that I wasn't to call the editor either!"

"Really?"

"Really."

"That reeks Ro. Give them a shout as soon as tomorrow. If he bothers you again, or if you feel wary, let me know, I'll say you made a complaint and 'warn' him, so to speak."

"Legally?"

"Off course!"

"Thanks Eamon. You're very good."

"Anything Ro, you know that. I always said I'd look after you."

Rowena jumped on the pause. "I know Eamon, since that night…"

"Yes…"

"Long time ago…"

"Look after yourself and I'll give you a ring before the Christmas."

"Do, please. Or come up for a drink, don't be a stranger, you've done so much for us over the years. Night and thanks."

"I will, thanks, night Ro."

She returned to the room and sat by the fire again. Not now, please not now; just as things were going well for her and Sandra, please don't let this be dragged up again.

She had been through more than enough; losing a father, a mother, a best friend, a sister. This was her time now, her and her daughter's time. She must defend it at all costs.

Nineteen

Rowena sat on the kitchen step out the back garden, huddled into her anorak against the morning cold. She pondered the talk with Carruthers the night before. A night's sleep had reasoned her mind somewhat; she knew that the facts of the case were there, in black and white. She always thought it would perhaps crop up in a local history book sometime but never thought a journalist would come knocking.

She craned her neck upwards, gazing at the top of the almost bare giant tree that gently swayed in the sharp December breeze. She always wondered how it managed to retain even a few leaves in the cold of winter.

The familiar sound of the pigeon echoed once more. Any time of the year, it was always there; cooing and hooting in soft rhythm over the years, always the same sound, the same speed, the same melody. It captivated her as a young girl, her mother used to play a game with her, seeing who would be the first to see the bird. Mary would join in, they would run to the end of the long garden and peer upwards, seeing a faint rustle and declaring that they'd seen it. It was the evil bird that always perplexed her, the big, bulging eye, long, open beak and a sharp pointed talon that singled her out amongst the three.

When she first saw a picture of a prehistoric pterodactyl at school she told the teacher one lived in the tree in the house behind her. Her school-friends laughed, her teacher smiled her gentle smile. Her mother told her as they walked up the hill from school not to mind them, that they didn't now what they were talking about.

She thought suddenly about that night, eleven years ago. Hallowe'en night. She shuddered, taking a final drag and threw the butt into the remnants of her mother's once fabled flower beds before stepping inside to waken her sleeping child for school.

"I'm sorry, say that again?!" Declan asked as he gestured to a passing Aidan to come into his office.

His eyes were aghast, wide open, a look of shock echoed in them.

Aidan mouthed a 'what' as Declan clenched a fist and mouthed 'James'.

"I see. I see. Ms. Brennan, I am shocked, I must offer you our most sincere apologies, I had no idea he was… no, no, I told him to forget... I actually specifically warned him against bothering any of the family…
yes, yes, he did come to me with the idea and I did expressly tell him to leave it be. We're a small paper, reporting the current issues affecting the area, I told him what was done was done, there was no place in The Forum for this story… yes, absolutely… yes… where do you live? Ok… again, I am so sorry and I will come down on him Ms. Brennan… he had no right…. What…? I'm not aware of any press launch, why…?" Declan slapped a palm on his forehead and threw his head back, eyes wincing as they closed.

"I see… I see… yes, yes well he had no right, no right whatsoever to do that… yes… questions…? On your family..? What, the photos…?. Oh you're…. yes, I'm actually flabbergasted… Ms. Brennan I am so sorry for last night, let me reiterate that he was under no instruction from this newspaper, he has been repeatedly told to drop it and I have set him other tasks to work on… yes he is well known… no, no you're right, that doesn't give him the right at all… I know, I know… ok. Ok. Ok. Ms. Brennan, once again we are so sorry and I can promise you that won't happen again. I will deal with him. No, no he's not in the office now…. What? Haha, well, I don't know… bit early…ok, thank you, thank you and I give you my word I will sort this mess out… thank you… and a Merry Christmas to you too. Bye. Bye. Bye. Bye. Bye…"

Declan slammed the phone into the cradle and stood up, hands on his hips.

"Jesus Mary and Holy Saint Joseph! I have to go out soon, but if that old waster comes back tell him I'm gonna rip his fucking balls off."

"Literally?"

"I swear, the way I feel at the moment… you know what he's after going and doing?!"

"I can kinda guess?" Aidan winced.

"That story he's working on, the murder case from millions of years ago, remember I was saying that there was a relation still living in the area? He only traced and knocked into her house last night reeking of gargle. A single mother, living alone with her daughter. He asked questions about her dead family in photos on the wall."

Aidan exhaled deeply and shook his head. Michael had eased into the room when Aidan spotted him outside and indicated for him to come in.

"The murder case?"

"Yep. He went up to a single mother's house last night and wormed his way in, reeking of gargle. Actually…" Aidan pointed at Declan, "where does she live? Up Michael's way I think, isn't that right, Jamestown?"

"What's her name?" Michael asked.

"Rowena Brennan," Declan replied, sitting back down.

"I know her."

"Really?"

"Yeah, lives on my road, up a bit. Nice woman, quiet, she lived with her sister who died some years ago. Has a little girl."

Declan sat forward. "I have to go up to her, apologise personally when I ring that drunk's neck."

"I can go up if you want?" Michael ventured.

"Does she know you well?" Aidan asked.

"Sorta. Quiet like I said, does her own thing. Know her to say hello kind of thing, my mam would stop and chat."

"Nah I best go up myself," Declan asked, "but maybe you can come with me? Friendly face and all that. Does she know you work here?"

"Not sure? If she did she'd have mentioned me?"

Darren had arrived back and stood in the doorway, camera hanging around his neck. He leaned against the frame, hands joined and smiled.

"I only arrived in but I know what you're talking about. Met James in the village, says he's on to 'something exciting'. The murder story, yeah?"

"Well he'd hardly be on his wife!" Declan laughed

"Poor aul Rosie!" Aidan sniggered. "Bet down big time!"

"Where's he now?" Declan asked.

"Was heading up Jamestown…"

"Oh Jesus he'd hardly go back up, oh wait, maybe gone to the old guy she also mentioned, Tony, she said he mentioned speaking to him. A witness."

Darren laughed. "Witness? How fucking old is he?! 190?"

"Not far off," Michael added, "I know the guy, to see like. In his nineties."

"Obviously those years in the nationals have honed his sense of sources." Aidan smiled wryly as he got up.

"I'm heading out," Declan said, "if he comes back tell him I'm gonna kill him. Last thing I need too, I've to begin typesetting the paper tonight. Up to me eyes."

"Sleeping in the attic room again tonight then?" Darren ruefully smiled.

"Yes. And alone this time! Work related!" Declan laughed as he descended the stairs. Outside in the bright December sunshine, his smile disappeared. The paper's reputation was on the line and he often questioned his own ability to hammer a point across. The rest of the small staff were singing from the same hymn-sheet, but Carruthers; he waved his experience and journalistic seniority over Declan as a mother would scold a child, knowing who had the upper hand and who knew better.

But did he know better? Was James Carruthers right? Was Declan wrong to dispute the story? What if he sold it to a national and it made headline news, took off; he would be a laughing stock, the self-taught, amateur newspaper editor of a small-time rag that let this pot of gold, that happened in his own back yard, slip through his fingers again and again.

He sat in the driving seat of his battered blue Fiat 127 and drummed his fingers against the wheel. Was he wrong? Or right?

'It wasn't meant to be like this…'

He looked at the shadow of the ruined church ahead of him, thinking back to the stories his father told him about the history of the area. This story was a part of the village's history, rightly or wrongly, it did happen, it did shape a major event, albeit one perhaps deliberately long forgotten. He decided to drop into his parents and mention it to his father, to seek advice.

His thoughts were interrupted by a rap on the window. Darren stood outside.

"Thought you might need this," he said as he handed a bemused Declan a black balaclava.

"What? What for?"

"In case people recognise you driving this heap of shite."

Declan burst out laughing as the echoes of the others cheering from the window above reached his ears.

"Tell you what, you can tell Andrea to wear it when you're in bed with her, how's that?" he laughed as he drove off, giving his colleague the fingers out the window.

A biting rain was falling as Michael was walking home up Jamestown Road. He had the collar of his navy three-quarter length jacket turned up and regretted not bringing a scarf out that morning. Cold. The evening light was dim but he could still make out the figure of James closing the door of Old Tony's cottage. He had his usual folder tucked under his arm and as he closed the creaky gate behind him, he noticed Michael across the road. He waved, indicating at him to cross.

'*Oh shit*'

James crossed over instead, barely looking to see if any traffic was coming.

"Was Declan looking for me today?"

"Yeah, he wants to speak to you."

"What do you mean."

"The woman you called up to last night rang."

Michael stood firm in front of him. Witnessing the events of some hours earlier made him angry, angry that James had tried to coax him into helping him with the story, angry that he had called up to Rowena Brennan's house last night. That was bringing the problem to his doorstep.

"Stupid bitch. What did she say?"

"I don't know but Declan was fuming."

"Pah. Fuming. Welcome to the real world of journalism, Declan…"

"He was annoyed that you called up to Rowena last night."

"It was out of hours, I can do what I want. I'm still working on that story, you know, for my own interests."

His eyes betrayed the obvious lie.

"I know her too James, she's a nice woman."

"And?"

Michael shifted nervously. "Probably best to leave her be."

"Are you a fucking emissary?"

"What?"

"It's none of your business, if Declan wants to talk to me he can, nothing to do with you. I gave you a chance to work with me on this."

"Yeah but Declan said…"

"Ah Delcan me bollix."

"I work in the paper too, she lives near me, it affects my work."

'*Ah shit my voice is quivering…*'

James leaned forward, almost eyeballing the young man, his breath forming a thin fog on Michael's glasses such was the ferocity of his exchange. His breath reeked. Stale. Cigarettes and drink.

"Let me tell you something you little bollix. I'm years in this game. Years! You only did your fucking Leaving Cert in June. Don't you DARE tell me, on a street of all places, how to go about my work, you hear me? I can have you dismissed from the paper like that!" He snapped his fingers and stood back.

James leaned back in towards a shaking Michael. "This conversation never happened, ok? Now you go home to your mammy and let us real journalists get on with our work. You know NOTHING about the real world…"

Michael stood rooted as James strode off, the young man's heart thumping in his chest, mouth drying up. James suddenly turned on his heels, walked right up to the shaken young man and jabbed a finger into his chest.

"One more thing, a word of advice. Don't pay so much attention to Declan or Aidan; they're fuckin' naive kids in this game, they've no idea of the big bad world of journalism out there. They're all in their twenties for fuck sake! Now you just concentrate on your press releases and interviewing shop owners who feed that fucking dog on the hill and leave the real work to the REAL journalists. As I said, we never had this conversation. But let me tell you, if you want to make a career as a journalist, get away from that rag in Church Street. Earn your corn somewhere else. You'll only get trampled underfoot. One day you'll understand that I'm right. They're fuckin' amateurs in there, you hear me? Amateurs."

He turned around and continued walking back towards the village.

Michael's heart hammered in his chest. His mouth was dry and glasses wet from the rain. Frantically he looked around, mortified in case anyone had seen the exchange. Headlights came and went and dark shadows of those going to and fro passed but not by him. He buried his head in the collars of his coat and shuffled off, legs shaking, yearning to get back to the safety of his home as quickly as possible.

He had never endured an exchange like that from anyone before, in any situation. This wasn't doing his confidence any good. He was shaken to the core and immediately questioned his choice of career.

'James was right, wasn't he. No he wasn't… oh God…'

All the way up the hill, the wind blowing in his face, the dark stormy clouds, enveloping an already twilight evening reflected his mood.

Had he done wrong in saying all that to James? After all, who was he to take it upon himself? Oh Jesus Declan was going to kill him, would he sack him? Warn him?

'Fuck it Michael, you shouldn't have got involved.' He repeated this mantra as he continued up the hill. He stopped in the newsagent to buy an evening paper, gazing at the by-line on the front page and wondering would he ever obtain that. A black mark against his name, at the starting point in his career; not good.

He sat silently worried after dinner. His younger siblings were excited about Christmas but the fierce breath and sharp finger of James Carruthers wouldn't leave his mind. He needed resolution. He needed to do something. Closing the living room door, he sat in the small seat by the phone table in the hall, his little red and black phone book in hand and dialled Aidan's house number.

"Everything alright?" Aidan queried after the opening pleasantries, detecting the quiver in Michael's voice. Michael sighed, heart beating and told him everything. When he put the phone down, he felt a great burden lift from his shoulder and a new found sense of confidence returned. He had survived his first skirmish in journalism and came through with an ally on his side. Aidan said he would ring Declan immediately and not to worry.

'He shouldn't have said that, he'd no right to talk to you like that, no matter about what he said about the paper, we'll deal with that. But he verbally assaulted you on the street. Not good.'

A new sense of optimism entered his spirit as he replaced the receiver and went back into the front lounge. He would still have to face James. But this time he had allies.

Twenty

D arren, Gerry and Michael stood outside the door of Declan's office as the argument ensued. Michael had brought the two outside up to speed on the latest chapter.

The paper had come back from the printers just before lunch and, as was the norm, all staff and contributors came in to review the latest edition. That was when James and Aidan were called into Declan's office.

Three voices raged inside the small room, the ajar window allowed those passing below an insight into the exchange. Baffled faces looked upwards before consulting their companions and continuing with their journey.

"He's gonna be sacked," Gerry whispered, "has to be now."

"Nah, don't know, warning maybe… a pound?" Darren ventured.

"You miserable bastard, a fiver, no tenner? Yeah? Tenner says he won't." Gerry added.

"You're on," Darren affirmed as he craned his ear.

Michael, while getting a laugh at the others eavesdropping, tried to make out as much as he could. Was his name brought up? What role would he play in the discussion, if any? Something slammed against a wall and James' voice was now the dominant one until Declan's rose above it.

"Who do you think you are?!" Declan roared with an authority at odds with his genteel demeanour. Those listening could visualise the embittered red faces, fingers jabbing, threats exchanged. Another slam.

Michael backed away into the main office, his heart in his mouth. What was to stop James emerging and swinging for him?

"They're coming!" Darren exclaimed as each abandoned their position and took up the first immediate stance they could think of as the door opened, Gerry rotating a screwdriver into yet another personal cassette player, Darren admiring a picture that hung on the wall. James stormed out.

"You proud of yourself you little tattler?! You'll get nowhere!" he shouted. James barged past those outside and thumped down the stairs before slamming the flimsy wooden door behind him.

Declan and Aidan emerged.

"You hear enough?" Aidan asked, an angry look on his face.

"What?" Darren replied, still engrossed mockingly in the picture.

"I'm studying the picture, lovely brush strokes…"

"He's a wanker!" Declan sighed as he called Michael into his office.

"Had a word with him, as you probably heard. Tore strips off him, told him it wasn't on knocking up to that girl."

"Did you mention when he spoke to me?"

"Yeah, course I did, wasn't letting him away with it, don't worry, didn't repeat exactly what you told Aidan, just told him it wasn't on and who did he think he was. He's on a warning anyway."

"What did he say?"

"About you?"

"Yeah?"

"Nothing, just guffawed and threw his pickled onions of eyes to Heaven. What did he expect? Experience or not, he can't go around throwing his weight around like that."

"And that's a lot of weight to throw around," Aidan added, walking in.

"That all he said?" Michael queried, relief filling his mind as he knew his side was being taken. "Because he was roaring out of him there, talking about me obviously."

"I didn't elaborate on what Aidan told me, he's a drunk anyway, always laying the blame elsewhere for his own failings."

"Forget it and don't let him talk to you like that again. You did well in reporting him, he knows he wont get away with it." Aidan added.

Declan nodded. "Exactly. Anyway, I'm going to head up to Rowena Brennan's house early this evening, do you want to come? To formerly apologise and the like. A familiar face may make her more accepting of it?"

"Sure, ok?"

"Grand, I'll drop into you first if you like."

"And James?"

"With a bit of luck he'll be hit by a fucking truck…"

"My uncle owns a haulage firm," Gerry offered with a wink.

The happenings of the last 24 hours washed through Declan's mind in a turmoil. *'It shouldn't be like this, we're only a small outfit. Christ I even typeset the paper meself, this hassle isn't for us…'*

As nervous as he was when Michael led him to Rowena's house, he refused to betray it. His mouth was dry as he repeated what he was going to say to her over and over. He silently prayed that the house would be empty as he rang the doorbell but the emerging light from inside and the shadow approaching the hall door pushed him back into a nasty reality he didn't want to experience.

Rowena recognised Michael and smiled at him, her eyes quickly darting towards Declan.

"Hi, Rowena, I'm Declan from The Forum newspaper, I spoke to you on the phone."

She smiled again and nodded. "Of course, of course. Everything ok?"

"Sure yeah, I wondered, if it's ok, could we come in? You know Michael?"

"Of course, of course, yes, come on," Rowena gestured as she stood back to let the two young men inside.

"Just in from work meself. You timed that well."

"Ah sure we could've given you a lift! I hope we're not interrupting your dinner?" Declan smiled as she escorted them to the front room and hastily turned on the Christmas lights.

"God no, will grab something later on. Tea? Coffee?"

Both accepted and surveyed the scene as Rowena busied herself in the kitchen, making small-talk as she popped in and out as the kettle boiled.

Declan's smile was permanent as he went through the proceedings one more time in his mind. He had everything rehearsed. Rowena entered with a tray of tea and biscuits, putting them down carefully on a small table by the window, in turn handing the tea to her visitors.

"I didn't realise you worked there too Michael," she added as she sat in the same armchair the evening she crossed swords with James Carruthers.

Declan and Michael sat on the sofa by the door.

"Just since June," Michael answered. "In college at the moment so working when I can."

"Michael's a great addition to the team," Declan beamed as he supped his tea nervously, and loudly. All three were silent for a moment as Michael surveyed the photos that hung on the wall. He remembered Mary, it was unusual to see her face again.

He admired the Christmas tree, an assortment of coloured lights mixed carefully with tinsel, balloons and a collection of decorations that looked like they'd been built up through the years. He spotted a hand-made lantern, remembering making something similar when he attended the local youth club as a child.

"You've a lot of Christmas cards," Declan remarked, nodding towards the copious collection.

Rowena, sitting back in her chair, at ease, glanced up at them. "You see the one nearest the window? The black one with Santy on his sleigh? That dates from 1985. The big one, with the Victorian scene? 1991. The battered looking one, well my late father gave that to my mother on their first Christmas in this house, many moons ago. I keep them. Makes me look immensely popular!"

"Good trick!" Declan laughed as he sipped his tea again.

Another brief silence hung in the air.

"Anyway," Declan volunteered, cupping his hands around the mug tight, "as you probably know we're here about James Carruthers. I just wanted to personally apologise to you for his behaviour. He has been reprimanded and…"

"How?"

Her question caught him off guard. He exchanged quick glances with Michael before placing his cup carefully onto the grey carpet beside his foot.

"Well, he's gotten a warning and ordered, if you like, never to contact you again."

"Ok but you can't stop him, can you?"

"Stop him?"

"Well what's to say he won't drop up, with more gargle on him, again?"

"Well, as long as he's working for us…"

"And if you sack him, he'll probably just devote all his time to this story as he calls it. What's to stop him following me when I put flowers on my mother and sister's grave? Or hanging around outside my work in the village?"

Declan swallowed. "Er, nothing, but as…"

Rowena's tone wasn't aggressive but her arguments were valid, testament to someone who had been thinking about the situation a lot.

"What Declan means…" Michael piped up, giving a relieved Declan a chance to gather his thoughts.

"What he means is, as long as he works for The Forum, he has been expressly forbidden to bother you, or follow the story. There was a heated meeting this morning with him. He won't want another black mark on his CV."

"Another?"

"He had some trouble in the past," Declan continued.

"Word of behaviour like this will not help his career, or any future employment he may seek, if you like, not that he'll probably get any at his age. He's a member of the Union, they can be contacted about him."

"Well I'll be contacting the Guards next time. I have an old friend stationed in Finglas, I told him about the other night."

"Ok, well as I said obviously we can't monitor him 24/7 but please, do let us know if he does bother you again. He shouldn't."

"I want him sacked if he does. Bother me again, that is."

Declan and Michael exchanged glances once more.

"Well we'll deal with him anyway."

"You'd better."

"We will. We're proud here of what we do at The Forum, we've built up a good base of support and we're hoping to expand and grow, we've a good relationship with the public and we want to keep it that way. We don't want this sort of publicity, you see, that's not what we're about. We're not a red top."

"Red top?"

"An English tabloid? Tacky? We're not one of them; like there's only a handful of us, I sell ads and typeset the paper as well, we're geared towards community and promotion of the community."

"Why is he working for you then?"

Declan signed as he lifted his cup back up.

"We took him on at the beginning, we knew his name but knowledge of his past came to light later. You see, aside from Aidan who studied in Scotland and Michael here who's studying journalism at the moment, we're not, as you might say, heavyweights. We're a simple operation but one which is, we believe, doing good things for the area. James Carruthers' name was like a star signing for us; a heavyweight, someone who did, initially, open doors, especially in advertising. He was near retirement age and convinced us he could do a good job, that he'd be an asset. A string to our bow."

"But if he had a past…"

"Well, like ourselves, not everyone is that knowledgeable of it. But, if I can phrase this in the best way, he has become, well…"

"A millstone?"

Declan smiled and nodded. "A good word yes, but as were evolving, he is too, but unfortunately on a different path. He wants his name in lights once more, to go out on a high and since his discovery of this story, if you will, he's been hell-bent on publishing it. But we won't.

"You see it's not our cup of tea. People want to read about the local football team, the new houses being built, Floppy the dog on the hill, the plan to redevelop Ballymun, they want to see themselves pictured in the pub making an arse of themselves. A century old, unresolved murder case, is not in our interests and I believe it's not in the interests of anyone else in the community, well not anymore, I don't think so anyway. Too much time has gone on. It's been buried in the past for a reason, according to his source no-one spoke of what happened for years afterwards, and only then rarely, if at all. If you know what I mean…"

Declan's last sentence was riddled with self doubt but one which he needed to deliver to Rowena. He had to make an impression. "So you see, I am not interested in running it, it's not what we're about."

Rowena nodded slowly, sipping from her tea and crossing her legs.

"What about other papers? He can go to them?"

Declan pursed his lips inward and nodded.

"Yes, but… well, I can't see the others going for it. There's a lot of people in the nationals who know about him. They'll push him away."

"We can't control what he'll do elsewhere, but from our point of view, he is not pursuing this with us." Michael interjected. He and Declan exchanged another glance.

"Devil's advocate here lads. It is, as much as I despise it being shoved into my life, a good tale. I'm surprised I haven't seen it investigated before, or written about, well since the originally newspaper reports, and of course relieved at the same time. What's to stop him penning something about it?"

Rowena sat forward and waited for an answer. The two men exchanged glances once more. Her eyes darted back and forward between them

"Well, being honest, we can't, he, well, he could go and write a book or something but it'll be nothing but conjecture…"

"Smoke and fire and all that." Rowena added.

"Yes, true, but, well, sources are at a minimum. What exists after that is rumour, self-belief and what was reported in the papers at the time. But, as long as he's with us, we will not entertain him, it's not for us, too heavy for us to get involved with and, of course, we are totally respectful to your family."

"Ok, well that's good to hear. It's not that I doubted your integrity Declan, or that of the paper, just unfortunate we're all thrown into this nasty mess. It's a nice paper, I do pick it up when I see it. Never knew you worked there, must have missed your name," she nodded towards Michael, sitting back again in the armchair and smiling. "I'll keep an eye out for your name from now on! It's good to see young people involved in a venture like that, can't beat the energy! Are youse all in your twenties?"

"We are yeah, apart from our friend James!" Declan laughed.

"Well you all have a good thing going there, I really hope it works out for you, well I mean…"

"That we won't go bust?" Michael smiled.

Rowena was flustered, red flushing her cheeks as she sought to explain herself through a smile. "I mean that it goes from strength to strength for you."

"Well we hope so too!" Declan beamed taking another biscuit.

"Listen, anyway, as a way of making it up to you, if you will, we want to invite you, as our guest, to the latest of the music shows we promote, down in the Bottom of the Hill. Only a small token but…"

He handed her a flyer.

"Oh, what's that?"

"We call it Forum Bands, we run it as often as we can, usually once a month, just showcasing local bands. Quite popular, held on a Thursday, the next one is next week, usually starts about eight or so."

"Oh that sounds good," she remarked, sitting forward, glancing at the black and white flyer. She let a slight laugh on reading the acts lined up.

"Sylvia and the Receptionists? The Prayer Preachers? Straw Hat?" She giggled.

"Oh you missed a treat last time, Cole Noak. Jesus, he was, eh, different!" Michael smiled.

"Who? Cole Noak, is that right?!"

"Yeah, well his 'stage name' as such. Won't be asked back. Into performance art, let's say." Declan mused, shaking his head slowly from side to side.

"Did none of youse know what he was like?"

"Sometime we kinda have to chase down acts who will commit to the evening, you know to fill the few hours. We don't always see them beforehand. Or they'd ring us up. Like a guy who says he sings and plays acoustic guitar, under the guise of Cole Noak, well, you wouldn't think anything, would you?" Declan smirked. "You'd think Jim McCann or Christie Hennessy or someone like that."

"Why what did you get?" Rowena laughed.

"An aul fella who came out in make up, leotard and an inflatable guitar. I shit you not."

Rowena threw her head to the ceiling laughing.

"I take it he's not coming back? I've never heard of any of these on the flyer but yeah, sounds good. My little girl is at her friend's birthday next Thursday would you believe, suppose I can organise for her to stay over. Thank you, God knows I need a night out!"

"Looking forward to seeing you there, and a friend of course. We're all big music fans anyway so we enjoy it. Anyway Ms. Brennan, thank you for your time, sorry to drop in like this but just wanted to express our apologies to you."

"Thank you for that, I appreciate it. Let's hope I don't see your friend again! Tell your mam I said hi Michael, lovely woman. Thanks for the invite to next week, I'll give my pal Susan a shout and we'll drop down."

"That would be brilliant, looking forward to seeing you there! Thanks again," Declan beamed, relieved.

She smiled as the two men walked up her path and closed the gate behind them before closing the door.

"You ok Sandra?" she called out to her daughter, busy watching a video in the other room.

"Yes Mammy."

"Ok, be in now, just having a smoke out the back."

Declan and Michael stood talking at Declan's car for some moments.

"I think that went down well. Nice girl."

"Yeah she's quiet, a decent neighbour anyway, my mam was fond of her mam. Hopefully that's the end of it."

"I think we did good…"

"You mean you. You did most of the talking Declan."

"Did I come across well, do you think?"

"Oh yes. Result."

"Please God," Declan replied as he bade goodbye and climbed into his car. As he started the engine, his mind wandered over the events that led him to Rowena Brennan's house. The first major complaint with the public, and such a delicate event. He flicked the switch for the windscreen wipers as he reversed the car and turned onto Jamestown Road. The rain was beginning to pelt down as he drove down toward the village, past the junction at Ashgrove House, by the bank that now stood where the elegant Gofton Hall once did. He turned at the Drake, down the dirty main street still littered with last night's soggy fast food wrappings and crunched empty cans of lager, noticing the taxi drivers sitting patiently in their cars in front of the War of Independence memorial, waiting for a fare they hoped would come as usual.

He turned by Rosehill House and the shoemakers cottage, waited at the lights across from the Spanish Convent, willing them to turn green before turning onto the dual carriage way, past the old abbey and graveyard and back onto Church Street before pulling up outside the empty Forum office.

He trudged slowly up the stairs, noticing how cold the place was. He turned into the tiny kitchen, taking a freshly made mug of coffee into the quiet newsroom, alone and in darkness.

Brief interruptions in the cloud allowed the bright silver moon to illuminate the room.

The silhouette of the cartoon medieval knight, part of the newspaper's masthead but painted onto the window by his father, stood silently by his own shadow. It's bright yellow paint was replaced by a sickly straw colour in the night light. Declan stood staring for some moments, gazing at the carefully painted knight with the oversize head and staff in hand, a physical symbol of the paper he evolved in the area he loved.

A guardian. A protector. A sentinel. Was that what The Forum was, or would become? What did the knight represent? Power? Dominance? Thinking over the recent events, he pondered the subject matter of what the avatar caricature meant. It was then it came to him. Fight. An ability to fight, to stand up for what the paper believed in, stand up for the truth, for the people of the area. A painting of fatigues long gone looking across at a ruined church and a graveyard that held bones going back centuries; both relics of the old in a town that was ever-changing, and not for the good. A dual carriage dissected the village.

More motorway madness was planned that would further carve a cold concrete swathe through history. The village was becoming unrecognisable from that of his youth. He remembered the beautiful red brick of Gofton Hall fall asunder brick by brick, to stand idle for years. Behind it, a new pub was nearing completion that would no doubt attract the youth of the village, they in turn ignoring the scant references to the past that would perhaps hang on the freshly painted walls. Scant, token references to Gofton, to Watery Lane, to the stream that once was the lifeblood of the place. He wondered what Mr. Heery would think if he could come back and see the place, his pub long gone and replaced by an ugly series of shops.

The Widow O'Donnell who ran the pub in later years, would she weep at the same? Would the Flood's be happy their two establishments were still serving thirsty punters albeit now known as the Drake and Bottom of the Hill? Mr. Brennan, how would he react to his field lost under the Casino cinema, since swallowed up by the supermarket?

The monks from the abbey over two millenia ago, would they baulk at the virgin greenery buried forever, never to return? The Luby's post office gone in favour of a car park. On the outskirts, St. Helena's House still standing remotely but now occupied by a rotation of groups and schemes, facing the green and black of Erin's Isle's GAA club as the players strove to be the best in the land. Across the street, the mysterious shape of building known as The Elms sat in silence, when once it served as a hospital for the cholera victims of the 1850s, now the secrets of its past were locked forever behind abandoned doors. A village that existed in the time James Carruthers was attempting to exhume. For what benefit? His own yes, but for anyone else?

It would be to the detriment of a young woman whose family had been part of that golden age. It served no purpose to rake up corpses that had long withered away, like the memory of the events James was desperately cajoling information from an elderly local for his own glory. Damn him, he's not even from the area. What good would it do anyone? It was a century ago. His pursuit of this story, long since closed and left in peace, would bring sorrow to this young woman and her girl.

No, no, no. He could not allow it. He loved the area to much to allow his name and that of his beloved paper to be associated with it. He sat down in the office chair as the moon vanished against behind the clouds, plunging the room and its painted guardian into darkness.

James poured the remnants of his can into the glass and sat back in his chair, reading and re-reading the pointers he had written down, his eyes squinting as the copious beers he had downed at home weaved their way into his thought process. Alcohol fuelled his angry mind. This was good stuff. A damn fine story. Fuck Declan, fuck the paper, fuck the lot of them; amateurs, children, they hadn't a clue. He had, he knew what it meant. James Carruthers, a man of vast experience as a journalist, he knew what was worth pursuing. They didn't know how lucky they were to have him on board, helping them, offering assistance yet they dare tell him what's worth writing about and what's not.

He was there after the Pillar was blown; he saw the carnage in Talbot Street after the Dublin bombings and he was one of the first to the smoking, deathly shell of the Stardust. He had pedigree. This was golden stuff, a gem of a story waiting to be read. If that shithole of a local rag didn't want it, he knew others would. They'd rue crossing him, trying to sanction him. He would destroy them. Tear them apart. He picked up the phone and dialled. It rang for an eternity. Eventually a weak old voice croaked a greeting on the other line.

"Tony, it's James. I need to talk to you again… it's not late, no… no it's not… were you in bed? Did I wake you?... You should get a phone by your bed then… what?... a phone by your bed, I said… a phone… look, I need to talk to you some more, there have been some developments… yes I know… yes I know… yes, like I said, I know that but you must have more to tell me?... what? No, I, yes, I mean, I am very happy with what you have given me but… let me finish… let me finish Tony… I need more information from you. Have you any newspapers, clippings, anything locked away…? You must have some stuff stashed away… no, I need more… I will call around to you, ok… what?! What?! What do you mean? I'm sorry Tony, no, I must have more, you must think harder… I don't care… your memory is damned good for your age, Christ sake all that you told me…excuse me? What? No, I am perfectly entitl… excuse me I am talking to you… I am talking to you Tony! Listen to me, I am the only one who listens to your ramblings anymore… what? Do not hang up on me, Tony, I said… no… no."

He angrily jammed his finger in the dial and whizzed it around again but there was no answer. James swiped the phone from the stand by his chair and lit another cigarette. He was not having that. He needed more. He would get more from that old fucker. He would have his day. By God he would.

Twenty-One

Rowena climbed the stairs and smiled as she recognised Michael at the top, sitting at a small table and taking the entrance fee from punters. "Hello. They have you doing the door I see!"

"I pulled the short straw. Will miss the first band, don't mind though, saw them before, they're shite. Shouldn't have said that, should I? Probably turn you off the night now!"

Rowena smiled as she fixed her hair that sat long and free, unshackled from the usual pony tail she wore. Michael noticed how attractive she looked. He had never seen her dressed up like that before. A long, wine velvet coat and high-heeled knee boots, her face made up like a classic painting. She was beautiful.

"On me own tonight," she continued.

"Where you not meeting a pal or someone?"

Rowena smiled. She noticed him looking her up and down. It felt good.

"Yeah Susan, couldn't make it, I said feck it though, youse were kind enough to ask me so I'd mosey on down. Sandra's at her pals and I've tomorrow off so gonna let loose!"

"No better place!" Michael replied, eyeing the people come up the stairs behind her. She turned around.

"I'd better let you be. I'll see you inside?"

"You will. Soon hopefully!"

She was made very welcome by The Forum; Declan introducing her to his sisters where he found out she had come down alone. He insisted on covering her drink for the night. When she protested, he waved his hand dismissively.

"No, you're our guest, we're delighted you're here, the least we can do Ms. Brennan."

"Rowena, please. Or Ro, always preferred that!"

"Ok, Ro. Enjoy though."

Michael joined them as the first band finished their set, an awful ruckus which he could hear outside. He handed the takings to Declan before buying a pint and, on Declan's instructions, a vodka and coke for his neighbour. He brought it down to her and sat in the empty seat to her left.

She wore a neat black patterned dress, accessorised with wristbands and a decorative necklace, and sat with her legs crossed. She looked relaxed, at ease.

"Ah youse are so good, thank you!" she beamed. "Though I won't have any more, feel guilty."

"Nah no," Michael added, "we're delighted you came down. Funny really, we're neighbours almost and today and the other day at yours is the most I've spoken to you I think!"

Rowena smiled. "Was thinking that meself, weird really. I know your mam alright, talk a bit to her. Ah sure, I just keep meself to meself, like it that way. So what about you? Aside from working here, what else makes you tick?"

"Well I'm studying too, you know and, well, just simple things, few pints with my friends on a Saturday, eh reading, music, films, going to Bohs…"

"You a Bohemian supporter?" she interjected, eyes lighting up.

"I am yep, good few years now."

"Ah right. I was there once."

"Really?"

"Yeah, ah good few years ago now, with, an old friend. We were standing out in the rain, he wouldn't fork out for a ticket under the roof."

"In the stand? Ah yeah, that's where I sit. Same stand, the wooden one. In fact the ground probably hasn't changed! Your pal a Bohs fan too?"

"Yeah, an old friend…"

Rowena swallowed some more of her drink and looked away, her eyes blinking is rapid succession as they darted around the room in front of her.

Michael smirked as he caught sight of Aidan, Darren and Gerry gesturing to him from a table beside theirs. Rowena caught his eyeline and turned around, the three men instantly adopting another pose.

She chuckled, throwing her eyes back in their direction as Gerry stood up gyrating his hips back and forth. Michael's face flushed with embarrassment; Rowena noticed and smiled gently. She leaned in close and said softly, "You know, I should just sit on your lap and really give them something to talk about!"

Michael's eyes widened, face reddened some more and a stupid over-excited laugh of nerves left his throat.

She leaned back and smiled, before shaking her head slightly and sipping more of her drink.

'Can't believe I said that…'

"Sorry, didn't mean to make you feel uneasy!"

"No, no!" Michael squeaked. "Not at all. Just a laugh!"

She smiled again and nodded, laughing to herself at her boldness. She was having the best fun in years. They sat in silence for some moments, Rowena smiling to herself as she sipped her drink and looked at the crowd around the room, Michael shifting in his chair and gulping his pint.

"So," Declan smiled as he pulled a stool under him. "Is this the Glasnevin end of the table?"

"Here we go!" Michael shook his head as Rowena's eyes widened.

"Oh now don't you start that too!" she chided.

"We're definitely Finglas our way. None of this Glasnevin shite at all." Aidan moved his stool over. "Did I hear Glasnevin?" he laughed. "A magical place, that Glasnevin, hops and jumps all over the place!"

Rowena pointed her two fingers, holding a cigarette, at him. "Now you're talking!" she giggled.

"Narnia has a better geographical description than Glasnevin."

"More Ballymun round that way anyway."

"Yeah, border dissects a green down by the local shops, I think it's there anyway. Glasnevin only magically appeared when the seven towers went up."

Aidan smiled and swallowed some of his drink. "I'm Aidan by the way, assistant editor, glad you could make it down. So sorry about all that stuff." He held out his hand to her.

"Nice to meet you, and thanks. Hopefully that's it now."

"He's as good as gone anyway," Aidan continued, sipping more from his pint.

"We've tried ringing his flat but nothing." Declan added.

"He lives alone?"

"Yeah, wife kicked him out I heard. No surprise really."

A large speaker on the small stage hummed as a guitar crackled. A man, dressed all in black and with shades approached the microphone.

"Oh wait up lads, here's fuckin' Bono!" Aidan smirked to Darren as Straw Hat began their set.

"They're going on early?"

"The Preachers bass player had to work late, they're going on last," Darren replied as he loaded a new roll of film in his camera.

"Rock and fucking roll…" Aidan surmised, draining his glass.

"Is that the guy who works in the post office?" Rowena asked surprisingly, pointing at the singer.

"No idea? You recognise him?" Declan replied, looking back and forth.

"I think it's him. Full of himself. I'll mention this to him when I'm next in!" She smiled. "So anyway," she began as the singer began singing a capella, "you said you're a small operation, do you hope to expand or anything when the paper takes off?"

Declan nodded and placed his glass on the table, leaning forward.

"Ideally yes. Small steps though, you know? It isn't a conventional place of work let's say. I'll demonstrate. Michael? Won't you tell Rowena, Ro, about the Christmas tree?" He smiled wickedly, winking at Rowena as she searched his face for a clue.

"What?!" she asked in surprise.

"Let's just say we're lucky to still have an office…" Michael murmured, a tinge of mortification in his expression.

"What happened?" A slight bemused laugh escaped her lips.

"I came back after lunch the other day," Declan began, " ran up the stairs, and the main office, the newsroom if you like, was thick with black smoke, windows wide open to let it out."

"A fire?"

"The intelligencia that work for me thought it would be great fun to draw, with marker, a Christmas tree on a large sheet of paper and stick it on the wall…"

"Ok?"

"…and use pictures of local politicians and themselves as decorations, baubles, that kind of thing. I still can't find out who decided to sellotape a candle to the top. A candle, by the way, that was lit."

Declan smiled broadly as he sat back, Rowena's shocked eyes on Michael now. He mumbled to himself and downed some of his pint. Aidan, laughing in the background, continued the story.

"We forgot about it, went to lunch in Wilde's. Came back, billowing smoke everywhere, the candle must have fallen and caught a bundle of papers on the floor beside it."

Rowena threw her hand in front of her mouth. "Oh you're having me on surely?!"

"No, 'fraid not. Lucky bastards." Declan smiled. "Whole place could have gone up."

Rowena roared with laughter. "And, like, they're still working for the paper?!"

Declan pulled his stool forward a little more to be heard and leaned in, chuckling gently.

"Well, like I said, we're a very relaxed crowd, probably a gang of messers, unconventional, but don't ever tell anyone that. Very serious about the paper but…"

"I know, you like a good laugh. Sounds hilarious, the thought of the politicians' photos stuck to the tree!"

"Yeah, that's it more or less. If the other aul fella was there he'd have had a conniption."

"Another one?" Rowena laughed.

"You better believe it!" Declan replied, draining his pint glass. "We dubbed it The Unforgettable Fire, you known that U2 album? Well we certainly won't forget it."

"Oh my God, a paper Christmas tree that caught fire. That is the best one yet, wait'll I tell your mam Michael!"

"What?!"

"Don't look so shocked, I'm only messing," she laughed as she slapped his leg. "Wouldn't do that. That is classic though, classic. I done a few mad things in my life but never nearly set my company on fire. There was times I wish I had, but anyway."

"Definitely don't tell his ma we all survived on boxes of crisps during the summer!" Aidan laughed, "she'll be giving him a packed lunch every day!"

"What do you mean?" Rowena smiled. "You lot get more eccentric every day!"

"We had a promotion going in the paper during the summer, free packets of crisps with tokens, that sort of thing. We had boxes and boxes of the things in the office, up to the ceiling. All one flavour. Cheese n'onion. Green packets. Christ we were dreaming about them." Michael replied.

She laughed and shook her head. "I love this. So funny! Can I have a job there?"

She offered her cigarettes to those around her before lighting herself one.

"So what did you get up to when younger?" Michael asked, breaking the pause in the conversation as Declan and Aidan began talking among themselves. The drink had put him at ease. He found himself strongly attracted to her, part of his mind convincing him he'd be in with a chance of some sort maybe. On another night. Just them. Alone.

"Younger?!" Rowena asked, two pin-straight fingers holding her cigarette at her lips as she stared at her neighbour.

"I am young! I'm only 29 you know!"

"I didn't mean…"

"I know, Jesus!" She smiled, shaking her head again.

'Has he ever been with a girl?!'

"Oh God, let me think…" She took a drag and stared up at the ceiling, smiling as she recalled a memory. "I was brought home by the Guards one night, I was rubbered, fell asleep outside the old graveyard over there. My sister, God rest her, was fuming, as the guard was her boyfriend at the time. Jesus, she killed me!"

"You on your own drinking?" Michael asked.

Her smile disappeared as she looked past him. "Ah no, an old friend of mine. A good friend… the Bohs fan actually, him."

"Do you still keep in touch?"

She smiled a weak smile and looked at Michael, eyes full of her own pity and images of her past. It was if an old memory had climbed from her subconscious and was now replaying it's full reel. She stared ahead into nothingness for a few moments. Painful.

'I thought I'd learnt to control it. Have I really moved on then if I still feel like this…' A jolt from the guitar brought her back to the present.

"Ah no, not anymore."

She took a few drags from her cigarette before turning back to him. She flashed an obligatory smile before excusing herself to go to the bathroom.

Inside, she stood facing the mirror, staring into nothingness once more.

'I thought I learnt to control it. It'll never leave me, will it, I blocked it away from Mary. I buried it, deep, why is my past coming back to haunt me…'

She looked back into the mirror and studied her own eyes. All the images were there from her past. In full view. The memories were always dormant, but ready to take over her mind at any time. Tonight a few were awakened.

'Oh to hell with it, not often I get a chance to mix like this. Fuck it, I'll deal with whatever in the morning...'

As she turned away her eyes caught something in the reflection, making her snap her head back to look.

'Not you again... just leave me be now. You're meant to be a dream...'

She bowed her head and gripped the sides of the wash basin tightly. Slowly she raised her eyes but the image she knew she saw was gone. It was that young woman and the child once more. She was in the white dress again, the white dress she only wore when something from her past flashed into her subconscious, as if something awoken an old memory. Like Michael asking about Ben.

A few extra drinks satiated the memories. She felt giddy, light-headed. She couldn't fall apart tonight. Not in front of them. The drink gave her extra confidence. For one night she was going to refuse to think about the past.

The crowded pub and the happy atmosphere lifted her, she tapped along to the selection of music on offer, laughing as various newspaper related stories got an airing and relished the warm, fuzzy feeling of a few extra drinks. It was good. She nodded to familiar faces, exchanged numbers with Declan's sisters and appreciated the honesty and fun of the evening.

Declan helped her back into her coat as the barman lazily called for everyone to clear the premises, nobody paying him any heed. At the stage, young men in the rudimentary rock uniform of rolled up jeans, floppy hair and oversize paisley shirts packed away their equipment.

"No, seriously, no need to call me a taxi. Thank you so much Declan, but I'm gonna go now, thanks anyway. Michael said he'd walk me up. It's been brilliant, I've really enjoyed it, thank you so much, your sisters are lovely, exchanged numbers anyway."

"Well we're delighted you came, thank you so much!" Declan beamed as he shook her hand. "Keep reading the paper!" he laughed.

"Oh I will, looking forward to the reviews of tonight, once I'm not in the photos though, hate the poxy things! Night and thanks again!"

She waved goodbye to the table as Michael opened the door to let her out first, Aidan and Darren making gestures once more. He gave them the middle finger and smiled.

"Oh Jesus, I'm a bit fuckin tipsy, nearly went on me arse down the steps in these boots!" Rowena laughed.

"You ok?!" Michael asked as he walked down behind her.

"Yeah grand. Fancy a chipper? My treat. Starvin'."

"You sure?"

"Oh for fuck sake it's a bag of chips. You are walking me home! Don't worry, I won't devour you..." She looked back at him with a wink.

"Unless you want me to!"

Michael's face was a myriad of expressions.

"Only teasing!"

The cold air was a relief to the smokey heat of the lounge.

"This is where I probably double in drunkenness!" Rowena laughed. "Cold air, always a killer."

"I never really noticed, doesn't have any affect on me anyway."

"Are you're only a young fella!" she smiled, punching his arm playfully. She closed her coat tighter around her, stamping her feet on the ground before lighting another cigarette. As she took the first drag she turned around and pointed, smoke in hand, to the dominating façade of Rosehill House that stood on a small hill beside the pub.

"Used to work there, for a while, not for too long though, menial work, a taxi place, taking in calls and all that. Just after my little girl was born, to bring in a few extra quid."

Michael nodded his interest. "That must have been boring?"

She sucked hard on the cigarette, expelling wisps of smoke through her nostrils which rose and disappeared into the chill of the night.

"You know something, the one thing that I really looked forward to, especially in the summer doing the night shifts, was seeing the sun come up through the window. Well not coming up through the window, I mean you could see it through the window. We used to get good summers. My Sandra was born in summer 1983, Jesus it was baking."

"Yeah I remember that."

"The following summer I mostly did nights, 1984, that was a scorcher too. All went tits up in '85. Weather-wise, I mean. But it was good, the morning air coming through the window and the sunlight appearing. So relaxing. So positive. The birds would start singing at 4am. Gave me real strength back then. I used to skip home, all so happy, have a cup of tea with my sister then she'd be off to work and I'd be looking after Sandra. I still like the nights more than the days. No-one really around..."

"Weren't you tired?"

"Nah, I'd nap when she did, then slept for a bit when Mary came home. Ways and means and all that stuff. Good times."

She swung round and pointed to a small cottage across the road that was once the gate house of Farnham Lodge.

"There? The shoemakers? Worked there too, for a week or so. Hated the place. Looking after orders and the like. Wasn't really a job."

They began walking and as they crossed the road Rowena pointed again.

"I used to go to discos there," she pointed towards the old community hall, the former church. "You ever in it?"

"The Barn Church? No no, never. Sure it's decrepid now, in bits. Junkies and the like hang around there."

"Been like that awhile now. Sad really…"

'Oh shit, I'd forgotten that, hadn't I…?' Years previous Lucy Jones tearfully blurted out to a devastated Rowena that she met Ben on the steps on that particular night. She refused to believe. She still refused. Lucy had a child, a small child, the same age as her own daughter. She was rarely seen much after that. Anytime Rowena saw her she would cross the street. But she had seen her early today, briefly on the street. She always refused to believe her claim. Bitch. No way. No way. She stared at the building for some more seconds, the ghosts of a past she wasn't sure existed repeating their liaison of that fateful Hallowe'en night eleven years ago.

'It's all coming back now…'

"You ok?" Michael asked as he dug his hands into the pockets of his coat. Rowena replied randomly, still fixing her gaze away from him.

"That parochial house, just behind the church, you know the one? The white one, just there…"

"Of course."

"Gobshites never included a stairs in the plans."

"How do you know all this?"

"Picked it up, my mammy was great for the local history, my sister too. I picked it up from them as I grew up. Heard bits and pieces and remembered it. Imagine, forgetting the stairs! C'mon."

She turned on her heels and linked Michael's arm.

"Chipper. Now!" she smiled.

They began walking briskly up the hill on the silent, damp street and ducked into the takeaway, the smell of frying onions and battered fish a pleasant one to take the cold December chill out of their noses. Rowena rested her elbow on the warm silver counter that ran the length of the display. Thick sausages and fish battered and waiting to be ordered were inches away behind the glass. She rested her chin on her hand. On the counter by the till was a plastic rack holding the latest issue of The Forum.

"There you are!" she smiled, still supporting her head.

"Fame, eh?" Michael joked.

She smiled softly and nodded.

"Really enjoyed tonight," she said, as she turned towards Michael.

"Good, that was the idea anyway."

"Thanks."

"Ah no bother."

"I was going to press legal action."

Michael eyes narrowed in surprise.

"Really?!"

"No! God you take things seriously don't you? I might have some fun with you!" She cackled as Michael reddened again.

As their food arrived, Rowena reached into her handbag and pulled out a ten pound note.

"I know where we can eat these!" she winked.

They stepped outside and she suddenly stopped, staring across at one of the buildings. Michael followed her gaze towards an unlit first floor window.

"What you looking at?"

She said nothing, staring at the window she looked out from so many times when younger. Ben's old flat.

"Ah, there, the insurance crowd upstairs there? That used to be a flat, a friend of mine lived there a while ago."

Michael nodded politely and began opening his food.

They continued walking up the hill, past the life-size crucifixion scene, its white figures glowing eerily in the neon light, past the church, the old barracks that now housed a bank before sitting on the wall of the car park that faced onto the taxi rank and memorial. A solitary driver sat in his car, watching them quietly as they ate.

"There used to be houses along the street here, you know," Rowena gestured, her hand full of chips as she pointed back down the street.

"My grandmother lived there for awhile, before they were flattened. Round about where the solicitors office is I think."

"Did she always live there?" Michael asked, concentrating on keeping the onions inside the baps of his burger and not on his jeans.

"No, she was raised, actually, up on Jamestown, the old house used to be there, long gone, she was raised there by an old woman and her family. Her own mother, my great grandmother, died you see, and they took her in as a baby. Her family lived in the same house years before, the cottage I mean, and my granny managed to rent it back some years later, until it was knocked, then she moved to a bigger house on Jamestown Road. Mammy bought the house I live in now when she got married, then Daddy got sick and died when I was very young, then Mammy some years after. I miss her. Mary took over the house, now it's mine. So, I suppose, a whole load of us living fairly close by. Do you follow? I'm waffling the ears off you, aren't I? The drink. I don't get out much."

"No no," Michael said, his interest perking up. "Which relation was the one that the trouble was caused over?"

Rowena didn't respond for a few seconds. "You mean the James fellah? That was my great granny, lived in that cottage down there, think she was an only child. Rowena was her name too. Her mother died young as well."

"How do you know all this?"

"The old woman who brought up my granny knew her and the family. You see the village was tiny then, everyone knew each other. As she grew up she learned, overheard from others about her mother, how she was derided and scorned. A 'loose woman' she was known as, poor divil. She heard the story about the murders and how her mother was meant to be involved in some way. The woman in Jamestown House, what was her name? Can't think of it. Anyway her, and her daughter, decided it best to tell her the truth. So it was passed on. My own mammy told Mary, who told me, well some of it, wasn't 'til she fell sick she told me all of what she knew. I suppose my mother wanted an end to it. Funny cos I've always been interested in local history, but I suppose every tale must have an ending and my mam decided the time was right. It was ended until that smelly big pile of shit knocked at my door."

Michael glanced back down the street, attempting to envisage the time she spoke of.

"So you know a good deal about it then?"

Rowena continued to look into her food as she ate.

"I know what I know and it's my business. I'm not getting at you Michael but it isn't anyone's business about my family. That's why I was so angry. None of his business, of anyone's business. My family's had enough hassle."

"Why you telling me?" Michael asked. "Like, it's obviously a sensitive thing to you?"

"Cos you're nice, I feel I can trust you and I know you're not going to put it all over the paper. I don't know, you and the rest of the paper team seem like honest decent people. Declan convinced me last week in my house that he had no intention of dragging up the dirt on my family's past. I was happy with that. Plus, I know now that if I hear any of it back, it'll have come from you. That's the gist anyway."

Michael was startled. "I won't, I promise."

"I know, I know, relax..." Rowena soothed as she turned to him and laid her hand on his. "I know you won't, you're nice."

"And do you know if the other Rowena may have been involved in the murders?"

"No idea. Just she knew the killer or something, a stranger who arrived in the village one day and disappeared just as quick. It's all in the papers, it was I mean. Don't know much after that, she died shortly afterwards, not sure when, well, long enough to have a baby obviously. She was kept out of the asylums while pregnant, I do know that cos my granny was told that by the woman up in Jamestown, she took Rowena into her care when she was expecting. God knows what way the family would have turned out if she was locked away. Actually it wouldn't have, she'd have died there, probably taken advantage of by some worker and that baby shipped off."

Rowena looked ahead a giggled.

"Fuck me, I can waffle! Where did that come from?"

Michael smiled back. "What about her father?"

"Don't actually know anything about him. Anyway you were sent away to these places for less back then. Maybe there was substance to the stories, hope not though, poor bitch. She's buried in the family plot over there, in the graveyard. I read some of the newspaper reports in the National Library, very open and shut case I think, unsolved anyway, they reckon he was some escaped soldier or something.

"No-one really said very much to the papers. One of the lads murdered had a clean break to his neck. Interesting though. Her name was never in the papers though, she must have had a transient part in the whole thing. Anyway she's rotten in that graveyard now. I used to spend a lot of time in there, would climb over the walls at night you know!"

"You're not going to do it now are you?" Michael laughed.

"Would ya fuck off! In this coat and boots? I'd break me neck. Though maybe if I take off the boots… hmmm there's an idea…"

Michael stared at her, fearful of her next move.

"I'm only joking young man. Jesus you're very tetchy! Those days are long behind me, I only go into the graveyard by the gate these days and with my girl."

"Still some interesting family history," he added.

"And that's how it'll stay. History. James Carruthers has no right prying into affairs that are not his. You finished your chips? C'mon, walk me home, I'm freezing…"

They got up and bundled up the empty chip wrappings, Rowena putting them into her handbag.

"I like reading about the history too." he claimed as she linked his arm again.

"Hope you don't mind? Just these boots?"

"No, no, course not."

"Don't worry your ma will never know you linked me home!" she teased.

She pointed at the huge boulder that sat in a circular brick enclosure just outside the shopping centre car park and once served as a fountain.

"I think there were houses there too at one point. I often wonder if the place gets bulldozed once day will the foundations still be there. Would they find things, like, I don't know, a toy soldier, an old hat, that kind of thing. Do you remember Gofton Hall? You must."

"Course I do." Michael replied, gazing over to the bank that stood in its place now.

"Bulldozed." She pointed to Ashgrove House sitting alone at the junction, now serving a compendium of businesses. In the freezing still of the night she saw her younger self thread carelessly out of the doctor's surgery, vomiting outside the hardware shop that was now occupied by a barber. She could recall the shop worker calling her a scaldy bitch.

That was the worst of it all. That moment. That horrifying sense of fear and powerlessness.

'I pass by these places all the time, why is it getting to me tonight? The drink…'

"That was another of the big houses too. Rosehill and St. Helena's are the last ones, all the others gone, long gone. Shame really. Would love to sit down and write a new history book on the area, a proper one. Talking to old people, their memories, that kind of thing, before they, well, die! Always love looking back… at certain things of course."

"The past is what makes us," Michael added.

"Ain't that the truth."

The conversation turned towards neighbours on the road, their opinions on certain people, who they likes and disliked. As they approached the cottages on Jamestown Road, the flashing blue lights of an ambulance and Garda car broke the dimness. The silent sirens were harsh, immediate, unnerving as they pierced the inky blackness of the night. A small crowd stood outside Old Tony's and at surrounding doorways.

"What's going on here?" Michael wondered, as two paramedics carried a stretcher out, a limp figure with mask over his face on it. A woman ran beside the stretcher, gesturing to a man at the gate who gave her the thumbs up and ran back into a neighboring house.

"That's Old Tony's house," Rowena pondered as she stopped and stared. "He must be ill."

A sense of relief washed over her in that instant. Relief, albeit with a twist of guilt. Tony was being taken away in an ambulance, the misfortune that befell the very elderly man was perhaps in her favour as if he were to die, that would put an end once and for all to his link with her family's past. The very man whose life bridged the generations of her family was lying flat on a stretcher, gasping for breath as he was placed inside the ambulance. She hurried a quick prayer, asking her mother to help her. *'Please Mammy, let that be it. I'm not wrong to ask this am I? I just want to let everyone rest…'*

"Jesus this would be great for the paper!" Michael exclaimed excitedly as he fingered his Forum ID in his wallet.

He began to cross the road but Rowena's linked arm pulled him back rigidly. He looked at her face. She said nothing, just shook her head slowly.

"But the paper…"

"I thought you wouldn't."

"What? No, no I'm not, I just want to see what's going on, old man taken away, nothing to do with…"

Her eyes, flashing wild in the omnipresent glare of the sirens implored him not to. He looked at her, then back at the scene, and nodded.

"You're right, we said we wouldn't pursue…"

He sheepishly regretted his burst of innocent enthusiasm.

"Thank you. I'm sure you'll find out tomorrow. You're on a night off anyway."

"A journalist is never on a night…"

"Oh fuck off will you spoutin' that!" she stated as she tugged at him again to continue walking. "Now walk me home like you promised."

They both turned back to watched as the ambulance drove off, its high piercing siren shattering the late night peace.

"That's a coincidence," Michael offered as Rowena stared at the ground as they continued to walk.

"Michael, what I told you, about my family, it's just general history, what's known and all that, maybe I shouldn't have been so quick to tell you."

"Rowena it's fine, I won't breathe a word of what you told me, I won't run off to scribble a story on it, you know that?"

"Yeah, just let it lie, please. If Tony dies then that's the last link gone, if you like. But will the other fellah run with the story somewhere else?"

"How? Hearsay and no tangible witness, or new evidence. He'd be dragging up rumour and newspaper reports from ninety-odd years ago, as Declan said to you the other night. No-one would want to run with that, and if he wanted to do a book, well based on what? Your, what, great granny doesn't feature in the old newspaper reports does she? So don't be worried."

"My, you know your stuff!" Rowena giggled as she squeezed his arm.

"Well I do like to use big words like tangible, evidence and newspaper."

Rowena threw her head back and laughed as they slowly continued up the Jamestown Road, greasy tarmac lit by the false warmth of successive neon streetlights.

"Don't turn out like Carruthers, promise me?"

"Course not, no intention of. Jesus."

"I just hope, well, want to get on with my life, you see, make something, protect my daughter. I was shaken when he turned up and mentioned it.

"But it's my story, and so long ago."

"Any decent reporter or author, interested in pursuing the story or whatever, would approach it differently. He's just weird, hell-bent on glory, no matter what," Michael added.

They neared the turn of their road and Rowena stopped. "Thanks for tonight Michael, thanks to the paper, I really enjoyed meself, God so long since I was able to go out and have a laugh, I needed it, I really did, makes a change from listening to Chris Barry or Larry Hogan on the late night radio, or Radio Sweden with that bloody jingle!"

"Gotta love that jingle!"

"Haunting isn't it?" Rowena laughed "I love it."

She paused for a moment, looking back down Jamestown Road. She cautiously grabbed his hands softly.

"Listen, do you want to come in for a cup of tea? Now before you shit yourself, it's a cup of tea."

Michael exhaled gently. The scent of perfume mixed with cigarette smoke in the stillness of the December air was exotic, exciting, captivating .

"Love to."

James Carruthers walked quickly up the North Road, not caring to look back but pleading for a taxi to drive by. Eventually he spotted one creeping along and struggled inside, breathless, as he slammed the door.

"How much to Ashbourne?"

The taxi driver smiled secretly at the fare. "£20."

"What?"

"£20. It's in Meath, outside my jurisdiction."

"Jurisdiction?!"

"Do you want to go or not? Long walk bud..."

James gathered his breath for a few moments.

"Yes. Yes, quickly…"

Twenty Two

"**A** history lesson and a half!" Michael smiled as he sipped from his tea.

"When I get a few drinks on me I begin chattering, no matter whether the other person is interested or not…"

"I was interested."

"I don't care if you were, you were listening to me whether you liked it or not!" Rowena laughed as she stood by the record player in the sitting room. A side lamp was on, along with the Christmas tree lights, forming a mellow surround as both relaxed in each others' company.

"What's your favourite Christmas song?"

"Has to be Fairytale of New York."

She scrunched her face up as she took a record out of it's sleeve.

"God no. This one."

She put the record on and the gentle crackle eased into the beautiful, soft and familiar notes of an organ followed by gentle guitar and a song he knew well.

"Ah, not bad!" he beamed. "A Spaceman Came Travelling. Yeah, a little gem. Why you like it?"

"It's amazing," she replied as she took her boots off and sunk into the opposite armchair. "So beautiful, those angelic notes then that chorus. But the theme too. A spaceman comes travelling, but he's using it to explain the story of the Nativity. I think it's wonderful, so powerful and clever."

She closed her eyes and tilted her head back as the chorus built into the familiar crescendo. The twinkling Christmas lights added a surreal atmosphere to the scene. A woman Michael barely knew a week earlier now was sitting curled on the opposite armchair, eyes closed, head nodding in time to the music. It was the perfect setting.

"Think of it," she added, "a spaceman travelling being the reason behind the story of the Nativity. Makes you think, doesn't it?"

"I suppose?" Michael lied.

She sat forward, feet on the ground, hands cupping the mug.

"Like, not that I'm into UFOs or anything, but such an interesting take. Who's to say a spaceman or some traveller of some sort hasn't come already, walked among us, altered things that we take for granted, our lives, our existence for example? You get me? How do we know? How do we know that my life, your life, Declan's, whoever, hasn't been altered by some traveller who's come and gone. We don't, do we? Maybe we only exist because of that traveller. Deep ain't it?!"

Michael pressed his lips together and nodded.

"I suppose. No one knows."

"Exactly! I like it, always did, the song I mean… have that album since it came out when I was a teenager, one of my favourites. Just such a wonderful story, and so bold too. But I like the thought of some other-worldly stuff now and again. When you're spending every evening at home with your kid, you read a lot, watch a lot of documentaries and so on. Kinda got interested in all that over the last few years. Like, did you ever hear of the fairy fort, speaking of supernatural things? Did your mam ever tell you?"

"I'm sorry, what?"

"Sorry just remembered this, my drunken mind works in mysterious ways. There was a fairy fort around here, ah years ago, I remembered old Mrs. Collins, the first resident of the road after it was built, remember her? She died some years ago, saying the houses were built on the site of an old fairy fort, and that it was bad luck, that kind of thing. Anyway years ago, I was only starting school I think, she told me her own mother had mentioned that a man appeared one day in it, she said it she heard it was the devil. Her mother worked in Jamestown House actually, remember the house I was telling you my granny was raised in for a bit? Located over there somewhere."

She pointed vaguely towards the window, Michael's gaze following her random and lazy throw of the arm. "Mrs. Collins mother was an English woman, legend goes it brought the area bad luck. Can't see how, but as we're on a supernatural theme…"

"Quite the opposite, you told me such a great story this evening, told it well."

"Nah, just the gist… but, we all have a book in us, isn't that what they say? Who knows, maybe one year, when Sandra's reared and safe on her own path, I may tell it, on my own terms. Not a drunk alco's. I may have come to terms…"

She stopped mid-sentence and glanced up at the photo of her mother.

"No. No I won't."

Michael nodded and swallowed the remnants of his tea. He could see the intoxicated Rowena becoming emotional very soon, he didn't want to be around for any tears. "Thanks Rowena, had better go though…"

"Ro."

"Ro, thanks."

She stood up when he did, a gentle smile on her face and her arms crossed.

"You want a sneaky drink? I've a few cans in the fridge?"

"I shouldn't."

"Ah go on you should. Sure you'd still be there if you didn't walk me home, wouldn't you? Pints piled up in front?"

"Guess so."

"Go on, one?"

"Twisted my arm."

"Sit back down then!" She winked as she gently pushed him back into the chair, leaving the room for a moment before returning with four cans, giving him two.

"Saves me making a second trip out."

She cracked open her can and went back to the record player.

"Tell you what, gonna change the record when this finished…" She fumbled with another record and squinted as she put it on the turntable, moving in closely to the grooves before smiling and placing the needle at a certain point.

"Stand for the anthem!"

The opening chimes Aslan's This Is swam from the speakers. A local band done good.

"Love this. Finglas in one beautiful five minute song. The words remind me of my friend, the one I was talking about earlier."

"The Bohs man?"

She looked at the wall in front of her, smiling as she nodded.

"Yep. Ben."

"Great tune."

"You were at the reformation show I gather?"

"Yep, great day, when the rain stopped."

"Never used to like them, always a U2 girl. But hey, times change you and music define your times."

The remained silent as the song faded out before the conversation began again about anything and everything. Music. Love. Life. The future. The past. Rowena hadn't had a conversation like it in years. She revelled in the chance.

She opened the window and leaned out to have a smoke, casually looking back in to continue the conversation.

"I never usually smoke in here, this room."

A drunk Michael couldn't stop admiring her as she quickly dragged on the cigarette. She was so beautiful.

"It's gonna be ok, isn't it, about James Carruthers?" she asked, as if seeking an assurance for something she was realising for herself.

"Yes, yes, sure we saw the aul fella carted away."

Rowena looked into the fireplace and back at the Christmas tree. She knew she should feel guilt about wanting him dead. But she didn't. She was confused. But wouldn't it be easier if Old Tony died? Easier for her, easier for her daughter. This night was perfect. Too perfect. Old memories resurfaced.

"Remember the old friend I was talking to you about, earlier, who brought me to the Bohs game?"

"Yeah?"

"Do you remember the chap that threw himself off the bridge? You were probably too young, don't know if you'd know."

Michael searched his mind, his eyes scanning the walls of the room as if the answer would be somehow printed on the cream painted wood chip wallpaper. "Kinda, maybe, I remember my mam talking about it. Was that him, your friend?! I do know a guy said he'd jump off the old water tower in the fields because a girl wouldn't dance with him years ago."

"The one just across from the red barn? Ah yeah, thought that was an urban legend! That's actually true?!" she chuckled. "But yeah, the guy on the bridge, that was him. Ben. Eleven years last Hallowe'en. My best friend. Lovely man. We'd had an argument you see, I hadn't seen him in a bit, then I heard…" She stopped as she realised this was the first time she had spoken about the event, outside of her late sister and Eamon. It felt cathartic.

"That's awful," Michael replied, searching for sensitive words in a mind swelling with alcohol enjoyment. "I didn't know, or think, sorry if I brought up bad memories."

"No no. Yep. Nasty, awful thing. He hung on a bit, you know, a few days. I'll never forget seeing him in the hospital, my God, never forget it. Took me forever to get over it, actually don't think I have in fact. Guilt. Guilt. And you know why?"

"The argument?"

She stubbed out her cigarette, closed the window and sat back in the seat.

"No, well, yes part of. It was because while he was jumping off the bridge, I, well, I was trying to do the same thing, you see."

She lowered her head, her voice suddenly soft. Michael's eyes widened and he clutched his can tightly, taking a long gulp. This was going to be tricky to hear.

"YOU were trying to jump?"

She stared down at her lap. She nodded her head slowly.

"I think you're the, what, third person to know about this? That I know of, anyway. Anyway, I saw an old mutual friend earlier today, in the village on my way home from work, hadn't seen her in ages, Lucy, an old school friend of mine. Weird girl. She has a little girl same age as mine. I remember us having an unmerciful argument after Ben's funeral. You see I was Ben's best friend and Lucy was mad about him, he was never into her but for some reason, well, I know the reason but that's neither here nor there, she claimed they shagged shortly before he killed himself, he jumped… anyway, at pretty much the same time as Ben was jumping, I was up that tree, you know the two big ones behind the houses? The one nearest mine? Well I scaled that, it was pissing rain, I was freezing, out of control, I'd just told Mary I was pregnant, you see…"

"And you were going to jump?"

"Yes. I was. God knows how I scaled the tree that night, wind blowing, soaked in me clothes. I couldn't handle it, you see, the…"

She stopped suddenly, looking up at Michael, realising what she was about to say. She pulled back from her train of thought.

"I… I couldn't handle being pregnant. Turns out my sister was making plans for us to move to New York. Jobs were secured and all that and me getting up the pole just ruined it. We had a huge fight, in the back garden, she went in, left me and I just got it into my head that I had ruined everything. I was sitting on a branch when I saw a torchlight, moving around and heard Mary call my name.

"I called back, she shone the light in my direction until she caught sight of me. Don't ask me how she kept her composure, talked me down. I was at some height, definitely would have broken a few bones at the very least, don't ask how the neighbours didn't poke their heads out, maybe with the noise of the wind and their telly, the bangers going off and all that.

"Anyway I eventually clambered down, slipping three times, ripping my top and ruining my jeans. She hugged me so tightly when I got back into the garden, then clattered me across the face! Fuckin' hard like, I can still feel it! Told me to cop on, think about what I was going to do. It was that moment, that moment, I realised I had help, that Mary would not leave me.

"Later that night when the phone rang, Mary answered, all I could hear was *'no, no, no'* and I knew, just knew, it was Ben, that something had happened. We got a taxi into the hospital but I couldn't go in, I couldn't see him… but I had to."

The silence hung in the air as the music continued in the background.

Michael didn't know what to say, he searched his mind, but knew he had to say something. "Jesus Christ Ro… so, both of you, were trying to take your life over a pregnancy. He probably over being with Lucy."

Rowena nodded, staring across at the Christmas tree.

"Your little girl was unexpected then?" he ventured.

"Was she what?!"

"And, the father?"

Rowena looked back at him, eyes narrowing slightly.

"My girl's father?"

"Yeah… was he around? Any help…"

Rowena looked away again, smiling gently. Despite all she was telling tonight, she still held some secrets. "No, he wasn't around."

She waved her hand as if to wipe the words away and start again.

"Anyway, Ben, he never regained consciousness after he jumped, I suppose poor Lucy carried that with her. Not as bad as me though, me best friend, but I know it wasn't that, or just that, well, I believe it."

"What do you mean?"

"That they slept together. I don't believe it. But still carry it. I asked Lucy again about it a year or two later, she blanked me, ran off. We hardly saw each other then, every time I did see her one of us would cross the street."

"Maybe you refuse to believe."

"Maybe I do. I'll never know. I won't be told anyway and I wont ask. I've my own girl to think of, doesn't matter Michael, long time ago anyway."

She could feel her heart in her mouth, that horrible, heavy leap that accompanied the sickening feeling in her stomach.

'Jesus I've just talked about it. To him! Why now? Why now?!'

"Can I ask something?"

"I suppose?"

"If he shagged her, well, why you so engrossed in that? You were friends, weren't you?"

Rowena nodded as she took a long swig from her can.

"I know what you're getting at, but, more to it. Too much more."

Michael searched her eyes as they blinked furiously and looked away rapidly. He was forming a picture in his mind but decided against pursuing.

"I walk over that bridge on my way to work," he eventually added.

"Yeah you would alright. Hate it. Always hated it since then. Too many memories. It overlooks the graveyard too, where me family are."

"Where's Ben buried?"

"Glasnevin. Anyway… sure that's me, eh?"

"Wow, never knew anything about that Rowena, sorry to hear it."

"Ah sure we all have our past."

Michael nodded and took another sip from his can.

"That's the problem, everyone has a past," he added as he excused himself to go to the toilet.

Rowena smiled as her gaze followed him.

'Feel at ease with him, why did I tell him all that? Why now? It had to be told though at some point, him though? I'll never understand why him, because Tony might be dying and the link could be broken…?'

He returned, motioning upstairs. "I was really quiet, didn't wake your kid."

"Too much information," she smiled as she stood up and approached him. "Anyway you'd be doing well to wake her. She's staying over at her friends."

She laughed as he shook his head, smiling.

"Dance with me," she asked quietly as she stood up.

Michael's eyes widened at this unexpected request.

"Wha'?"

"Dance with me Michael, just a quick dance. I don't think I've ever had anyone dance with me, properly.

"Never had many boyfriends, none I can recall dancing with. Please don't be confused, I just want to dance, haven't done since my girl was born, took a lot out of me, to say all that tonight."

She stood in front of him, a vision of beauty in a flowing dress, dark hair and doll-like features embellishing the perfect red lipstick. Her smile was inviting yet simple. Her eyes... captivating.

Alcohol flowed through his mind, desire, yearning awakening. He looked her up and down once more as she gently laughed and went over to the record player and cued up the song. She stood in front of him once more, head cocked to the side slightly, slight smile and raised eyebrows that asked deftly would he accompany her. He stood up as the song faded in, backing vocals gently cooing as the tune began to take hold. She smiled and buried her head in his chest as the song began in earnest and they slowly shuffled from side to side.

"I'm a brutal dancer," he softly admitted.

"So am I."

She felt safe huddled into his warmth, her eyes closed as her feet slowly moved on the carpet. His grip on her was firm, warm, inviting and secure.

He momentarily closed his eyes and let his mind wander in the moment. Such a beautiful moment. He was aroused but the sensual relaxation of his mind overcame such thoughts. He wished the song to go on forever.

He gazed at the photos on the wall as they shuffled gently, wondering what it was like for her to be alone, raising a young girl in a house once filled with chatter and laughter. No wonder she was so scared. What she held dear, those beautiful smiling faces in the photos could no longer help her with. Her banal and quiet life was threatened by a brute outsider who wanted to pry, to expose, to pull apart what family she had left.

Rowena could feel a tear escape and trickle down her cheek as the song played softly behind them. What she cherished was in the open, questioned. No-one would harm her baby, no-one could mar her baby's upbringing. What Sandra needed to know she would know in her own time and when she decided to tell her. Old Tony, if he died, that could only be a good thing, couldn't it? It wasn't right, yet felt right at this very time.

The song faded as both regretted the loss of this precious moment that only they would ever know or share.

Rowena stepped back, wiped her eye and gingerly sniffed as she smiled up at Michael, her arms wrapped around him once more.

"Thank you…" she whispered as she leaned up and kissed him.

Michael closed his eyes and relished the short moment.

"Thanks Michael, for walking me up and, well, the chat, haven't chatted like that in a long time. I miss it, company, not just male company, well I never had it to be honest, not after I became pregnant with Sandra, rarely had a man since, and never before…" she blushed and winced.

"Oh God, sorry, I'm rambling, I don't mean… sorry, I'm making a show of myself, aren't I?"

He kissed her once more softly and smiled.

"No, no, Ro no need to tell me anything. I know what you mean. The company. Chance to talk. I know. And I appreciated it too."

"Did you?"

"Yep. Got to know you didn't I? That can only be good. And every single thing you told me shall remain with me and never be told to anyone else, you have my word."

She smiled, leaned forward and kissed him again softly on the lips.

"Thank you. Really, thank you. Lovely thing to say. God knows I've had a lack of them."

They stared at each other for some seconds, minds in turmoil, minds eager to give in, but resisting. He was quite handsome, she thought. Lovely looking chap. Someone had to break the moment up; neither wanted.

Michael shuffled awkwardly.

"Anyway I best go. Thanks Ro…" he added softy, searching her eyes for a reaction. She beamed as she reluctantly released her grip on him and held his hands.

"Thank you really! And thanks for walking me home. Cup of tea and beers was the least I could offer… eh, I won't mention this, well the tea, to your mam, not that I see her all the time, our secret? You know the way people talk. God, Michael, I'm going on again, it's the fuckin' drink, and the dance will always be ours, yes?"

"Absolutely," he whispered back.

She watched him close the garden gate behind him and offered a small wave before she closed the porch and hall doors behind her and stood with her back against the hall door, arms still crossed, head bowed as she ran through her thoughts. She hadn't felt that comfortable with anyone in a long time. She knew because her tongue ran away with itself. She smiled and went back into the room.

Why now, though? Why tell so much to someone she barely knew? Was it because he was out of the loop so to speak? Someone with no knowledge of her past, someone who wouldn't judge or care? She didn't know but it felt such a relief to talk. She knew nothing was really solved; her mother and sister were still dead and the past would always be there in the background, but she felt better than she had for a long time.

'One more drink before bed. To hell with it.'

Michael poured himself a pint of water and stood sipping it in the kitchen, trying to take in all his close, yet, until recently, distant neighbour had told him. *'Why me? She must trust me, was it drink. Will she regret telling fucking me of all people that...'*

Whatever the reason he would abide by her request. He felt good.

Twenty Three

"You were lucky I was on tonight!"

The barman placed another fresh pint in front of James.

"I knew your uncle well, Old Davy Whittle, that brings back some memories."

James smiled as he took the pint in his shaking hands.

"Couldn't say no to Davy's nephew!"

The barman smiled as he bid goodnight to another punter who slipped off his stool and out the side door. James had flung the £20 fare at the cab driver and crossed towards the pub he remembered. The barman was shutting up, James pleading with him for just one drink.

'I've come a long way, am staying below in the hotel. I used to come here as a kid with my uncle, I'm away first thing in the morning, just thought I'd poke my head in…'

The journalistic gift of blagging worked to his advantage this time as he began to tell the elderly barman of his uncle who once owned a cottage just around the corner. He spoke how he used to be brought in on his summer holidays with his cousin, eating crisps and drinking bottles of lemonade while his uncle supped a quick pint inside. The barman loved the nostalgia, stood by to allow James in and pulled a few late pints.

"The place hasn't changed, the village that is."

"Nah, thankfully, the odd estate here or there but still a one-horse, one road town!" the barman smiled.

James skulled the pint back quickly, hand shaking, trying to steady his nerves. "Thanks, thanks for that."

He placed some pound coins on the counter, stubbed his cigarette out and struggled off his stool.

"Bye now, good to see you, if you're ever around again do drop in."

James didn't answer, instead waddling out the door and standing outside, lighting another cigarette in the winter night.

He barman smiled and shook his head. *'Yep, I do pick them…'*

James stood outside, glancing back up at the pub. The Hunter's Moon hadn't changed a bit since he was last up this way.

Across the street, the last of the regulars from the original village hotel staggered out into the cold night, shouting and laughing back at each other as they each made their separate way home.

The church across the road was as he remembered it, the forgotten parish hall as forgotten as it ever was. He turned to walk away from the village, past the rusted iron walls of the seed depository on the same side.

James had pondered his decision to come back to Ashbourne. He needed to get away, but here? Revisiting old haunts; to see once more the crumbling cottage of his uncle silent, neglected and derelict, sitting cold and alone in the field atop the hill that the road to his right now weaved towards.

He thought of Old Tony, realising now that he was reminiscing just like the old man whose house he had left in a hurry. He turned and walked up the long road. It reminded him of the incline toward Rowena Brennan's house. Warm Christmas lights twinkled here and there in the windows of the new houses which climbed the hill with him. He glanced across at them, remembering playing in these very fields in the fine and sepia summer evenings of his memory of as youth. Endless fields that stretched for miles and miles. The road up to his uncle's cottage was just as steep, but narrower, rougher than its current layout. *'All changed, just like Finglas. I just have to see it again, once more, then it has to end…'*

His body began to shake as he pushed the creaking gate aside and stumbled through the high grass and nettles, before shoving open the rotting blue door. He felt his way along the cold, damp walls until he reached a room at the back.

There he squatted down in a corner, his hands covering his face as if in deep meditation, before carefully removing the long carving knife, sticky with Old Tony's blood, and placing the blade on the on the floor beside him. He held onto the handle, shaking, his mind awash with a mixture of emotions.

He looked down at the knife, catching a faint glint in the dim moon light that filtered through the broken panes beside him. He had carried that in his jacket. It could have fallen out at any time. Anyone could have seen it.

Years ago he sought solace in the fields surrounding the battered old cottage. This night he sought solace of a different sort. He felt for the knife once again, carefully running the tip of his finger along the blade.

His mind was drawn back to those moments in the cottage in Finglas.

The look of fear on Old Tony's face as James ranted, raved and swiped ornaments and delicate photo frames from the mantle piece, mocking how the old man dried his clothes by the open fireplace.

'What have I become?! What have I done?!'

He lowered his head as the anger rose deep within. His mind was awash in an alcoholic haze but his thoughts on this matter had never been clearer.

'All his fault. It's all his fault things have turned like this.'

He began to sob as he realised there was no way out. No way. He turned his wrist toward him and held the blade on it. He couldn't face what he knew he had to.

'I need to finish this…'

Rowena stopped dead as she listened to the radio report.

"...an elderly gentleman attacked in his home in Finglas has died. He has been identified as Tony Salinger and lived alone for…"

She placed her hands on the bottom of the sink, submerging them in the dishwater as she let out a sigh of relief. Relief tinged with guilt but maybe, just maybe, it was all over now. She opened her eyes as the report continued.

"…the Gardaí are appealing for a man seeing entering the house late last night to come forward…"

It had to be Carruthers. He could be out of the equation too.

The mood was sombre in The Forum on the grey cold morning. Hangovers didn't help. The small staff were gathered in Declan's office.

"What are we going to do?" Darren asked.

Declan was staring out the window, his eyes tired and mirroring a drained sensation within.

"Stupid bastard…" Aidan mumbled.

"And I passed there last night," Michael added, "saw Old Tony being carried out in the ambulance, no idea though what had happened inside."

"What time was that at?" Declan asked.

"About, what, half an hour after I left the pub last night I suppose. We got chips, ate them on the car park wall then rambled up. Unreal though…"

"Did she, Rowena, say anything when the Tony guy was being carried out?"

"No," he lied, "not a word."

"The Guards definitely said it was him?" Aidan asked, a question he knew was useless.

"A neighbour heard a commotion, used her key to get in, saw Tony on the floor, he gasped out Carruthers' and the paper's name to her before she called the ambulance. She read the paper, our paper that is, knew what he meant. Guards were on to me as soon as."

Declan's desk phone rang, the shrill tone sending a shiver down his spine. He glanced at the others, weariness, dread and the unknown in his eyes.

"Hello The Forum? Yes? Yes, this is he. Oh hello Guard… yes… yes… what? What? Are you kidding me… ok, ok, thank you… yes, we'll be here all day, do we need to go over to you… yes, ok, ok, that'll be no problem… thanks Guard, thanks, thanks…"

Declan replaced the receiver and buried his head in his hands.

"What?!" Aidan asked.

"Old Tony died from his injuries in the early hours. James is being charged with manslaughter at least, well when they catch him. They want to talk to us all about the story. Tony managed to string a few words together and explain why James was there, mentioned that accursed story. It's going out on the national media now."

They all sat in stunned silence in the room, each one wondering what the latest events would mean for them.

"The paper's fucked!" Aidan spoke, slamming his notebook on Declan's desk.

"Wasn't sanctioned by us," Darren glumly added, "he was working off his own bat…"

"Guilty by association," Aidan replied. "People will hear what they want to hear. The oldest resident of the village killed by a fucking alco, who works for us, doing our line of duty, so he says. He's fucking destroyed us."

Aidan got up from his chair and kicked the wood panelled wall in frustration. Michael stood rooted to the spot as he thought of Rowena, his blood cold. He thought of her words, that if Tony were to die that would be the last link gone. She wasn't to know what was going on inside though, no-one was.

"What about Rowena Brennan?" he asked, voice shaking.

"The guards will no doubt be in touch," Declan surmised as he stared blankly out the window. He stood up abruptly, rubbing his hand over his head.

"Ok, we need a solicitor, this is gonna get messy, Carruthers has no way out, he's gonna drag us down. Prick. Jesus as if I haven't lost enough hair already," he smirked weakly

"Christ my hangover's bad enough…" Aidan mumbled as he left.

"Do they know where he is?" Darren asked.

"No, they've put a description out anyway."

The bodies melted away, sombre thoughts kept to themselves.

"Declan, sorry, should I tell Rowena? I walked her home last night."

Declan thought for a moment.

"It should come from me, though she probably knows, it's been on the radio apparently. Look drop in and tell her she's nothing to worry about, we're the ones in the shit, they have all his notes and the like so they know what he's been chasing, they'll no doubt just want a statement from her about it."

"Yeah ok, I will."

The noise from a Christmas film in the opposite room blared cheerily as Rowena stared out the open window, pulling sharply on a cigarette, breaking her non-smoking rule in that room.

"I really can't believe this," she snapped, "there's going to be a Garda car outside my house, people will want to know why. Oh God, everyone will know."

"You can go down to them, they have all the details."

"That's it. They have his notes, his findings, his work so to speak. The coverage this will get, Jesus it's gonna be dragged up again."

"Not necessarily…"

"Ah will you stop!" Rowena spun round in her slippers as she stared down at Michael who was shifting nervously in the chair.

"Course it's gonna be brought up. The murder that led to another murder ninety years later. Jesus Christ, and before Christmas, my poor girl. Christ when I saw him taken out last night, I thought, presumed, hoped it was a heart attack, of his own accord, if you know what I mean, not this. I got a shock when it said on the radio that he had been attacked, but… Jesus, not this!!"

Michael sat silent, staring out the window behind her.

"When this hits the papers, when Carruthers is caught and I reckon he will, it will be about an old alco journo, who used to work for the nationals attacking an old man for the gist of a story. Aside from the transient details, I don't think the bones of your story will be aired or need to be aired. Have you ever seen it happen before?"

Such a difference to the perfection of the previous night.

Rowena took a drag of the cigarette and glanced at him, eyes narrowed.

"Either you're learning incredibly well in that college and paper, or you're incredibly naive."

Michael swallowed hard. He reckoned she knew, as he did, it could well be the latter. She tapped the remaining ash of the cigarette out the window and closed it before walking over to him and grabbing his hand.

"I'm sorry Michael, I didn't mean that," she smiled weakly

"It's ok, you're right though."

"I can shoot me mouth off sometimes. What's your paper going to do?" she asked, head bowed as she fingered the cigarette box for another.

"Well Declan's going to talk to the Guards today, take it from there, get it straight that he wasn't acting on our authority. You've a friend who's a Guard, didn't you say that?"

"Yeah, yeah I do."

"Give him a ring?"

"Yeah, will have to. And me? What about me though? I'm the only other person involved."

"You'll be ok Rowena."

She sniffed an ironic laugh.

"Declan should be up here, solicitor or not, he's the editor…" She jabbed the cigarette towards the window. "And after such a good night last night. Typical me, eh? Jesus Christ, this family is cursed alright."

Michael eased towards the door, prickly, sick sweat on him. Last night's tender moments were well and truly crushed.

"I'd better go Rowena, sorry about this. Declan will be up, he was always coming up but we both reasoned if we waited 'til he came back, you'd have heard from someone else."

"I heard it on the fuckin' radio anyway. It's ok, I see the reasoning, Jesus his head must be fucked. Such a nice guy."

She smiled and hugged him gently.

"I thought this would be over. Michael, will you tell the police what I told you, last night like, the story of my family as I knew…"

He tried to think cohesively.

"Rowena, I don't know, probably not, but, well, how would I know about it? If you get me? For all anyone knows, you never told me a word of it."

She nodded and patted him on the shoulder.

"I know, I know, sorry. Not your fault Michael, not your fault, we're all in this together. Youse at the paper were very good to me in mopping up Carruthers' mess. Ah look, let's see what happens, eh?" she smiled.

They stared into each others eyes for some moments but nothing could replicate the previous evening. They smiled wistfully as Michael began to move. She waved as he left the house and closed the gate behind him, before turning up towards his own house. She wondered what his mother would say, about why he was in with her during the day. Suppose he'd have to tell her maybe.

Michael's mother was all talk about the latest incident, plugging her son for information on James Carruthers. He never mentioned Rowena, or her connection, or that he had walked her home last night and spent some time in her house. If she asked he would tell, but he wasn't going to volunteer information or he would never hear the end of it.

Rowena had dialled the number of the Garda station and as the dialling tone chirped, the doorbell rang. She stretched the cable and opened the door slightly. It was Eamon. She quickly replaced the receiver and let him in.

"These phones are fuckin' great…" she mumbled as she gestured for him to come in. As he sat down in the front room, she was worried by his face.

"Eamon, why didn't you tell me?"

"Ro, I just came on duty, checked the reports and all that, and saw the incident report. I came up to you as soon as I could. It's an awful mess."

"I know, I know, a reporter from the paper told me, he's just left."

"Was he involved in the story?"

"No, no just works there but he lives down the road. He and the editor called up to me the other day to apologise."

"Has the editor been in touch?"

"No, not yet, reporter said he's meeting with a solicitor but was acting on his instructions to tell me, if you like. Are you investigating Eamon?"

"Well, a man got killed, everyone's involved, though if you're dragged into it…"

"Will I?"

"Well you may be asked to give a statement about the other night, when he called up. Anyway if you are involved, I wouldn't worry at all, just give your statement, as far as I know some of his notes were scattered on the floor."

"His notes about my family, an investigation he had no right to delve into."

"Well, that's neither here nor there."

"Here nor there? Of course it's fuckin' here nor there; it involves my family, if this, and it will, gets into the papers, so will my name."

"I doubt that."

"When it goes to court, my name…" She threw her hands in the air. "Jesus, you've the look of a detective, typical suit! Fuck sake, what a sight!"

"My own car though."

"Ah some nosey cow's gonna see you walk out."

"Ah here you're getting ahead of yourself, being…"

"Paranoid?! Haven't I a right to be?!"

"Tell them your library book was late!" he smiled.

Rowena chuckled, waving him away. "Ah, Jaysus Eamon you always had the solution, hadn't you?"

He smiled and glanced at the picture of Mary hanging on the wall.

"You ok Ro?"

She followed his glance.

"Yeah, I'm ok, always hits me this time, you know. Imagine, her anniversary again next Tuesday. Ah I make the best of it for Sandra, but she talks about her auntie fondly. She was very good to us, Jesus Eamon, when I think of what she gave up for us, to help me raise Sandra."

"New York you mean?"

"Yeah, broke the poor girl's heart, God we had some fierce arguments, but, she dusted herself down and was like a mother to me. She looked after me when mammy died, then when I should have been able to make my own way, stood by me and helped raise her niece. She doted on Sandra, kept Ben's name out of the local gossip too, like we agreed, wouldn't be fair on his folks. God love them, they still don't know they've a grandchild.

"God I often wonder was it me that caused the cancer, you know, all the burden on her shoulders."

"Ah Ro no, you know it wasn't."

"Ah you know what I mean, the stress, the let down, the heartbreak, she had her dream and I helped shatter it. We talked about the three of us going one day but, well…"

"Ro, her forty a day habit caused the cancer, you now that."

"Yeah but still, she was so let down by me, so upset. I'll never forget the night I told her, then Ben goes and kills himself. God, what a time."

"Does Sandra ever ask about him?"

"No, not for years. She knows he's in Heaven with Mary, that his name was Ben. I showed her a photo of him and she was content. Hasn't mentioned him in a long time."

"Well look, I have to get back, but don't be worrying, it won't be as bad."

"Ok. Thanks Eamon."

"What you doing for Christmas?"

"Here, as usual, then my cousin and her kids are coming over, they'll stay the night, will be nice. I'll always have Christmas here, as long as Sandra wants anyway."

"Is Santy coming?"

"Oh I hope so! I really do. If she's acting, she's doing an Oscar-nomination style one. She's always been her own girl if someone told her in school, she'd brush it off if she didn't like it!"

"Like her mother!"

Rowena laughed. "Cheeky man. Thanks Eamon thanks."

"It'll be ok Ro. Trust me."

Rowena smiled as Eamon left. Her mood was lifted slightly, was it enough?

She went upstairs and sat on the bed; her mother's bed, Mary's bed, now her bed, gazing out the window at the cold night and drawing the shape of the tree that looked down on the house with her finger.

'Is this a curse, is this something more powerful that I don't know of or understand? All I was doing was getting on with my life, keeping my head down and now this. What will I do, what will I do… poor Sandra. School, kids can be bastards…'

She coughed hard as the wind lifted the scant leaves of the great trees, the sound filtering in through the small top window that she had left open. She stood up, pulled the net curtain back and rested her hands on the windowsill.

All around her she could see the lights of houses, the dull shadows of the two big trees looming, the ancient wood, skewered solidly into the soil, it's roots spreading and unwinding like thin, skeletal fingers, an appendage of that ghastly bird that sat silently for time immemorial, pointing down at a succession of frightened and confused people through the years.

She coughed again, held her chest as it tightened and glanced at the dark hulk of the tree. She recalled Mary's illness, the fit of coughing that led to a trip to the doctor, the hospital and the ultimate diagnosis. She wrestled the half-full pack from her jeans pocket and scrunched it in her hand, thin card, a film of clear paper, gold foil and carefully wound sticks of tobacco submitting to the anger in her tightened grip.

'It's got to end. No more. Leave my family in peace. It ends now. My daughter deserves a good life, a good family,'

Declan shook hands with the Guard as he closed the door behind him.

"You ok son?" his father asked, standing in the kitchen doorway of the dark hall.

"Yeah dad, thanks. I'm going to head into the office for a bit, take my mind off things if I can."

"Be careful."

"I will, let me know if his photo comes up on the news."

"I'll be watching son."

Declan closed the front door of his parents' house behind him, deciding to walk the short distance down. Production of the paper had been deferred, he knew everyone in the village would know why. They had no option but to, out of respect, out of the incessant queries of the Guards who trawled through the small offices thoroughly and out of an inability to physically do the job. He ignored the collection boxes shoved into his path by jovial volunteers outside the shops as he kept his head down and walked towards the iron bridge. Tinny Christmas songs played their warm and well-worn tunes from hidden speakers as he passed the shops. A flurry of snow was swirling in the shrill wind, around him children excitedly grasped at the weak strands as he paid no heed to their faces and squawks of delight. He only stopped when a gentle hand touched his shoulder from behind. Declan turned to see the friendly face of the head librarian standing behind him, a sympathetic smile on his face.

"Ah, how are you?" Declan whispered almost, accepting the tall and thin man's hand. A thorough gentleman, well respected around the area and one who passionately supported and bigged up the paper to all he encountered. A man of words, like himself.

"God almighty it's terrible isn't it?" the middle-aged man said in a soft, polite voice. "Shocking stuff. Are you ok, the lads too, anything I can do for you?" He respected and in turn was respected.

"Hasn't hit us yet, sure early days, even we don't know the full story... God knows what will happen."

He nodded and noticed some prying eyes of those passing turning on the young editor. The head librarian stared back, his hand still firmly grasping Declan's, a challenge almost to anyone who dared think ill of the local newspaper editor. "Well look, you know where I am, give me a ring or drop in anytime. Whatever happens I hope you have some sort of good Christmas."

Declan smiled, his eyes watering as he once more shook his hand and patted his shoulder.

"God bless now," he added before walking by the crossroads and into the library across from the shopping centre car park. Declan smiled. An absolute gentleman. One of the good ones. He continue don his own path, turning onto the bridge and passing the ruined and almost forgotten abbey as he continued towards the office. The metal walkway bounced almost as his footsteps neared the path of Church Street once more. Looking up, the yellow painted knight looked down at him through the grill on the oversize helmet.

'Jesus I need you now…'

He struggled with the lock. He quizzingly examined it inside as he flicked the latch back and forth. Looser than normal. He must get it replaced. He trudged up the stairs and flicked on the hallway light, going straight into the kitchen to make a coffee. He watched the kettle rattle as it reached boiling point, smiling at the memory of an old French teacher who debunked the myth that 'a watched kettle never boils', urging his students to 'watch one next time, it'll boil…' He lazily stirred in his coffee, taking a quick sip before walking down towards his office and opening the door.

Thoughts of being able to keep doing this were swimming through his mind.

'Look what this paper has done…'

He switched on the light and dropped the cup, cursing loudly at the sight that greeted him. James Carruthers was sitting in his chair, dishevelled, reeking and clutching, in his right hand, a knife tinted with red.

"How the fuck?!"

Carruthers staggered up, waving the knife dangerously, a demonic gleam in his eyes as he approached Declan from round the desk. Declan stared down at the knife and uselessly backed towards the door.

"You open the door I'll fuckin' cut you! Sit down!"

Declan backed into the chair, terrified, as his assailant hovered over him

"What are you doing here James? You're wanted…"

"Don't you think I know that? Look what you've driven me too!"

"What?!"

"Me. Attacking an old man. Leaving him for dead on his floor."

Declan shook his head, eyes wide in surprise.

"He's dead James, he died."

Carruthers eyes widened. "A murderer. You've made me a fuckin' murderer!!"

"How have I…"

"Shut up!! Shut up!!"

The maddening elderly man leaned in over Declan as he tried to disappear back into the seat. Carruthers stood back up, throwing one hand on his head while he dangerously waved the knife over Declan.

"All I wanted was to go out on a high, all I wanted was one final good story, one final time. It was a good story, a fuckin' great story, you hear me? A fuckin' great one! And you ruined it for me. You ruined my chance, my big, final chance. Why? Why did you stop me? Why did you not let me write one big, final piece on that bitch's family?! It was gold Declan, you see that?! You stupid bastard, it was gold!"

James turned away and Declan, sweating heavily, glanced at the window. The blinds were drawn. His eyes darted around the room looking for something, anything, to get him out of the predicament. James swung round again, holding the knife right at Declan's eyes.

"I knew my stuff, you see? I knew about good writing, good journalism, that story would have made the fuckin' paper unstoppable. It would have launched it properly, then I'd be gone, and you could do what you want. I wanted to HELP you, you see, HELP YOU!!"

"But you spurned me, asked me to write about cake sales, taxi spaces, a new motorway planned, when all the time I was sitting on a goldmine!"

James expression was a manic one, his arms flailed wildly but he kept a firm grip on the knife.

"And what was I reduced to?! Skulking and hiding in a cottage in Ashbourne, about to slit me own wrists… me, after all I've done. Then it came to me, it came to me."

Declan could feel his heart in his chest.

"What?" he stammered, mouth dry, bowels churning.

"That I'd be able to get away, take myself away from this, away from being hounded. But I'd confront you first, let you know one more time how much of a useless, self-important fucker you are. You know NOTHING! NOTHING!"

He swiped the knife back and forth in front of Declan's face, causing him to cry out in fear.

Carruthers laughed. "Well, it looks as if I have my big story, my big adieu, doesn't it?! And it's all your fault! All yours! You and this accursed shithole of what you call a paper. YOU could have just let me write it!"

"What happened James? With Old Tony?" Declan stammered, his heart palpitating furiously.

"He wouldn't give me any more information, I don't know, my mind, I drank a lot, I lost my cool, did he name me? He must have named me!" he seethed.

Declan nodded. "Old bastard. Well that fuckin' story has raked up another murder. There'll be two more!"

Declan's heart almost stopped. "Wh-what do you mean?!?"

"You think I can let you walk out here after this?! You think I can walk out of here after this?! We're fucked too, Mr. Editor. A fitting end to a murder story that started in 1902! This has consumed me; your staunch refusal to allow me to pursue this had dominated me, when I sleep and every waking second of my bloody day!"

Declan closed his eyes as he thought unthinkable thoughts; a tear escaped as the madman standing over him took control and was about to end both their lives.

"I'm taking myself out of this, but you're fucking coming with me!"

Declan opened his eyes again as James raised his hand over his head. He shook his head from side to side, mouthing 'no' repeatedly.

James had a look of venom in his eyes, a look of evil as the hand that gripped the knife shook.

'Any second… any second…'

Declan was stuck to the chair, too afraid to try and save his life. He closed his eyes, conjuring happy memories in his mind rather than stare at the manic face of the man about to claim his life.

Twenty Four

The unnerving calm was what struck Declan the most in those seconds. Life had slowed down, not a sound was to be heard. He felt warm, comfortable, secure, safe. His reaction to the fear of the inevitability of losing his life ceased. Memories that seconds ago thundered in his head, visions of people long gone, people he loved in the present, people he never got to say goodbye to, no longer concerned him. Serenity overcame him. Whatever happened him now would no longer matter. He shook his head, his eyes skewed tightly shut as he wished, begged, whatever God was there to grant him a few more seconds of this peace, a peace he had never felt in his life before.

'Please please please…'

There was a silence, a calm. He felt his mind lift, his body rise.

'Am I dead? Is this it? I sense nothing…'

He open his eyes slowly, wary, very afraid, not sure what he had heard, not sure whether he was alive or dead. The familiar wood panelled office filled his vision, the glare from the limp overhead bulb causing him to squint.

'Heaven…?'

He saw James Carruthers slumped against the wall in front of him, wheezing, the knife on the floor by his side as he clutched his chest with both hands. Fear was in the old man's eyes, as he reached out with a hand to his prisoner. Declan stood up, legs almost buckling under him, awash with relief and tears of joy. He was alive. Good God, he was alive! He let out an uncontrollable sob as his heart began to race once more.

The tables had been turned. James Carruthers was struggling to breathe. A heart attack? Declan looked at the helpless man, crumpled in a pathetic heap on the floor as all serenity and peace left him. Anger welled inside. Fear, betrayal, cowardice spite, hatred…

"YOU want me to help you? To help you?!" He shook, towering over the crippled and suddenly vulnerable man. More feelings rose from deep inside him; remorse and the most powerful, revenge. His mind churned as he lost control over these emotions. He lay kick after kick into the now hapless James Carruthers, not forcefully, but enough to satisfy his immediate outburst of anger before collapsing back into the chair, head in hands.

He gathered himself and reached for the phone.

"You better hope you die right there you old bastard."

Carruthers face was a sickly grey as his eyes rolled back into his head.

Declan held the receiver in his hand, watching the pathetic sight crumpled on the floor, gasping for breath; the very man who moments earlier could have ended his existence. His eyes shot open, they locked with Declan's as his rasps grew heavier, his eyes wider in fear, his mouth trying to pronounce unheard words. He reached a hand out, unashamedly and pathetically, begging for help from the man he was ready to kill.

Declan starred back at him.

'I'll leave him die. I'll let him die there, he would have let me…'

He put the phone back into the cradle and stood up as James rasped for help. He left the room, turning into the newsroom and staring at the yellow painted knight. He focused on the brush strokes, remembering the day they had carefully being painted on. He envisaged them being scrubbed off as the paper shut down and the office was taken over by another company. This is what lay ahead for the paper, his paper, if this path continued.

This was not how it should to be. This was not what he or the paper stood for. James had met his karma. That was sufficient. No need for anyone else to suffer. He returned to the room and dialled the emergency number as James began slipping into unconsciousness.

Darren waited outside The Forum offices as James was taken away in the ambulance and the scene recorded, along with the testimony of a very shaken Declan. He tried to urge the small crowd to disperse a few times, aiming his camera at the gathered faces, a deliberate move to intimidate. He had no time for gawkers at this scene. Curious faces began melting away as they realised they didn't want to be pictured near the scene. Declan and Eamon stood at the door for some more moments after exiting, talking as Declan indicated he had someone to take him home by gesturing at Darren. They shook hands and he approached Darren's car.

"Just get me out of this fuckin' place…"

Darren started the engine up. "You want a beer?"

"I want to go home, but, not yet?"

"We can just drive…"

"That sounds good."

They were silent as the car pulled away and turned down the dual carriageway. Darren eased the car to a halt at the lights and turned to his editor.

"Are you ok?"

"Yeah, yeah. I rang my folks, they want me to come home but I don't want to yet."

"What did the Guards say?"

"He's fucked, definitely now."

"Your word against his?"

"He mumbles to the paramedics once they calmed him down and treated him at the scene, told them and a Guard the basics, said he wanted it all to be over. Handed himself in, sobered up I guess and saw how lucky he was not to be left for dead."

Darren turned to him. "What do you mean?"

Declan continued to stare out the window.

"Nothing… "

Darren nodded, half understanding, half not wanting to know.

"What you going to do now?"

"Sleep tonight, sleep tomorrow. We've a paper to get out."

Darren turned to Declan, surprise etched on his face.

"Are you serious?!"

"Deadly."

"After all this?!"

"It's done isn't it?"

"Yeah but…"

"Yeah but nothing. I can put something, maybe, in the next edition, deal with it immediately and get back to work as soon as. Better that sitting at home."

"Counselling?"

"Offered to me."

"You should take it."

"I don't know, this thing began and ended so quick."

"Yeah and it'll hit you in five, ten, twenty years."

Declan grunted and gazed out the window. "I'll get through the next few days first."

"Don't mope now."

"I won't. I will act on it, I promise."

"Ok."

"Where we going?"

"Haven't a clue?"

"On the Phibsboro Road anyhow…"

"Keep going?"

"Nah don't be wasting your petrol."

"You want to get some food and eat it in the car or something?"

Declan smiled. "You know something, I'm suddenly starving."

"Adrenaline."

"Where's that?"

"What?"

"Adren… oh wait, sorry, though you were talking about some take away or something…"

Darren laughed as he drove the car past Cross Guns Bridge and turned up Leinster Street, pulling in at the side of a chipper.

"Come on, let's eat and we'll have it in the car."

"Maybe, I might go for a pint in Hedigan's after… if it's still on offer?"

Darren smiled.

Rowena sat staring at the Christmas tree, it's lights and collected decorations reminding her of better times.

"You think that's it?"

"Yeah. He's at death's door I hear, confessed anyhow," Michael answered.

"Poor Declan."

"I know. Couldn't believe it."

"What an evil prick."

"You know something, no-one would probably have known until one of us opened the office doors on Monday. Could have been Aidan, Darren, me…"

Rowena nodded. "Doesn't bear thinking about."

"He's going back as soon as the Guards are happy enough to let him continue. Wants to get a paper out as soon as, according to Darren."

"Are you for real?!"

"Yep. Says it will help him put a lid on it, he might make a statement in the paper, hopefully that will close it once and for all. Said he'd rather do it as soon as than wait. Get it done, enjoy Christmas if he even can, rather than let it slip into January, and Declan hates January! I kinda agree with him."

"Jesus."

Both were silent as Rowena leaned forward and stoked the fire she had lit that afternoon. Upstairs her daughter and friend played happily, blissfully unaware.

"What about you?" Michael eventually asked, sitting forward and clasping his hands, hoping his face was one of sincerity.

"Gonna have a drink tonight, keep Sandra out of school maybe, just the two of us. Do a lot of walking, praying."

"Don't let it ruin your Christmas."

"I won't, Jesus I won't, nothing will do that for me. Do you realise the relief I felt tonight when I heard the full story and knew that bastard was fighting for his life?! I hope he dies, Michael, I'm sorry if you think that's cruel but I hope he dies. He raked over the bones of my family to fulfil his own desires, one old fucker dead and another murder and cowardly suicide prevented by a heart attack that the right moment! I definitely believe in God now!"

"He was all wound up, had drank and smoked a shit load, fled from Old Tony's to Ashbourne in a taxi I heard, drank more, got a late cab back. His body just said 'fuck this' and kicked back. At the right time."

Rowena laughed and sat back in the chair.

"Instant Karma got him. I just hope he dies…"

Michael nodded and remained silent as the sound of laughter carried from upstairs.

"Do you fancy a drink?"

"Eh, ok, tea?"

"No a drink? I don't usually with Sandra at home but one will be ok. Just to help the nerves."

Michael nodded and watched her as she sprung from the chair and left the room.

Darren and Declan walked through his parents' front door to be greeted with an avalanche of hugs and tears.

"I needed to think mam, just for a bit."

"Have you not heard?" his father asked, ignoring the mild stench of beer from his son's breath. He deserved a pint or two.

"No?"

"Just on the nine o'clock news; a man arrested this evening on murder and attempted murder charges in an office in Finglas has died. Some Guard called up to tell you."

"Eamon or something?"

"That's the one. He's dead, son."

Declan and Darren exchanged glances. Wry but exhausted smiles crept onto their faces as they both accepted the offer of mugs of tea. Declan bowed his head, closed his eyes shut tight, a final effort to squeeze the horrible memory of that moment from his mind. He opened them, exchanged glances with Darren. He nodded and led the way into the kitchen.

Michael let Rowena bury her head in his shoulder as the presenter read the news report. She sobbed and sobbed.

"It's ok, it's over now..."

Michael fixed his gaze at the tv. A token camera outside the now deserted office with customary Garda standing watch outside. He thought of what his parents would say to him when he got home, how they would caution against returning and express utter shock. He knew what to say.

Rowena stood at a distance as the small group of mourners left the graveside, a priest dutifully fulfilling his obligations. She had to be there, she had to see the rotten old bastard dropped into the ground. She began to move away, through the corridors of forgotten tombs and overhanging trees blocking what little December light filtered through. She left the gates of Mount Jerome cemetery behind and went for her bus. Her mother, grandmother, great grandmother could rest again. She had a daughter to rear. As she waited, she opened her purse and smiled at a photo she always carried. Her, Mary and her mother. Happier times, time to make more memories.

Twenty Five

Declan closed the door behind the two Guards and went back upstairs to his office here the other staff members were still gathered.

"Wasn't so bad," Aidan surmised.

"He's confessed everything before he died anyway, not implicated anyone. Still, the paper's name will be linked for a while. I was delighted when the Guard said James said he was working off his own bat and not ours."

"A contrition as he stared death in the face?" Aidan wryly asked.

"If so, there was a modicum of decency in the man."

"Will we publish a statement?"

"I've drafted one that we're co-operating fully, the usual stuff. Just plough along. Try to put it behind us. I'll drop up to Rowena Brennan tonight, she's knows the gist anyway I gather?"

Michael nodded.

"Well I'll just confirm it's definitely over for her."

"How are you doing?" Darren asked.

"Just need to keep moving, I'll enjoy Christmas and see what the new year holds. If I stop it'll be the worse thing I can do."

Aidan nodded in agreement. "Look, if you do need a break, we can easily take over things."

"Typesetting?" Declan smiled.

"Ah for fuck sake… is there anyone we know…"

"Lads, I'll get this issue out, it's the last before the break. The break will do me good. We'll see what the new year holds."

"It's over, I just knew it when I heard the report first. For my own sake I couldn't relax 'til I saw the fucker's coffin drop into the ground. His part in this is in the ground with him. If some other hack wants to rake it up in another ninety-one years let them, I'll be dust by then," Rowena commented.

"He didn't offer much to the Guards before he died, about you like. Said he was working on a story, I'd be very surprised if they took it further. He was his own worst enemy. You just played a transient part," Declan replied.

"More than transient for me, I can tell you."

"I'm issuing a small statement, in the paper."

"I want no part of it, no mention, no nothing."

"I thought so."

"Just let it lie for me. Are you ok, after all, you know…"

Declan smiled and nodded, looking around the room, warm with a pre-Christmas glow and cosy fire lazing in the grate.

"Something I would never wish for anyone to go through but I will probably relive it at some point before I go see someone about it. All happened so fast. Thought my heart was about to burst. But, when I opened my eyes, and saw him there, helpless, begging, I was empowered… it gave me a strength to take command."

"You should of let him die there."

"The thought occurred, but, if I did, he wouldn't have told everything, the Guards would have had to dig to find why he was in that situation. Plus I like to think I'm a decent human being."

Rowena nodded. "A super human being for going through that! Good thinking though. I'm glad he's dead, well, seeing as we're being frank!" she laughed.

"Ah sure… think I'll give up this paper game," Declan smiled, eyes dropping to the carpet. Rowena's eyes widened.

"Ah no don't, youse do a great job."

He smiled and looked back at her, turning his empty mug round and round in his hand.

"Then again maybe not!"

He said his goodbyes and started up the engine of the car.

"Then again maybe I will…" he murmured as he drove off.

"Maybe I will…"

The next edition of The Forum hit the streets, a heartfelt, almost apologetic editorial from Declan summed up not only the area's horror, but their own abhorrence at having been associated with the perpetrator. Declan urged the readership to not let the actions of a staff member, working independently of the paper's directive, sully what they had built up in reputation. He recommitted himself to the production of a quality newspaper for the area and hoped the foul deed would not get in the way of the paper's evolution. Only time would tell. He wished for the year to be over.

Michael stood and applauded as Bohemians left the field, themselves milking the congratulations and plaudits having just beaten their great rivals Shamrock Rovers 2-0. The victorious red and black clad players shook hands with the defeated team in green and white hoops; victorious bodies grinned from ear to ear, fists pumped the air as the desolate opposition sauntered off the pitch, heads bowed, the jeers of defeat ringing in their ears. Today belonged to Bohemians. Fans exchanged salutations and slapped each other on the back as they bade farewell to Dalymount Park before Christmas. The towering floodlights, blazing down on the pitch stood guard, their warm glow indicating to all from miles around that battle had just finished. To the victor went the spoils; post match pints in the bars underneath the antiquated wooden stand never tasted so good. Hastily purchased Christmas presents of jerseys and scarves from the shop were tucked safely under coats as men and women sipped their drinks, discussing the on-field activities that they just witnessed, a zeal in the conversation that comes with every dismissal of a great rival.

On the walls, sepia-toned images of great teams of the past watched the celebrations carefully. Their ghosts mingled with those associated with the Bohemians of today. They watched from the walls, most wry smiles, arms folded, oiled hair, serious expressions, proud and defiant as they waited for the shutter to click. Their spirit would never die even if the bodies did.

Michael stood by the pitch for some moments, breathing in the fresh, sweet post-game scent of damp grass tinged with crisp, December air. A haze hung over the ground, foggy dews of condensation escaping from the mouths of excited spectators as they relived what they had witnessed in the ninety previous minutes.

The crowd were dispersing on the other terraces, away fans grumbling and facing into a Christmas with a derby defeat. Flags were untied from the red crush barriers on the terraces, their owners stepping carefully down the steps of the concrete tier as they sought to store them for another day, another battle. Very soon the individual bulbs of the giant floodlights would slip into darkness and the famous old ground would sleep until after Christmas.

Michael stood near the bar sipping his pint and chatting to an old friend from the nearby row of terraced cottages that sat in the shadow of the old ground. Victory was sweet, they exchanged Christmas greetings and he made his way out to the cold and damp lane behind the ground, turning down what was commonly and unofficially known as Dalymount Lane before stopping and looking back, the noise of regaling and joyous fans in the cosy bars echoing into the silent air. This was one of the good nights in Dalymount Park.

He turned around, walking slowly by long forgotten hulk of a mews that was partially hidden by the back garden wall of number 1 Dalymount. The dirty, scuffed and weathered bricks were long abandoned and stood silently, the usage within the walls long forgotten from modern memory. A thriving undertaker business was once run from the premises, the mews housing horses and carriages. Decades elapsed and generations of Bohemian FC and Ireland supporters filed past the neglected yet grand two storey edifice. Elegant, Victorian era brickwork still fought to shine and be noticed under almost a century of grime and desertion.

The match had been a form of escapism for Michael. He glanced back one more time as he entered onto the North Circular Road before continuing on his journey to catch the number 19 bus. A nice win. A nice few hours to forget the chaos of what had gone on in his life of recent.

Rowena decided to keep Sandra off school for the remaining few days before Christmas. It was a short week for the school but she reasoned on someone mentioning the murders to her daughter, who was all excited about the holiday. As she sat sipping tea on the back step, the wind whipping her hair into an unholy mess, she decided to ring the school first thing in the morning and tell them she was unwell. She would instead take her into Dublin to see the lights, maybe another trip to see Santy in Arnott's this time. She would shield her as best she could, praying that by the time she returned after the break the news would have blown over. She looked at the outline of the bird in the tree, just about visible in the dimming twilight and smiled.

'"You're a bastard, you know that, bird?!" she muttered. "Mock me, point at me. It's Sandra you'll never get. She'll have a good life away from this ..."'

Declan drove aimlessly, his mind questioning his decision to return to the paper the so soon, every word of this statement re-read in a tumultuous mind.

'Have I done the right thing? Have I said the right thing...?'

He turned off the road at Violet Hill, passing two abandoned and hidden whitewashed cottages, the only remaining trace of the once thriving village at Finglas Bridge, itself long swallowed up by progress. He drove up the hill, past the house where rumour told about the woman who kept her daughter locked up. He grinned as he remembered the story, another mysterious tale of the area; whether true or not, he pondered whether someone would try and pursue it in the future, just as James Carruthers had done. Would more lives be ruined, would a future editor of The Forum have a decision to make on a story that no-one else probably cared about?

He continued in silence past Washerwoman's Hill, the Botanic Gardens and onto the Phibsboro Road. He replayed the recent events in his mind again and again, trying above anything to convince himself that the worst was over; that the paper would move on and leave the stagnant episode of James Carruthers behind. It would be good to be free of him. The young team he had assembled worked well together, mature for their age. There would be no more worrying about whose door James was about to knock on, no preparations for fraught arguments he knew would happen on certain days. No embarrassment as he stumbled through the door, dishevelled and unshaven, reeking of stale beer and still drunk. James was dead. That nasty chapter of the paper's existence was buried with him.

'The paper will be ok, won't it? Won't it?'

He continued on through Phibsboro, passing a 19 bus travelling in the opposite direction laden with Bohemian football supporters returning home. Past Doyle's Corner, Broadstone, Temple Cottages, Constitution Hill and onto the quays where he crossed the Liffey and turned onto Usher's Quay. Traffic was light, the roads quiet. The unique smell of the hops from the Guinness brewery reached his nose as he wound the window down slightly. For all his years he was rather unfamiliar with this part of the city. He noted the street

253

names with interest and filed them away in his mind. He drove past Usher's Island, the decaying shells of once grand houses that evolved into tenements just about standing, their roofs long gone, exposed interior walls damp and dank, the faint remnant of wallpaper once carefully picked and later admired fading away with no-one to notice.

He swung a left onto Watling Street, another left onto Island Street.

On one side a block of boxy old flats, on the other premises of various descriptions behind crumbling walls; faded lettering on iron gates hard to read now. He continued driving, up past the Gothic splendour of John's Lane. He stopped finally at Christchurch, parking the car in a decrepit plot of land that served as a car park, serviced by a man with a limp who promised the sun moon and stars. He walked down the steep hill and stood under Christchurch's famous arch. From somewhere, maybe within, he could hear a carol service. It comforted him, attributed him the solace he sought in his mind.

He slipped into the building and, for the first time in years, picked a silent pew and began to pray. He sought deliverance from the scene that day in the office which seemed to be re-running on a loop in his mind; forgiveness for the desire to leave James Carruthers flailing helplessly on the floor, guilt for having put himself in that position in the first place, regret for the episode that had affected his small staff, anger for perhaps ruining the life of an innocent single mother, all the time seeking answers as to whether he handled it well enough.

Most of all he begged for strength. The strength to stand tall, to rise from his knees and continue with not only his cherished newspaper but also with his life. Insecurities coursed through his veins, he gritted his teeth and clenched his clasped palms together repeating 'please please please' again and again in his mind.

'It wasn't meant to be like this, all I wanted was to start a small paper, it wasn't meant to be like this…'

Again and again he begged for the strength to continue.

'It would be easy to walk away, wouldn't it Lord? To just close down the place and melt into obscurity. But they'd know in the village though, they know me, my family, would they point or stare, would they whisper… what would they think of me… 'there he is, look, the editor, his journalist killed a man, wasn't it awful… that young girl lives up off Jamestown, ah you knew her ma…'

They will tut behind me in the supermarket, in the street, in the pub. Lord, I need help…'

The angelic vocals from the carol service weakened his resolve. He bowed his head, let go and silently weeped.

He held back no more, he needed this release.

He needed this paper, by God he needed it so much, it must move on from this, it simply must. But could he?

Christmas morning was beautiful and clear, a crisp, a serene frost, still air and gentle mist that benefited the day. Greetings were exchanged with neighbours as Rowena and Sandra left the house for morning mass. Jovial offers of lifts were politely declined, the morning was very pleasant and the sharp, cold air would do her and her daughter the world of good.

Sandra was excited about the visit of Santa the night before; whether she was continuing to act or genuinely believed Rowena didn't care. She delighted in listening to the patter of feet run down the stairs in the early hours, the slight click of the light switch and the barely audible gasp of pleasure and surprise. Small moments, a brief moment which may never come again but one in which Rowena mouthed a silent 'thank you' to her mother and sister as she threw back the covers and lazily put on her dressing gown.

The frost added a Christmas card look to the shiny morning. Rowena couldn't remember a white Christmas, the closest she got was delightful mornings like this one. She took a deep breath and exhaled slowly as he daughter skipped along beside her. Beautiful, just beautiful. The angled and abandoned old house once owned by a manager of the industrial estate whose ground it was built in peaked out over the ugly concrete wall, its roof tinged with a soft white. She often wondered what would become of the house. She could never remember anyone living it in but often you could see window blinds, yellowing and still, unmoved for years. Behind it, the yellow crane that cumbersomely moved huge mental tanks around the depot glistened in its own covering of frost. She remembered staring at the crane moving as a child, fascinated, but as she grew up it became just one of those things; always there and probably always would be.

As they passed the little newsagent, open this Christmas morning such was the savvy of the elderly owner, knowing panicked parents would need batteries, she smiled as she recalled how her unexpected pregnancy and ultimately Ben's death put paid to the little job she managed to wrangle in there.

The shop hadn't changed; perhaps another one of those things that would always be there.

As they approached the village she told her little girl again that her ancestors once lived in a tidy cottage near the church. She asked her to close her eyes and picture the scene, a real quiet village. Sandra stopped and squeezed her eyes shut.

"I can see it mammy, I can see it! So old!"

Rowena laughed. "Well on the way to the church after the graveyard I'll show you where I think it was, would you like that?"

"Yes mammy, thanks!"

They crossed the footbridge, turned back towards the dual carriageway and followed the path by the two tiny cottages until they were at the steps of the old graveyard. Cautiously they climbed, frost still packed onto the old steps.

The Nether Cross greeted them in the morning chill, it's severed pieces clamped together, an instant reminder of the time Oliver Cromwell's troops passed through the village but continued on without incident. It still stood this day, and would for many more Christmas mornings as the village continued to change.

Rowena led her daughter silently to a neat grave near the wall. She placed the small selection of winter blossoms on the grave and said a silent prayer. Sandra read the inscriptions on the headstone, counting back the years as she did every time, the names fading slowly as the years rolled back.

"Mammy, is there more people buried in here than are named?"

Rowena blessed herself, kissed her two forefingers and tapped the headstone with them. A ritual she always carried out.

"Well my Mammy Annie and sister Mary, Granny Lily and Grandad Bill, her mammy Rowena and her mother, Lily too or Elizabeth. Probably a few more in there but that's all I know of."

"What about your daddy?"

"He's with his own mammy and daddy love, he wanted to be buried with them," Rowena squeezed her daughter's arm tighter.

"Is there any more room in the grave?"

"Don't know sweetheart, it's very old."

"Where you will go Mammy?"

Rowena laughed and again hugged her daughter close to her.

"Hey, you little messer, it's Christmas Day, don't be worrying or thinking about that, y'hear?!"

Sandra smiled. "Only asking!"

"Why though?"

"I think it's lovely isn't it, that the whole family are together?"

She took a hasty look around the graveyard. She had such a history here. Funeral after funeral, drunken nights crying over her mother's grave, the last place she saw Ben alive and the place where her daughter was conceived. She wondered if the ghosts were wandering the stones, looking at her now, smiling, calling out, or just silently watching. One day she would know. One day so far away.

She shuddered and took Sandra's hand. "Let's go love, we'll be late for mass and I have enough of graveyards and the dead this Christmas."

She led her to the gate once more. As she stopped to let an elderly couple enter, bidding them a swift salutation of the day as she did, she glanced over at Rosehill House, taking in a sight that the bones of those resting behind her would have also seen when they visited the graveyard in their time at Christmas. The village had changed, but that one, tiny, insignificant line of sight remained. She smiled and thought of her relatives, at peace in the earth behind her. Christmas Day and family, wasn't that what it was all about? She glanced back at the grave again. Family. She looked at her own little girl, placing her hand on her shoulder and guiding her down the steps as they crossed the carriage way and made their way up the main street for mass, but not before stopping in front of the red-brick office building and telling her daughter all about the old cottage that once stood right there.

Father O'Brien led the packed church in prayer and hymn. The sun beamed through the tall, narrow windows as tiny atoms of dust danced in their light. The creaking confession boxes that smelled constantly of varnish welcomed the bright light that illuminated their dark exterior. Children randomly played with whatever new toy they were allowed to bring out of the house as Sandra read one of the many brass plates on the pew, asking for prayers for those long since departed. Rowena always thought of those names at Christmas, people she never knew but whose names became familiar to her over the years as she attended mass with her mother and sister. Who were they? Where did they live? Did anyone care anymore?

The elderly parish priest gave his blessing and the congregation filed down the narrow centre aisle before forking into two separate doors.

Outside, laughter and chatter filled the air; the condensation of conversation forming a haze over the freshly cut and combed heads of the men and new hairdos of the women. A scene that occurred every Christmas morning in the village. As the years declined, the faces grew older, eventually disappearing. Families dispensed in different directions, down by the carpark at the back of the church past the abandoned parochial house, down the main street, across the iron bridge which passed the graveyard, through the lane separating the church from the local girls school, the delightful mural painted years before by Declan's father being ignored, but this time by excited children and mothers hoping the meat wouldn't be ruined in the oven.

Rowena exchanged greetings with a neighbour, chatting for some moments under the cacophony of church bells. She occasionally glanced up at the bells, well hidden in the tower and clanging a joyful tune from underneath a pointed, copper-green roof topped off with a cross.

Her mind drifted away from the conversation the Christmas Eve following Ben's death; no matter what Mary did, Rowena could not come out of her stupor. Mary had made the house cosy, lit fires in both downstairs rooms and played some Christmas records before tuning in a carol service on the radio. She was upbeat, making sure Rowena had a task around the house, offering to accompany her to his grave should her younger sister wish. She remembered her younger self smiling, sheepishly and with pain, as she appreciated what her sister was doing and tried to keep up with her good cheer. This would be the last Christmas with just the two of them, the following year Rowena would have her baby. The thought terrified her, but she was strangely subdued. She thanked Mary, had dinner with her and they sat together in front of the fire watching television. She could have rebelled, curled into herself, but she remembered the eerie peace as the carol singers drifted to their door.

She wished her sister a goodnight as they let the last embers of the fire fade away and she went to her room, took out some paper and began writing.

Scrawling at first, then a structured story. She thought about scribbling out the scrawlings, but left them, taking random words and constructing a feverishly wrought story, amateurish, hastily thought out episode set around the very same church on a Christmas Eve.

As the neighbour continued to speak of her husband's ailments, and how she thanked God he is out of hospital for 'the Christmas', Rowena tried to piece together the long forgotten memory.

The plot, if there was one, was buried in her mind, but if was about a mother and her child; maybe she wrote it as a solace in the early stages of her own pregnancy as she and Mary faced and uncertain new year, one that would ultimately bring joy but at the time it scared the hell out of them.

'The Christmas Bell', Rowena silently mouthed as the neighbour warbled on. She nodded her head when required, maintaining eye contact as she recalled the church bell falling in the story. She couldn't think of any more but it was a solemn link to a past where she was at her most vulnerable. But she remembered the effect it had on her as she dotted the final sentence and sat back on the bed. She read and re-read her piece, feeling something dark lift from her, as if that self-penned piece just flowed from her mind and was cathartic in channelling her doubts, her pent up and buried sorrow.

She smiled to herself at the feeling. She drifted off to sleep and awoke the following morning; bright, crisp and sunny just like the present day, and for the first time since those awful few weeks, she smiled at her sister and hugged her warmly. She could feel Mary shake as they embraced, holding onto each other for some moments but enough to allow Mary a brief release. It was a good Christmas, she remembered. Uncertain times ahead but a nice few days.

Out of the corner of her eye two faces grabbed her attention. Ben's now elderly father she recognised instantly despite his shock of white hair and unhealthy colour, but the woman; his mother? Was that Mrs. Hedderman? She looked so old, much older. Her heart leapt. There they were talking to a woman of similar age. There they were facing another Christmas without their son, another Christmas without the knowledge that they had a grandchild. The wafer-thin memories of her short story came into her mind again as she glanced down at her daughter, and back at Ben's parents.

The neighbour bade her a Merry Christmas, Rowena replied likewise but was relieved she was gone. She stood on that spot for some moments, eyeing up Ben's folks. She squeezed her gloved hand on her daughter's shoulder, who in turn looked up and smiled at her mother.

Family.

She glanced back in the direction of the old abbey and graveyard, hidden behind the overgrown memorial and rusty green railings.

'Isn't this is what Christmas is all about… family…'

She thought of her own family all at peace in the graveyard. She thought of Ben, lying alone up in Glasnevin, maybe a journey too far for the frail couple.

They nodded and shook hands with the woman they were talking to and made to turn round for home. Another old Finglas family. Generations of the Hedderman family had lived in the area, just like her own family. Rowena glanced back towards the graveyard again. She knelt down to meet Sandra's eyes.

"Sandra, do you remember me telling you about your daddy, and how he died, long ago?"

"Yes Mammy," she replied, eager to get home and back to her toys.

"Well I'm just after seeing his own mammy and daddy over there, and they don't know about you…"

She stopped suddenly. What was she doing?! Why now?! She looked back at Ben's parents, moving slowly away, his father's arm around the mother.

Sandra looked up, turning her head around. Her eyes widened excitedly.

"What do you mean Mammy?"

Rowena remained silent, a variety of scenes playing through her mind. The value of a family had been going through her mind a lot since the hassle with James Carruthers. What was there to lose? What was there to gain though? She could very well easily confuse her daughter and bring back heartbreak for Ben's parents. She glanced back at them again.

'They deserve to know about their granddaughter…'

She automatically took her daughter's hand and approached the elderly couple. Her heart thumped and she could feel it's sickening, unnerving taste in her mouth. This would either solve a lot of issues for both her and her daughter, or blow any solace they and Ben's elderly parents had acquired since his death. *'What am I doing? What am I doing?'*

Despite the cold morning air, beads of sweat formed on Rowena's forehead. She stopped just as she reached the elderly couple. She ran her tongue across her lips as Sandra looked quizzingly up at her mother.

Rowena swallowed hard, looked down and smiled at her daughter. She had to try. They deserved to know.

"Excuse me, Mr. and Mrs. Hedderman?"

IV

1902

Twenty Six

Matthew Whyte was missed at work. His money was missed in both Upper and Lower Flood's as it was in Heery's.

Neighbours reported hearing an argument. Gossip reached fever point as the burly men of the village assisted when Constable Scollard broke down the door of the cottage while others watched. The stench caught the RIC man unawares, the sight that greeted him in the chaotic small room enough to send him aghast against the wall, searching for a hankerchief to cover his mouth. Joseph Ryan arrived in behind him.

"Oh sweet Jesus," the doctor muttered, exchanging horrified glances with the young constable. "Close the door!" he ordered, repeating the order more forcefully as the shaken constable clambered to shut the door. "Constable, we need to find his daughter."

Scollard shook his head wildly, and stood up straight, smoothing his uniform as he urged the doctor to keep the door shut behind him. He stepped out into the sunlight again, women still wearing shawls of mourning for Robert Hart, questions angled at him by varying voices as he kept his head bowed and urged them to make way as he begun the brief journey to the barracks.

"Look at his face!" a middle-aged woman gasped.

"He's after findin' him dead, isn't he! Is he dead Constable?"

"The peeler's after findin' him dead!"

"Another one, another one dead!"

The voices blended into a communal shout of random declarations of anger as he kept his pace. William Scollard was beginning to curse his posting to this supposedly 'quiet hamlet'. How he longed to return to his native Kerry with his wife and infant child. Finglas was meant to be a handy number, the odd labour dispute, a fine for drunkenness, a slap on the wrist for those living in dirt by the graveyard. Not two murders, possibly now three by an unknown hand.

He removed his helmet as he wiped the sweat from his brow and ascended the few steps up to the barracks. Standing against the door frame of the small porch, Sergeant Linden's face was as pale as his constable who didn't need to update him on the latest development. "Another?"

"Dead sir, but, no sign of a wound that I could see. Head wasn't twisted either, like the Farnham patient. The doctor's with him, could be natural?"

"He was a heavy drinker and hard worker, so that's true. Was his daughter around?"

"No sir."

"We'll have to find her. Check up in Jamestown House, she does some hours there from time to time. Anything else?"

"His belt was undone, he was in a bedroom."

Sergeant Linden nodded grimly.

"I'll go down to the house, you get on up to Mrs. Devine and see if you can find her. Rowena's her name, the daughter. Jesus Christ, William, we have to get to the bottom of this to appease that mob out there. That lot don't understand the extent of how we have to do things. They just want results, blood even. We need to solve this. I don't want to end up like William Rogers," Scollard added, referencing an unpopular predecessor who fell foul of the locals, he and his family burnt out of the original barracks that now served as the tenement at the bottom of the main street.

Constable Scollard nodded, donned his helmet and mounted his bicycle, scooting around the corner and up towards Jamestown House as the gathered mob hollered after him. Sergeant Linden took a deep sigh and glanced out the window at the angry and frightened villagers. The pockets of men talking in a huddle through cigarette smoke worried him.

Rowena instructed the hackney driver where to take them as they climbed onto the cart in the early morning sunshine. The driver looked her companion up and down, his face half hidden by a growth of a beard, a cap pulled low over his eyes. Rowena noticed his interest.

"My cousin," she described.

The driver looked back at her, eyes narrowing and shrugged, signalling the horse to move. He didn't care once he had the fare. He didn't need any aired suspicions to come back on him, the peelers needn't know about his alcohol scam. He decided to keep silent and declare ignorance. Not his problem.

The male passenger closed his eyes in relief as they pulled away from the village, past Rose Hill House, the Farnham Lodge gate house and the woods. Down towards the tiny village where the stream met the Tolka, the cart ambling past quietly and dutifully, one of many to approach the bridge on any given day.

He looked away from them, towards the sound of the gushing Tolka, back-dropped by plentiful trees of deepest green and felt his mind slip, just as before, unconsciously, to a scene he was not sure was happening. His eyes narrowed as they focused on an old mill sitting by the river right in front of him, but only existing in his mind's eye. Faceless folk stood outside, mill sacks on their humped backs as the daylight shone brightly. The river gushed loudly with authority, yet with a peaceful serenity he wished he could escape to. The men looked toward him but past him, signalling to others unseen. A peaceful moment, not like the violent, abrasive one of the Maypole he conjured previously.

He lowered his head and pressed the palms of his dirty hands into his eyes, raising his head slowly back onto the scene, but it had vanished. He lowered his head again as they passed the row of tiny cottages and the Royal Oak pub before the curving road took them over the bridge as they began a gentle ascent past the big cemetery within whose walls prince and pauper lay side by side. The ghosts of O'Connell and Parnell continued their powerful orations to the pale shadows of their fellow deceased; their words going unheard amongst the living and the heroes of tomorrow who would one day rest alongside the fallen leaders of the past.

Parnell lay at rest above unknown quantities of cholera corpses, Rowena's ancestors among them. Dumped, without ceremony, to rot and be forgotten for all eternity? Pointing to the sky, the round tower over O'Connell's crypt kept watch over the landscape, a sentinel to those interred around it. He closed his eyes and felt his tired mind slip once again, the sounds of hammering and random orders barked in his ears. Workmen long gone chipped away with crude tools as they perched cautiously on scaffold as the tower rose slowly from the ground. People stopped to watch as they walked by, relatives of those buried craned a sorrowful neck skyward in awe of progress. In his mind he could see the scene clearly, but as he opened his eyes and all was gone; quiet, eerie in the early dawn. Had he been there, just as he was at the old mill or at the fight by the Maypole? Where they real events, real events in which he bore witness too? He bowed his head, trying to make sense of the senseless.

'What is happening to me now…'

Rowena nudged him from his thoughts, leaning in and smiling to his face. She winked. "It's going to be better now, just you and me and the future. No-one can touch us again…"

He wondered where they were heading though he knew his road took them into the city. His heart felt joy at the prospect. He was moving away from the village. Regrettable, though necessary, but he was heading into unknown territory with the very reason for his abandoning of the chosen village, that damned girl with the hold over him.

He was in enough danger because of her. He thought back to the woods, when he had failed to resist her once more. He should have, but he couldn't. He dropped his head lower at the thoughts, the consequences. But she was beautiful. What had he done?

Phoebe Hedderman stood watching Rowena and her companion climb on board the cart in the early morning air. There was something about him. Something familiar; she could not see his face from her position outside her home but there was something. His walk, his gait, his height alerted her senses. She shushed the crying child in her arms as she watched him take his seat beside her old friend.

'That walk…'

She remembered being approached by a stranger outside Heery's.

'Ah it can't be…'

He asked did she know Rowena Whyte.

'But he's long gone, isn't he, he must be…'

Rowena and the most wanted man in Dublin, together. Still in Finglas.

'Holy mother of Jesus…'

She walked forward as the cart pulled off, stopping outside the entrance to Rose Hill House, watching as they crept away slowly. That was him. That was the stranger. She stood rooted as gentle whirls of dried dirt whipped up under the wheels.

"Girl, what are you doing?"

She darted around, following the voice. Mr. Bayly was at the gates of Rose Hill House.

"What are you doing girl?" he demanded a second time. He always went for a walk first thing and was surprised to see one from the tenement just standing there. He was suspicious.

"Sorry, sir, I just…"

"Just what? Speak up?"

"That man, on the cart. I know him from somewhere."

Mr. Bayly's brow furrowed as he followed her gaze, not that he could see much from that distance.

"Well what about it? What about him? A labourer?"

"I've seen him before, up by Heery's sir."

"And?"

"He was a stranger, he asked me a question."

"What are you saying girl? What is your name?"

"Hedderman, Phoebe Hedderman, sir."

"Well what are you saying Phoebe?"

"He was a stranger, he asked me, some days ago, about the girl he's gone off on the cart with, Rowena Whyte sir, just before the murders started."

Mr. Bayly's eyes widened.

"You didn't recognise him, at all, from the village, when he spoke to you at first?"

"No, no sir, he was a stranger, he spoke very differently. I couldn't see his face just there but his height, his walk, the same."

Mr. Bayly stood beside her.

"You're from in there, aren't you?" he asked, gesturing with his eyes back to the flaking paint of the White House.

"The old barracks? Yes, sir."

"Are you a truthful girl?"

"I am sir, yes…"

Her expression was one of surprise tinged with horror. Something had startled her. Charles Bayly looked back up the hill of the main street at the scant people out and about in the early morning.

"I think you must talk to the authorities," he ventured.

Phoebe looked back at him, her blue eyes wide with excitement and dread.

"Should I?"

"Yes, yes of course; a terrible thing has happened in this village of recent, if you have some suspicions we must let the authorities know?"

"Yes, yes sir, let me bring the baba back first though."

Bayly nodded. "One thing, Phoebe…"

"Sir?"

He looked down at the ground, and clasped his hands behind his back.

"You are going to tell the police some serious things, alright? Brush your hair, have a wash and change your dress, or I will give you one from inside if you wish. Too many times the poor have been dismissed.

"Make yourself presentable, that dirty dress simply won't do. I'll accompany you to the station. Maybe best not tell anyone else inside, yes? Not even your family?"

She nodded. "Thank you sir."

She scurried back inside the building. His voice was comforting, assuring. She felt safe. Confident. Charles looked across at the two-storey dwelling adjacent the graveyard. He had never liked the place, never liked the people who lived inside the fourteen room dwelling and who threw the contents of their chamber-pots and rubbish over the wall of the cemetery. He would prefer if it was pulled down. His own family had a vault in the graveyard and here was this precious place of rest sullied by the carry on of vagrants. He recalled the night in April eleven years earlier, when the building was an RIC barracks. A constable became trapped inside when the two-storey building was set alight, perishing, his grave not far from Charles' own family vault.

He loved this area, had lived in Rose Hill house almost thirty years and he had invested heavily in its land. If trusting an inhabitant of that awful tenement was what it took to rid the village of the recent curse that befell it recently, then so be it. He didn't want to bear witness to another public upheaval on the forces of law and order.

Rowena paid the driver the two shillings and seven pence fare for her and her companion as they disembarked at Cross Guns Bridge.

"And something else?" the driver, a heavy set bearded man asked, his hand out for the customary tip.

"Never trust strangers," she winked, "especially those who know about your distilling racket and that you visit a certain lady every once in a while, you wouldn't want your wife finding out, would you?"

The driver stared at her for a second, glancing at her companion who sheepishly looked down at the cobblestones.

"I have my secrets…" he began as he flicked the reins, "and you have yours. Let's keep it that way."

He took another glance at the mysterious person with her. He studied him for a few moments before turning the carriage around and continuing on the return journey. Paranoid thoughts of extortion and blackmail filled his mind as he considered what certain others in the village may do should they find out he was the recipient of a substantial reward.

'To hell with it. Not my problem. I'm happy with things as they are…'

The carriage completed its turn and he began the drive back to the country village, his suspicions as insignificant as the sight of another horse and trap on the country road that morning. Rowena took her companion by the hand and led him across the cobblestones.

He looked in awe at the road ahead, filled on either side with elegant and identical red brick houses, the noise of early 20th century business and activity filled the air. The countryside had given way to a small metropolis. Smaller streets branched off along this main road. Horses with carts clopped and trundled by, piles of dung spread around the shiny cobblestones as an oncoming tram dinged and approached with haste.

Behind him people sat lazily by the Royal Canal, children jeering an elderly man, dressed in too heavy clothing for a fine summer's morning, as he sat on the bank, ignoring, or perhaps failing to hear, their hastily arranged songs berating him. He sat quietly, staring down the waterway as it pierced a gentle path towards the sea.

Rowena led him further down the busy street towards a large junction, passing shops selling a variety of wares as the well dressed and those in labourers attire mingled. Tidy, identical cottages lay to his right as he spun his head around repeatedly, trying to take in everything possible. At their doors, some women stood chatting, occasionally glancing up at the new arrivals before returning to the strands of their conversation. Brass doorknobs were cleaned with gusto, urchins running to and fro shouting and playing, criss-crossing women in elegant clothing floating past them with ease. Tucked behind the cottages lay the tram sheds where unseen drivers and conductors met, drank tea and studied timetables before they clocked on for their busy shift. There was far more people in this town, people who didn't pay him a second glance or care who he was. He felt a surge of freedom.

Rowena grabbed his hand and led him further across the cobblestones, past the gentry on their morning stroll who looked upon her with disgust. He tried to draw a response from her but she said nothing, just continued on, her grip on his wrist strong. They left the row of cottages behind, sturdier and more modern than the ones back in Finglas as she led him to the crossroads at Dunphy's Corner where the public houses did a roaring trade. As the road continued past the junction and on towards the viaduct, the curves of the mountains loomed more clearly now as they sat neatly between grand houses either side of the road as it stretched toward the city.

His sense of freedom surged, his confidence grew and another feverish spell of giddiness overcame him. A quick slip here, a run down that street there, and he could, he would, be free!

"Look!" Rowena's delighted squeal pulled him from his thoughts.

"What?" he asked, confused.

She let go of his wrist, and pointed to the window of the public house on the corner. He walked over a few steps. A playbill. He looked back at her.

"Look!" she urged.

He moved in closer.

He felt the colour drain from his face as he slowly read the heavily-printed letters. Simple words, but strong in their meaning. The sketch was accurate, minus the beard growth he how wore. Height, weight estimation, all canningly accurate. Underneath, in big, imposing letters was printed;

WANTED
REWARD OFFERED

"Didn't I tell you? Didn't I tell you to trust me?"

She smiled gleefully as he stared at her. His heart beat heavily. He ran his fingers over his light beard.

"Oh do you not think they haven't thought of that? Why do you think they've shaded in a beard on the sketch?"

He studied the etching once more.

"There's more on the poles over there, and the shop window over there…"

She pointed vaguely in various directions, his paranoia palpable.

"I am offering you safety. But you must tell me your secret. Come now, let's go! It's time!"

She tugged hard at his wrist as they turned right, up a similarly busy road adorned with quaint shop-fronts and dominated by a huge church that lay ominously ahead of them, forking the road in two and with scaffolding surrounding the spire as tiny workmen feverishly toiled to complete the construction. As they walked up towards the church a number 19 tram emerged from the depot, clanging a stark warning as the driver waved at the two pedestrians to move out of his way. Standing at the back and holding on tightly the conductor peered down at them from under his peaked cap, his ticket machine swung neatly across his great coat as a soldier would do preparing for inspection.

He locked eyes with the male stranger, noticing his bemused expression, before turning to walk through the carriage and converse with his driver. At the entrance to the depot, similarly attired men stood near idle, grand trams, smoking and laughing. The skyline was carved by electric cables stretching toward the city. He smiled wanly at the lone tram as it trundled by and made way for it's destination.

'Beautiful…' Noise. Business. Life. He liked it here, but he knew every step, every person who glanced at him, a stranger in this town too, added to his peril.

"I know a place we can stay for the night."

"What?" He stopped in his tracks, the sense of dread returning. No, no, now he was to be free of her.

"Stay. For the night. We'll be safe. No-one can touch us, while you're with me, you know that? You need to protect me now."

"Protect you? What do you mean?" he asked.

She smiled and moved in close to him.

"Protect me. I'm safe now, amn't I? And Daddy, he can't hurt us anymore. We can do what we want. He won't hurt me again."

Two women dressed in unseasonable heavy, dark clothing and wearing hats worthy of an upper social standing passed silently by, watching them and passing whispered comment before they crossed the road, gentlemen doffing caps in recognition as the duo continued on their journey back to Halligan's Dairy on the road to the city.

Rowena ran on carelessly, her hair trailing back in the freshening wind that had whipped up as they passed a row of grand houses with large gardens to the front. Thick, mature trees, bursting with summer foliage loomed out over the railed walls, casting vast circular shadows across the path and onto the cobblestones. She stopped at the entrance to a lane that sat snugly between two such houses. The cobblestones continued up the narrow thoroughfare that she led him up as she hummed a distant tune to herself. The top of the lane opened up to reveal a sports field with a small wooden tiered stand. To their left, at the very end of a back garden, sat an odd two-storey building, an elegant mews, with fine brickwork and finish. A long window-like opening sat atop the structure, right in the middle and set in behind three tiers of a brick frame. This unusual and ornate building stood out from the house which it sat behind.

"We'll stay the night here, maybe bit longer than one night," Rowena suggested.

"In here?" he asked surprised.

"Better than the woods, do you think? We can hide here. No-one will look here. And you can protect me. We'll be very safe. The old woman keeps horses here and carriages. She does funerals you see, she lives here with her daughter in that big house there," she explained, pointing to the house that shared the garden.

"Daddy knew her, did some work for her a few years ago. She's old, kind, foolish. She'll never know we're here."

"Are you not going to ask her to stay?"

Rowena laughed. "Oh you silly man, the police are looking for you, aren't they? I can't ask her, I won't ask the old bitch. We can sneak in, stay, then we'll move on maybe, find a better place, an old house that no-one lives in. That can be our house, maybe we'll follow the little canal, sail a little boat down," she smirked, "and we could sip ale with the other tramps who sit at night drinking under the big viaduct, though if you were to be found they'd hang you from it, so best stay with me, right?"

He remained impassive as he cursed her again.

'Am I being naïve? How can she be in command of this?'

The grounds were quiet, a carriage sat inside the building and two horses, silently eyeing the new arrivals. Distant shouts of children echoed from the school at the far end of the lane and houses behind. It was a very built up area. He was taking a great risk.

"Enough!" he barked, wrestling his wrist away from the young girl's grasp, almost sending her tumbling in the process.

"What are you doing?!" Rowena hissed.

"I am going away on my own. Do not follow me again. You have done enough for me, you have drawn me into too much already, I do not need this, I must be on my own."

Rowena shook her head slowly, mockingly, and circled him.

"Oh you fool, after all I have done for you, all I have helped you, hidden you, fed you, and you're going to leave me helpless in the big city?"

"I must go."

"Oh go, then, go on, go… but you don't know this city. You don't know it at all. You don't know anything, do you?"

"I know enough."

"You'll be found and jailed, if you're not caught first by angry mobs!" she whispered and grabbed his hand, placing it on her lower stomach.

"Think of the baba, think of the little baba…"

He looked at her flat stomach then at her eyes which blazed.

He pulled his hand away.

"You cannot be with child."

"Oh I can. Our baba you see, a magic baba from a magic man."

"You cannot be," he repeated calmly.

She moved closer, her eyes boring into him, her breath reeking in short gasps as she whispered "But I am. I am. I have been left with child and you need to stay with me. I know! I KNOW!!"

He turned to walk down the lane.

"No! No! Don't run away bastard, I need you now! You have a responsibility!"

He stopped. Primitive bitch. "You are not with child. Leave me be."

"I am you bastard, I am!"

"Your body is not showing, how can you know?"

"My Mama said she knew I was growing inside her the moment I was put there, I know too, I can feel the baba."

"You are foolish," he retorted, "you are young."

'What if she is... I should never have. Time to end this'

"I am a woman! I know you, bastard! You must stay with me. You must. I will be locked away, in a fucking mad house for being with child. You have to stay with me. Do you understand? It's me and you now, forever! No-one will help me. If you help me I'll help you. Remember what I know about you!"

Her words ran through his mind. "Run away then, run away!" Rowena shouted after him, her shrill voice echoing down the lane. "But I'll tell them. I'll them all. The fairy fort. I saw everything! I'll tell them! I'll tell them exactly what I saw, the whole palaver!"

He stopped, turned and walked with intent back to her as she stood rooted, visage alive with the threats she had just made. He grabbed her two wrists with such force her face jolted in shock. He slammed her against the wall of the mews, causing her to cry out in pain. Anger rose within him.

"The fairy fort! Tell me what you know!"

Her face remained rigid as he bore over her, his height intimidating her, his face gnarled in question and disdain. Her eyes darted around, trying to see behind him. All she could see was a dog, licking sporadically at the cobbles, glancing up at them occasionally

Her ears listened for other voices, a cough, anything to alert someone and stack the cards in her favour again. He squeezed her wrists. They hurt.

"Answer me you stupid woman, the fairy fort?"

Frightened as she was with this sudden turn of events, her face broke into a smile and a laugh, irking him as he shook her violently.

"Tell me what you mean! I know of the fairy fort. Tell me what you know of it!" He eyeballed her, his clenched teeth and snarling face right up into hers. "Tell me what you know, once and for all and we can put an end to this!" He had to hear her words. He must know for definite now what she knew. Enough was enough.

She stood on her toes, her stained teeth forming a wide smile as she searched his eyes. She saw anger. Panic. She was still in control.

He lifted her from the ground with his hands still clamped tightly around her neck, causing her to choke as he dragged her up against the wall. She uttered a gasping cry of pain.

"Tell me Rowena! Tell me! Now!"

"The fairy fort," she whispered painfully, "where the fairies live, where their world is. I saw you there, you appeared in the fairy fort." Her voice rose in intensity as she continued to gasp the words, her eyes blazing and a look of fear forming on her face. She pointed at her neck. "Please..."

He relaxed his grip around her airway slightly but she was still held firm against the wall. She took in some gulps of air.

"We were told as childer that one day someone would come back from the fairy world into this, but we were told it would be a woman, not a man. Not a man who just appeared, in a bright light from nowhere. I was walking nearby and just saw you, fall, from nowhere. I just watched you."

He stood back, releasing her from his vice-like grip as the words sank in. She dropped to her knees, breathing in huge gulps of air with relief.

"For long?!"

She looked back up at him, her hands rubbing her neck. "Long?"

"How long did you watch me?"

"A few minutes? I don't know, I don't carry a watch. Are you from the fairy world? Were you taken by them long ago and returned?" She clambered to her feet, the colour returning to her face.

He had to deal with her now. "What do you believe?"

"You're not from my home. You don't speak like anyone, you appear confused. You let me lead you around, give you shelter. Then you give me your child, you let me think you're a devil, but you're too weak to be a devil. Then you kill like a devil! Who are you?! Not from this world are you?!"

"Why did you not tell the old woman, tell anyone, what you saw?"

"They'd have me put in the madhouse if I told them what I saw, I told you that. When I saw you appear, it was magic. I knew you would be of use, I knew you were here to help me. Did Mama send you? I killed a boy to help you and you try to get away? I hid you, kept you safe, lied to the peelers about you, I am carrying your baba, I must know who you are and you will tell me. I know, bastard, I know."

"What do you want from me?" he pleaded, his eyes showing desperation.

"To tell me the truth," she simply asked, "I have your child in me."

"I could not have put it there."

"You fucked me."

She stepped forward, placing her hands on his shoulders.

"You will be the daddy."

"It could be the child of any man…"

She slapped him across the face, pushing him back.

"Yours. I need it to be yours, you hear me? I need the child to be yours. I have a feeling of a child in me. I need to know what the father is! Tell me! But I need this to be your child, you will accept the child or I will finish you!"

He pushed her back. She was manic, spitting as she spoke, venom on her tongue, arms flailing wildly, madness setting into her.

"Why my child? Why do you need this to be my child?"

"It simply must be…"

"You are but a young girl, you have lived a sheltered life in that village, you know nothing of what is out there save for your penchant for getting people into trouble."

"Oooh you use such big words! Aren't you the devil? Aren't you?! You appeared, like magic, like a devil. A weak devil."

"No I am not your devil, or any devil."

"You appeared in the fairy fort, from nothing. I saw it, I saw it, everything. What kind of spirit are you? A Pucá?"

"I am no spirit and I have tired of you. You were never meant to be involved. My plans have altered dramatically since you came into this scenario and I have found myself in hiding.
"People have died, people who were never meant to. People who were to live, to have led their lives. This is your doing. By interfering you have their blood on your hands. You have, as you say, seduced me; if anyone is the devil, child, it is you."

He grabbed her by the arms and slammed her back against the brickwork, placing one hand over her mouth to stifle her protestations.

"Now it is time for me to go. This was not meant to be. My experience here has been one of fear and terror and hiding like a criminal. Because of you."

He threw her against the wall again and cupped his fingers over her throat. Her face was one of terror, mouth jerking open as her brown eyes bulged.

"YOU were never meant to be there!"

His face was one of venom, emotions released and aggression, anger, disgust. An anger he had never experienced but one which had overcome other emotions. An anger borne of survival. Spectres of dreams past danced in his brain, urging him on, urging him to kill this feeble, stupid woman.

"YOU were never meant to be there!"

He gritted his teeth as he squeezed tighter, Rowena's hands uselessly trying to free her neck from his pincer-like grip, her legs kicking wildly as he raised her off the ground with his strength. Her hands sought something, anything to save her life but they found nothing. Her eyes widened. Sweat poured from his brow as he tightened his grip even more, his teeth barred in a snarl as unchecked emotions and pent-up aggression was unleashed. Soon she would be no more and he would be free to explore, to live and disappear. All his pain, his suffering, the effort to see this place and time would be worth it. She would die in moments. He would be free.

"YOU were never meant to be there!"

Tears streamed down Rowena's eyes as they rolled back into her head, her porcelain face displaying an unhealthy pallor as the life began draining from her. In her mind she saw her Mama, her beloved Mama. She was smiling at her, arms outstretched, urging her daughter to come to her, to feel no more pain, to plunge into her waiting, comfortable arms and feel a protection she hadn't felt in years. Behind her mother another woman stood still, the gentle smile of the woman a second source of comfort to the dying Rowena. At that moment Rowena knew the woman belonged to the fairy fort from many years ago. Now she had come to claim her soul.

"YOU were never meant to be there!"

'Time to let go… there is nothing here for me anymore, the devil is killing me, I'm coming Mama, Rowena is coming…'

The constriction on her neck suddenly released its deathly grip. She slid down the wall towards the floor, the brickwork scraping her dress before she hit the ground with a painful thud, gulps of air forcing their way down her throat as, through blurry eyes she saw her devil hit the ground beside her, his eyes closed, a syrup of blood beginning to seep from the side of his head. She closed her eyes again and held her aching neck as her lungs screamed and accepted the welcome oxygen. But she caught sight of another.

The young man threw aside the plank of wood he hastily liberated from the football ground and rushed to Rowena's aid.

Adrenaline and quick thinking had saved Rowena's life. Arms shook as he gathered the young woman in his, screaming for help until people began to arrive slowly.

Twenty Seven

A crowd had gathered as he was led out the door of the Mater hospital into the bright sunshine. His shackled hands made an attempt to shield his eyes but the grips of the two policemen on his arms were too strong. In front of him, two curving wings of concrete steps led down to Eccles Street where the angry crowd had begun to jeer and shout. Newspaper reporters scribbled furiously in note pads and shouted questions at the beleaguered prisoner

He was escorted cautiously but quickly down the steps, his bandaged head dull with pain, towards the van. Beside the vehicle, Charles Bayly and Phoebe Hedderman stood impassively, Phoebe's eyes widening as he approached down the steps.

"Constable, that is far enough," Mr. Bayly requested, behind him a thin line of police separating the prisoner from the crowd.

"Phoebe, come on," he gestured to the young woman who remained rooted to the spot. "Now girl, we must hurry!" he barked as she almost ran to his side.

In front of her, flanked by two DMP officers, he stood; clean-shaven, washed, hair combed neatly. She recounted in her mind the scene again, when she was approached by the man who now stood manacled before her, asking did she know Rowena Whyte. It was unmistakably him. He was no longer a threat, but a man imprisoned, his eyes reflecting defeat. He stared back at her, himself thinking back to when he questioned the validity of approaching her outside the public house as the girls behind him mocked. Now this insignificant woman was to play a significant part in his story.

"Well, Phoebe?" Mr. Bayly asked, his hand on her shoulder.

She glanced up at the elderly landowner and back at the prisoner. Her eyes darted down toward her feet at the borrowed shoes he had let her keep.

She nodded.

The young constable by the van shifted nervously. "I'm sorry miss, I need to hear you say yes or no."

"Yes, yes, that is the man."

On hearing her words, those gathered within earshot began to shout once more as he was bundled into the back of the vehicle.

"Where are we going?" the prisoner demanded, a quiver in his voice.

"To Finglas. You are a much sought after man there."

His heart sunk. "Why take me back?"

"I have my orders."

"But I will be in danger…"

"I have my orders."

"Please, anywhere."

"Shut up, y'hear? You are in no position to question me. Get in!"

His head lowered as more DMP officers climbed into the back beside him. He felt a tear escape as the vehicle jolted and turned over the cobblestones of Eccles Street.

'All is lost…'

From inside the hospital, Rowena stared out the long, narrow windows as she watched Phoebe identify him. She was to be discharged too, into the care of Mrs. Devine who hastened to her side when news reached Jamestown House of what had happened. Rowena pressed her hand against the window as her imprisoned devil was taken away. He had not told her who he was, what he was. She must know. She had to know before he was hanged.

Reverend Martin Hackett stood by the window of the parochial house, hands behind his back as he gazed across the garden walls towards Rose Hill. His eyes were narrow on his craggy, pale face.

"Is everything you are telling us true?" Sergeant Linden asked Rowena, seated on the armchair, notebook in hand. His eyes often glanced at her neck, purple streaks around it, the mark of her own suffering.

The young girl, sitting forward in the opposite armchair behind the large fireplace, cold, grey and unused in the summer heat nodded her head and rubbed her fingers over each other.

"Yes, sir."

Reverend Hackett's voice, a strong, authoritative one boomed in the room, the high walls giving it extra resonance.

"This is a remarkable tale girl, a remarkable one."

He turned around, his face cast in an intense look.

"You are talking about a man, the identified murderer, who appeared from thin air. Think of what you are saying girl, think about what you have told Sergeant Linden. Repeat your words in your mind."

Rowena exchanged glances with Linden. The sergeant nervously licked his lips and fingered the fringe of his carefully combed hair back into position. The smell of his hair-cream in the musty room embarrassed him.

"I am telling you the truth. Everything. The stranger is the man you want. The murders. I witnessed them. Phoebe Hedderman identified him."

"Why didn't you come forward sooner?"

"He threatened me; said he would kill me, kill others. He made me hide him in the house, he forced himself on me in my house, and in the woods, left me with a child…"

"What happened your father?"

"My father found him in my room hiding, beat him, and he ran. The murdering coward ran away, ran to leave my drunken bastard…"

"Language in my house!" the cleric boomed.

"He left me, let my drunken excuse of a father punish me, take his anger out on me. The village whore he called me then threw me on the floor, said I deserve to be beaten back to hell, and then his face turned a bright red, his eyes rolled in his head, he clutched his chest and fell on me. Dead."

The two men were silent. She glanced at the floor.

"What makes you think you are with child?" the police officer asked carefully, hoping to take control of the situation away from the clergyman.

"I am a woman, I know… I know. My mama knew with me."

Sergeant Linden shifted uncomfortably in his chair and wiped the sweat from his brow before sitting back, elbows on each arm of the chair and outstretched fingers tipping off each other.

"Ms. Whyte, you have made some extraordinary statements to us about this man, who has no real name you say, and who, you also say, appeared in a fairy fort up by Jamestown House. May I remind you…"

"That I am not to be trusted?" Rowena asked, standing up. "That I am a fool, a stupid whore a stupid bitch…"

"Language in my house!"

"Father I must say. I am not liked, I am laughed at, mocked, am at the butt of some cruel comments about my mama, thought of as dirt, the village slut, one who cannot be trusted."

She approached the clergyman and grabbed his hands, his eyes darting back at her and the RIC officer with unease.

"You must believe me. You must believe every word I have told you. You say my story is fantastic, it is unbelievable, but you are a man of God, you know of the evil of the devil."

"This man cannot be the devil."

"Devil he may not be, but a spirit, a ghost, someone evil who came to our village, murdered a young man, murdered the fool in the mad house, made me cover for him, made me lie to the sergeant here, involved me in this evil bidding and left his seed in me. He almost murdered me too were it not for that man who ran in and saved me. I have suffered at my father's hands too, please believe me. "

"Do you realise what you are saying girl? What you have told me?"

Reverend Hackett shook his hands free of Rowena's grip and stretched his arms out wide, raising and lowering his hands slightly as he emphasised each word; "...that he appeared from thin air! Thin air!"

He turned to face out the window once again and slammed his hands on the window sill. He stared impassively for some minutes, the sound of the grand clock the only noise echoing in the large room. Pictures of Jesus and his mother looked down on the scene. Three teacups sat used on a small table, Rowena hardly having touched hers.

Two months into his new posting and Martin Hackett was facing a situation of outrageous consequence. Word would spread, the village was tiny and people would hear and expand on the tale. They would seek solace and deliverance from him. He must think. What to do with the girl?

"May I go?" she enquired softly.

"Sergeant Linden will escort you to Jamestown House, Mrs. Devine will put you up for now. We have not finished with you."

She blessed herself, smiling slyly as she walked behind the police officer. It couldn't have worked out any better.

As they stepped out into the gardens, the sergeant grabbed Rowena gently by the arm as they passed under the shade of a great tree.

"I will say that I have never heard such a tale. Never. But listen to me. This will go to a court of law, you will be asked to testify and do you think for one moment that the story you told me and the clergyman will be believed?!

"Ms. Whyte, this is a murder case, murder, think of that. It will make the newspapers, there'll be reporters from the Freeman's Journal swarming around. In court, what makes you think a judge will not throw you out? Condemn you to the asylum?! This case rests on you saying you witnessed these murders, but also that the man you are accusing appeared from thin air if you like! Think Ms. Whyte, think."

Rowena swallowed and looked around. She spied the Reverend Hackett still at the window, staring rigidly at her.

"I am telling the truth. Yes, I may end up in Farhman or Belle Vue or wherever but that is my story; a true story and I am sticking to it. You will get no other tale from me, 'cos I have no other story, ask me 'til my dying day and I will tell you the same story again and again and again. It is the only story you have. Ask your prisoner. He was caught trying to kill me!" Her finger jabbed at her chest.

"I am the villager here, he the stranger. Three men are dead now, two because of him, and well, I'm sure my father confronting him put paid to his heart. You are the peeler, what do you believe?"

"The story you told inside, it's incredulous!"

"It's the only story I will tell. It is what happened."

Mrs. Devine's voice was firm, her stare steely.

"Rowena will indeed remain with me. She has been in my employment, I will not allow her to be put into Farnham or Belle Vue or any other madhouse in this God forsaken area. She can stay with me, continue to work while she can and I will look after her. Give me what I need to sign. This house used to be an asylum once, did you know that? Fitting isn't it that she should move in? Fantastic story or not, she has a right to it; a right to be heard and listened to. And a right for her baby to be brought up in a good home. I have played a big part in this, sheltering him, I have since gone down to the barracks and identified him in his cell. Let this be my penance. Rowena may be touched slightly by the hand of God, that we know, but what else have we to go on? He is saying nothing, is he?"

"I do not want to bring trouble or whispers to your door…"

"I do not like the girl, I cannot abide her at times but she is the daughter of an old friend of mine who I loved very dearly.

"She is without a father now, she has no one. I will be her guardian. I will give her bed, board, some work, I will look after her. She will not go into an asylum in Finglas, or any asylum. I will lock her in her room before that happens and go to the bishop if needs be. I must make amends. I will have my way."

Sergeant Linden and Reverend Hackett swallowed hard as they listened to Mrs. Devine. She was a very well liked and respected woman in the village. She held sway. Old school and matriarchal.

"She will stay with me. I will see to it. Do what you want with her house, she may never live there again. I take full responsibility for her from now on."

Both men stood up from the dining table, the incessant ticking of the clock the only sound before they bade her thanks and goodbye.

"If you insist, we will do as you wish," Robert Linden said, "but I must investigate."

"I do insist. She has seen enough hardship, hasn't she? And I've no doubt he will accept all charges. Caught in the act, trying to kill the girl in a brutal fashion. That young man who saved her, you should pin a medal on him, and he using a heavy timber from a sports field to prevent him from killing her! Now do what you have to do and let this terrible event be over once and for all. I will keep Rowena on a tight leash, I will raise her baby with her. She will not be committed."

"May God be with you," Martin Hackett added as he made for the front door.

Both men were seen out into the beautiful sunshine. She closed the heavy door behind them and stopped to look at the photograph of the handsome man once again. A weak smile crossed her face as she thought of what her life could have been, how she badly wanted to his bride and be the one at his side as he left the small village and made a new life for himself and his wife in the Liberties area of Dublin all those years ago. Is he still alive? Has he grandchildren? His own parents were long dead; kind people, hard workers. Oh Ben, she whispered, before clearing her mind and calling for her own daughter.

Kathy sat looking through an upstairs window, the huge tree with burgundy leaves just in her line of sight, but today the evil bird was hiding from her, not making himself known. He had delivered on his promise.

Word spread through the taverns, throughout the great houses and in the fields that the murderer was in a cell, transported back from Phibsborough at the request of the sergeant. The people living in the cottages at Finglas Bridge said that the van had trundled by in the dead of night after he spent a night in Mountjoy before returning to the barracks where he was held now, safe from everyone, sitting securely, out of harm from those he terrorised, if all but briefly. Talk continued into the evenings and in the public houses. Anger hung over the village like a shroud, the innocence of a slow, quiet life shattered. How he had terrorised that young girl. A fool, a cheap woman she may be but a young girl; one of their own, forced to cover for him, to hide him. He was described as the devil incarnate. Resentment grew. Hatred. Tales abounded about his origins, how he appeared out of thin air. A demon? A pucá? Was the devil in the village? Schoolchildren feared passing by the stone bridge spanning the stream in case they should see the devil, but was he walking amongst them?

Childish talk in the schoolhouse was that the devil appeared and was in the village. Women prayed and sought comfort from Reverend Hackett. They prayed to the idols in the small church at the bottom of the hill. They prayed for Phoebe Hedderman who had taken to not coming out of the room in the tenement. She didn't want to be seen, to hear questions asked of her about the man. Reporters from the Freeman's Journal knocked on doors and questioned those in Heery's or Flood's two pubs, but no-one spoke. The village closed in on itself.

The men talked on their breaks from the fields, servants and maids whispered to each other as their employers eagerly folded the thin sheets of the newspaper to see what was being said about the situation, what the official line was. Robert Hart's father had to be told to leave the barracks or face arrest himself. He demanded to see the face of his son's murderer. He took to nights in Heery's and Flood's, drink enthusing his talk of revenge and justice amongst those similarly inebriated.

Finglas became a tinderbox. A wild plan was honed in the pubs amongst the men, but not discussed with the women or the authorities. He could be taken from the barracks at any time. They needed to confront him. Make him pay. The young boy was a good kid, the poor fool a sad individual, Matthew Whyte a drunkard but still, one of their own. He tried to take the girl's life too. It had to stop.

What right had he to be hanged in Dublin? It was a Finglas issue and it had to end in Finglas.

Robert Hart's mother and brother blessed themselves at their slain son's grave and walked slowly towards the Catholic gate. Edward had his arm around his grief-stricken mother's shoulders. As they passed the Nether Cross she stopped and turned to her son.

"I know there is talk."

Edward furrowed his brows in surprise. "Talk...?"

"Yes, talk, that is all I'll say. I know the men are planning something."

She placed her hand on her son's heart. "Do what you must. Do it. But let me know what. I want to be there when he breathes his last."

"Mother, we..."

"Do it. I won't say a word to anyone, just let me know what is happening. No-one else need know. Go now, I'll follow."

He nodded and descended the steps quickly. Mary Hart stood in front of the Nether Cross, tracing ornate yet faded carvings with her two fingers.

"This is my town," she said, "my town, my family's town, we have been here years, you will not destroy us!"

She smashed a fist into the cross, drawing blood from her leathery knuckles. The wind rustled the branches of the tree beside the ancient artifact.

'The birdsong, it's gone, the song has gone out of the village, a terrible deed is to be done to right this wrong...'

He sat on the hard bed, the tiny square of light allowing the bright moonlight into his room. He searched for what stars he could see, wondering would he ever see them again as a free man. All he had planned to do, all he had planned to see, all his plans... gone.

He never bargained on seeing the inside of a hospital, of a prison van, of Mountjoy Gaol and now a tiny cell in the barracks back in Finglas. Everything had all gone wrong, so badly wrong. He stood up, placed his hands on his hips and walked towards the tiny window. He traced the stars he could see with his finger on the dirty glass, the moonlight keeping watch on all below. How insignificant all this seemed to the great celestial plan.

He bowed his head and thought back at everything that had passed.

'An utter failure, no memory of me, no marker shall commit my triumph to eternal recognition. It was never meant to be like this, never. I should be free now, free to walk and talk as I desire, away from trouble, away from harm...'

He mulled over his thoughts of escape, an idea he quickly dismissed at the start of his imprisonment. *'I could not get away from the girl, how am I going to escape shackles and cells...'*

He repeated her name over and over again in his head. Undone by a young woman. Undone by misfortune, undone by the wrong person being in the wrong place at that time.

'How funny this old world is, how much chance plays a part in the path of life. What a peculiar time to live in, but I had to see it, to breathe the clean air, to look upon flesh and bone for myself. Yes I have succeeded, but I have also spectacularly failed...'

He thought of the child Rowena claimed he would father. A child never meant to be born. He lay back on the hard bed, sleep overcoming him as the ghouls of dreams he still experienced awakened once more to mock him. He tossed and turned, struggling to cope with what those dreams would bring, with what they would bestow on him.

As he dreamed fitful and horrific dreams, a small band of men met at the lodge behind Gofton Hall, awakening wives told to go back to sleep where necessary as they quietly dressed and slipped out of their abodes, grabbing hold of whatever implement was necessary. Now was their best chance.

Twenty Eight

The woman and child encircled him, their arms casting a ring as they shuffled around his wretched body. Behind them skeletal spirits mocked and danced around a small fire. From within the fire the fool and young man emerged, hands out as they begged him for deliverance. They loomed over him, eyes bulging, mouths agape, silently pleading with him. As they drew closer, their mouths formed harsh, evil grins and their hands turned, cupped and half-closed as they wrapped their bony fingers around his neck. He could not move, could not cry; all the time the woman encircled him, her eyes wide and smiles forming on her face, which began to change slowly but unmistakably into that of his tormentor, into his reason for failure. He was no longer looking at the features of a woman long dead, woman who once had a role at the fairy fort many centuries ago. but into the elegant features of Rowena, adorned in a brilliant white, unending dress. Tears were streaming down her face as she held a tiny baby in front of him...

His reluctant slumber was violently disturbed as he felt his back slam hard on the concrete floor. Eyes wide open, he couldn't see what was happening in the darkness of the cell but he knew there were others in the room, surrounding him. From the distance he could hear shouts. The burst of light from a flaming torch blinded him momentarily as the kicks and punches reigned in on his helpless body. He screamed in pain but the assault continued for what seemed an eternity until a sole voice barked that they should move.

He could hear more shouts, angry shouts, a declaration; "We will have him!" before he almost slipped into unconsciousness. He felt his limp body being dragged across the floor, down steps, out into the open. Garbled voices swam around him, all melding into one. The body odour from those who carried him was pungent. Dust lifted in the trail of the footsteps as his lungs rejected their tiny, dry particles but still he was dragged. His whole body was lifted from the ground as the footsteps quickened. He raised his head but, face down, could not make out where he was being taken to.

He could hear the stream, gushing peacefully in the now broken silence of the warm night, a calming oasis amongst the uncertainty surrounding him, the gentle hissing of the torch being doused.

Steps were climbed, a gate clanked open and his body was turned slightly, giving him enough time to look up and see the distinct outline of a tall celtic cross in the moonlight. He was thrown to the ground, landing heavily as more kicks reigned in on him before being dragged across the muck, over graves that in this moment no-one blessed themselves for passing, his flailing legs banging painfully off headstones as numerous lanterns lit the path he was being dragged along. The low voices were muffled to his confused ears. Someone loomed right in front of his face, speaking directly to him. He couldn't make out the words but he could smell the stale ale from his breath. More punches, harder kicks as he pleaded for them to stop, his lungs struggling to expel the dust and dirt particles he inhaled.

"Keep him quiet! We don't want the world to know!"

He was hoisted from the ground and thrown into something hard, his legs dangling over one side.

"He's too fucking big!" one voice exclaimed as the lanterns moved closer to him. Someone's boot was wedged into his mouth, causing him to try and inhale gulps of air in panic as the owner pressed his leg down slowly. He was unsure as to what was happening, confused as his legs were hoisted up and bent; painfully, awkwardly until the snap forced a howl of agony from deep within his gut. His eyes bulged with terror and pain as the second leg was broken, his body trashing wildly in search of relief, escape, anything to take him from this torturous hell. He bit hard into the leather boot, silently but uselessly pleading for a mercy by now he knew would never come.

The pain seared back to his waist and up his spine as his shattered bones were pulled and dragged into position inside the container he now lay in.

"Join them you bastard! Join them in hell!"

He heard those words clearly.

The man removed his boot from his mouth and leaned in over him, smiled wickedly in the light of the lantern, his unshaven face cackling. He spit into the stricken prisoner's face.

"You don't have any cloven hoofs do you! We're gonna give ya the punishment you deserve!" He moved away, saying 'Do it'.

Now was the stricken man's chance. He barely unleased a weak, pitiful and pleading cry before something was slammed down over his head, plunging his world into absolute darkness. He lifted his hands but they struck solid wood. He heard hammering, behind him, below him, at the sides. He couldn't see anything. His hands clambered blindly as he felt around him. Wood. All wood. He was being nailed into a wooden container. A casket, a coffin.

Panic surged from within, he found his voice and began croaking, desperately trying to scream and force the lid from over him as his broken bones emitted a horrendous numbing ache of their own. He couldn't kick anymore, just punch and slam his hands at the wood.

'The bastards, the evil, primitive bastards!'

He panicked, hands thumping on the wood as he screamed for help but his captors continued their duty quickly. He felt the coffin hoisted, seemingly dangle for some moments before being dropped violently and roughly. A similar yet louder noise above him made his own casket creak and almost broke the lid. The incumbent coffin removed from the covertly reopened grave to accommodate his tomb was rolled back into place, sitting on his. Then a succession of dull, terrifying plods began. He listened intently. He was being buried alive.

He hammered with his fists on the coffin lid, cried for mercy as the thuds continued and became less audible as the earth packed up. If he hammered and cried long enough, maybe the constable would arrive and be alerted, he would be dug out, saved, live …

The coffin lid groaned under the weight. He gasped for air, punched, anything to try to free himself. He knew it was useless. The bastards. His lungs heaved. His shattered legs burned with unmerciful pain. He urinated through pure fear. His eyes were wide open but he could see only the pitch black of the darkness. There was no escape. He would die here and die here soon. All training and calmness let him. He was a crying child. Lost forever, never to be seen again, never to be discovered; nothing guaranteed but for his body to give out and skin to wither away, bones to grind to dust over the centuries.

His great journey, the greatest journey ever undertaken by man, would end here. In failure with nothing of this new world learned. He sobbed softly. Blackness. Silence save for the gnawing of rats outside his tomb. No way out. He dreaded every waking second that was left in his life, one to be snuffed out in a backward village.

For what? Trouble. Murder. Fear. Pain. Now a lonely death, a revenge carved out by locals.

Rowena. Rowena. Her name echoed in his mind again and again as his lungs audibly searched for the stale, depleting air tinged with the odour of his sweat and urine. Above him, the earth of the forgotten yet disturbed grave was patted and moulded back into shape, not expertly but enough to fool anyone who would casually glance in that direction in the coming days.

No family mourned the grave with the greasy, faded tombstone. The grave digger, over a few free drinks in Flood's and a few greasy pounds told the conspirators the best place. An old, forgotten grave by the wall. Three coffins were buried in there long ago. Plenty of room for more. He worked under the cover of dark, knowing every inch of the graveyard. He would have it ready but needed men to lift out what remained of the top coffin. It was in decent shape, pulled out roughly and with effort and simply pushed back into the grave when all was done.

The lanterns were snuffed out as the keys of the graveyard were handed back to the grave digger who slipped back inside his cottage and back into bed, his wife deep in sleep and unaware of anything at all.

The mob nodded and grunted at each other, a silent pact that no more was to be said of this. The matter was over. Standing outside the graveyard, looking on but doing enough to stay out of the way was Robert Hart's mother. She quietly slipped away into the darkness, as quickly as she arrived, nodding her head and smiling.

The RIC officers interrupted from their sleep by the small mob were pinned back into their room and prevented from coming to assist, all done in darkness so no-one could be identified, barricaded in as the mob set to work, to be rescued next day by Reverend Hackett following the early morning discovery of an anonymous message pinned to the parochial house door. Enquiries would come to nothing. Every man claimed they were sound asleep, unknowing wives and those who didn't want to know vouching for their husbands. The prisoner had vanished, been taken from his cell, but no-one would tell by who.

Stories abounded, tall tales told by children that he was indeed the devil and had vanished in the dead of night, gone back to hell, as quickly as he had appeared in the field that June day. Others told that he escaped through the tunnel and was safe in the castle by the North Road.

The police officers took to Upper and Lower Flood's, buying punters drink as they did in Heery's and beyond in the Jolly Toper, in the village at Cardiff's Bridge and the Royal Oak at Finglas Bridge. RIC officers from the barracks in Ashbourne questioned Evaline Devine, sister of the kindly old woman in Jamestown House. Did she know anything? Did her sister confide? She knew nothing, had heard nothing and pleaded with the officers to leave her to continue her work in the Hunt house.

William Scollard and Robert Linden quietly hoped the veil of silence would continue, that tongues wouldn't be loosened. The drink was accepted, silent nods affirming that there was no ill feeling held over the RIC officers. What was done was done. The problem was at an end. It was to benefit all.

Martin Hackett thundered from the pulpit, warning those who bore a guilty secret that eternal damnation would await them. His whiskey bottle comforted him at night as he stared out the window across the fields, trembling hands clasping each topped up glass as he mumbled *'not in my town...'*. Wives prayed furiously to their God to deliver their husbands from such torment. In the Protestant church, Eleanor listened as her own vicar preached a similar warning.

'There is no place in God's house for those who harbour guilt or knowledge of a wrong...'

Fellow Protestants whispered and pointed as she made her way out of the church, people she would briefly stopped to chat too after Sunday service now keeping a distance. *'Does she know? She was there when he came to the house. She must know something...'*

She fixed her bonnet on her head which she kept lowered as she began the walk back up the hill. She seriously thought about returning to Lancashire. *'To what? Anything, better than these secrets and whispers.'*

Lips remained tightly sealed as days passed into weeks, months... the authorities had no choice but to close the case. Robert Linden did what he had to but he wanted an end to it. The conclusion drawn was that the stranger had simply disappeared.

Time would pass and the village would gradually move on. Rowena Whyte would be seen sometimes rambling through the woods by the stream or sitting by her mother's grave, her expanding belly cause for some derision and disgust that she wasn't put away by some.

'It's his baby! The murderer's!'

'She should be taken into the back street and 'ave it cut from her!'

'She should be locked away, that cursed unborn is a reminder of what happened!'

Others were more sympathetic.

'It's not her fault, poor soul!'

'He took advantage of her, made her play along!'

'She's one of us!'

Matthew Whyte was buried in Prospect Cemetery with his own family, Rowena wanted nothing to do with him or the grave. Mrs. Devine attended mass with her head held high, she had nothing to be ashamed of anymore. She was duped and sucked into this awful episode, by giving Rowena a home she felt he had atoned for her sins.

Memories faded, newer generations deliberately unaware of any mysterious stranger, or his disappearance by unnamed assailants in the dead of night. No more would the episode be spoken of, out of shame, fear or disgust. Pockets of rebellious old women would confide in a grandchild but details were sparse. The story would wither, die and be expunged from memory, maybe to be sought again in generations to come, but by then it would be too late to find out the truth.

In the graveyard, he lay still, terrified and in unbearable pain. The first hour ticked into the second as his searched his soul for help, for salvation. Where he came from religion was long dead, but in this time religion was at the core of existence. He remembered prayers from his education and they came to him. He knew they could be of no use but if they offered him comfort.

For all his training, his personality, he was a wreck. Alone, so far from home. The hopes, dreams and aspirations he had desired in coming here would never be reached. He thought of the consequences of his being here. People had died. Robert Hart should have gone on to be a powerful man in society, he was meant to; how he could have changed the world around him if he had been allowed to live. Rowena... how altered her life would be now. Would she end up in an asylum? Carefree days of wandering through the village and woods behind her. Her knowledge of him, would that be shared, written about, passed on? Or would she be dismissed and locked away?

Had that one, unplanned event in the field by Jamestown House altered history forever? Would others follow, did someone else follow him on his journey, someone who could be walking in the village now, or was that person one of the kangaroo court who buried him in the ancient cemetery, knowing it would be better if he was dismissed from history forever?

Rowena claimed to carry his child. If she did, the lineage of her family would be changed forever. What would the child be like? How would it develop, grow? What would it be told? Would it know its mother or be removed from her? Would it be told by its mother of the father. The child would grow, spawn offspring of its own, a troubled line that should never have existed. A new line would emerge into the future and evolve as the decades and centuries passed. He had altered history, he had altered time, what would be the consequences?

The ghouls of his dreams stood erect and tall, looking down on his pitiful body, the colour in their faces a watery pale, their eyes fixed, retinas searing ahead as they watched intently from behind darkened visors. Thin fingers twitched at their side, lips were licked over and over again. Their faces betrayed no emotion, nothing similar to the ghouls they would become in dreams of the future, from the past. They watched silently, staring ahead, waiting, pondering, selfishly wondering. The woman, a pagan priestess from many centuries ago stood by, watching the life ebb out of him; a pagan priestess who had opened the very portal he travelled through but millenia before, a portal fed by the burning branches of the cherished yew trees that once grew aplenty by the monastic settlement. How fitting, how fitting...

Tears filled his eyes again. Tears of acceptance. Why, why this. He closed his eyes, his tortured mind drifted as the lack of air began to play tricks with his mind. The lack of oxygen to his brain releasing stored yet forgotten memories into his consciousness.

'...they could never know, they could never understand what brought me to their home. What turn of events that led me to mingle among them, to feel their sun on my face, to drink the same cool water, to gaze in awe at the stars in the early morning light. I could never be revealed. They would never understand, they could never understand who I was. I am not of them, not the way they are now. Coming here to this place was the fulfillment of a dream,

a dream conceived in times past but one that remained for eons just that, a dream. But for me and those who surrounded me, a dream no longer... no one will realise, no one in this pathetic village will know of whom walked among them or how they played a huge part in the most significant voyage ever undertaken. I arrived shrouded in mystery and will depart with that mystery unknown... it was not meant to be like this. This was never meant to happen. Others may have followed me, learnt from what I had hoped to learn... but all has changed now. So be it, my mystery will die with me ...'

Pockets of air gulped into his lungs as his heart thundered in his chest, his body rising in search of whatever air remained that was to dissipate quickly. He tried once more in vain to lift the lid from the coffin, confusion abounded in his head, dizziness swept over him which lifted and spun his body around even though he was lying flat in the cold ground. His head shook from side to side as the last of the air swam down his throat, into his lungs, barely helping their raging quest. He could hear his body making unnerving sounds, the panicked gulps of air forcing a noise from his throat that was unnatural yet uncontrollable. *'Rowena... Rowena...'*

Her name was the last thing his dying mind processed.

Rowena woke to a dull sky. Her mind played out strange dreams to her like a film reel in a picture house, dreams she could not understand. She opened the curtains and looked out the window at the land below, her feet cold on the wooden floorboards. She noticed a little rain was starting to fall. The pleasing scent of the breakfast cooking made her stomach grumble. She picked up the hairbrush her new guardian had given her and began to slowly brush her hair. She would go down to the barracks today and inform the sergeant that she must see their prisoner. She must know. She must know the truth. She bathed last night, Kathy had given her some powder to disguise the choke marks on her neck. She smiled as she pulled on her new white dress and fixed herself in the mirror. She hummed the song again, tried to remember the name and exact words, but it didn't matter anymore.

As she descended the stairs, she became aware of the hushed whispers from the dining room. She peeped her head around the door and Constable Scollard, on hearing the polished floorboard creak, looked up from the chair. Mrs. Devine sat in front of him, her face white, her eyes startled as Rowena glided in. The young girl took one look at the constable's face, it was ashen and the cup and saucer shook gently in his hand.

"Rowena, dear, I didn't hear you come down the stairs..." her guardian began, looking nervously back at the RIC officer.

"Why are you here?" Rowena pointed at him. "I've told you everything, I told it to the sergeant and priest."

"He's not here for that reason, Rowena. Sit down, child. Please." Mrs. Devine gestured to a chair. Rowena looked at the shaken constable.

"Something is wrong, isn't it? I need to talk to him today, you know, I must speak with him.."

The constable stood up, straightening the tunic of his uniform. "Something has happened, Ms. Whyte, last night, at the barracks and..."

Rowena clenched her fists and let out a scream that startled both the adults.

"No, no you see, I must speak with him, I need to talk to him today..."

"Ms. Whyte..."

"No, no, don't tell me, you bastards! You bastards!"

Mrs. Devine cried out at the young woman but Rowena left the room, running out into the courtyard. She ran and ran until eventually throwing her self onto the ground. She lay on her back crying as the rain fell on her, knowing that her stranger, her devil, Ben, was gone from her life for good.

Twenty Nine

The snow fell gently on the grey monuments and headstones around her, the disappearing wooden beams that once held the roof of the church forming neat, soft white lines against the cold grey stone of the walls.

Rowena stood by her mother's grave, huddled in a warm coat given to her by Kathy Devine. Her swollen belly made it too hard for her to sit on the cold muddy ground anymore. She patted her stomach, rubbing it from time to time as the December snow fell around her, the intense heat of a baking summer a memory. Mrs. Devine noticed the young woman had withdrawn into herself, a shadow of the person she once was. She rarely spoke anymore, hardly smiled, never sang her childish tunes as she withdrew deeper into herself since she that day she fled Jamestown House. The constable and Mrs. Devine had followed her out and simply said that he was gone. They wouldn't elaborate despite her sobs, just repeated he was gone. The RIC man wasn't going to volunteer theories or wishful thinking. That is all she had to know.

Rowena rejected their advances and arms of protection, wandering away toward the village instead in a daze, ignoring or nor noticing glances and whispers directed at her. She sobbed gently, gazed around at nothing and grabbed her belly before crashing to her knee in the middle of the crossroads. Women stood and watched, men spat their tobacco and grunted as they joined the watching circle. Some men filed past, heads lowered; men with a secret, men who didn't want to be reminded and who wished her to an asylum so they themselves could move on and forget.

'*Poor aul soul… God help her.*'

'*Ah she's not for here, she's for the madhouse.*'

'*She knows more than she's lettin' on.*'

'*Leave her be, go on, walk away, let her, let her alone.*'

Rowena would never know of him now, never again speak to him, never know who he truly was. She never spoke of her strange companion, or how he first came into her world, to anyone. She would have to live with unanswered questions in her mind, never to know who her devil was; was he indeed a devil or a messenger?

The man she had taken into her life, she had even killed for him, a guilty secret she would have to live with forever, to find out why he appeared from nowhere. He had turned on her, almost killed her, that encounter being the last time they would be in each other's company.

He had disappeared in the night. He would be put out of people's minds, forgotten, but not by her. She never got her answers. She never got an explanation as to how a man can appear in a burst of flame in a sunny field outside the village she grew up in. She would have to live with her questions, walking the roads of life with them unanswered to her.

Rowena walked slowly through the headstones after kissing her two fingers and laying them on her mother's cold marker for some seconds, gazing again at names she had read time and time again, wondering at abandoned graves with leaning, faded and greasy headstones who lay under there and why they weren't mourned anymore. She stopped at a very neglected old grave by the wall, not too far from her family plot. Undisturbed, ancient, unloved.

The ancient graveyard had a serene look in the winter snow. Her bootsteps made a gentle, crunching noise as she walked among the buried dead. Everything looked so clean, so pure, so innocent. The Nether Cross stood guardian over everything within the holy walls, as it would stand for many years more.

She gazed down again at the lonely grave for some moments before turning to walk away, descending the steps to Barrack Lane by the side of the tenement. Head down under the gentle fall of the snow, she shivered as she crossed over the river.

'Are you there, devil, are you under this bridge?'

As she turned up the hill she spied Phoebe Hedderman coming out of Rose Hill, tying her warm coat around her. Phoebe had been employed by Charles Bayly since the summer, since she identified her Ben, since she took away Rowena's chance of an explanation to all this.

On seeing Rowena she stopped, the two girls of similar age staring at each other for some moments. They stood on the road in front of the cottages on Barrack Street, saying nothing, just looking as the icy stream gushing under them. Phoebe lifted her skirt and began to walk past Rowena but the pregnant woman stood out in front of her. She grabbed Phoebe's wrist, placing it one her stomach.

"You feel this? You feel this Phoebe?!"

Phoebe nodded, her eyes wide, her mouth agape.

"This is a bastard. I am carrying a bastard, you know that? A child who will grow up fatherless, because of you. You! You and your mouth, who the hell are you to go about meddling?! I hope you think of what you have done every waking second of your life!"

Phoebe shook her head wildly but said no words.

"Won't you remember these words?!"

"But, he tried to kill you…"

"But you put him away. You. You and Mr. High and Mighty behind his castle on the hill there became the saviours of the village. Unless he escaped, maybe he's after you, Phoebe."

"The man who saved you though, he called the police…"

"Yes, the peelers who were tipped off by you… but maybe the stranger did escape, maybe he'll come after you, maybe you're next to carry his child and be killed by his hand. Maybe he'll succeed!"

Phoebe let out a sob and broke free of Rowena's grip, running towards the pitiful building her family called home.

"Run, you bitch, run away and live with your conscience!" Rowena laughed after her. "He's gonna get you!" she sang before turning and continuing her journey past her old home, now occupied by a young family, towards her grander new one.

She paused outside, staring at the freshly whitewashed walls as she recalled visions of her Mama chasing her outside the door, laughing with her, holding her, embracing her.

Deep inside her, she knew her devil was dead. She just knew. Dead like her Mama, like her Daddy. All dead. She was alone now. All alone.

The snow began to fall heavier as she turned by the post office and on towards Jamestown. A tear escaped and fell down her cheek.

V

Timeslips...

Thirty

Early Winter, 1041

Resplendent in her finery, the woman was lowered into the grave close to the monastic settlement that lay by the crystal stream and the grove of yew trees.

Those gathered huddled in the shrill east wind, animal skins occasionally tugged tighter over their shoulders in an effort to detract from the biting cold. Rain began to fall as the body gently rested at the bottom of the grave. Trinkets surrounded her as symbols of her status in society; a large oval brooch of bronze, silver and gold stood out.

Standing near her grave her son ran his fingers thoughtfully yet gently over his silken beard which protruded from underneath a rough cowl. To some there he was a stranger, to others he was their leader. The beautiful woman, sought by kings and warriors alike throughout her turbulent life, had passed on and he saw it his duty to inter her near her place of birth. As he departed, he chuckled wryly to himself and allowed a glance back at his mother's grave. In times to come and should her grave ever be discovered, people will wonder just who she was. He grimaced as he signalled to his men that they must begin the covert journey back to safety. They needed to sail as soon as they could.

November 12, 1800

The stagnant stench of the dank rising tide against the river walls stung her nostrils as she skipped over the cobbles and up to the doorway of the tavern. She hated going in the main door but there was no answer at the service door round the back. She sighed as he heard the usual drunken shouts from inside and swallowing hard, entered. She skipped in lightly, head bowed and made her way as quickly as she could to a small wooden door to the left of the bar. The relief of being almost there was cut short when she felt an arm grab her waist and roughly pull her onto a lap.

"C'mere luv, how are ye today?"

She glanced hurriedly.

She closed her eyes as shouts and jeers went up from across the table as Billy planted a disgusting, rum-reeking kiss on her cheek.

"So when you gonna play with me then?" he laughed as the others around whooped and jeered. His free arm began roaming and she fought to break free of his grip. Billy was the reason she got this job. The previous hired help of the rooms above fell foul of his drunken lust one night when he cornered her in the back lane. Or so the story went. Poor Mary gave birth around nine months later and was last heard of on working the streets for money.

She fought against his grip, vainly until the form of the inn matriarch loomed in front of him.

"Let her go or so help me God I'll have you thrown into the Liffey!" Mrs. Connor barked. The young girl smiled and felt huge relief as the grip loosened as she scurried past her employer into the rooms at the back. The middle-aged woman made her way to the door of the inn to pay the driver who had brought the young girl back to her work. Handing him the required fare she asked did he want a meal before his return.

"No ma'am, best get 'ome quickly, it's cold enough now!"

"But it's such a long journey?"

"Thank you kindly, but I must make way," he replied, bidding her goodbye as he urged the horse forward, its shoes creating a loud and curt clop on the cobblestone street.

Mrs. Connor returned inside and deftly closed the door.

"How are you, child?"

"Saddened, ma'am."

"It is hard, yes, the death of a parent, particularly a mother. I'll visit her grave with you one day of my choosing, if you would like."

"You're awfully kind, ma'am. She is buried in the churchyard back home, in a new plot my father bought."

"A lovely gesture, I'm sure. Had you a good journey back?"

"I had thank you, very cold."

"There's a sharp wind out. He has been cursing it, though I dare to assume he would be used to it..."

"Has he, asked for me, ma'am?"

The elderly lady nodded as both women exchanged looks for a brief moment.

301

"Yes, he enquired as to your whereabouts and said he was deeply saddened to hear the news of your loss. He would like to pass on his condolences to you. I have his meal ready, you may bring it up to him now, if you wish? Would you like some food yourself first?"

"No thank you, I ate at home before I left."

"Warm yourself by the fire then?"

"It's best I get back, I think. I missed enough time here, thank you ma'am."

Mrs. Connor nodded and smoothed her white pinny down. Her greying hair peaked from under a plain white cap.

"Very well, then, let me take your coat and get your apron from the kitchen. But he is very busy with his charts at the moment. Do not wait longer than you should. He will dismiss you as usual. Well, as usual as can be expected."

"Thank you ma'am."

The matriarch took the coat and turned around quickly, avoiding any more eye contact as she scurried down the steps of the corridor and into the kitchen beyond, beckoning the young girl to follow. She quietly placed the silver tray of a meal, cutlery and a mug of ale into her hands gently.

"Go now, he waits."

She took the tray, the small candle secure in its holder to light her way and softly climbed the polished and creaking stairs. Her employment forced her to expedite the climb though she longed to put it off as much as she could.

She swallowed hard and bit her lip as the nerves took hold. A gentle light seeped from under the door in the dimly lit corridor and she knocked softly, hoping he wouldn't hear.

"Enter."

She pushed the handle down skillfully, as she balanced the tray and walked into the small room, just as she had done so many times before. He sat there in his chair, his back to her, at a desk that faced the window that looked out onto the quay side below. In front of him lay rolls of paper and numerous instruments of his for his task, instruments that were alien to her. He glanced over his shoulder.

"Leave it over there," he ordered, gesturing to a small table at the far side of the room.

He glanced back over his shoulder, then turned sharply, causing the legs of the chair to screech on the highly polished floor.

"Rowena."

"Mr. Bligh, sir."

"William, I told you. It gladdens me to see you, child. Please accept my condolences on your mother's passing."

"Thank you, sir."

He stood up from the chair, smartly dressed, the soft light in the room adding colour to the usual pale palour of his stern expression. His receding hairline was brushed away from his face. He had, at that moment, the kindly demeanour of an old schoolmaster. She knew that not to be the case in reality.

"I was told you wouldn't be back until the morn?"

"I came back tonight, sir, to be sure of the early start in the morning."

"William, please, like I told you."

He smiled softly and glanced at the meal placed on the table at his request.

"Another fine supper. Will you join me, girl?"

"I mustn't, sir, I must return below."

"Nonsense. Five minutes won't be any harm. If the housekeeper enquires I'll see you right."

She admired the warm crackle of the fire in the hearth, warming her bones after the long journey from the countryside in the shrill evening air.

"You look cold, dear girl. Please, accept my chair, pull it up to the fire and keep me company while I eat. I do miss the company of people who I can converse with outside my task at hand here."

She smiled nervously and did as requested. He had an imposing presence. He took the tray over to a small table on the other side of the room and sat firmly down facing her and the fire.

"Do you pray, child?"

"Yes sir, I do."

He nodded and stretched out his arms on the table, resting his elbows behind his plate and joining his hands together.

"You will join me in a prayer before I eat, yes."

"Yes, sir."

He smiled and nodded as began a short homage of thanks as Rowena bowed her own head, occasionally opening one eye slightly to watch him. His brow furrowed as continued, carefully pronouncing every word before a rousing climax. He raised his head and tucked the white napkin tight into his collar, looking down again at the meal and raising the knife and fork with intent.

"Tell me," he asked as he began eating, "I see you every day since I've come here and I know so little about you. I like to take an interest in those who share their lives with me. Where do you come from?"

Rowena glanced into the fire, nervously wringing her dress as she softly replied.

"A small country village…"

"Speak up or be damned girl, I can't hear you."

His voice was firm with authority. She startled at his order, swallowing hard as she repeated, louder. He was a known disciplinarian, feared, reviled, yet admired and praised equally. She knew his past. She never let on to Mrs. Connor though, she kept that knowledge to herself. That was a long time ago.

"A small country village, sir," she asserted.

"A village you say?" he nodded with genuine interest as he pushed a generous amount of meat into his mouth with the fork.

"I assumed, quite wrongly of course, that you were of the city. But, yes you speak differently to the others. Your accent is richer, softer. I find the accent of the Dublin people quite harsh and abrupt. Tell me, where?"

"Out in the country, a good distance away, across the river."

He nodded again as he gulped some drink.

"Does this country village have a name?"

"Yes sir, it does."

"And?"

"It's called Finglas, sir."

"What's that? Finglas? I see. Is it a nice place to live?"

"It is my home, sir, a tiny place, some big houses here and there but mostly cottages, like mine."

"Hmmm," he added as he continued to stare into his food.

"I may come for a visit with you one day. Even I need a break from the sea. The country life is not like the sea, to state the obvious. No excitement, but, alas, quiet and contemplating. I like a break now and again. How do you amuse yourself in a tiny town like that?"

She smiled softly. "There is much to do, places to walk, rabbits to chase, a huge woodland…"

"Woodland, you say?"

"Yes, sir, so peaceful too."

"I'm with you on that one, I will admit, a bit of quietness does one the world of good. It is good for the soul, sometimes a man needs time alone."

He was silent for a long minute as he continued to concentrate on his food. Chewing loudly, he looked up at her.

"Country village, you say. Are their fairs? Games, like in an English village?"

Her eyes lit up, honoured by his delicate interest in her personal life.

"Why yes, sir, every summer, a fair, with games, dancing around a maypole…" She looked down at her lap.

"Go on, girl?"

"Well, it is a fair, drink does be taken and a lot of boisterous palaver does go on. It is not good for women late in the evening, the men do, the men…"

"Out with it!" He had a hint of a smile on his face as he chewed, waiting on her next answer with interest. She signed wistfully and heard her heart beat in her chest. Why was he asking her all this, now? But she daren't defy him. Not him.

"The men drink a lot during the day and do seek, well, a companion, if you will…" Her cheeks flushed and she looked down into her pinny.

He snorted and swallowed a mouthful of ale.

"Discipline!" he barked as he slammed down the mug on the tray, startling her. "I know all about men and the weakness for women. Ale too. It's a potent mix. The best of men do away with their senses.

"You just have to look at the blackguards down the stairs in the tavern. Oafs, the lot of them! Have you family? Brothers, sisters, that kind of thing?"

"Yes, a sister, Mary and brother William."

"A fine and noble name!" he smirked as he sat back in the chair, pausing between mouthfuls. He smacked when he ate, making rudimentary noises perhaps commonplace in his trade. Her mother had taught her how to eat with dignity, with her mouth full. Her mother would have scolded William Bligh.

"So how did you end up in employment here?"

"My mother, sir, she knew the house-keeper, I worked in one of the great houses in my village, she recommended me."

"And a fine recommendation too!"

He stared at her for some moments as he finished his meal and drained his mug. "How did she die, Rowena?" He leaned forward on the desk, cupping his hands when he pushed the plate aside.

She closed her eyes, her fingers wringing her apron as she tried to hold back the tears.

"She got very ill, sir, dirty water from the stream you see. A few people have died from it."

"I see," he nodded as he glanced out the window.

"Is anyone addressing the matter?"

"Sir?"

"Addressing the matter, erm, is anyone looking into the cause of the dirty water…"

"I don't know, sir."

"Hmm, well, it needs to be addressed or there will be an outbreak, an epidemic. Cholera, I gather. Can devastate communities… may God's hand lead your mother to Heaven."

"Thank you, sir."

He stood up and walked slowly towards her. Around his neck hung a small pendant and he noticed her eyes rest on it. He glanced down and took it in the palm of his hand. Rowena automatically stood too.

"Sit down girl, I am a husband, a father, I am human. I'm William in this house, not Captain or Lieutenant or whatever else they bestow up on me."

"Yes, sir."

He walked over to her and leaned forward, holding the open locket before her. Inside was two tiny pictures.

"This is my wife, Elizabeth, or Betsy as I call her, and my four children. A fine family I have. I miss them."

Rowena stared at the two pictures. "Your wife is very beautiful," she ventured, glancing up at him with a faint smile before her eyes darted back down to her lap.

"Tell me, Rowena, what is your age?"

"Eighteen, sir."

"As I guessed. Tell me, Rowena," he repeated as he walked back towards the desk, casually glancing at his charts before looking intently out the window as the cold rain fell steadily from the night sky against the assorted panes. She sat still, awaiting his question with uncertainty. How long more would he keep her here?

"Do you find me intimidating?"

She swallowed hard again. Her mouth was dry.

She stared into the fire, considering an answer. A careful answer.

"No sir, of course not."

He walked slowly back towards her, his boots stomping on the floor.

"Stand before me, Rowena."

She straightened her dress, clasping her hands tightly in front of her as his curled finger gently lifted her chin up.

"Do not fear me, Rowena, I mean no harm or ill toward you."

"Yes, sir."

"William…"

She stuttered his Christian name out, fearing Mrs. Connor would fling open the door and scold her for addressing the guest beyond her remit, yet wishing she would do so and get her out of the damned room.

The back of his hand softly brushed her cheek, causing her to gasp. He placed his other hand on her shoulder. She shook slightly as her heart raced.

"You are a lovely girl, a lovely girl. Very kind and polite. Do you know in all my years of marriage I have never looked at another woman. Even in Tahiti when the native women were lavishing what-nots on the men, I never looked at them, I just went along with the general gaiety of the occasion. I had to be on my best behaviour, you see, I had a mission to succeed in. The women there, the curse upon my men."

His voice trailed off and he turned around, clasping his hands behind his back as he walked back toward the window.

"I am a man, first and foremost Rowena."

She began to perspire, licking her lips as she sought to control her urge to run. He remained silent for some moments increasing her palpable nerves.

"Do you know why I am here, Rowena?"

"No sir…" she lied.

He waved his hand across the window as he continued to stare ahead.

"Many ships have been damaged or wrecked as they sail into Dublin Bay, you see, on the sandbars that build up under the surface, it's always been a problem. Do you know what a sandbar is? Well, it's just that; a bar of sand built up underneath and can trap or damage ships if they hit it. I am to chart and map the bay, you see, and develop ideas to improve the accessibility of the port. It's a very important task."

Rowena was perplexed by his enthusiasm for his work here. He barely afforded her a glance as he spoke confidently while looking at his charts.

He had a big ego, she had heard of that.

"A breakwater, girl, stops the full force of the tides coming in… anyway, that's my job here, to make recommendations, to look at that, to improve the harbour so it can continue to trade and attract larger merchant vessels. The wintry weather is ideal for assessing such structures, I think. Improvements can, and will, be made, of course. The winter is cruel yet ideal; all the different and risky patterns and tides, helps me observe. But I've gone to sea in worse."

He turned around, blinking quickly as he licked his own lips.

A faint smile crossed his face. "That probably means nothing to a country girl like you, eh?" She nodded uncertainly.

"Do you know much of me, Rowena?"

She swallowed again.

"That you are an important man in the navy, sir, that is all I am told."

Two lies. Two lies to a man of the reputation of William Bligh. She silently said a quick prayer. She was adhering to her duties, she told herself. It was not her place. He sniffed and smiled, nodding his head slightly as he looked into the fire.

'The Bounty bastard' they all said of him; 'the Bounty bastard…'

He looked her up and down and slowly approached her again. He took her hands in his. A common servant girl, that was all she was to him. She would be forgotten in time.

"You hands are clammy Rowena," he said softly as she avoided his eyes.

"It is warm in here, sir."

He raised her head again by curling his finger under and chin and lifting slowly. "Thank you for your conversation, I appreciate someone, normal, to talk to now and again. I may call on you again for a snack or some other sustenance. Make sure it is you who brings it to me, understood?"

Rowena nodded, continuing to avoid his eyes. He placed his arm gently on hers. "Do not be frightened, I will not harm you, Rowena, you know that?"

"Yes, yes sir." They stared at each other for some moments, his grip tightening as she prayed for him to dismiss her. He released her arm and turned back towards the desk.

"Go now, girl, take the tray with you and be away to your duties," he waved.

"Yes, sir, William."

"Good, good… go now."

Her heart heaved in relief as she gathered the items and made for the door.

"Thank you, sir."

November 4, 1874

The cart pulled up outside the big house, the long journey through muddy country roads which gave way to shiny and slippery cobbles almost reaching a climax. Children ran to and fro, playing games on the streets as mothers watched from steps and chatted among themselves while their men worked in the brewery or on the railways.

Ben stepped down from the cart, his hand guiding his new wife as she daintily pulled her skirts up and stepped down onto the worn cobblestones outside their new home. Maria settled her new pink skirts and, wiping her hands down her side, stood back at gazed up at their new home.

The unending hum of the city could be heard around her. Ben stood with his hands on his hips, his new address offering a challenge to him. The silence, calmness and solitude of his previous home had been replaced by hustle, bustle, noise and chatter. He looked around, nervously almost, hoping he had made the right decision.

"Want me to take these in for you? It'll cost extra."

Their cab driver gestured to the two scruffy cases lying awkwardly in the cart. Ben glanced at him.

"No, we'll manage," he replied as he swung the cases down effortlessly on his own; muscles from working the land helping him easily move their belongings onto the ground.

He paid the man his few pence and watched as he moved away, the horse clopping along. He felt he should offer him some food, some drink, but had nothing to offer. He placed his arm around his new bride's shoulder.

"Here we are…"

She smiled weakly back at him, her expression betraying uncertainty. She was used to the city life, but tonight, her first night of marriage was different. She was alone, with her new husband, in a strange new house, a house they would share with many others. Two women approached them, offering their blessings on the couple, their names went over Maria's head as she took in the scene.

Children gathered round, Ben dismissing one who had begun to dig in his pockets. "Away with you, go!" he ordered in his rich north county Dublin accent, softer and more pronounced than the harsh, grating dialect of the locals in Watling Street. His wife was softly spoken but her tones reflected those of their new neighbours. She smiled, tugging on her new husband's forearm.

"They're only children Ben…"

"He was trying to pick my pocket!"

"It's their way, isn't it? They're poor people 'round here. Throw them a shilling. Ah go on!" she chided. "Go on, make an impression!"

"Of someone who throws their money around?! Money I haven't got? I just paid the cab driver."

"No, of friendliness, these people will be living around us now. We may need their help at some point."

He sighed and dug into his coat pocket, flicking a shiny coin into the air as the small band of children cheered and squealed as they sought to capture their bounty.

"Now isn't that better?" Maria asked as her handsome young husband smiled his wide grin from beneath a stately moustache.

"Come on, let's go in," said, holding his arm out for her to link.

Together bride and groom walked up the steps and through the green door with the flaking paint and under the fanlight, two of it's small windows smashed.

As they entered, Ben looked back out onto the busy city street; a world away from his family homestead in Finglas. He thought, just one final time, of the young woman he once shared long walks with in his younger days. This was the life he had chosen, here was home now.

March 23, 1903

Mrs. Devine muttered silent prayers as Rowena's coffin was lowered into the ground on this crisp spring morning. Beside her, Kathy held her mother's arm tightly as the elderly woman's two sons stood behind her. Reverend Martin Hackett mumbled as if disinterested through the ceremony.

Constable Scollard and Dr. Ryan made up the rest of the small funeral party. Outside the cemetery, a small band of gawkers had watched silently as the coffin was carried through the gates. Charles Bayly stood watching through an upstairs window in Rose Hill.

Inside her musty room, Phoebe Hedderman said a few silent prayers as others gathered at the door or hung out their windows to watch the small cortege make it's way from the church and across the bridge to the graveyard.

'It is finally over…'

She blessed herself as she attended to the baby, refusing to join the others who urged her to come look. It was a funeral everyone wanted over as quickly as possible.

There was an air of relief in the village as word spread that Rowena Whyte had died in childbirth. Another chapter in that grisly summer ended forever.

Mrs. Devine said a few final prayers as Reverend Hackett stood after the service for a respectable amount of time before melting away, waving away the children who danced around him on the street asking was she really dead. He glared at the nervous mothers who instantly called their wayward urchins to behave. Kathy threw a small flower in on top of Rowena's coffin, repeating her mother's action as they blessed themselves, the young woman nodding to the grave digger who saluted back, donned his cap and began to fill in the grave as the funeral party filed away to a waiting cart.

"I'm proud of you child," Mrs. Devine said as she patted her daughter's arm. "Letting us bury her in the white dress you gave her. She looked elegant, beautiful, at peace. She deserves that. No matter what anyone else thinks in this godforsaken place, the poor girl deserved to be laid to rest with dignity."

Sitting in the large living room of Jamestown House, Eleanor rocked the newborn Elizabeth to sleep as she gazed out the window. She had grown tired of the questions asked of her in the village, adhering Mrs. Devine's request to ignore them.

'Where did he really go… he's living up in Jamestown House with 'er, isn't he?'

She always lowered her head and scurried along quickly. In her elegant church on Sunday, she pretended not to notice the glances and whispers. Those few short days had perhaps changed her life forever. She couldn't leave Mrs. Devine now, as she had planned to do. She had to stay, to help the ailing woman and be at her side. The last few months had taken their toll. She resigned herself to settling in Finglas for life, hopefully raising a little baby of her own. Maybe her own child would help someone in many years to come.

311

She could just wonder as she spied the cart return to the courtyard in front of the house. She got up from her chair quickly, placed the infant in the cradle and rushed out to help her good friend in.

"That's it done now, Eleanor, the poor cratur laid to rest now. God help her."

September 16, 1913

Elizabeth Whyte hid by the side of Heery's with her friend Sophie Harper as the mob walked up the hill. She had stayed too long in her friends down by The Elms on Church Street. Mrs. Devine had told her to be home early, that trouble was in the air, the farmers were angry and the unions were stirring it up. Ever since the attack on Butterly's farm, when strikers attacked their fellow labourers who refused to fall in line with their beliefs, an air of unease simmered. Elizabeth listened intently as Mrs. Devine told her family about the situation, telling them to stay clear of the village for a few days.

"I've no time for any of that carry-on, none at all. Stay well out, you hear me?" she directed her son.

News had filtered through of the two men killed in the baton charge in the city. A new dread gripped those in the sleepy village as word spread that the Lockout dispute had spread to Finglas. Hushed tones abounded as neighbours discussed what could happen.

Wives bigged up their husbands who sided with Jim Larkin and those who wanted nothing to do with it didn't offer an opinion. Wives of those who needed the work and would by default be declared scabs stayed out of sight, terrified of the reaction. The city was divided, up in arms, a melting pot of anger.

Scab. Bloody scab, drinking in Upper Flood's, and they were serving him! Perry was his name. Word had spread and men began picketing the premises from earlier in the day when Elizabeth had gone to Sophie's house after lessons. She had dallied too long and as pleasant day turned into muggy evening, more people gathered at the junction.

"What's happening Lily?" Sophie asked.

"It's the men, they're going to fight I think!"

"How will you get home Lily?"

Elizabeth shook her head as the fading light brought an eerie caution to the village. "I'm afraid to go by the fields in the dark... but I have to go."

Sophie gripped her friend's arm. "No you mustn't Lily, you'll get caught in the fight! I'll get my daddy to bring you home," Sophie offered, unaware he was in the crowd.

"Nana Devine's gonna kill me!" Elizabeth quivered as she watched.

Sergeant Brennan and Constable Barry swallowed nervously as they observed the mob. Speeches were now being given randomly, Elizabeth recognised the name of Larkin. Drink had been taken. Some men had sticks, others rocks. The atmosphere was about to boil over.

Elizabeth cowered by the side of Heery's, afraid to move, afraid to pass the mob, afraid to run through the fields or by the north road as others continued to approach from various directions. Above her the birds sang their evening song innocently, the trickle of the stream continued abated as tensions rose. As she watched the police left, returning to the barracks.

Elizabeth stood up and smiled.

"Look Sophie things must be getting better, the police are going away!"

"Go now Lily, run home now quickly, while you can still see the road!"

"I will Sophs, go home yourself. I'll go now!"

Elizabeth watched as her pal's golden hair trailed behind her as she sprinted down Church Street. She listened for the sound of the door shutting before she made her own attempt to go to the safety of her home.

She crept out of the shadows at the same time the two officers emerged from the barracks with rifles.

As she passed the simmering mob, gathering at the junction she heard the smashing of glass and shouts erupted as bodies swayed and ran in all directions. She screamed, placed her hands over her ears and tried to run but she was surrounded on all sides. Tears streaming down her face, she stood rooted, frantically looking around her for a way of escape. More glass was smashed, the incessant roar of drunk shouts and garbled voices colliding in her young ears as bodies brushed brutally off her.

A loud crack dominated the noise. A brief, shocked silence befell the crowd as three more cracks followed in quick succession. Elizabeth threw herself to the ground and was trampled underfoot by the fleeing, roaring cacophony of male voices as the crowd fled.

She remained face down on the ground, crying and hurt as silence once more descended on the crossroads. From her left, she could hear someone groaning. She lifted her head, screwed her eyes in the dim light as she heard footsteps run towards her. She could make out the fallen figure of a man and someone rushing to his aid.

"They've shot him! They've shot him!"

Elizabeth got to her feet.

"C'mere girl, quickly!"

Her feet took her towards the two men more in fear than thought.

"You bastards! You shot him! Paddy! Paddy can you hear me?" the youth roared.

"Hold his head!" he ordered as a terrified Elizabeth fell to her knees, cradling the stricken youth's head in her lap.

The police turned away and returned to the barrack.

"Where are you going?! He needs help!!"

"What's happening?" Elizabeth cried, tears running down her face.

"They've shot Paddy Daly in the back, the bastards! Can you hear me Paddy?"

"Will he die?" Elizabeth quizzed, shaking with fear, not fully understanding what was going on.

"That scab, that bloody scab!" the angered man continued as footsteps approached. Sergeant Brennan and Constable Barry returned.

"Another one?! Not happy with killing two in the city, you want another innocent man dead?" he roared.

"Get away from him!" the sergeant roared.

"We've got to get him some help before the crowd returns," he whispered to his young constable.

"I shot him..."

"We'll talk about that later. Just say nothing and help me get him to Farnham. Girl! You girl, what are you doing here?"

"Trying to go home sir, I got caught in the crowd."

"Where do you live?!"

"Jamestown House, sir."

"Away with you, this isn't a place for you!"

"Remember what you saw!" the man shouted. "Remember that Paddy Daly was shot by these bastards! Tell everyone!"

Elizabeth froze, fear controlling her every nerve.

"I said go home child, you saw nothing here! Otherwise we'll jail you!" Sergeant Brennan ordered as Elizabeth turn and ran past Gofton and Ashgrove, past the cottages and fields, only stopping to gulp down air as she clambered by the briars and hedgerows in the darkness. In the distance she could hear the sound of a horse and cart. A lantern dangled and grew brighter as the vehicle approached. She stood transfixed, throwing her hands in front of her face as the cart stopped.

"Elizabeth, thank God!"

Michael Devine jumped from the cart as his mother blessed herself.

"Elizabeth, where were you?! We heard the noise!"

"Gunshots," her son added.

"Are you ok?" the elderly woman asked as the young man lifted the crying child into the seat. She sobbed as Mrs. Devine wrapped a shawl around her and the cart made to turn back to the house.

"The boy was shot down," she cried as her guardian comforted her.

"Who?" her son asked, head darting around to face her. "Why was he shot?"

"Enough, take us home!" his mother barked.

"Daly, Paddy Daly, shot by the police!" Elizabeth sobbed.

"That accursed Larkin," the child's guardian muttered. "I knew something was happening tonight. Whispers in the village earlier. Then I heard the faint cracks and I knew they were shots…"

"He's a good man," her son interrupted as he drove the trap furiously toward Jamestown House.

"Two men have been killed, maybe young Daly too by the police and all because of this Larkin and his union. What has the world come to?!"

"He's fighting for us all."

"Oh isn't he just! Fighting being the very word. Fighting and blood and tears and all in front of a young girl alone. You may have your Mr. Larkin, son, his world has no place in mine. Come on, get us to the house."

The only sound from the three people on the cart was young Elizabeth's sobbing.

"You're not to go down to the village again until this has all passed, you hear me Elizabeth?"

Elizabeth nodded.

"I promised your mother I'll look after you, every waking second of my life, and by God I will."

The cart trundled on as Mrs. Devine thought long and hard. The world was changing, her area was changing, nothing was the same for her since those murders eleven years ago. Finglas was no longer a peaceful haven away from the dirt and noise of the city she was born in. Now politics brought the two even closer and with it an air of discontent, frought with bloodshed and fear.

She didn't like what this world was becoming. She longed for the more peaceful times. She yearned for a return to the old values. This was not a world to raise a young child safely in.

Elizabeth would remain in the house and be schooled there. She could have lost her this evening; how could she explain that to Rowena when she met her again at the point of her own death?

June 13, 1962

Mr. and Mrs. Collins shook hands with the foreman as he handed them the keys to their fresh new home, still smelling of plaster and paint, the concrete of the new roads and paths of what was known as Jamestown Estate almost snow white.

The first shoots of the newly sown lawn were emerging from the levelled soil and the foreman laughed as he lined the beaming couple up outside the front garden wall for a photograph. He clicked the shutter and rolled on the film, urging them back into position for another shot, 'just in case'.

The middle aged couple surveyed the new row of semi-detached houses that stretched from Jamestown Road and away in a perpendicular direction. Behind the houses across the road, the shell of the once grand Jamestown House stood lonely among the overgrowth, used sporadically for various ventures over the years but destined to crumble or be demolished, it's once lush gardens and grounds annexed and the vast majority buried under concrete. Slight remnants remained, two big burgundy trees that once lined the drive up to the house still stood behind the row of houses Mr. and Mrs. Collins would now live on; older, more random trees still stood around the ruins itself as the once ample fields stretched wayward and forgotten, themselves too to be soon buried under new estates and roads. Gone was the orchard, buried was the well, demolished were the small homesteads that dotted the surrounding area.

Mrs. Collins sighed as she remembered the stories her late mother Eleanor told her about the House, how she lived and worked there for some time, nursing a young child who she would watch roam and play in the fields for hours.

'Everything changes,' she once told her young daughter, in her broad northern English tones, *'sometimes you got to let go of the past...'* Mrs. Collins smiled at the thought as she knew that every morning she could look out the front bedroom window and see the grand house her mother lived in and that, albeit hidden under layers of concrete, she may even be tracing the same footsteps.

'Some things should never be let go of...'

A time yet to come...

They stood gasping as he stepped into the breach, the brilliant illumination showcasing his brittle body being thrown around as unimaginable screams haunted their ears.

They tried to help him, to end the experiment and recover him but as they fought frantically they knew it was hopeless. The power was too strong. All they could do was helplessly watch him as he collapsed onto green grass on a sunny day. One of those horrified in attendance squinted as he stepped forward; he could swear a girl was nearby, watching everything.

The image disappeared and the power overloaded the laboratory, ensuring a definitive end to project and an inability to return him safely. He was a pioneer, an explorer, the first one to accomplish successful time travel, but at what cost...

Epilogue

2006

The dull rumble was an unusual sound, an uncommon one causing heads to turn. The hollers and shouts that accompanied it worrying. A hazy soup of dust rose slowly into the sunshine and drifted out past the shell of the new apartment block that was under construction.

Construction workers stood rooted to the spot, frozen, some with their hands clenched behind their hard-hats.

"This can't be happening!" the foreman shouted, "this can't be fucking happening!"

The dust began to clear. Shocked onlookers gasped as hands were thrown up in front of mouths, others shouting obscenities at the beleaguered builders.

Foundations had been disturbed, weakened wall cavities strained beyond the capability to bond centuries-old brickwork together any longer and crumbled under the stress. A once solid wall crashed onto the ground below, stagnated soil following in a dirty, shadowy waterfall.

Lurking within the collapsed stonework and soil were the remains of broken coffins. The bones and tattered rags of those interned having daylight shone on them after many years of rest. The workers remained rooted to the spot as members of the public began to rush over, shouts and abuse breaking the eerie silence at the old graveyard.

Building work on the new apartment block, on that tiny piece of land wedged between the dual-carriageway and ancient cemetery had caused the broad outer wall to collapse. Those first on the site were stopped in their tracks as a long-dead skulls smiled up at them, the shattered remains of the rotten caskets strewn around the corpses' ragged remains of clothing. Other coffins balanced delicately as they protruded from the exposed yet still firm and undisturbed soil almost like fingers stretching out. They too could tumble and disintegrate at any time. One casket that had come loose lay almost upright against the remains of the wall before slowly sliding sideways towards the ground. Two workman automatically lunged to halt its decline; as they did the weakened lid slid off. They allowed it to crumble beneath them. As they unwillingly gazed inside the exposed tomb they both stopped and stared, exchanging gazes to each other as they slowly lowered the lidless, crude and rotten simple box to the ground. They stood silently, mouths agape, hands trembling at their side as they stared at the skeletal remains inside.

Scratched heads, frightened expressions and a quickly taken macabre mobile phone photograph surrounded the newly exposed corpse, a corpse that remained where it had been placed in the coffin many years before, though not in the traditional manner of a body laid to rest.

These bones were of open palms and curled fingers pushing upwards. Shin bones splintered awkwardly, knees raised and a body twisted in effort and strain. The skull was turned sideways to it's left as if the long dead remains was calling for help.

A young apprentice collected the shattered bits of the lid and turned them over, calling excitedly as the others scrutinised what looked like weak scratch marks on the inner lid.

A few passers by had infiltrated the scene, squirming in through weakly enforced barricades despite a lame command to stay away. They stood just as shocked as all gazes were directed downward to this strangely contorted body; the body of someone who looked like they had tried to escape their tomb.

Unnoticed and only feet away another complete coffin lay almost sideways, sitting on a mound of earth, the one that lay under it smashed and the bones scattered and exposed. The more recent burials perched precariously as they poked out from the undisturbed compacted soil of the original grave.

Amid the confusion, the coffin that leaned slightly on its side escaped immediate attention as panicked working hands immediately tried to put the bones back into what was left of the rotten casket that splintered underneath. The coffin sat, its occupant, still inside the wooden tomb but with the lid torn off, the corpse in a ragged white dress not at peace anymore as the bones of her beloved mama lay open to the sun only feet away, awakened from a young death to be at the mercy of a cruel world her daughter had hoped she was finally rid of.

On the main street, Rowena stood silently outside her office, in a dream as a colleague returning from lunch broke the news of what had happened. She let the conversation go over her head. She prayed and prayed but deep down she knew. She knew. The apartments were being built against the wall of the graveyard she once sat against on that darkest of nights, where feet away her family's resting place lay silently amongst many others.

She turned to the young girl blabbering beside her.

"Can I have a smoke?"

"What?! I didn't know you smoked?"

"Please can I have one?"

The girl handed one over and lit it for her as Rowena dragged long and hard on the cigarette, her first in years. She had given them up shortly after she was dragged into the story with The Forum thirteen years previously. She needed one now. Badly.

The other girls gossiped away as she slipped out of their company, walking down the street, not stopping until she had crossed the dual carriageway and stood at the junction where the graveyard and new apartments lay.

Her hand shook as she finished the cigarette and threw it through the railings of the neat housing estate that had risen from the rubble of the Spanish Convent which had itself replaced Farnham House. She folded her arms and crossed over, intent on her face, hiding the fear that turned her stomach inside out. She did as others had done, stepping over cones bonded by yellow tape, squeezing in through the wire fencing until she stood at the horror scene.

The wind caught her hair and blew it over her face as one of the workmen noticed her. He called to his foreman, busying on his mobile phone, and he waved at her to move as the young builder pleaded with her to move away as the site was dangerous. She turned her head slowly to him, smiling but remained in her spot.

The foreman ended his call and rushed over to her.

"You must leave here, it's not safe, this is a construction site, you have no business being here!"

She turned slowly, the sound of an approaching Garda car in her ears as the foreman barked at her to move.

She remained impassive, just staring at him. She looked back at the mess in front, eyes darting back and forth as she did some calculations in her mind. Her stomach dropped in a sickening heave as her worse fears were realised. A few plots were affected. Including the one holding her family. She felt tears well up from deep within her, a primeval howl urging to escape as once more she set eyes on her mother and Mary's coffins, balanced delicately in the soil, ready to fall at any second. Her eyes dropped at the splintered and shattered caskets and scattered bones that lay askew around her.

She gazed at the skeletal figure in the ragged remnants of the white dress, the long dead relation still lying peacefully but now for all the world to see.

"Please, move, now! Out of here!" the foreman barked as he began another call on his phone.

Rowena turned sharply, her face changing to one of venom. She swung a hand out, sending the mobile phone flying from his hand as it bounced onto the ground, coming to appropriate rest in the gutter.

"Who do you think…" he began but Rowena followed up with an unmerciful smack across the face that send him stepping backward, eyes wide in shock.

"That…!" she pointed, tears welling up and emotions taking over, "that there, right there, is my family plot! That coffin sticking out on top, that's my sister! Underneath, my mammy. Those shattered, my granny, great granny and whoever else! And you ask ME who the hell do I think I am?!"

She shot forward, eyeballing the shaken foreman as she spat the words into his face. Onlookers gasped, voices raising in disgust and support of Rowena as other builders remained frozen.

"That is my family plot! How many other plots have you destroyed?!"

She swung at the foreman again, her wrist was caught thought by someone behind her.

"Ro, please…"

She spun around to see Eamon.

"This will do no good," he urged as the cacophony of voices urged her to hit the shaken man.

"Eamon, look, Eamon, that's my plot! Look!!"

Eamon glanced over, eyes surveying the devastation.

"You can't be sure…"

She wrestled her arm free, pointing back towards the site.

"Don't tell me I can't be sure, I've been at that grave all my life. Look, Eamon, look, there's Mary's coffin, look, right there, on top! Look!"

She was almost manic in her speech, her arms flailing wildly as Eamon took another look. His eyes fixated on the dirty casket before gauging the precise spot from the trees in the background. He could always tell where Mary was buried as he passed by each day on his way to Finglas station.

'Oh sweet fuck…'

Rowena turned away and hit the foreman hard again.

"Are you going to do something about this?!" the stunned foreman shouted at the uniformed Guard standing nearby.

Eamon shot him a look.

"I didn't see anything, did you Ruairi?"

"Sir?"

"I said, I didn't see anything, did YOU, Ruairi?" Just out of Templemore, the young guard swallowed and shook his head.

"Did ANYONE here see that woman hit the foreman?"

Angered and supportive shouts from the gathered members of the public hollered 'No' with excitement.

"I don't believe this!" the foreman roared as he stepped towards Eamon.

Anger rising, Eamon grabbed him by the lapels of his sweaty shirt under the hi-viz jacket and swung him around to face the devastation.

"You see that?! You see THAT?! Look! You did that, your team did that! They are the deceased of this parish, look, dead people, look, those coffins sticking out, you see those two there, right there?! That's that lady's sister and mother! The top one was my girlfriend, you see! She was my girlfriend! And you DARE talk back to her like that?! You DARE assume the poise of the innocent party?! YOU will pay for this you little bollix, you hear me?! You will PAY for this!!"

Eamon shoved him away and he tumbled, landing beside the coffin with the girl in the white dress.

"Her!" Eamon continued, as he pointed at the skeletal remains of Rowena Whyte, "that's her relation! Take a good look you prick, go on, take a good look at that poor soul!"

The foreman, terrified of the manic detective, obeyed him and stared at the ghastly site. Eamon's heart heaved with anger and adrenaline.

'Fuck it, I don't care. Too much PC for my liking these days…'

"I ask again," Eamon shouted as he addressed the crowd, "after the disgusting event we have seen today, caused by this crowd of shites in hard hats here, did anyone, I repeat anyone, see that lady or me lay a finger on this prick?!"

Laughter erupted, a few cheers went up as a chorus of 'no!' carried on the wind. He looked at the shell shocked workers.

"And if any of you ever want to work on the sites again and earn fucking massive wages for destroying heritage and tampering with the dead, did you see anything?"

Heads shook, denials mumbled as Eamon nodded and turned to Ruairi.

"Arrest the foreman, he'll answer for this."

"For what?!" the foreman squeaked.

"Wanton destruction of a heritage site and desecration of the dead! It wasn't bad enough you concreted over the ancient wells discovered when digging the foundations here or pressured the archaeologists to move the Viking skeleton so concrete could be poured over the site, now you cause this!"

"My solicitor will..."

"Your solicitor will cost you a fortune and you'll still be punished over this you fool. You're not getting away with this!"

A cheer went up as the foreman was meekly led to the squad car.

Eamon turned back to Rowena, standing still, head turned to one side as she stared at the rubble.

"Are you ok Ro?"

"No, I'll never be after this."

"Damn right."

"But thank you, thank you Eamon. I know that fucker will be eating his dinner tonight with his family but thank you so much for making an example of him."

"He needed it. Mary. Your mother, your family."

She nodded. "Will you get into trouble?"

"I couldn't give a fuck now..." he smiled, his grey hair catching in the wind. "I'm sick of this job, too many people getting away for nothing. I'm thinking of finishing up early."

"For what?"

"I've some money saved up, I've been paying into a pension plan and a few other accounts. We've been thinking of moving down the country, just to get away. We've always liked Sligo. Too much bad shit happening on the streets, so disheartening when those you painstakingly build a case against give you the fingers as they leave court on bail, only to offend again. I can't take it anymore. This," he waved at the rubble, "this got my goat. The dead can't even remain in peace now."

He glanced up at the apartment shell.

"Like, whoever granted permission for this ugly box to be built between the road and the graveyard wall should be shot. Disgraceful."

Rowena nodded and stared back at the mangled corpse.

"You know something," she smiled.

"What?"

"I owe Lucy Jones a pound…"

"What?"

"Him there, him," she nodded towards the distressing site of the broken and twisted skeleton.

"Years ago, in St. Canice's primary, an old friend of mine bet me a pound that there was a man buried alive in the old graveyard. Her granny told her or something. Of course I bet her, cos it could never be proven. Well, there he is."

Eamon gazed down at the contorted bones, brow furrowing, detective mind ticking over. He placed a hand on Rowena's shoulder.

'The murderer vanished didn't he…'

"Ro, remember all that trouble with The Forum newspaper and…"

"Don't," she said softly, glancing up at him.

"You don't know what I was going to say…"

She smiled weakly.

"The story died again when Carruthers keeled over in the office over there."

She nodded towards the old Forum offices, the painted knight still adorning the window of the empty building but now a weak, sickly pale yellow. Rowena often thought about Declan, the paper's staff and Michael who had moved away some years previous. The Forum didn't last long after the Carruthers incident. She never saw or heard of Declan again after that. She always wondered was that incident a catalyst in closing the paper.

"Just let it die again. Who knows how he ended up like that. Maybe he had an accident, broke his legs, unconscious, people though he was dead. Buried him. That happened a lot, you know? I'm sure there's a good explanation. Don't read into it, what's the point… you've more to worry about here."

Eamon nodded. In time the bones would be tidied up and stored, the wall rebuilt and the disturbed remains reburied and blessed once again.

"Let me take you home Ro, this isn't a pretty sight. I'll get this fucker back to the station then drop back for you."

She nodded and smiled. *'Hope you like that Mary, he did you proud there, he did us all proud…'*

She turned away from the wooden coffins sticking out of the soil and looked down on the girl in the dirty white dress.

'And who were you, I wonder… not granny, I remember her funeral, she was in a purple dress. You must be great granny.'

She nodded and smiled, gazing back across at the old Forum office.

'YOU were the cause of the trouble then, you poor dear, all the hassle with Carruthers. Rowena's your name, like mine. Now you can't even rest in peace love.' She stared down at her great grandmother's remains, two Rowena's face to face over time. *'Poor girl. Poor, poor girl'*

Eamon gently touched her elbow. He was always very good to her.

"I'll be back in five or so. You hang on or do you want to walk to the village?"

"I'll hang on here. Say a prayer. I want to watch over her..." He nodded and got into the car with the shaking foreman and young guard. Rowena looked back down at her namesake and smiled.

'I've you to blame for me posh name…'

She stooped forward, slowly placing her fingers on the tattered dress, tearing off a small flailing piece and placing it in her pocket. She looked upon the long dead face, her hands still joined in eternal prayer, rosary beads clamped within the bony fingers. She placed her own hand on that of her great grandmother and closed her eyes, bridging generations and finally, she felt, closing a tale once and for all.

She kissed her two fingers and placed them on the mouth of the skull.

'Rest in peace Rowena…'

His phone beeped on the table beside him, interrupting his study as he looked away from the old dusty register. He put his glasses on, brow furrowed as he read the words before picking up his desk phone to call his friend back. This couldn't be true. *'You're joking… seriously? When, like an hour ago?!'*

The brief conversation with Rowena confirmed his fears. He sat back in his chair and signed, glancing out the window as Glasnevin cemetery lay in his gaze. Of all people, he knew the sanctity of the dead, the respect they deserved, the peace and dignity that was expected. He pulled his tweed jacket from the back of his chair, folded his glasses and placed them in the breast pocket beside the motley and ever-present collection of pens.

Stepping out into the sunshine the historian fumbled for his car keys, his mind in turmoil over what he just heard. There would be hell to pay over this.

'The mangled corpse though, that would be worth investigating... this I gotta see...'

The hollow eyes of Rowena's skull gazed at those of the contorted skeleton as her coffin remained leaning on the mound of earth it came to rest on. The flimsy container bore no identification, giving no hint as to who the twisted shape was, where he had come from, the child he fathered, but today both he and the young woman who witnessed his arrival on that hot June day in 1902 lay feet apart, the closest the two had been together in one hundred and four years. It meant nothing to anyone there. Even the deceased woman's great grand-daughter could only skirt on a thought that crossed her mind. No-one would ever realise what this meant. But now the ghost of Rowena could stop searching aimlessly throughout the area. Time had reunited her with her mysterious stranger. The circle was closed, the portal finally sealed.

author's note...

This story merges fact with fiction; characters, locations and events all intertwine to create a story purely borne in my mind.

The riot of 1913 in Finglas village actually happened, young Paddy Daly was indeed shot on that balmy September evening. Most peculiarly, William Bligh did visit Dublin and was billeted in quarters overlooking the Liffey for some months, his brief to chart and suggest a way to minimise the danger to shipping in Dublin Bay.

The grave of a Viking-era lady of significant social standing was unearthed as the lands around the old church were being excavated for the construction of new apartments; alas the collapse of the cemetery wall unfortunately occurred also but please know I used artistic license to embellish this event for the story.

Most personally, The Forum newspaper once existed, albeit briefly, in the early 1990s and the bar the protagonist James Carruthers, staff mentioned are based loosely on the actual people, with their blessing.

What characters existed and which ones were fiction? Well some are obvious and some may surprise you should you do some research. Others make brief cameos, fleeting appearances dotted throughout the whole story. A glance through the Thom's Directory of 1902 or a stroll through the old graveyard by the ruined church may throw up some surprises.

That is the beauty of a story like this. To reveal who was who is pointless. If you want to research and work it out, by all means do. But if you don't, well, let their appearances remain a mystery to you throughout the whole tale as fact intertwines with fiction.

44859968R00186

Printed in Poland
by Amazon Fulfillment
Poland Sp. z o.o., Wrocław